A CITY LOST TO MAN

It existed on a crumbling parchment and in the legends of Bronze Age tribesmen. It lay on an ancient slave route that time and the desert had long buried. To some it was a sanctuary; to others, a place of death, guarded by a warrior race that had once been the scourge of the Sudan.

Yet, as they plunged deeper into the secret heart of Africa, James and Jon Paul Jacobson began to see the oasis as something far more than legend. For their sister's trail led straight into the limitless waste around it. And the trail was littered with human bones.

Also by T. W. Hard:

SUM VII

OASIS

T. W. Hard

A DELL BOOK

Published by
Dell Publishing Co., Inc.
1 Dag Hammarskjold Plaza
New York, New York 10017

Dell ® TM 681510, Dell Publishing Co., Inc.

ISBN: 0-440-16544-X

Printed in the United States of America
First printing—August 1985

*To Gretchen,
with fond memories of
our family, our childhood, our home.*

Wide Africa, doth thy sun
Lighten, thy hill unfold
A city as fair
As those which starred the
Night o' the older world?
Or is thy rumor . . .
A dream as frail as those
Of ancient time?

Alfred Lord Tennyson, 1829

AUTHOR'S NOTE

The oasis of Bogadez is fictitious and does not occur anywhere on the African Continent. References to a similar oasis called Zarzura, however, appear in early twentieth-century accounts of Sahara exploration. It was thought to be somewhere in Libya, though never found.

T.W.H.
San Francisco, 1984

PART I

Life under the wing of a fly is better than sleep in the grave.

Arab proverb

1

They had been crawling for nearly an hour, following a narrow spit of a trail that led through the dry shrub bush country of the Northern Frontier. A thorn jabbed her right knee, making her wince with pain. She stopped long enough to gently disengage it, then inched forward, not daring to make a sound. Her heart pounded like a piston and her breath came in quickening gasps until at last she found she had to remind herself to slow down, to breathe easy, to relax.

Blond, blue-eyed, and elegantly slim, at twenty-seven she was a beautiful woman, oddly out of place in this hot desert country, one hundred twenty miles from the nearest phone. Dressed in faded jeans, a khaki shirt, and dusty Adidas, her hair pulled sternly back and tied with a brown ribbon, she was in sharp contrast to the black man who crawled in front of her clad only in a tattered cloth.

A yard ahead, she saw a string of ants and gritted her teeth. Damn the luck, she thought. But the Turkana had moved past them without flinching. Unless she wanted to ruin everything, she would have to go through them as well.

She could feel the insects crawling up her ankles and under her jeans; and her skin recoiled at their touch. She took a deep breath, waiting for the bites to come. A sharp burning pain erupted from her calf. Then a second. She suppressed a cry. A third stung into her abdomen. She moved more quickly now, almost bumping on the heels of the man in front of her. What have I gotten myself into this time? she wondered. And is it worth it all?

The African stopped. For a long moment he crouched motionless, his eyes wide with excitement. Suddenly he pointed to a small clearing in the desert brush. She squinted into the distance. The sun had already begun to dip toward the western horizon. Another hour and it would be too dark to shoot. Reaching down, she instinctively checked the barrel of her 250mm Telephoto lens.

The Turkana let out a soft cluck. She looked up in time to see a movement. In the late-afternoon shadows, the leopard had been almost invisible. It was carrying an antelope in its mouth and it hesitated for a second, staring directly toward them, then moved stealthily across the clearing toward a large acacia tree. Leaping into the lowest branches, it spread out along a limb and surveyed the area below.

The African began crawling forward. She followed, almost afraid to breathe, afraid the cat would hear the pounding of her heart. She had been trying to photograph the leopard for a week. The Turkana had carefully constructed a blind overlooking the creek bed where he thought the lair was hidden, but each time they had approached it they had made a sound, or the wind had been wrong, or somehow they had scared the cat, for until this evening she had never seen it. A few faint tracks in the sand, once the half-eaten entrails of a gazelle, were the only evidence they had found.

The light was fading fast. They'd have to hurry. Then, abruptly, the blind was ahead of them and she crawled into the thick thornbush enclosure. Carefully she rose to her knees. Poking the barrel of the Telephoto through the bush, she sighted through the Reflex lens. The scene was magnificent: the pure blacks and yellows of the leopard, the dark contrasting shadows of the tree, and the sun, red and swollen, dropping slowly in the background.

The cat was a big male. As he reared up on his hindquarters and yawned, she shot off five photographs in rapid succession. Each click of the shutter was followed by the rapid electrical grinding of the automatic motor drive, a sound soft in volume but unnatural to the stillness of the Northern Frontier. The leopard turned his head and looked toward the blind. Had he heard? Panicking, she looked toward her guide. He held up his hand for her to stop.

A minute passed. Finally the leopard dropped his head. The Turkana nodded and she brought the barrel of the camera up again. Quickly she checked exposure, distance, and speed. It

was a reflex for her now, and she smiled to herself as she remembered the time she thought she'd taken her most spectacular sequence of elephant photographs. She'd been in Africa only
a month then. Standing atop a high ridge, she'd come upon the
rival herds so suddenly that she'd hardly had time to get the
camera up before two great tusked males were locked in combat. The cows were screaming; the baby elephants milling about
in a frenzy; and the young bulls, taking advantage of the chaos,
were mounting any female they could find until the entire area
was filled with fighting, trumpeting, mating elephants.

She'd run off thirty-five photographs through the motor drive
before she'd discovered that she'd forgotten to load any film. By
the time she'd gotten out a new roll the elephants had disappeared in a forest of thick brush. The memory of it made her
flush. She'd been so angry and disappointed that she'd cried. It
was a costly lesson. But she'd become a better photographer for
it. She would never make a mistake like that again.

She checked the film-loading mechanism, then squinted back
through the lens. The leopard changed positions and began
grooming himself. She triggered off five more shots. Suddenly
she realized that the Turkana was clucking wildly to get her
attention and pointing directly in front of the blind. She
scanned the brush, searching for the source of his excitement.
Her eyes widened. A female leopard had come out of a den
hidden somewhere in the creek bed. Following closely behind
were three cubs tumbling over one another at every step. She
sucked in her breath. This was the moment she'd been waiting
for. This was what made it all worthwhile. Moving quickly, she
brought the camera up, peered through the Reflex lens, and
began to click off shot after shot of film.

Without hesitation, the mother leopard leaped into the tree
and stiff-shouldered her way along the branch toward the male.
He rose to his full height, snarling. With an indignant swat, she
backed him off the limb. Leaping to the ground, the male took
one look at the three cubs charging him then sprang back into
the tree. By now the female had jumped to the ground with the
antelope in her mouth. Sauntering to a comfortable spot, she
dropped her prize. The cubs were on it in an instant with much
ferocious growling. After eating they romped like kittens, stalk-

ing each other, then spitting and snarling as they frolicked in
the dust.

Even through the viewfinder they were adorable. Their fur
was sleek and smooth, their eyes black, filled with playful curiosity, and their ears were enormous in proportion to their
heads. They looked as if they belonged in some children's zoo,
and she smiled affectionately as she watched them.

Within twenty minutes, she'd finished her third roll of film
and she couldn't have been more pleased. Already she could
imagine herself back in the offices of *National Geographic* or
Audubon where editors would pore over her work, marveling.
She'd been working on a book on the Northern Frontier for
some time now. These last sequences might be just enough to
finish it off.

Nodding to her African companion, she bent her fingers in an
"okay" sign. At his full height Molo barely came up to her
chin. Large copper earrings hung from his earlobes. His hair
was matted in a protective cap of dried mud with an ostrich
feather poked over his left ear. He wore little more than an old
piece of blanket around his waist. Yet despite their differences,
he was completely devoted to her. It had been the same with all
the Turkana. They had taken her into their tribe first with suspicion, then with caution, and finally with admiration and affection.

The sun slipped another degree beneath the horizon. She
made a sign to the Turkana that it was becoming too dark to
shoot. He nodded, holding up his hand in a sign of caution. It
took her a moment to understand that he was trying to alert her
to the movement of the leopards. Slowly he lowered his head
until his ear almost touched the ground, then clucked, pointing
his finger just beyond the perimeter of the blind. She looked
toward the tree. The male leopard was gone! Good God! Did he
mean the big cat was right outside, moving toward them?

She craned her neck, searching the narrow opening of the
blind. The mother leopard and the cubs had disappeared and
she could see nothing but empty bush. The Turkana rose silently to his feet. He made a quick motion with his hand, pointing to the doorway of the blind. It was time to get out—quietly
and fast!

Setting the exposure wide open to counterbalance the fading light, she frantically loaded a new roll of film. She tried to swallow but her mouth was dry as cotton. If the leopard was stalking them, they had no way to defend themselves. She carried no weapon. The Turkana had only a walking stick. Maybe if they found her half-eaten body, at least they'd discover her last photograph, she thought, chuckling nervously. A tight close-up, barrel of 250mm lens stuffed into the leopard's mouth. Red patch, tongue of leopard; white ridges, leopard's teeth; dark thing, photographer's hand *inside* of leopard!

They had only gone ten yards when the Turkana stopped in his tracks. Something in the maze of thornbush ahead told him that danger was near. There was no warning growl, only a flash of yellow. The guide took a faltering step backward. The big cat stood before them, blocking the path. His fangs were bared, his tail twitched ominously.

Very slowly she reached for her camera. Shooting half by instinct, she adjusted the distance from zero to ten feet and triggered the shutter. The moment she heard the motor drive, she realized her mistake. The sound resembled a growl. The leopard froze. She was close enough to see his eyes dilate, to note how he gathered himself into a tight ball just before he sprang.

Molo eased himself protectively in front of her. "Eeeaaahhh!" he screamed, trumpeting like an elephant. He bent over, shifting his weight back and forth, and waved his stick as if it were a trunk. Reaching down, he grabbed a handful of dust and threw it over his shoulder, mimicking an angry bull elephant. Stamping his feet violently, he trumpeted again. "Eeeaaahhh!"

The leopard looked at him with surprise, grunted once, then leaped to the side, retreating into the brush. She could hear the photographs reel off inside the camera. Ten, eleven, twelve, she counted; then the leopard was gone.

"Oh, Molo!" She gasped. "That was wonderful!" She reached forward and hugged him. Her hands were trembling. Embarrassed, he shrugged his shoulders as if to say acting like a furious elephant was just part of his normal working day. Turning, he bounded along the trail that led back toward the Land-Rover.

As she followed him at a steady jog, a broad grin spread across her lips. The evening had been worth everything. The leopard family would be among the most charming photographs she'd taken, and this last sequence might be the most dramatic work she'd ever done. She prayed they'd all come out, that she'd gotten the focus and exposure right.

The best photographs always seemed to come by accident when she least expected them. Yet such accidents occurred only after endless hours of careful preparation. She couldn't possibly count how long she'd spent trying to get the animals to pose, waiting for the light to be just right or the composition perfect. In reality, there was little luck, she thought. If you worked like hell, you made your own breaks. And if you were photographing two herds of elephants mating or a leopard crouched before you on a narrow path, you made damn sure you checked exposure and lighting and distance and film.

It was ten o'clock at night. She'd finished writing her last letter of the evening, this one to a fashion editor in Rome. One of the Turkana boys would walk it to Tula Gorda, a tiny outpost of a town six hours away, in the morning. The letter probably wouldn't get to Italy for another month. Yet it was one of the prices she paid for leaving civilization behind. Still, she wouldn't have traded what she was doing for the world.

There had been a time, shortly after finishing college, when she'd considered modeling as a career. She'd majored in art and discovered, much to her chagrin, that unless she was willing to teach, no one wanted to hire a woman with a special interest in nineteenth-century French Impressionism. On a lark, she'd interviewed with one of the big modeling agencies in New York and they'd liked her. In six months she'd done two television commercials and a score of magazine spreads, including a cover for *Vogue*. But she was far too restless for such work. She wanted a career upon which she could put a creative stamp of her own. Then one day, working with a photographer friend, watching his prints develop in the darkroom, the idea had come to her. Photography was the perfect extension of art. Everything she'd learned about the composition, the lighting, the colors of the French masters, could easily be applied to film. In a way, film was the photographer's canvas; the camera, his brush.

She'd started slowly, taking a job for Peter Illes, one of the better-known fashion photographers in New York. For a year she'd worked as an apprentice, waiting for the weekends to do her own work. She'd shot everything in sight—still lifes, babies, friends, friends' dogs, an alley filled with garbage cans. If the subject had a peculiar shape or looked interesting or the sun played across it in an intriguing fashion, she'd photographed it. Then one October she'd come upon a group of horses playing in a field. It was early morning and she'd caught a golden sun rising above the horizon, the fresh dew sparkling on the grass; the horses, coal black, galloping across a meadow, backdropped by a forest of red and yellow leaves. Illes told her it was one of the best natural sequences he'd ever seen.

Two years later she'd had her own exhibit in a small gallery in New York; part fashion, part nature, with a few still lifes thrown in. The critics had given her good reviews, stating that her real talents lay in wildlife photography. There were hundreds of photographers who could do good fashion work. What she needed was an area of specialization, and gradually she'd begun to concentrate more and more on natural subjects.

Shortly after the opening of her show, she'd gone to hear a lecture at Columbia University given by a British anthropologist working in Kenya. She'd been intrigued by the slides Dr. Ruth Parker had shown. Afterward she'd gone up and introduced herself. Some spark had ignited between the two from the very start. The next day they'd gone to lunch and Ruth had invited her to come to Kenya for a visit.

She'd spent a week there first, returning later for a two-month photographic safari through some of the game parks. When she went back to New York with a collection of one thousand photographs, she realized that she was hooked; there was no place in the world like Africa and no country like Kenya. She'd conceived the idea of her book then, a photographic essay on Kenya's Northern Frontier, one of the last outposts of old Africa, bordering on the vast deserts of the Sudan. Here there was no television, no jet aircraft, no antibiotics. Here the tribes such as the Turkana still went half naked, hunted with spears, and lived in huts plastered with dung.

It had taken her a year to set up the trip. She'd arranged to do some fashion work in Rome and then she'd gone on to Africa. She'd been in Kenya now for four months. Except for several brief jaunts to Nairobi to replenish supplies, she'd spent most of the time in the Northern Frontier.

As she sat in her tent that evening, she thought about the day's events and the close call with the leopard. How far she had come in four years! When she first graduated from college, she'd never imagined that this was what she'd be doing. But she was happy, and for the first time she truly felt she was doing something important with her life.

She sealed her letter, decided against writing one last note to an old college friend in New York, then walked out of the tent and took a small canvas chair by the fire. She poured a cup of tea from a pot nestled in the coals and surveyed the compound. The Turkana village had begun to settle down for the night. She could see a small fire next to old Kamani's hut. Next door, the two infants inside Lolomanu's dwelling were finally quiet. Across from the central fire she could hear the murmur of six young Turkana warriors, still fresh from circumcision, boasting of daring and bravery in the ceremonial hut. When she looked up, Molo was standing before her.

"Is everything all right?" he asked in Swahili.

She nodded, trying to choose her words. "Upcountry" Swahili, a simplified version of the language, was spoken in trade by most of the native tribes across Kenya. It was not difficult to learn; she had mastered the essentials in six weeks.

"Thank you for the afternoon," she replied slowly. "I think you saved my life."

He laughed. "It was the *shauri*, memsaab, the will of God."

"But how did you know the leopard would run when you acted like an elephant?"

He cocked his head with a sly grin, his black eyes glistening. "I knew we did not have much of a chance if I sounded like a gazelle!"

She smiled.

"Is there anything I can get for you tonight?" he asked.

"No. No, thank you."

"*Kwaheri,*" he said. "May you have pleasant sleep."

"Good night," she replied.

She sat for another half hour gazing absently into the fire. There is only one real disadvantage with this work, she thought. Sometimes during the months of isolation, she became terribly lonely. There were times at night, as she wound down from the activities of the day, when she yearned for a man. It was not so much a physical desire as a longing for companionship, for someone she could share her thoughts with. Funny, she reflected. Beneath her desire to succeed, beneath all her courage and bravery, was a small vulnerable spot that sought a home, a family, a safe refuge. She kept it in the back of her mind, but more and more these past months it seemed to intrude on her thoughts. Ruth Parker in Nairobi knew that feeling. Ruth had spent years trekking through Africa on her own and had warned her about the feelings of loneliness and isolation that occasionally came upon you in the bush.

If she really thought about it, she was not sure why she had never married. She'd always been able to pick and choose her men. But as her work began to absorb more and more of her time, her social activities had declined. Given the right man, the right time, someday she would marry, but right now, nothing was more exciting to her than being out in the bush photographing dangerous game.

She stood up and started back to her tent. Closing the canvas curtain, she began to take off her tennis shoes. A cow bellowed inside the *boma*. The hoarse cry rang in the night, then was suddenly stifled. She thought first that it was reacting to a wild animal stalking beyond the protective thorn fence enclosure.

What next? she wondered. Maybe back to Rome for a couple of fashion jobs, then New York for a little magazine work, and then . . . *then the book.* If she could really put together a photo essay on Kenya and the Northern Frontier in a single volume and do it better than any other photographer ever had . . . That was the challenge! That's why she was doing it in the first place, wasn't it? She wanted to leave some distinguishing mark behind, some handprint that showed she was here. And she was close. So close to accomplishing all she'd set out to do.

She reached down to massage the painful spot on her leg where the ants had bitten when she heard the scream. It was a long terrified yell ending in a gurgle. She'd never heard such a sound before, but even then she knew it was the cry of someone dying. She leaped up and ran to the doorway of the tent.

There were more shouts. They seemed to come from all around her. Dark forms hurtled by. In the blackness of night, it was impossible to tell what was happening or who was who, only that people were running frantically across the compound. A bright light sprang from one of the huts beyond the central clearing. Good God, old Kamani's hut was on fire!

Molo came running across the compound toward her.

"Molo, what is it?" she cried in Swahili.

"Run, memsaab," he shouted. "Devils! Demons! Run for your life!"

Before she could gather her wits, her eye caught the glint of a blade. She heard a swishing sound and saw Molo collapse to the ground. His severed body trembled in uncontrolled spasms.

For a moment she was numb. She tried to scream, but found no voice. Out of the darkness emerged a huge figure covered in black. Red eyes stared at her through a narrow slit in a head-dress that covered his face. The figure lunged for her, his sword still dripping.

She sprinted around the tent and darted inside, searching desperately for a revolver buried beneath her clothes. There was a hacking sound as one of the tent poles sagged in. She heard a cry and shouts in a language she couldn't understand. From across the compound came more screams. My God! she thought, struggling against panic. What is this? What's happening?

Her mind groped frantically for some way to escape. Her Land-Rover was parked just outside the fenced enclosure. If she could somehow fight her way out to the vehicle, perhaps she had a chance.

With trembling fingers she grabbed the revolver and cocked it. The shadow of a figure moved across the side of the tent and stopped. The form was silhouetted by the rising blaze of fires and it loomed above her, raising its sword. She fired three shots in rapid succession through the canvas, but they had no effect.

The blade fell. A second guide rope severed and the tent began to quiver above her. She fired at the shadow again, realizing too late the body was not where she saw the reflection. There was a splintering crack as the third guide rope snapped and the tent collapsed on top of her.

2

It was Monday. For an April morning in New York City, the day was already hot and saturated with humidity. By nine o'clock the usual commuter rush had begun to dissipate when a sleek black limousine pulled up to the corner of a busy Midtown East Side street. The door opened and a middle-aged man carrying a briefcase stepped out. He paused for a moment, studying the huge, imposing building that rose seventy-two stories above him. Yet whatever pleasure he derived from gazing upon the magnificent curve of black glass and steel was short-lived. Glancing at his watch, he realized he was late.

He slammed the door of the limousine and started quickly across the sidewalk, entering the building's tall revolving doors. The limousine pulled out behind him and disappeared into the traffic. For the moment, for the brief ten seconds it took this man to cross the sidewalk and enter the rotunda of the Trans-Oceanic Airlines Building, he could have been any average New York businessman. Except for the intense blue of his eyes and the slight graying of his temples, there was nothing particularly distinguishing about his features. He was of medium height. He wore a conventional three-piece pin-striped suit with a J. Press tie. For all practical purposes, he was a man bent on escaping the city fumes and hurrying to his job.

"Good morning, Mr. Jacobson," the doorman said.

"Good morning, Jake," he answered. "Your family all right?"

"Yes, sir, doing fine, sir." The black man smiled.

"And Rodgers?"

Rodgers was the doorman's eldest son. Jacobson had helped provide the scholarship funds that enabled the young man to go to college.

"He's doing well, mighty well, sir. Made him an A paper on poetry. Good writer, he is. And your family, sir?"

"Fine, thanks." The businessman nodded as he disappeared inside the closing doors of an elevator. The doorman picked up a small telephone next to his station and dialed a number. "Mr. Jacobson is on the way up," he announced. He turned and watched the elevator blink steadily upward, first to twenty-seven, then to forty-eight, then on past sixty-four.

On the seventy-second floor of the TransOceanic Airlines Building, seventeen members of the board were seated around a long mahogany table. A secretary poured a cup of coffee and looked nervously at her watch. Only the large armchair reserved for the chairman was empty.

Abruptly the tall panel doors at the end of the room swung open. Instantly everyone rose to his feet.

"Sorry for the delay," Jacobson said. He walked briskly into the room, nodding to assorted individuals around the table. The secretary handed him a small typewritten page that outlined the agenda for the meeting. Pushing his briefcase aside, he studied it for a moment, then took his seat at the head of the table.

For the next hour, Michael Jacobson directed the meeting like a general, planning corporate strategy, reviewing profits, listening to suggestions from the board.

Based on the prospects of a poor spring quarter, the vice-chairman made a motion to raise fares on transatlantic flights. Jacobson argued against the proposal. Competition with Pan Am and Air France on the New York-to-Paris run was keen, and he did not want to lose their edge, which was based on dependable schedules and an affordable price.

During the fifteen years Jacobson had been president and chairman of the board, TransOceanic Airlines had gone from a carrier with a negative cash flow of 15 million dollars and a reckless expansion program to a conservative, steady-growth airline serving forty-five countries, with twenty thousand employees and a fleet of fifty planes. Jacobson had been the first to suggest the purchase of the new Boeing 747s. Likewise, he had been the most outspoken against the fuel-inefficient Supersonic transport. On his recommendations, the company had affiliated with a hotel chain, formed under a subsidiary corporation called World American Inns. Through package travel fares and prearranged hotel accommodations, the subsidiary had shown a nice, continued profit. Now the company ran thirty hotels in twenty-five countries. Instinctively Jacobson had known what the traveling public wanted, and he had always tried to keep their desires uppermost in his mind. Through his leadership TransOceanic had become one of the most successful airline companies in the world.

They were midway through the meeting when one of the tall panel doors opened and Jacobson's secretary came unobtrusively into the room.

"I'm sorry to interrupt you, sir," she whispered, presenting a small yellow envelope, "but I think you'd better see this."

Jacobson nodded and took the telegram. The words "DELIVERY URGENT" were stamped across the envelope.

The members of the board leaned back in their chairs and relaxed. Interruptions of this type were a frequent occurrence. They knew Jacobson liked to keep a close touch on the pulse of the corporation. Often sudden problems required an immediate decision. Probably the telegram was another nuisance request from one of their offices in Paris or Rome.

"I'll be just a moment," Jacobson said. He wanted to dispense with the telegram quickly and get back to the meeting. As his eyes glanced across the message, they suddenly became riveted to the words. A shadow crossed his face.

"Gentlemen—" He tried to clear his throat. "I'm afraid I must leave . . ." His words trailed off. Slowly regaining his composure, he rose to his feet. "Vice-Chairman Miller can continue with the agenda."

He started to say something more, then stopped. Turning, he

walked out of the room. The doors slammed solidly behind him.

Outside the board room, Jacobson clawed for air. His heart pounded inside his chest. His legs felt as if they would buckle. He stood for a moment, trying to calm himself, then walked unsteadily down the hall to his office. He pushed his way into the large plush room and shut the door.

On top of his desk was the photograph of a young blond girl, slender and lithe, dressed in a riding jacket and breeches. She was standing in front of a black horse, its head wrapped around her shoulder. The contours of her face were beautifully formed. Even in the photograph her blue eyes shone in their intensity.

The buzzer on the intercom rang. "Mr. Jacobson, are you all right?" his secretary asked.

"Yes, I'm all right," he answered. For a moment, he welcomed the interruption. But as quickly as it had come it was gone, and now he was left in silence with only his clean, neat desk, the yellow telegram, and the photograph of the beautiful young girl and her horse.

"Should have been married by now," he muttered. "Married with a couple of children and a nice home in Westchester County where I could come and see you on the weekends and watch your family grow."

But in his heart he knew that was not her style. She would never have been satisfied with such an existence. He knew that it was the difference about her that made her so special, the way in which she fought life, the way she bucked and argued against his authority much more than did her three elder brothers and one younger brother. More than any person he had ever known, he thought, unless it was himself. And that, he thought, was perhaps why he loved her most of all.

As he stared at the photograph, a memory came back to him. She was a small girl, cradled in his arms. He was sitting at the helm of his sailboat, manning the wheel while his three older sons worked the sails. In the sunlight, the golden color of her hair sparkled and dazzled like spray. She was soft and graceful and gentle, and every time she laughed, she made him smile. What an absolute gem of a child she was.

. . . And then he recalled a time when she was older. Jacobson had been watching a horse show from the stands when she fell off at a jump. He remembered how he had leaped over the rail, running out across the ring to help her. He could still recall the fear in his heart, the same pounding, frantic feeling he felt this morning, only it was so much less then than now, for she had not been hurt and it had come to a good end. After he had dusted her off and made sure she was all right, he had helped her back on her horse. She had gone back and ridden again, and this time she'd won a ribbon and he was as proud of her as he'd ever been.

. . . And then there was a time one night when she was parked out in the driveway with her first high-school boyfriend. It was long after midnight. He remembered getting out of bed and looking out his window in the moonlit night and seeing the shadow of two figures embracing inside the car. It was then that he first realized she was growing up, that she would be steering gradually away from him toward a destiny of her own. But not this, he thought. How could it happen? How could it come to this end?

He reflected briefly on the meeting in the conference room. Hell, they could run the company without him. The question now was, What could he do? What options did he have? Where could he turn for help?

He would have to tell his family. He could bring his sons together to discuss a course of action. But how in the hell was he going to break it to his wife?

He stood up from his desk and walked out into the hall.

"Miss Johnston, get me the limousine," he said. "I'm going home."

She looked at him with concern. "You sure you're all right?"

He started to nod, then shook his head. "If we get a call in the next half hour from the State Department, pipe it into the limousine telephone. Otherwise you can reach me at home. I'll take the elevator down and wait for the car out front."

She noted an expression of exhaustion flood across his face. He looked suddenly very worried and very old.

"I'm sorry, sir, is there anything I can do?"

"I wish there were," he answered. "Just tell Miller he'll have to run the company for a while. I'll make some kind of formal announcement this afternoon."

He turned and started for the elevator. The secretary called the limousine, then watched out the window until a long black form pulled up to the front of the building seventy-two floors below. In another instant Jacobson had climbed into the vehicle and was gone.

An hour passed before Miller entered the room.

"Meeting went fairly well," he said. "Mr. Jacobson all right?"

She frowned. "I'm not sure."

"The telegram?"

"I think so."

"Business?"

"No, I don't think so."

He thought for a moment. "When the old man read it back there, I thought he was going to collapse. I've never seen him look so upset."

"Yes, sir," she answered. "Whatever the message said, it disturbed him deeply."

"Something with the family?"

She shrugged. "He didn't say."

Miller walked into Jacobson's office and laid the copy of the agenda from the board meeting down on his desk. As he started to leave, he noted the small yellow telegram.

Reaching down, he picked it up, fingering it cautiously. None of my business, he thought. It was probably a bit of privileged information that he shouldn't be interfering with. Yet perhaps there was something he could do, some way in which he could help.

Unable to control his curiosity any longer, he opened the folded message. He stared at it for a long time in disbelief. His eyes squinted and then he shook his head.

"Jesus," he exclaimed. "Holy Christ."

The cable was from Nairobi, Kenya. The message read:

Routing 57XXAB KENYA to USA COPY
Department of State, United States via Embassy
Washington, D.C.

Message to Mr. Michael Jacobson, Esq.
President, TransOceanic Airlines
TransOceanic Building
New York, New York

Approved for Transmission. Nonclassified.

REGRET TO INFORM YOU YOUR DAUGHTER DI-
ANA JACOBSON MISSING ALONG THE NORTH-
ERN KENYA BORDER STOP WHEN LAST SEEN
SHE WAS WORKING WITH A TRIBE IN THE
NORTHERN FRONTIER STOP POLITICAL UPRIS-
INGS AND BANDS OF ABYSSINIAN RAIDERS IN-
VOLVED IN RECENT BORDER CLASHES INDI-
CATE THAT SHE MAY HAVE BEEN KIDNAPPED
OR KILLED.

3

They'd gone out through the Golden Gate on a beam reach, the
thirty-six foot sailboat heeled over so far that he thought once
her mast would break. The captain was a tall, deeply tanned
young man of twenty-nine. His crew, a red-haired woman and a
dog. They sailed outward for an hour until they reached the
Potato Patch, that treacherous shoal of shallow water which
guards the entrance to San Francisco Bay. Then the ground-
swell became too big and he turned the boat around. If he'd
been by himself, he would have handled it easily, but the girl

was prone to seasickness and he didn't want to ruin her afternoon.

Coming back, they passed beneath the great double pillars of the Golden Gate, its expanse soaring far above them like some fantastic reddish crown. He was tempted to raise the spinnaker when he heard the deep-throated blast of a tanker surging through the bridge behind him.

"We've got company!" he shouted. The dog perked up its ears and barked. There was a noise from the galley as the woman pushed up through the stairwell. She was dressed in a bikini, with a white shirt wrapped around her shoulders. "What did you say?" she yelled. He pointed in the direction of the freighter then checked the wind. They would have to come about.

"God, what a crew," he muttered. "You"—he nodded toward the mongrel and shook his finger at it—"you sit here all morning and when I need someone to help with the sails, where are you? Chewing on a bloody bone."

"And you?" He smiled at the woman now emerging from the stairs.

"The captain wants food," she answered. "The cook was in the galley."

She took a piece of sandwich and stuffed it into his mouth. He put his arms around her and kissed her lightly on the neck.

"You'll make your stripes yet," he said.

"Thank you, cap'n," she answered. "But I think you'd better sail a bit more to the left or we're going to find ourselves impaled by a rather large boat coming up on your stern."

He glanced back and laughed. The freighter was now steaming full bore through the gate. She was a giant hulk of a vessel, a hundred times the size of the sailboat, and she was churning down upon them, throwing out a great showering wake from her bow.

"Sail over power." He snorted.

"You may have to explain that to the Coast Guard," she answered. "I don't think they've even seen you."

"Try waving." He grinned.

The freighter was close enough now so that he could read the inscription ASPERIA on her bow. She was flying the flag of the Netherlands. As she bore down upon them, there was another deafening blast from her horn.

He felt a surge of excitement, measured the distance until the freighter was almost upon them, then swung the bow of the sailboat sharply out of the way. The great hulking mass of steel passed less than a hundred yards off their port. He glanced up at the towering bridge and saw a dozen sailors standing along the railing looking down at them. They were all clapping and cheering. He was puzzled for an instant, then saw that his companion had slipped off her shirt and the top of her bikini and was waving it up at them. She stood in the golden midday sun, her firm taut breasts exposed to the wind, and he couldn't help but marvel at her body. Her name was Page Sinclair and she was five feet nine inches tall with slender legs and long flowing red hair.

"You crazy?" he shouted, half in shock, half in amusement.

"Just wanted to say hello!" she yelled back at him.

"That's one hell of a welcome!" He laughed. He stood up and applauded her along with the crew of the *Asperia.* She was one of the most fascinating and unpredictable women he had ever known.

As the ship churned by, he turned the sailboat directly into its wake. They tossed wildly through three sets of waves. Once the last trough passed he swung the vessel eastward again and they proceeded with the wind at their backs. In half an hour they had crossed Raccoon Straits and dropped anchor off Angel Island.

"You want another sandwich?" she asked.

"No, but I think you could give one to the mate."

The dog was up on its hind legs begging. She threw it a bit of bread, then disappeared back down the stairs toward the galley. He remained on deck, securing the anchor and furling the sails. The boat rocked gently in the shelter of the island. It was a gorgeous day—blue sky, scattered clouds, the water bright and sparkling. To the west the wind had begun to blow wisps of fog over the Marin headlands, the mist spilling through the ridges like streamers of cotton.

"Well, it's your watch, Ahab," he said to the dog as he finished tying a line around the mainsail and moved down the stairs into the galley.

Page was lying on one of the foam beds in the forward cabin.

"Prepare to repel boarders." He grinned.

"I think I have a better idea," she answered.

He could feel his pulse begin to rise and a weakness flood into his legs. He moved in beside her and lay down.

She took him in her arms and kissed him lightly, then ran her tongue along the corners of his ear. With her right hand she began to gently undo his shirt. She had placed her bikini top back on and he pulled the strap off her shoulder, watching the soft pink breast emerge from beneath its cover. He touched the sharp demarcation of the nipple with his finger. He could feel the saliva begin to build up in the back of his mouth.

"Jim, I love you," she said.

"All you want is more grog," he murmured, smiling.

He watched her for a moment, saw the corners of her mouth begin to pout, and knew that she was going to be serious again. For the past month she'd been putting increasing pressure on him to marry her. He'd been fighting off the suggestion, pretending he didn't know what she was driving at or, when she actually tried to pin him down, saying that the time just wasn't right. At twenty-four, Page Sinclair was already a spectacular woman, a leading buyer for one of the San Francisco department stores and well on her way to a successful career. But there was something about her that made him hold back. Women like Page were meant to be treated casually, he thought, for when you really fell in love with them, something would foul up and then you'd be left with that terrible old hurt that came upon you in spasms and never really left you alone. He'd been in love once, deeply in love, and somehow it had gone wrong. He knew that he never wanted to feel that sense of loss again.

"James, I love you," she whispered.

He kissed her softly.

"Jim, I want you to tell me that you love me too."

"You know I do."

"Thanks," she answered sarcastically. "You really sound convincing."

"How else could I put up with you?"

"Bastard."

"Now don't get huffy."

"Jim, I want to marry you."

He frowned his long deep frown and she knew what his answer was going to be. She lay back down and stared up at the ceiling of the boat. He tried to nuzzle up next to her but she pushed him away.

"The company asked if I'd like to transfer to Seattle. It's a brand-new store. It would be an opportunity to move up."

"If that's what you want, go for it," he answered.

"That's not the answer I wanted."

"Page, I—"

"Bastard."

"You said that before."

"This time I meant it."

"Jesus, Page," he said. "I don't know what the hell I may be doing six months from now. If I break away from the firm, I'll be on a starvation diet for the next couple of years. You like all these trappings, the boat and the condo and all the rest of it, but I don't know how you're going to like me poor. And if it's something I have to do, then I don't want to drag you into it, especially if it means passing up some hot opportunity in Seattle. What the hell else can I say?"

"I'm not sure I believe you."

"Well, it's the goddamned truth."

"Maybe staying here is something I want to do."

"Then don't push me."

"Your father will never let you go hungry, you know that."

"Christ," he answered angrily. "There are some things that I just can't ask my father to do for me. One of them is to support me at my own career. I chose architecture. If I want to leave the firm and go out on my own, then I'll have to do it myself. Thank you."

"And what about Nicole?"

"Nicole is in the past," he found himself shouting. "That's over and done!"

"But that's partly it, isn't it?"

"No . . . yes." He nodded slowly. "I guess partly. It's just that there are some things going on now that I'm not quite sure about, and it doesn't make sense for you to get involved with a lot of variables, especially not at the expense of your own career."

"Then, Jim, I'm going to leave you," she said.

He had heard her say it before but it was the first time he'd noted the tone of desperation in her voice. He thought now how much he wanted to lie down with her again but he pushed the impulse aside. Suddenly he felt hemmed in, claustrophobic. He had to get air.

He got up slowly. "I think we're drifting," he stalled. "The anchor must have broken loose."

He walked back through the galley and up the stairs. The dog was on the back section of the stern staring down at some small fish dancing across the surface.

Jesus Christ, he thought. I've already been through this once. Married and divorced at the age of twenty-five. I bring this girl home and my brothers will give me a long lecture on what happened to Nicole and remind me how uncertain my future is and how I can't afford to get tied down right now, and, damn it, they're right. If I'm going to lose this tall redhead with her long legs and beautiful breasts, then it will have to be.

Five minutes later she came up the stairs dressed in jeans and a large bulky sweater. He could see that she'd been crying.

"James, I want to go home," she said.

"Page, I'm sorry," he muttered. He turned and began hauling up the anchor without saying anything more.

Four hours later he was waiting in the terminal at San Francisco's international airport for a nonstop flight to New York, trying to piece together his father's urgent call.

4

He paid the cab and watched it disappear. For a long moment James lingered outside the Westchester estate, taking in a landscape familiar since childhood. The five-acre lawn spread out

behind the Tudor mansion in gentle sloping contours that ended
at the farthest perimeter in a forest and a lake. It was Tuesday
evening. The sun had set; the last blush of day disappeared in
deepening shadows. The grass smelled freshly mowed. Tall
manicured cedars swayed softly in the breeze. How long has it
been since I've last been home? he wondered. Three years?

The estate was a testimony to his father's achievements. Few
people outside the family knew all of the things the elder Jacobson had accomplished. You could read about a number of them
in *Who's Who*. Pilot and squadron commander of the 144th
bomber group out of London in World War II. Heavily decorated. Graduate of Harvard Law School, cum laude. He'd
banked his first million by the age of thirty-five and been offered
the presidency and chairmanship of the ailing TransOceanic
Airlines, making him the youngest chief executive in the airline's history. Now, at fifty-seven, he was still hard-driving, te-
nacious, remarkably successful.

All of this was fine, James thought, unless you were his son.
As he turned toward the door, he began to feel some of the old
pressures rise up again: the pressure to succeed, the pressure to
excel, the pressure to compete with his older brothers, pressures
that had been ingrained in him since he was old enough to walk.
His two older brothers had followed closely in the Jacobson
tradition. Both had been outstanding college athletes and had
done extremely well in school. James had had more difficulty.
He'd tried hard, but grades had never come that easily. Diana,
on the other hand, had rebelled almost from the very start. And
Jon Paul—the youngest brother—was already a problem. Well,
it happens in the best of families, James thought. What was the
saying, from rags to riches to rags again in three generations?
He took a deep breath, rang the doorbell, and greeted his
mother with a hug.

They gathered at the dinner table that night just as the family
had done when the children were growing up. Each had his
allotted spot. James's father occupied the head seat at the end of
the table. Diagonally across from him was his oldest brother,
Michael Junior, now a professor of economics at Yale. Next to
him was Donald, a rising partner in a prestigious Wall Street
law firm. To James's right sat his youngest brother, Jon Paul—a

sixteen-year-old junior in prep school. At the far end of the table was his mother, a beautiful stately woman, tall and angular with gray hair and warm brown eyes. Only the seat usually occupied by his sister was empty. Yet even then, his mother had set a place for her, as if by some miracle she might suddenly arrive.

During the dinner all of the brothers asked questions of concern. James wanted to know about Diana's disappearance. Donald quizzed his father if there had been any word. Michael Junior queried about a search. But the elder Jacobson fended them off, stating that he didn't want to discuss the matter fully until they had eaten. Then as coffee was finally passed, he leaned back in his chair and searched the faces of his sons.

"The telephone calls have been futile," he began. "It took twelve hours for us to reach the Kenya Minister of Foreign Affairs. He was of little help. Neither was the United States Embassy. William Simpson at the State Department could only offer his regrets. Apparently there was a semblance of a search. Some planes were sent out to fly over the area where she disappeared, but they found nothing. Part of the problem is that no one knew exactly where she was or what had happened. They *thought* she'd been working with a particular tribe in the Northern Frontier District of Kenya. Native reports indicate that she disappeared in a raid. Some bodies were found. None of them identifiable. . . ."

There was a long, silent hush inside the room. James looked over toward his mother. Her face was passive and withdrawn.

"Of course, Washington sent a note of sympathy. They offered to arrange an investigating party, but there's a time delay and I don't think they can really be much help. There's absolutely nothing else to report. They think she was killed. They're not sure. Not absolutely." Jacobson paused, glancing around the table.

"The question is, Where do we go from here?"

"We don't have a whole lot of options." Michael Junior frowned. "For the next day or so maybe the smartest thing to do is wait. You told me yourself that was what the State Department recommended."

"Maybe the damn thing is just some kind of awful mistake," Donald said. "When was the last word you received from her?"

"Six weeks ago she sent a postcard. She mentioned that she'd gone down to Nairobi for some kind of medical attention then was going back to the Northern Frontier. About a month ago, we received this in the mail. . . ."

James's father opened a small felt pouch and took out an object that at first glance resembled a songbird's egg. It was a round, bluish stone. In the light, it radiated a deep, sparkling fire. As he passed it around, his sons examined it one by one.

"Out of curiosity, I took it down to a jeweler," Jacobson reported. "It's a blue-black sapphire of very rare composition. He'd never seen anything quite like it. Polished and placed in the proper setting, he estimated its worth at about ten thousand dollars."

Donald whistled loudly. "Where the hell did she get it?"

Jacobson shrugged. "I don't have the slightest idea. But look at the flat surface at the end. It's cut and engraved with some type of marking."

The top of the gem had a small hole drilled into it as if it could have once held a tiny wire or chain. Across one face was a finely carved etching that appeared to be the outline of a desert palm.

"What does it mean?" James asked.

Jacobson shook his head. "She sent a note with the package. Said she wanted us to keep it for her until she came back. There was nothing else of interest."

"Strange," Michael Junior replied. "You think she was involved in some kind of smuggling?"

"No, not Diana." Jacobson scowled. "It would be very unlike her."

"Then perhaps a gift?"

"Who knows? She certainly had plenty of suitors," Donald interjected.

"Maybe the Duke of Yorkshire." James smiled, referring to a man who had been after his sister for years.

"Or that guy who offered the diamond bracelet that she wrote you about. The perfume heir. What was his name?"

"Or the race car driver. Wasn't he supposed to have gone to some tour down in South Africa?"

"Boys! Enough!" their mother said harshly. She glowered angrily from the end of the table.

"Mom's right," Donald said. "It's interesting, but it doesn't offer much help. But I agree with Michael. I think we should wait. Something's bound to turn up."

"How long do you wait?"

"Until we hear some news."

"And what if there is no further news?"

"You cross that bridge when you come to it," Donald answered.

Jacobson looked across the table toward James. "James?"

The architect frowned. "Perhaps someone should fly out there to see what could be done. It might be worth a plane trip to check it out."

"I've thought of that," Jacobson answered. "Certainly it makes more sense than sitting here trying to make connections halfway around the world. Especially when you don't know who you're talking with or what the hell to say."

He glanced down the table toward his wife. She was a woman who rarely showed emotion. In front of the boys she'd exhibited few tears. Now she held herself well. He could tell from her expression that she, too, was in favor of waiting. But the next thing he said made the look of concern on her face deepen.

"I was thinking that perhaps I should go myself."

"It's premature," Donald argued. "What could you do that someone else couldn't? You don't know any of the languages. You'd only jeopardize your own life, especially if it's some type of border skirmish. Then we'd have two members of the family missing, instead of one." The lawyer shook his head firmly. "To be quite frank, I don't think it would be wise."

"Perhaps," Jacobson said. "But what if several of us went? Can any of you break free?"

"I'd go with you in a second, Dad, if I thought it would do any good," Michael Junior said. "The hardest thing to do now is nothing. Even tomorrow you might get a telegram saying she's been found and everything's all right. We need something more substantial to go on."

"How about the rest of you?"

Donald shook his head. "I'd have a heck of a time getting away on such short notice. I think we should wait until all the information is in before we make a move."

"I'll go!" a voice cried. The three brothers turned sharply and glared at the sixteen-year-old boy.

Jacobson smiled. "I know." He nodded. "Except I don't think your mother would approve."

Jon Paul started to protest but Jacobson cut him off.

"Then it's unanimous, we wait," he said. The two oldest brothers nodded. Jacobson could see the faint traces of relief smooth across his wife's face. Only James sat quietly, deep in thought.

The tall grandfather clock rang the hour of ten in a slow and melancholy chime. Jacobson was on the telephone speaking with William Simpson of the State Department. The governments of Ethiopia and Uganda had been contacted. It did not seem to be a political kidnapping. No one had any additional information.

He hung up the receiver. Upstairs, he could hear his wife and older sons talking quietly. Maybe his sons were right. They all had good judgment. The hardest thing to do was wait. He tried to remember other cases that he'd read about. Several years before a senator's son had disappeared off the coast of South America. Jacobson remembered it now because he had wondered at the time what he would ever do if it had happened to one of his own family. The young man had been working on some anthropological studies off Surinam. He'd ventured out with a fellow researcher one day in a native canoe, trying to cross the mouth of a large river. The story was that a wave had swamped them. They spent the night in the water, then the next morning tried to swim to shore. Neither was ever seen again. The official statement indicated the men had drowned, but rumors persisted for months that they had made it to shore and been killed by hostile tribes. Missionaries in the area said there were sightings of natives wearing the men's glasses around their necks like charms. Others coming out of the jungles reported that they had seen the men's shrunken heads.

He heard a noise on the stairs and looked up to see James enter the study. James saw the expression of torment on his father's face and put his arm around his shoulder.

"I hope we didn't let you down tonight," he said.

Jacobson shook his head. "You boys never let me down. I needed good honest answers and that was what you gave me. It's about what I had come up with. We wait for now and if nothing turns up, we consider sending someone over there as our representative. I can look for someone tomorrow."

He smiled grimly and gripped his son tightly on the arm. "That's why I wanted all of you to come."

James stared at his father, searching into his eyes. "I know it hurts you, Dad. Diana was the one you loved the best. She was the most creative of us all. It nearly killed me when I got your call. It was as if something inside of me had suddenly died. I can't imagine her—" He stopped abruptly, realizing he was going to say something that might upset his father.

"Raped and murdered?"

James nodded. "Yes . . . if you put it in those words. I don't even like to think about it."

Jacobson placed his hand on his son's shoulder. "Well, maybe everything will turn out all right. You going back to San Francisco in the morning?"

James shook his head. "I thought I'd stay until we heard some news. I took off a week."

"How's work?"

"It's all right," James replied. "We just finished a large project designing a sixty-four-story building for the Bank of California down in Los Angeles."

"Sounds impressive."

"Yeah," James answered. "I got to work on the garage."

Jacobson smiled. "It's a hell of a thing when I only get to see you like this." He brushed his fingers through his son's hair. They started up the stairs. "I just finished talking with the State Department. There's still no news."

"Dad, why don't you let me go?" James said abruptly.

Jacobson stopped and stared at his son. There was a long silent pause. "No . . . no," he finally said. "Your brothers are right. Let's wait another couple of days."

Far past midnight, after all of his brothers had said good
night and his father and mother had finally gone to bed, James
walked down into the study. Remembering a portfolio of his
sister's photographs, he crouched down and withdrew a large
folder from a drawer inside the desk. Very carefully he laid it on
the table. Slowly, almost reverently, he opened the cover and
began to leaf through the pages. The section was titled *Africa,*
the photographs were large black-and-white matted prints.
There were beautiful shots of leaping gazelles, of giraffes wandering across dry and lonesome flats, of strange natives with
pierced lips and mud plastered on their heads, wearing thick
bead necklaces.

He came across a newspaper article that his mother had cut
out weeks before and pasted into a page of the book.

New York, UPI. Among the most talented of the new female photographers, Diana Jacobson's collection at the
Wanesworth Gallery is a fresh and artistic look at Africa.
Her composition is superb and her use of natural lighting
cannot be equalled. No other photographer has captured
the spirit of the country quite the same way. She has
braved disease, natural disasters, and hostile tribes for
some of the most unique pictures of Africa in the past
decade.

As he finished, he heard a slight movement. Turning, he saw
that his youngest brother had entered the room. Jon Paul was
barefoot and in pajamas.

"Jon Paul, why aren't you asleep?" James asked sternly.

"Couldn't," the boy answered. He looked at his brother imploringly. "You mind if I sit up with you for a while?"

"No, I guess not," James answered. He turned back to the
scrapbook and continued thumbing through the pages.

Jon Paul sat down next to him and began studying the portfolio. "Jim, I want to go with you," he said.

"You crazy?" James answered. "Your brothers are right. We
should wait."

The boy looked at him and frowned. "You're the only single

one of the bunch. You were closer to Diana than any of us. Dad couldn't possibly go, he's got too many obligations here. Besides, he's too damn old. You know that neither Michael or Donald are eager to leave their families. I think we should go and I don't think we should wait."

"And what brought you to this remarkable conclusion?"

"Because that's not just anybody over there, James. It's Diana. What if she needs us? What if she's in trouble and needs us now?"

"Well, then, we'll send somebody over to see."

"Nobody will do as good a job as we can."

"We?" James studied his younger brother. "Dad says that you've been having some trouble in school."

"Poor attitude."

"Who told you that?"

"The school psychiatrist."

"And what are you doing about it?"

Jon Paul shrugged. "I'm just not very interested. I mean, James, all this history and math. I guess I'm just bored."

"And what about all this damn drug stuff?"

"It was no big deal. I was smoking marijuana with some friends out behind the gym and I got caught. That's all."

"You've still got a couple of weeks of school left this quarter, you know."

"Yeah, but I could always make it up next year. Or in summer school. Whenever."

"And what do you think Mom would say?"

Jon Paul nodded gravely. "We'd have to break it to her very gently."

"You're too young and you'd just be in the way."

Jon Paul's eyes widened. "Then you have been thinking about going?"

James shook his finger at him. "Yeah, thinking. Come on, it's late. Go to bed."

"Well, think about what I said, would you?"

"About going?"

"About *me* going."

The boy muttered good night and climbed the stairs. James was left in the study alone. When he thought about it, a lot of

Jon Paul's arguments made sense. James *was* single. The timing couldn't have been more perfect. He had just finished the Bank of California project and although there were some loose ends, he had no pressing assignments.

He stood up and crossed the room, searching through the wood-paneled bookcase until he found a world atlas. Thumbing through the pages, he located a section on Africa and looked up Kenya. Along the northern border of the country was a flat, rectangular district that butted against Ethiopia and the Sudan titled the Northern Frontier.

"Geography," he read. "Flat and arid with scattered desert mountains. Rainfall less than ten inches per year. Inhabitants: desert nomads herding goats and cattle. Major cities: none. One hundred thousand square miles poorly mapped. Many parts still unexplored."

Good God, he thought. How do you find somebody who's vanished in the desolate reaches of Ethiopia or the Sudan? Where do you even start?

5

Jon Paul Jacobson sat in the middle of the history class at Farnham Military Academy. It was two in the afternoon and Mr. Boyd, the instructor, had launched into a lengthy discussion of Lincoln's unsuccessful bid for Congress in 1858 as the "split rail" candidate. There were twenty-two members of the class, all boys. The term military academy merely referred to a heritage of military preparation years before. Now the boys wore their uniforms only once a month for drill. The rest of the time they dressed in sports coats and ties. Half of the students were boarders who came from outside the area, some as far away as Wisconsin and Oklahoma. Others, like Jon Paul, at-

tended the school on a daily basis. Farnham had a reputation
for preparing students superbly. In fact, the prep school had
placed students in reputable universities for years, the most recent graduating class sending no less than eleven seniors to
Harvard. When his father had first discovered that Jon Paul
was becoming a problem, he'd pulled him out of a local high
school and sent him to the military academy in the hope it
would provide him some direction. He had thought about
Andover or Exeter for the boy, but his wife didn't like the idea
of his leaving home for a boarding school quite yet; there'd be
plenty of time for that when—and if ever—he attended college.

When Jon Paul chose to apply himself, he could easily be one
of the best students in the class. During the winter quarter he'd
become interested in a friend who'd been bitten by a rabid bat.
For a student project he'd written a masterly report on the
complications, incidence, and frequency of the disease, which
his biology professor had said was in the top of the class. "A+.
Fully a college-level report" was the comment.

On the other hand, when he wasn't interested, he tended to
become careless. He finished ahead of all the other students on a
math final, but was too lazy to check his answers. He'd been
given a C−. The only grade lower at the academy was an F.

Of average height for his age, Jon Paul was stockily built
with sandy hair and hazel eyes. Like his older brothers, he was
a good athlete and excelled in wrestling and track when he
chose. For the most part, however, he had no patience for the
repetitive practices required to become a top competitor. He
played at sports with no real desire to win.

This particular afternoon he was doodling on a piece of
scratch paper, half listening to the instructor, his mind occupied
with that singular topic on which he seemed to concentrate
almost constantly these days—*sex*. Had his own sister been
raped?

It was a pretty awful thing to have happen, especially to one's
sister, yet there were things about the act itself that puzzled
him. If a woman was raped from the front, what was she doing
with her arms and legs? And more important, how did you keep
from getting kicked in the balls? Maybe it was better accom-

plished from the rear, he reflected, but he wasn't entirely sure if the female anatomy allowed you to enter from that direction.

He let his mind wander a little farther. The problem was, if you raped somebody you didn't know, what if they were having their period? He knew women wore such things as Tampax. If they were wearing one and you stuck it into them, would it block the passage? And what about diseases? You'd have to wear a prophylactic, for sure. And for double sure, you wouldn't want to impregnate her, especially if you didn't know her. Raping could be fairly tricky, he thought. You almost had to interview the woman before you tried.

"Hello, there, I'm going to rape you and I was wondering if you were having your period or had been exposed to any diseases recently . . . ?"

And what about the panty hose and underwear. How the hell would you get that stuff off? The closest thing he'd ever come to raping was grabbing Marcia Johnston, a girl two years older, on the tit, and she'd knocked the hell out of him with a blow to the jaw.

It wasn't that he was completely inexperienced. He'd had sex before. Twice. Once he was third in line in a group endeavor in which one of his buddies had rented a room in a sleazy New York City hotel and they'd all got drunk one night and for one hundred dollars she'd taken on all seven of them. He couldn't remember much about it except waiting in the bathroom with the others for his turn. The room was dark and he couldn't see much and he thought it was funny as hell listening to the others grunting and panting and moaning . . . until it was suddenly his turn. Afterward someone had suggested washing off with some after-shave lotion—"to kill the bugs"—and it had burned him for a week.

The other time he'd had sex was in the backseat of a car with a girl named Sally Foster who worked in one of the local pizza parlors. Word had gone around the school that she was an easy lay, and he'd finally screwed up his courage enough to ask her out for a date. She'd smelled like pepperoni and sliced tomatoes. Just at the critical moment, he couldn't get his damned prophylactic out of its package. When he finally did, he wasn't sure he'd put it on right. He'd sweated that one for a month and even now when he occasionally saw her at the pizza parlor, he'd imagine her being pregnant. *"Dad, there's something I've been wanting to talk to you in private about. . . ."* God, his father would have killed him.

A spitball launched across the room landed on his cheek with a plop. He wiped it off his face and felt a flush of anger. He'd thought at first that it was Roger Pearson, a fat whiny slob he'd love to have an excuse to punch. But it was his old buddy Thomas Patterson. Rich in fantasy and poor in experience, he and Patterson had gone into the city one day and snuck into one of those porno parlors on Forty-second Street. And there was a woman named Marlena Juggs who'd starred in a movie called "Sweet Pie." She had the most exquisite body they'd ever seen.

They loaded their hot, panting bodies into one of the small booths and began feeding the machine quarters. They saw Marlena Juggs undress, saw her step over and embrace a man, saw her take his clothes off, and . . . then he remembered seeing something move down below the screen. They hadn't noticed it, but there was a hole large enough for someone to stick his head through. As they were watching the film some pervert was looking through the hole, salivating, watching them.

"Mr. Jacobson!" The words came out of a fog. Jon Paul had the terrible feeling that he'd been asked a question.

He looked up, his face flushed. "I'm sorry, sir . . . could you please repeat the question?"

Mr. Boyd was a stern, elderly man with white hair. When he became angry, his face turned very red. Jon Paul noted a faint warning glow of crimson start across his cheeks.

"I said, Mr. Jacobson, who was the President of the United States when Abraham Lincoln was running for Congress?"

"James Buchanan," Jon Paul answered. He remembered that from reading his homework.

"And who won the senatorial race for Congress in Illinois in 1858?"

"Abraham Lincoln," Jon Paul answered.

"Wrong!" Boyd snapped. "Stephen Douglas won the election. Lincoln was defeated. If you'd been listening you would not have missed the question."

Boyd paused and glared at Jon Paul. "I think you'd better stop by the desk after class, young man."

The boy squirmed in his seat. He glanced across the room and saw Patterson smirking with suppressed laughter. Stopping off at the teacher's desk after class usually meant a special assignment of additional homework. Damn it, I should have been paying more attention—as usual, he thought.

For the rest of the hour, Jon Paul tried to follow the lecture as best he could, taking copious notes. At the end of class the door opened and the principal's secretary walked into the room to hand Mr. Boyd a note. He read it quickly, then stood, discussing the lecture with some of the students. Jon Paul waited quietly until they had finished, then finally stepped up to his desk.

"You wanted to see me, sir?"

Mr. Boyd nodded. "Jon Paul, what am I going to do with you?"

"In what respect, sir?"

"How do I get you to pay attention?"

"I'm sorry, sir, it won't happen again."

"Three times this past quarter I've asked you a question and you've been off somewhere. I can't have that in my class."

"Yes, sir."

"I would like you to write a special report on the impact of the election of 1860—*if* Stephen Douglas had been elected president. Ten pages. And I would like it in a week."

"Yes, sir." Jon Paul groaned.

"History is extremely important, Mr. Jacobson, whether you like it or not. Many times history repeats itself. You get a certain perspective of where you're going and why you are where you are."

"Yes, sir."

"You are a bright boy, Jon Paul. When you're not paying attention you set a bad example for the rest of the class."

"Yes, sir."

"I don't want it happening again, ever."

"No, sir."

"Miss Merriewell just brought a note. You're to see the principal."

Jon Paul looked surprised. "Now?"

"That's right."

Oh, no, he thought. What have I done now? He thanked Mr. Boyd and walked down the hall, his heart in his throat. He searched his mind for possible sources of difficulty. He'd hidden all the rest of the marijuana. It was unlikely anyone had found it. He could feel his pulse hammer in his temples. But the principal didn't call you in on a special occasion just for an idle chat. What if they'd found his stash? Then what the hell would he do? It would be immediate expulsion. They'd already warned him once. And if he was expelled, then what? He'd run away. Go to California. Maybe James would put him up. He'd have no other choice.

He walked into the principal's office and announced his presence to the secretary. Biting his lip, he took a seat in the reception room. He waited for what seemed an eternity. Finally came the sound of voices from behind the office wall. The door suddenly opened. He was astonished to see his older brother walk out.

James looked at Jon Paul and grinned. "You got some packing to do," he said. "We're leaving for Africa in the morning."

6

It was on the last leg of the flight, on the long Cairo-to-Nairobi trip, that James began to realize the immensity of his task. Below him the broad sand reaches of the Sahara slipped steadily away, replaced first by dry and arid mountains then the green carpet of the African veldt. There were no roads, no cities, no evidence of inhabitants. Occasionally the brown line of a river snaked across the terrain but there was little else to break the monotony of his vision. The grandeur of the land, the great pockets of desert, the endless unbroken plains stretched out beneath them for as far as the eye could see.

They had just finished their in-flight breakfast. Jon Paul was staring out of the window watching the great expanse below. James turned toward him.

"How you doing?" he asked.

"Just glad you invited me along," Jon Paul answered.

"If I remember, it was your idea." James smiled.

Jon Paul frowned. "I want to help, James. How in the world did you pull it off?"

"I think if you'd been at the top of your class it might have been easier. As it was, I needed to convince both Mom and Dad you could be useful to me. That maybe if we spent a couple of days together, I could help you sort a few things out."

Jon Paul bit at his lower lip. "That bad, huh?"

"They're awfully concerned about you," James answered. "You're the baby of the family and Dad doesn't feel he's given you enough attention. He thinks all of us older brothers made things too difficult for you. He's worried you're going to end up throwing your life away. You made them real happy by telling them you weren't sure you wanted to go to college."

"Who the hell would take me?" Jon Paul scowled.

"Then why don't you get your grades up?"

Jon Paul began to fidget nervously in his seat. "It's just that I hate school, I guess," he said.

"What do you hate about it?"

"You sound like the school psychiatrist."

"No, come on, get it out."

"I just don't like it. I don't like the work, the memorization. I don't like half the kids. A lot of them at Farnham are just rich snotty guys who've never had to lift a finger in their lives."

"Yeah." James smiled. "Kind of like you, eh?"

"I guess," Jon Paul murmured.

"Look, just figure it's a rough time in your life and you've got to get through it. You've got the talent. It's up to you. I didn't like school either, but I knew I had to make the best of it so I could get to where I wanted to go in life."

"That's part of it, James," Jon Paul replied. "I mean, you

and Michael and Donald always knew where you were going. I
don't have any idea what I want to do."

"You've got a job application to turn in?"

"What do you mean?"

"I mean just relax. You've got plenty of time to make that
decision. Lots of people don't know until they get to college. I
didn't have any real clear-cut idea about architecture until my
senior year."

"So what did Mom say?"

"She was dead set against you going. I told her you didn't
have a lot more important things to do at home. That we should
turn your predicament into an advantage. Maybe you'll even
learn something."

"Yeah, maybe." Jon Paul scowled.

"Well, Jesus, Jon Paul, what the hell did you think they
would say? You run close to trouble all the time and sooner or
later it's going to catch up with you. Your grades are lousy. It
makes it really tough to defend you. Just don't let me down
now. This isn't going to be any picnic."

Jon Paul frowned. "You know, James, this is the first time
I've ever felt the family was depending on me. Dad never seems
to really care."

"Of course he cares. He depends upon you all the time."

"I've heard all that before." Jon Paul shook his head. "He
depends on me to keep my grades up, to do well in school, to
excel in athletics. But you guys have already done all that. I
don't think Dad did much more than grunt when I showed him
my best paper this fall. I got an A plus on that, you know."

"He's been awfully busy."

"That's just the point," Jon Paul answered. "There's eleven
years difference between you and me. You know what I heard?
That I was a mistake. That they thought they couldn't have
more children when I came along."

"Who told you that?" James scoffed.

"I overheard Mom talking with Dad one day."

"Well that's absolute nonsense, and even if it was true, what
the hell can anyone do about it? Now, quit feeling sorry for
yourself and grow up. We've got a lot more important things to
do."

James picked up a magazine and tried to read, but his mind kept wandering back to his own adolescent lack of direction. It was Diana who had first suggested architecture. "God knows," she had told him, "you want to be an artist, you're going to starve for the next forty years—even if you can paint like Renoir." Before that he'd thought about illustrating, advertising, and number of other forms of employment, none of which held any real interest. Unlike Jon Paul, however, he'd never gotten into any real trouble during his high-school years. He'd been too afraid to. When he'd received a D once on a report in European history he'd managed to keep it from his family for weeks. Yet it wasn't until his senior year in college that he'd taken his first architectural course and discovered where his real talent lay.

It was Diana, too, who'd warned James about working for a large firm. "If you're not careful, you're going to get swallowed up and lost out there," she'd said. And, of course, she'd been right. He'd been something like number thirty-six in a firm of eighty. Had the situation been reversed, Diana would have gone out to San Francisco, started working on her own, and said to hell with everyone else. Yet Diana had always been more courageous than James. Or maybe impulsive was a better word. And it was this same courage that had taken her off to Africa and gotten her into trouble. And now Jon Paul seemed more impulsive, less socially adapted, than either of them had ever been. It was funny, James thought, how each member of the family had wandered a little farther away than the last. Michael and Donald—perfect students, popular athletes. Diana and James—more artistically inclined, less conformist. And now Jon Paul—the caboose, seemingly fighting authority at every turn.

When James thought about it, he was not exactly sure why he had been so quick to volunteer. In days past he was the one of the family who was prone to temporize and think things out. His action was much more like something his older brothers would have done, and he'd been surprised when both had suggested that they wait. But they had their families and it had fallen on him to take up the slack. And then he remembered the sadness in his father's eyes when he spoke of Diana's disappearance. When he saw that, he knew no matter what happened, he would have to go and try to bring her home.

As he sat pondering, the smell of smoke suddenly caught his attention. He glanced around nervously, afraid for a moment that the plane was on fire. To his chagrin, he found that Jon Paul had lit up a cigarette. The paper was flimsy and hand rolled, the aroma smelled like burning rope.

"Jesus Christ!" James exclaimed. He reached over and slapped the cigarette out of Jon Paul's mouth. His voice was harsh and angry.

"What the hell do you think you're doing?"

Jon Paul glared back at him with a sudden air of defiance and bent forward to pick the cigarette up off the floor.

"Put it out!" James roared.

"Come on, James, I've been smoking these for over a year. I thought you were being a buddy."

"You know what they do to people over here with this stuff? They put them in jail and throw away the key. What in hell have you got for brains?"

"You bastard," Jon Paul said beneath his breath.

"You want to go home this afternoon? I'll get you back on the next flight so fast your head will spin. Now give me the damned things. All of them."

Reluctantly Jon Paul reached down into his overnight bag and pulled out an open package of cigarettes. There were perhaps a half a dozen haphazardly rolled sticks inside the pack.

"And the rest of it."

"That's all there is."

"Come on, Jon Paul." James glared at him. "You're not dealing with some two-bit prep school kid. Give me the rest of it."

Jon Paul glowered back at him, then bent down and rummaged around before finally producing a small metallic film can. James took it, unscrewed the cap, dipped his finger in and smelled it.

"What are you going to do with it?" Jon Paul said with alarm.

"That's the first bloody place a customs agent looks, Jon Paul. In a film can. God, how can you be so dumb? I'm going to do you a favor and throw it away."

"That's all I brought," Jon Paul said with dismay.

"Let's get something straight, right now." James clenched his teeth. "This is *my* trip. You're here because *I* invited you. No other reason. While you're with me you'll do as I ask. If you don't like it, hit the road."

Jon Paul glared furiously at him.

"You can be a real asshole, can't you?" James said.

"Just taking after the rest of the family," Jon Paul answered.

"Go screw yourself," James replied. "You want to go back home? Try me!"

He stood up and angrily walked back to the restroom. He was gone only long enough to dispose of Jon Paul's stash. When he returned he glared at his brother, trying to control his rage. Got to be patient with him, he thought. He'll come around given enough time.

Glancing out of the window, James swallowed hard, trying to fight the nervousness that steadily rose up inside him. As each mile slipped away so, too, his confidence had begun to ebb. He'd convinced his father that he would find Diana and help straighten out Jon Paul. Then he'd been bold, reassuring, and confident. Now he was not so sure. Jon Paul was going to be more difficult than he thought. And the strange land below him looked more hostile and impenetrable than he'd ever imagined. Damn it, he reflected. What in the hell have I gotten myself into?

When he looked up the seat-belt sign was on and the plane had begun its descent. They banked once and circled the city of Nairobi and then they were down, taxiing toward the terminal.

7

They checked into the New Stanley Hotel. After lunch James and Jon Paul spent an hour at the U.S. Consulate. The information given was disheartening. There was little additional news. They were further referred to Wilson Tomboya with the Kenya Department of State. By two o'clock they were en route to the capitol building of Kenya. The taxi brought them to a modern glass structure that rose some twenty stories in the newest sector of the city. On the sixth floor in a large central office they found the Minister of Foreign Affairs.

The African was a thick black man with a barrel chest and deep widespread eyes. He wore a dark suit and white shirt, his neck seemingly stuffed into a collar two sizes too small. As he spoke, veins bulged widely across his temples.

"Please sit down," he said politely. "You have come a very long way." His expression changed to one of concern. "I have spoken with your father. I am sorry. Very sorry about the news."

James stared at him, hanging on his words. "Is there any hope?"

Tomboya frowned. "A year ago we lost a young man from the United States. He was from California, working with the Peace Corps. The natives came to the district commissioner saying that a witch doctor had put a spell on him and he was killed.

"Six months later he turned up in South Africa. The consulate notified us that he'd had some kind of mental breakdown. Nerves, they called it. He was flown back to the States. The parents were very grateful."

Jon Paul glared at him. "That's not our sister, Mr. Minister."

Tomboya shrugged. "You must understand, gentlemen, it is a very primitive world here. The people, the country, the law, all are totally different from what you are used to. Order here in the bush is often based on tribal custom."

He shook his head. "With the boy at least there was some hope. With your sister . . . ?" He paused, staring over at Jon Paul. "I'm sorry. I wish I could offer you better news."

"We want to see for ourselves," James persisted.

"Your sister was what you call in America very *independent*. The last time this office heard from her was six months ago when she requested a permit to go up into the Northern Frontier and do some photography. She wanted to spend time with a tribe up in the Akasi area, a desolate tract across from the border of the Sudan. Her request, of course, was denied. You see, we can't have a single woman of her, well, complexion running around the desert. It could cause a great deal of unrest among the tribes, you know. But somehow she managed to get a permit. Bribed somebody, I'm told. It was very much against my wishes."

Just like Diana, James thought. She would figure some way to get around the red tape of governmental policy. The more difficult it was, the more she would enjoy it. "We've come a long way, Mr. Minister," he said. "I don't intend to go back without running down every lead. Was there any evidence of a political motive? Perhaps a kidnapping with some ransom? You see, we could arrange to have some money—"

Tomboya shook his head. "Sir, you are not talking about the civilized world. Your sister was in the Northern Frontier. A chief needs a new wife and they go on a raid. The village where she lived was burned to the ground. The report listed seventeen bodies. All charred. No means of identification. Usually it is riders from Abyssinia."

"Your sources?"

"The report was filed by the district commissioner at the request of the United States Embassy. We flew some planes over the area. But there was nothing. No signs of life."

"What did he expect to see, some lady waving a bikini?" Jon Paul whispered.

"Shhh," James hissed at him.

"What good is an air search going to do?" Jon Paul spoke up. "If she was taken hostage or kidnapped, you're not going to see anything from the air. What kind of ground search was performed?"

Tomboya glared at him. "The government does not have enough funds, sir, to go chasing around after every lost person in the desert. We have dozens of incidents like this every year. Half the time the people show up a couple of days later and they were never missing in the first place. Usually a report is filed. The district commissioner did go into the area and investigate. We know there was a raid. It has taken time to collect the data. The first reports came in a month ago—"

James's, voice rose. "My God, man, she disappeared a month ago and you didn't contact us until last week?" He sat back stunned. A dull haze seemed to permeate his mind.

"Gentlemen, you have to realize that your sister was one hundred twenty miles from the nearest telephone. In the bush word travels by foot. One tribe passes information to another. Eventually someone crosses paths with somebody coming into town. There is no telephone to pick up and call for help."

"This village where she was last seen," James said angrily. "Have you been there?"

"Myself? No."

"Then how the hell do we get there?"

Tomboya shook his head. "You will have to write for permission from the government. The permits might take several weeks, *If* they are approved. To be quite honest, I would advise against it."

"Well, then, what in the blazes are we supposed to do?"

"I have talked with your father." Tomboya answered flatly. "There are a hundred thousand square miles of desert up there. Many of the tribes travel by camel. There are places where even a Land-Rover cannot go. You ask me what you can do? Go home, gentlemen. I'm sorry about your sister, but go home."

Jon Paul eyed him scornfully. "Say that perhaps we were able to get permits, say that by some stroke of luck your government did make it possible for us to go up there. Then what would you advise?"

"Well, then, sir, it would still be very difficult because you would need a guide, and there are perhaps only one or two men that know the country in all of Kenya. White men, that is."

James's interest perked. "And they are . . . ?"

"One is very old. I understand he is living on a ranch now and in his seventies. The other is a Swede. A white hunter named Lundstrom. But I doubt you'll find him very satisfactory. Since our government stopped the hunting of big game, many of the safari hunters left the country. Others became farmers. He's become—how shall I say it?—a drunkard." He scowled. "Perhaps you can find him down at one of the bars in lower Nairobi."

"You give us a great choice." James stood up. "One old man and one drunk. Thank you for your time."

He shook Tomboya's hand and started out the door. Outside the room he grabbed Jon Paul by the shoulder.

"What the hell were you trying to do back there, get us kicked out of the country? Our very fate may be hanging on that guy's hands. Now, damn it, keep your mouth shut. I don't care how you feel."

"How the hell could they search a place by air?" Jon Paul replied. "I got the feeling he couldn't give less of a shit—"

He stopped suddenly. Tomboya's huge shadow loomed behind them.

"Gentlemen, before you go I think there is something both of you should see." His voice was cold. He led James and Jon Paul back into his office. Reaching into his desk, he drew out a large manila folder. Opening it, he spread out a stack of photographs upon his desk.

James hesitated, suddenly afraid of what he was about to see. Jon Paul stared curiously at the prints. They stood for a moment in silence.

It took a few minutes to overcome the shock. The first photograph was of a dead native with one leg chopped off. The second, a man with his hand amputated; the third, a body with no head. James turned away and did not look at the photographs further.

"Why are you showing us these?" he asked angrily.

"Because this is the work of Abyssinian raiders. I don't want you to leave here with false hopes. They ride camels and carry automatic weapons. They dart across the border, killing and maiming practically everything in their path. Only a few young women do they spare. They always castrate the young males."

He looked sternly from James to Jon Paul. "You see, gentlemen, I don't think you would be successful with an entire army. If I were you, I would turn around and go home. If your sister is lucky, she's dead."

"I know," James answered grimly. "You see, that is why we came. If there's one chance in a million that she is alive, she needs our help."

8

In the bar of the New Stanley Hotel, James learned more about the Swede named Harold Lundstrom. After several inquiries, he found that Lundstrom had migrated to East Africa shortly after the war. Known for his drinking and harsh treatment of the natives, he had started out as a farmer, then turned to hunting and prospecting in the Northern Frontier. But the one big strike he had always hoped for had somehow escaped him. Eventually he came back to Nairobi and tried to settle down. Gradually boredom and alcohol had consumed him. In his best days he was unpredictable and moody, prone to sudden outbursts of temper. At his worst, he was an angry, embittered drunk. In recent months, James was told, he might be found in any one of a half-dozen bars in lower Nairobi.

After dinner, James and Jon Paul checked three of the more popular bars with no luck. The fourth bar was a place called the Zambesi in one of the roughest sections of town.

Nightfall descended upon them as the taxi sped through the central section of the city. Tall, modern apartment buildings flashed by, replaced soon by two- and three-story structures

with tin roofs and panel walls. The street lights became farther
and farther apart. The road narrowed to two lanes. They turned
at an intersection and the pavement ended. The taxi jarred up
and down over a rough dirt road. Crowds of natives stared at
them as they passed.

"Not a good place for tourists," the taxi driver said.

James nodded. "We'll make it quick."

They drove for another fifteen minutes, winding through a
series of narrow roadways that led like a maze into the rookery
of the city. Few other cars passed. People here were scantily
dressed, some clad only in blankets or robes.

The Zambesi bar loomed at the end of a dark, empty intersection. It was an old two-story frame building with a single
lighted sign.

James stepped cautiously out of the taxi. Jon Paul slid across
the seat and started after him.

"Better wait here," James said. "If Lundstrom is in there, I'll
try to get him to come back with us to the hotel."

"I want to go with you," Jon Paul replied.

James shook his head. "Looks too rough down here. If
there's trouble I want you to make the taxi driver leave, do you
understand?"

A frown of disappointment flashed across Jon Paul's face.

"Come on," James said. "If something happened to you, Dad
would kill me."

"And what if something happens to you?"

"Well, then I guess he'll kill *you.*" James smiled. "Wait here,
I'll be right back."

He started across the street. A group of blacks lounged in
front of the doorway. As James moved toward them, they
parted, opening into a narrow lane. One man leaned on a spear;
another was barefoot, covered only by a blanket. They watched
in silence as he passed.

Pushing his way through the doorway, James choked at the
rancid smell of stale beer. A thick haze of cigarette smoke hung
below the ceiling. He had the vague impression that the room
was packed, that there were tables filled with people in darkened alcoves along the wall, but in the dim light he could see
little. Passing between two tables, he made his way to the bar.

An Asian with a stained turban was pouring a drink.

"I'm looking for a man named Harold Lundstrom," James said.

The bartender stopped and eyed him suspiciously. "Here sometimes," he answered.

James reached into his pocket and pulled out a Kenyan five-pound note and set it down on top of the bar. Instantly a dozen heads turned to watch. A low, hushed whisper sprang up around him.

For a second, James wondered about Jon Paul outside, if he would be safe, how he could make it out of the bar if he ran into trouble. He had an uneasy feeling that the choked, packed atmosphere was about to explode.

"Drink, sir?" the Asian said.

"Just information."

The bartender took a rag and began wiping the bar in front of him. He had made three circles by the time his hand reached the money and curled it underneath the rag.

"Corner table," the Asian answered.

In the dim light, James could see a white man with blond matted hair. As he approached the table, he noted a faint scar across the man's face, partially breaking the contour of his lip. He was a huge man, a head taller than the black and two Asians who sat next to him. A bottle of Scotch was half finished on the table.

"You looking for me?" the blond man growled.

"Your name Lundstrom?"

The Swede was unshaven. His shirt was stained and wrinkled. Up close, James could see that the scar, which ran upward from the corner of his lip, extended into his eye. There was a faint gray color to the tissues. The eyelid never fully closed.

"I have a business proposition for you," James said.

"Sit down." Lundstrom grunted, kicking a small stool out from beneath a table.

He whispered something to the three men next to him. They stood up and quickly left, disappearing into the darkened room.

"There is a section of Kenya called the Northern Frontier . . . an area called Akasi. Can you take us there?"

Lundstrom's jaws tightened. "Who's us?"

"Myself and my sixteen-year-old brother."

"You crazy? That area's been closed for months. Very dry, hunted mostly by the Turkana and Somali. There's little game left up there."

"I'm not interested in hunting, Mr. Lundstrom."

The white hunter looked at him closely. "Photography?"

"No," James answered. "I'm looking for my sister. She disappeared a month ago from a small native village in some kind of a border raid. I'm told she was probably kidnapped by Abyssinian raiders. There have been no traces of her. If she's dead, we'd like to find out. If she's alive, we'd like to bring her back."

Lundstrom leaned back in his chair and shook his head. "That which you ask me to do is impossible."

"I can make it worth your while."

"Not interested."

"Ten thousand dollars in cash if you take me and double that if we find her and bring her back."

"Alive?"

"Preferably."

"Is the woman attractive?"

"Very," James answered. "Good figure, blond hair, blue eyes."

The huge man looked incredulously at James, then threw his head back and burst into a harsh laugh.

"I spent five years walking around in the godforsaken desert. Lost my eye there, I did. Poked out by a Somali spear. Swore I'd never set foot in that devil's hole again and now you offer me ten thousand dollars to look for your sister. Ha!" he snorted. "Your sister must have been quite a woman, sir. Quite a woman."

"Lundstrom, I offered you a business deal." James said angrily. "Are you interested or do you want me to find someone else?"

The Swede took a long drink from his bottle and stared at the American sitting across from him.

"You must be prepared to find your sister dead, her skin stretched out and drying on a *boma* like an animal hide, her hair hung around some black man's belt like a trophy. You must be prepared for that, and if you're not, I think you had better turn back and go home."

James met the fierceness of his stare. "If she's dead, I don't think it will make much difference how we'll find her, will it?"

On a sudden impulse, James reached into his pocket and pulled out the small felt pouch that his father had given him. He shook it open and spilled the blue stone out upon the table.

"Ever see one of these?"

Lundstrom stared at the stone in disbelief. "Where did you get this?" he cried.

"I—my sister—" James started, but Lundstrom was on his feet, his hands tearing into James's neck, squeezing his breath away.

"By God, man, where did you get this godforsaken stone of hell? Speak up before I break your neck!"

Lundstrom's right hand broke free. With a roar, he swung his fist against the side of James's face in a blow that sent him spinning backward. Half dazed, he crumpled to the floor.

At the same moment the table overturned and James caught a fleeting glimpse of the small blue stone bounding across the room. Two dark forms leaped out of the shadows, scrambling for it. A gunshot roared from somewhere above him. One of the figures tumbled over, sprawling lifelessly upon the floor. Lundstrom stood over him, his pistol drawn, the barrel still smoking. Everyone in the bar froze.

What happened next flashed by so fast that James almost missed it, yet the events so startled his mind that he would remember it for days as if it had happened in slow motion.

The crowd parted as the largest black man James had ever seen emerged from the darkness. He was dressed in a blanket, his hair greased with reddish ocher. His movement was a single fluid motion. A spear flickered across the room. Lundstrom grunted, his chest impaled as if it were butter. His left hand groped feebly for the shaft. The pistol in his right hand discharged twice into the floor. Sinking slowly, he fell to the ground. His hands and feet quivered in one last spasm of life.

A gunshot fired off somewhere behind James. Another table overturned as two men spun past him, locked in combat. He wondered for a moment what had happened to the blue stone.

Rising to his feet, he tried to shake the fogginess from his mind. A turbaned figure loomed out of the shadows, knife raised, aiming for his chest.

James had a split second to see death pass before his eyes, to imagine his body penetrated by a blade from an unknown assailant in a derelict bar when a bottle crashed down, shattering over the man's head. He sank to the ground. Jon Paul was standing behind him.

"Jon Paul, Christ . . ." James gasped.

"We've got to get out of here," Jon Paul cried. He grabbed his brother by the shoulder and pulled him toward the entrance. A spear splintered in the wood just above the boy's head. People scattered in front of them, running in every direction. A volley of gunshots broke loose.

Midway past the bar James was able to get his feet underneath him. Jon Paul charged forward, bolting through the door. James reeled after him, knocking two men over as he reached the entrance. As they ran into the street the taxi pulled away from the curb, tires spinning, accelerating crazily.

Yelling frantically, Jon Paul sprinted after it but the vehicle was too far ahead. In a moment the car was gone, two red tail lights roaring away from them in the darkness.

"Holy shit!" Jon Paul exclaimed. "What do we do now?"

James staggered after him, still holding his jaw. A group of blacks poured out of the bar. There were scattered shouts and then the entire mob advanced toward them.

"I think we'd better get the hell out of here," James murmured.

He turned and led the way, darting down a long alleyway. A shadow loomed in front of him, and he knocked someone over trying to pass. They raced down the road to an intersection and then down another street. By now James was breathing heavily. He stopped once, trying to rest, then heard the sound of scrambling feet. Ducking into a side alleyway, they began to run again.

James swore at his own fatigue. They were no match for the slender wiry shapes that pursued them in the night. As they rounded another corner, they could hear footsteps steadily gaining.

"They're still on us." Jon Paul gasped.

The two sprinted ahead in one last frantic run. Finally James could go no farther. He grabbed Jon Paul and spun to a stop, trying to catch his breath. A tall dark form bore down upon them.

"Better take him," James whispered. Clenching his fist, he lunged out of the darkness but the man blocked his blow as if he would brush aside a fly. Jon Paul rammed into his midsection and tried to throw him to the ground. In an instant the youth found himself pinioned between two strong arms.

"It's all right, bwana," a deep voice said. "I'll help you. Come quickly."

The sound of scattered shouts sprang up behind them.

"This way!" the black man exclaimed.

Taking in a deep breath, James turned and followed. Jon Paul trailed closely behind. They ran for a block, then darted into a small doorway. Pounding footsteps hurtled by. There were wild shouts. Dark forms carrying spears sprinted past them. Gradually the sound of the searching mob became fainter. Off in the distance the warble of a police siren echoed through the streets. The noise grew steadily louder.

The black man stepped out from behind the doorway. "I think it is safe now," he said. He was lean and muscular, covered by a single blanket draped across his shoulder. The luster of a copper bracelet glinted from his left arm. His earlobes hung down practically to his jaw under the weight of heavy earrings.

"You want to go up to the Northern Frontier?" His eyes flashed brightly in the darkness. "Perhaps I can help."

"Who are you?" James asked.

"There is time for that later. Tell me your names and where you are staying."

James introduced himself and Jon Paul then gave their room number and hotel.

"Follow this road until its end. You will find a small store. Use the telephone and call for a taxi. The storekeeper is an Asian who speaks English. I will meet you later."

"But how will I . . . ?" James started to question, but the man had already turned, his form blending into the shadows of the night.

9

It was nearly midnight when they reached the New Stanley Hotel. James staggered into the room, poured himself a drink, and sat down. Even then he could still feel the clattering of his heart. He smiled at his brother.

"Well, I owe you one," he said.

"What happened back there?" Jon Paul asked.

"I showed Lundstrom the gem. He leaped from the table, tried to strangle me, then belted me across the chin. The stone dropped to the floor. Someone went for it. Lundstrom shot him. The next thing I knew he had a six-foot spear through his chest. I had just made it to my feet when I saw somebody coming for me out of the shadows. Your timing couldn't have been more perfect."

"I was afraid you might be in trouble," Jon Paul said. "When I heard the first gunshot I asked the cab driver to wait. He was getting pretty edgy. I hope you don't mind me not following your orders . . . *sir.*" Jon Paul flashed James a mock salute.

James slapped him on the back. "Have a drink." He grinned. "I think you've earned it."

James sat back in the chair and mulled over the night's events. Lundstrom dead. The blue stone gone. But why? What was there about the gem that had caused such a violent reaction? They'd only been in Africa for twenty-four hours and they were both lucky to be alive.

After half an hour passed there was a faint tapping on the door. When Jon Paul opened the door, he stepped back in surprise.

A tall black man in a white shirt, slacks, and a tie stood in the doorway.

James stood up, regarding him in bewilderment.

"I am Lasiri," the man said, smiling. "May I come in?"

The voice sounded familiar, yet James had expected someone in a native blanket with bare legs and sandals.

"By Christ, man, I didn't recognize you," James exclaimed.

"I've changed my dress from mine to yours." He grinned. "Let us say each serves its purpose depending on the locale."

"I think we owe you our lives tonight," Jon Paul said.

Lasiri shrugged. "Sooner or later we all owe our lives to each other, my friend."

As Jon Paul led him into the hotel suite, James now noticed three things about the man that seemed unusual. First, his English had a strange British accent that made James think he must have studied in a European school. Second, his earlobes had been cut away from the rest of his ear so that they hung in loose slings of flesh used primarily to carry earrings. In the darkness of the chase, James had only faintly perceived this. Now in the bright light he noted that earrings had been removed and the slings of flesh were pulled up over the ears to keep them from dangling freely. Third, an odd set of tattoos were etched across the man's right temple like the tracks of a bird.

Lasiri shook Jon Paul's hand. "You are brothers?"

"Sometimes he thinks we are." Jon Paul smiled.

"And yourself," James asked. "Your English?"

"Two years at Cambridge."

James shook his head. "I would never have expected it in a thousand years."

"No, probably not," Lasiri answered. "But, then, many are educated now. Just because this country is black does not mean that we are all ignorant savages."

"My apologies," James replied.

"No offense," Lasiri said. "Perhaps I should fully introduce myself. I am called Lasiri, though my full tribal name is Lasiri Jamba Mzonbili. I am Masai. I was educated through the twelfth grade in a small mission school in Nieri. I did very well in school. Afterward I spent two years at Cambridge attending college, then returned to Africa. There are few jobs for an educated man to earn much money unless they are in hunting or

politics. I took up with the white hunters. I could track fairly
well and my English was an asset to the English-speaking cli-
ents for I could explain to them certain characteristics of the
game. When the government closed down hunting, I, like many
others, found myself without a job. Tonight I was sitting at the
table next to Bwana Lundstrom. I heard your proposition. I
would like to help."

James studied the man carefully. The sleek lines of his muscles seemed hidden behind the shirt and tie. Except for the
strange shape of his ears and the tattoo across his temple, he
could have passed for any "civilized" man back in the States.

"In your conversation with Lundstrom you mentioned your
sister had disappeared from a small *boma* in the Northern Frontier," Lasiri continued. "If your offer is still good, I would be
willing to go up there with you."

"The man I offered to pay was a white hunter," James answered cautiously. "I was told that he knew that area very well.
We would be paying for some expertise."

"You were also paying for a very treacherous man who might
or might not have taken you if he was sober. You see, my friend,
the color of the skin should not make a difference in your judgment of talent. I have spent many years up in the Northern
Frontier. Some of that country belongs to my people." He
paused. "Do you know why Lundstrom was speared back
there?"

James shook his head.

"The man was one of Lundstrom's trackers. Lundstrom shot
him in the stomach and left him for dead during a safari. Do
you know why? Because he tracked a very big elephant into
some heavy bush. Lundstrom pushed after him with a client.
The tracker had not predicted the elephant would circle around
behind them. The elephant charged and wounded the client,
making Lundstrom look like a fool. In a rage, he shot his own
tracker, then left him to die. It was an unforgivable breach of
conduct. The man has been waiting to get even with Lundstrom
for months. That is the type of man you would have offered ten
thousand dollars to. Do you know why they were chasing you
tonight?"

"Undoubtedly they thought I was carrying more gems."

"Hardly," Lasiri retorted. "They wanted to be sure that you would not testify against them."

"Then they would have killed me?"

"Dead men do not talk."

James sighed and leaned back in his chair. "Are you asking for ten thousand dollars for saving my life? If so, I'll pay you a reward and you can be off. Right now the only thing I care about is finding my sister."

"I understand," Lasiri answered. "It is also important that you hire someone who can speak the languages and take you into the Northern Frontier. Before you make any further plans, why not fly up and have a look at the village where your sister was last seen? There's a mail run that goes up toward Lake Turkana in the morning. We can make a day's trip of it and be back here tomorrow night."

"How much would I owe you?" James asked.

"No charge," Lasiri answered. "We may find enough tomorrow to convince you not to go any further."

"Like what?"

"Traces of your sister. Some evidence of exactly what happened. If you can be ready, we can leave at seven in the morning."

"Christ." James shook his head. "This is the first progress we've made in twenty-four hours."

"Twenty-four hours, Bwana Jacobson?" Lasiri answered with a frown. "In this country progress sometimes takes thousands of years!"

He turned toward the doorway, winked at Jon Paul, then exited.

Jon Paul stood up, emulating Lasiri's posture—sticking his chest out, feeling the flex of his muscles underneath his powerful young shoulders. Maybe, Jon Paul thought, maybe I will have my earlobes cut and a fine tattoo etched on his temple. He wondered with amusement how he would ever explain it to his friends.

10

The small single-engine plane lifted off the runway into a beautiful African sky. Except for scattered clouds drifting low on the horizon, the air was crystal clear. James watched from the back window as the city of Nairobi vanished rapidly behind him. Jon Paul sat next to him, his eyes glued to the glass. As they climbed steadily upward, James began to admit that many of his original doubts about Lasiri's competence were diminishing. The Masai had met them at seven in the morning outside the New Stanley Hotel. He was dressed in typically Western fashion, wearing sunglasses, long pants, and a white shirt. Now he sat easily in the front seat of the airplane, his tall frame bent beneath the superstructure of the cockpit.

"The flight will last a couple of hours," he said above the noise of the engines. "The pilot has agreed to let me show you the country. Give you some idea of what we're dealing with."

The plane darted westward, passing over long miles of open grassland. Soon the great Rift Valley came into view, cutting down from the plains in a broad, deep gorge that stretched out for two miles before it rose in a steep escarpment on the opposite side.

"One of the great geographical landmarks of Africa," Lasiri said, turning toward Jon Paul. "Runs for several thousand miles, all the way up into Egypt and the Mediterranean."

As they approached the rim of the valley, Lasiri pointed toward a small clearing at the edge of the escarpment. The pilot descended in a gradual bank until they were flying no more than two hundred feet off the ground.

"Two o'clock to your right," Lasiri shouted. "Masai village."

James could see a series of low gray huts surrounded by a bush fence. A herd of cattle milled restlessly beneath them.

The plane dipped one wing, circling over the village. Natives rushed out of their huts, gazing upward. A broad grin spread across Lasiri's face. Jon Paul stared out of the window in time to see the Masai wave up at the plane and then they were over the edge of the escarpment, the great cliffs descending down to the valley two thousand feet below.

They turned north, following the direction of the valley floor. Ahead, a large lake shimmered beneath the morning sun. As they flew toward it, great droves of pink birds took off the water, scuttling away beneath them.

"Flamingoes!" Lasiri exclaimed. James watched in amazement. There were thousands of them. The splendid color of the birds reflected off the water like a wave of pink fire.

As he marveled at the changing pattern of colors, James began to forget the deadly earnestness of their mission. Soon he was like Jon Paul, his head pressed against the side of the window, watching the grand display of nature below.

Half an hour up the Rift Valley they banked again, climbing steadily above the rising escarpment until the plains flattened out beneath them. There thousands of animals dotted the flat grassland. The pilot descended, running close to the ground as herds of wildebeests scattered before them. Small groups of zebra darted here and there among the running animals.

"Ho!" Lasiri suddenly cried. "Look there, below us." The pilot banked to the right, passing over a solitary tree. A dozen vultures flapped furiously off the branches. For an instant James thought he saw two golden animals bounding off beneath them.

"Fresh kill," Lasiri said. "The lions follow the migration, cleaning out the weak and wounded."

James looked over at Jon Paul. A broad grin had spread across his brother's face.

"It's fantastic."

They climbed again, flying steadily around a huge thunderhead, then continued northward. Below them the flat grassland disappeared, replaced at first by thick, impenetrable brush. Then the dry desert mountains of the Northern Frontier came into view.

Another hour passed with little change. Occasionally a road ran like a thin penciled line between the valleys. Vegetation was sparse. Here and there a dried streambed wandered down from the mountains, carrying with it a narrow row of trees.

As they flew over a mountain ridge, Lasiri pointed to a broad desert below. The plane banked and James could see a landing strip of red earth carved into the ground. Descending rapidly, the pilot circled once, then landed, taxiing to a stop.

"I'll be back here to pick you up at five," the pilot said. He waved and took off, continuing his mail run northward toward Lake Turkana. James watched the plane until it became a tiny speck in the sky.

As he glanced around, he suddenly realized they were in the middle of the most desolate country he had ever seen. Scattered leafless trees crowded either side of the landing field. There was little else. Except for a single fly that buzzed around his head, there was nothing to break the African stillness. Already it was hot. The sweat slowly began to ooze off his brow. James's thoughts returned to the incredulous realization that his sister had not only passed through this country, but had lived here.

"Well?" he said. He could feel a growing sense of impatience.

"We wait," Lasiri answered. He moved over to a tree and leaned against it in the shade.

"For what?"

"A limousine." Lasiri grunted.

James glanced at him with a scowl.

Fifteen minutes passed before they heard the faint cough of an engine chugging off in the distance. It sputtered and groaned, gradually drawing nearer until an old, dusty flatbed truck came into view. The truck pulled up to the edge of the shade tree and stopped.

"*Jambo,*" Lasiri said in Swahili. "Hello."

The driver was a black youth probably not much older than Jon Paul. Lasiri talked to him for a few minutes in Swahili.

"We will pick up a couple of trackers in town," he said. "Then we will go to the area of the burned *boma*. The boy reports it is several hours drive from here."

James looked at Lasiri with a bewildered expression. "You arranged all this last night?"

"No, bwana. This is the airport limousine. He hears a plane and he comes out to pick up whoever has landed."

James shook his head and laughed. He had seen nothing during their descent that even suggested a town. And now he began to realize that their fate was completely in Lasiri's hands. He could rage and fume impatiently, but neither Africa nor the Africans would change. They ran things their own way at their own speed.

A mile and a half from the airstrip they came to a small desert outpost composed of a single dusty street with five or six mud-baked houses. At the side of a building two camels were tied to a post. Except for a dozen dogs and a few natives sprawled in the shade, no other inhabitants were visible. The road stretched off into the desert in two empty tire tracks that finally disappeared in a shimmering mirage.

The truck stopped in front of the only store. An Asian wearing a white robe and turban greeted them at the doorway. He shook Lasiri's hands as if they were old friends, then led them into his shop. They moved through the dimly lit room containing numerous colored fabrics, rolls of printed cloths, and various pots and pans. In a small room at the back of the store they sat down around a wooden table. A servant brought small cups of tea. James and Jon Paul listened as Lasiri conversed with the storekeeper in Swahili. The Arab was middle-aged, heavyset, with yellow, uneven teeth.

"Bwana, I do not like what I hear," Lasiri finally said. "My friend, Ali Hassan, whom I have known since I first came to the Northern Frontier, runs the only fabric store for several hundred miles. The natives travel here to purchase cloth, and he is able to keep up with much of the local news. He says that he has met your sister. The Turkana had a name for her: *Nywele Thahabu*, which means the 'golden one.' He says that she was well known in these parts and the natives would often come through town and ask where she was located so that they might go and gaze upon her. The raid occurred about four weeks ago. The district commissioner came up a week later and investigated the story but never went out to the village."

James shook his head. "No wonder we couldn't learn anything."

"It's very strange," Lasiri continued. "The story was first that it was Abyssinians because there are often similar raids this time of year. The raiders will come down and make off with the cattle and women. It is easiest for the district commissioner to file this type of report, you see, for then he does not have to undertake any further investigation."

"Jesus." James gritted his teeth. "It all fits."

"He says there was *one* known survivor," Lasiri said. "An old woman who had been left behind for dead. She is staying in one of the nearby villages. Ali Hassan says that most of the cattle from the village were found the following day. That, too, is strange."

James frowned. "I'm not sure I understand."

"Because, bwana, the Abyssinian raiders always take cattle. Had they made a raid upon a Turkana village, they would not have left them behind."

They had been traveling for two hours. The truck bounced along a narrow roadway barely visible on the hard-packed ground. James sat in front of the cab with Lasiri and the driver. Jon Paul stood up in the flat, open back of the truck, hanging on to one of the side rails. Next to him were two wiry black men covered only by blankets. They were from a neighboring Turkana village and they had come into town to trade. For a few dollars, Lasiri had persuaded them to join the party to act as trackers.

Every now and then one of the Turkana would grunt and tap his spear on the side of the truck and the driver would make a turn, sometimes following an invisible path. A herd of impala leaped off in front of them, swallowed quickly by the desert bush. They saw little else. The country was harsh and desolate, covered by endless miles of shrub acacia.

They were running parallel to a small dry streambed, following a single poorly marked trail when one of the Turkana began banging furiously on the side of the cab. The driver brought the truck to a stop and then they saw the herdsman. He was tall and thin, dressed only with a short gray cloth that dangled to his knees. He leaned on a spear, standing in the shade of a thick bush. A dozen mangey cattle lay in the shade beside him.

Lasiri stepped down from the cab. Very slowly and elegantly the herdsman left his position and ambled over to greet him. They touched fingers, spoke a few words in Swahili, then the man walked around the truck, looking inside. After completing this inspection, he returned to Lasiri, crouched down, and began speaking in a rapid dialogue punctuated by numerous clicks and grunts.

"His *boma* is just beyond the ridge," Lasiri translated. "The single woman survivor is living with them. He says to leave the truck and follow him."

In a long desolate valley they found a village surrounded by a thornbush enclosure. At a corner of the fence the herdsman bent over and pulled a section aside. Crouching, they passed through the opening.

By James's count there were fifteen squat, dung-coated huts, each no more than five feet tall. A dozen dogs rushed out to greet them, barking furiously. Dark faces peered out from the dwellings. The herdsman led them to one of the huts and shouted something. Three women emerged from the darkness. The oldest was a thin bald woman with sagging breasts. Her neck and arms were covered with coils of wire.

Lasiri greeted her with a touch of his fingers, motioning for her to squat down next to him. The rest of the village came cautiously forward until Lasiri and the old woman formed the center of a crowd of nearly twenty people.

As they talked James tried to listen, brushing madly to keep the flies out of his eyes. Several naked pot-bellied children crept up to the edge of the group. The flies crawled across their faces, concentrating at the corners of their lips and eyes. Even the adults seemed unbothered by them. The villagers stared at the two American brothers and did not move.

My God, James thought. Diana working in these conditions! He'd known that the villages were primitive, yet the squalor was something that her photographs never fully showed.

"The old woman says she was living in the village during the raid," Lasiri translated. "There was no warning. Before she knew it, the village was overrun with shadows. She could hear the cries of her people being murdered in the night. . . ."

Lasiri stopped now, listening intently. As the old woman

spoke, her voice rose, trailing off into a wailing quiver. The rest of the women took up the call in a weird, frightened chorus, then stopped. For an instant there was no movement, no sound. Everyone was completely still.

"My God, man, what did she say?" James cried.

Lasiri spoke in a whisper. "She said that a shadow came up to her like a demon in the night. He was dressed in black. She could see only his eyes. They were the eyes of a devil, and when they looked upon her she felt that she was going to die."

The Masai stood up. Nodding to the gathered assembly, he shook several hands then began walking toward the opening in the fenced enclosure.

James and Jon Paul hurried after him. "Lasiri, what is it? What is wrong?"

"It is all very strange," he said quietly. "The Turkana are not a superstitious people, yet she describes the raid as if it were carried out by ghosts, demons who came and disappeared into the night."

"And Diana?"

"Your sister lived in a tent just inside the enclosure. The old woman says she remembered hearing a woman's cries for help."

"Then she is dead?"

Lasiri rested his hand upon the American's shoulder. "They buried the remains of the villagers two or three days later. The old woman does not think there were any other survivors, but your sister's body was not among the ones they found."

James could feel his heart skip a beat. "Then there is a chance!"

"Let's go out to the burned village," Lasiri said. His lips were set in a tight, grim line. "There are still a few details that I need to understand."

On a small plateau looking out across the desert they found the remains of the village where Diana Jacobson had lived. The truck stopped at the outer perimeter of the ashes. There was still a visible ring of scorched ground where the thornbush fence had been. A Land-Rover lay on its side, wheels blown, its insides charred and disfigured as if it had exploded in the heat.

Lasiri stepped down from the truck and shouted directions to

the two trackers. They spread out and began searching the
ground. Jon Paul walked over to the Land-Rover. The seats
were gone, the canvas top nothing but a few shreds of burned
fragments, the steel frame twisted and bent.

"It looks as if it was bombed," he muttered. "James, you
think this was Diana's?"

James nodded grimly. "Probably the fire." He turned and
followed Lasiri, moving slowly through the debris.

"Huts here," the Masai said. "I count between twelve and
fifteen. The village probably had a population of thirty or forty
people."

One of the trackers grunted and James moved toward him.
He pointed to the top of a burned piece of wood. It was the
remains of a tent stake. A seared end of nylon rope was still
fastened to the wood.

James could feel a lump slowly growing in his throat.

"I think this is where your sister slept," Lasiri said.

They moved slowly through the debris, turning and sifting
the ashes. Jon Paul let out a startled cry. Reaching down, he
discovered a half-buried camera lens.

"Do not expect to find too much," Lasiri said. "After a raid
such as this, neighboring tribes will come and pick everything
clean. They might have taken her camera and tried to sell it or
keep it as a souvenir. Hyenas and vultures first, then people
combing over the ground taking whatever they can find. What's
left becomes community property."

Outside the burned perimeter they discovered a row of a
dozen mounds.

"These are the grave sites," Lasiri said. "Bodies buried by
other tribesmen."

James nodded grimly.

As he walked back through the debris, the faint odor of
smoke came to his nostrils and he could smell the death of the
place. Suddenly he felt sick.

Lasiri searched back through the ashes but could find nothing more. Half an hour passed and then one of the trackers
whistled from the edge of the plateau. A dry creek ran next to
the *boma* in a thin ribbon of sand. There in the soft dust the
tracker pointed to a smudge. The signs were faint and hardly

discernible, yet the Turkana began to stop here and there, showing where certain telltale markings were. The two trackers searched the streambed for nearly fifteen minutes, then came back to Lasiri, and all three entered into a deep discussion.

"There are camel prints there," Lasiri said. "The trackers think a party of twelve men came over the sand here." Lasiri followed their course with his hand. "They moved across the narrow embankment, then stopped, probably waiting for night, probably watching. Then they spread out and converged on the village."

"They can read this in the sand?" Jon Paul asked with astonishment.

"The Turkana can track a bird in the dust or chase down the jumps of a grasshopper," Lasiri answered. "What is hard for even me to see here, they read like a book."

The trackers moved away from them searching for further signs. Suddenly a sharp whistle broke the silence.

One of the trackers was crouched in the sand, speaking excitedly.

"Something dragged here," Lasiri translated. "Something heavy . . . something like a body."

The trackers continued following the signs. Abruptly one clucked with satisfaction. Leaping up on top of the bank, he moved into a narrow area shaded by a grove of acacia trees. There he pointed to a small mound. The earth was of the same texture that James had noted in the graves back at the burned village.

James swallowed hard. So she's dead, he thought. They raped her and killed her and dragged her here to be buried. He looked with concern toward his brother. He wanted to tell Jon Paul to turn away from what they were about to see.

"Hang on, boy," he said grimly.

They watched as Lasiri and the two trackers began removing the soil on top of the grave. Little by little they sifted off the upper layers, digging steadily downward. When James saw them stop, he knew they had discovered a body. His thoughts pattered dizzily in his brain. Well, at least we've found her, he told himself. And the whole terrible matter is resolved and we can go home.

"It's all right. It's not her!" Lasiri cried.

James rushed over to the grave. The body that now lay uncovered had been partially preserved in the desert heat, the tissues dry and dehydrated. The man was naked, buried in Egyptian fashion, arms crossed upon the chest. Clutched in the fingers of the right hand was a curved, jeweled knife. Lasiri reached down and slowly pried the blade loose. Brushing the dirt away, he examined it in the light.

"It's been a long time since I have seen a knife like this," he said.

Then he did a strange thing. Taking the knife, he bent over and slipped the blade between the body's clenched teeth. Twisting it sideways, he pried the jaw open and looped his finger down into the cavity of the mouth, drawing out a small, roundish object.

James watched in astonishment. At first he thought it was a piece of flesh, but as Lasiri began to clean the object, he could see that it had a hard surface to it. With the last wipe of the Masai's fingers, it began to shine and sparkle with a radiance of deep blue fire.

James took the stone from Lasiri, rolling it over in his hand. A small notch had been drilled into one end as if to accept a tiny chain. On the back was a faint etching that appeared to be the carving of a desert palm.

"Jon Paul!" he exclaimed. "It's the same stone Diana sent!"

"The stone of the oasis," Lasiri answered. "The sapphire . . . blue . . . water . . . life . . ."

"But in the man's mouth?" James gasped.

"Placed there, given to this man to carry with him into the afterworld. As a token to pay the gods for everlasting life."

Lasiri took the stone and bent over, gently inserting it back into the dead man's mouth. Keeping the knife, he motioned for the two trackers to cover up the grave.

"Good God, man. You're going to put the stone back?" James exclaimed. "Do you know what it's worth?"

Lasiri frowned. "In your country, thousands. Here . . . nothing."

"But that's crazy."

Lasiri glared at him. "The man who would take this stone would be cursed for the rest of his life."

James felt a surge of uneasiness rise up inside him. What was it Lundstrom had called it before he was speared? The stone of hell? And Diana? Where had she found it? Robbed from a dead man's grave?

"And you believe this?" he asked incredulously.

Lasiri regarded him with a scowl. "As much as I believe in the sky and the sun and the blackness of the night. . . ."

11

On the airplane heading back to Nairobi, James stared out across the setting sun, watching the shadows grow across the vast African land. For some time he had been puzzling over what they had seen. They'd found the village where his sister had been working. The discovery of the tent stake and camera lens left no question in his mind. But their talk with the only surviving woman had disclosed nothing, only that strange demonlike figures had attacked the village in the night. And they had discovered the grave of a man who Lasiri thought was one of the raiders. A man who carried a jeweled knife and was buried with a blue-black sapphire in his mouth. But where is the key? he wondered. Is my sister alive or dead? And if she'd been kidnapped, where had she been taken and by whom?

He turned and looked at Jon Paul and he tried to imagine what it would be like working their way through the long desert shrub, following tracks of raiders who left no more signs than the etching of the wind.

Yet the thing that bothered him the most was the change in Lasiri. The guide seemed strangely quiet and upset, far different from the cocky, almost swaggering man who had led them into the plane that morning. And while Lasiri sat brooding, James could feel an unrest come upon him like an ominous dark shadow of the fast-approaching night.

Once they reached Nairobi, Lasiri escorted them back to the New Stanley Hotel. In the lobby he paused before he said good night.

"Bwana, we had talked yesterday about some kind of financial arrangements to try to find your sister."

"Yes, of course," James answered.

"I am not sure it would be fair," Lasiri said.

James looked at him with surprise. So that's it, he thought. He's going to try to ask for more money. He's shown us a few things to whet our appetite and now he's going to try to get as much out of us as he can.

"We had offered ten thousand to Harold Lundstrom," James said firmly. "If we find my sister, the offer is the same for you."

But the next thing Lasiri said took him completely by surprise. "No, that's no good."

"Then twenty thousand," James said angrily. "Name your price!"

"It is not the money, Bwana James; I don't think I can help."

James stared at him with astonishment. "But why? We've seen the burned village. We know the raiders were there. We could follow them in the desert."

"If it was Abyssinian raiders, I would say yes. They're usually always good for some kind of bribe. We could go up into Ethiopia and spread the word that we were looking for a white woman and we would be willing to buy her back. If she was alive and she was there, word would soon get back to us that someone had seen her. The Abyssinians are keen on bargaining. Women there are treated like cattle, and there is no woman who cannot be traded—for a price."

"But this?" He raised the jeweled knife. "I think the wisest thing might be to forget your sister and go home."

"Christ!" James cried. "We've come all this way and you tell me to go back to the States? You're no better than the Minister of Foreign Affairs."

"Perhaps," Lasiri answered. "But I tell you this because I am not sure that there is anything I can do."

"I don't understand," James protested.

"I don't understand either," Lasiri replied. "I will try to talk to some friends here in Nairobi; perhaps they can help. It's not easy to track down spirits who drift off in the night."

"That was no spirit that we unearthed back there in the ground!" James said angrily.

"I'm not sure which way to go, bwana." Lasiri glared back at him. "East, west, north, south? I don't even know where to start."

"Then what the hell are we supposed to do?" James replied. A long, tired look dragged across his face.

"Something which you in your country do very poorly, bwana."

"And that is?"

"Wait."

12

James and Jon Paul waited. And when the first day passed and then the second and the third, and there was still no word from Lasiri, they could feel a growing sense of impatience. First, James became angry and then worried that something had gone wrong. They were eating breakfast on the fourth morning at the Thorn Tree Cafe when the waiter came over and interrupted them.

"Bwana, there is someone here to see you."

At last, James thought, Lasiri finally has some word for me. He looked up hopefully, expecting to find the tall Masai. But the person whom the waiter brought back to the table was not Lasiri. Rather, a heavyset Caucasian woman hobbled toward them with a cane.

"Mr. Jacobson?" she said.

James stood up to greet her.

"I'm Dr. Ruth Parker from the Nairobi Museum." She held out her hand. Her voice had a faint British accent. "I knew your sister and I wondered if we might talk."

"Of course," he exclaimed. "Please join us. Please sit down."

As she eased herself into the chair beside them, James studied her. She had grayish-red hair and a tanned face. He judged she was perhaps in her mid-fifties. There was nothing pretentious about her manner. She wore no makeup, no jewelry except for a small gold cross at her neck, and was dressed in a plain plaid suit. Yet James did not find her unattractive. Behind a pair of dark glasses were deep green eyes that darted back and forth between James and Jon Paul as they introduced themselves.

"Diana talked often about her family," she said. "You see, she was a very special person to me."

"Yes, yes, go on," James urged.

"I'm an anthropologist," she said. "It was almost a year ago that your sister came to me for help. She wanted to photograph one of the Turkana tribes during a very special ceremony and I gave her some assistance with her permits. We'd met in New York some time back. We became good friends, and often she would come over to chat or stay with me when she passed through Nairobi. Diana is a very talented person. I admire her greatly."

"That's very kind of you to say," James answered.

"I was horrified to hear what happened in the Northern Frontier, horrified to hear that she may have been killed or kidnapped or taken away. I thought perhaps I might be able to help."

James's eyes narrowed. "We'd be interested in anything you can tell us. But how did you know that we were here?"

"Lasiri," she answered. "I've known him ever since he was a child in school. I helped him with the scholarship to Cambridge. We have worked together on many projects. He told me that you flew up to the Northern Frontier. He told us what he wasn't sure he could help any found."

"We were just about thinking he had abandoned us," Jon Paul said. "He told us that he wasn't sure he could help any further."

"He comes from a very intelligent, proud tribe, Jon Paul," Ruth replied. "For a long time the Masai would not work for the whites; they considered it degrading. I don't think he wanted to lead you up into the Northern Frontier again without getting more specifics about what you had found. He told me about the burial and he showed me the knife."

"Yes, yes," James answered eagerly. "And what do you make of it?"

Ruth Parker reached into her purse and pulled out a smudged piece of paper. "I thought you might be interested in this," she said. "I took several notes."

She took off her dark glasses and replaced them with a pair of bifocals. Then she began to read:

"We had been traveling for nearly a week on the fringes of the desert when we came upon a strange town built from stone on the very edge of a long plateau. There was a fresh spring here and we stopped for the night, freshening up on our water supplies. The town was run by perhaps thirty Arabs and a mixed combination of blacks and various tribes who assisted with the functions of crops and herding cattle. When I asked with great surprise how such a grand stone structure could be built here, the Arabs replied that it was part of a caravan route coming out from the interior, and that there was a whole series of such oases located each within five or six days' march from the other, leading all the way to the coast. It was obvious that there was no great source of treasure or riches at this particular oasis, and when I asked where their trade came from, one of the men took me onto a large knoll and pointed out across the desert to a tall, distant peak shimmering like a mirage. It was what he called the Devil's Tower. Beyond that was a magnificent city, far greater than the one in which we resided. There was great treasure there, he said.

"I asked him if I could go there and he shook his head and said no, that it was out of bounds for Christians. But who lived there? I asked, and he replied in a strange way that it was a tribe of lightskinned peoples who looked like

Arabs but wore veils and who were very dangerous and not
to be bothered with.

"The next afternoon he came to me with great excitement and pointed out upon the desert and there I saw a
great caravan moving in a ghostly procession through the
sand. There were fifty or sixty camels and a number of
captives bound around the neck. As they drew closer, I
saw that one of their captives was a very lightskinned
woman with long blond hair. . . ."

"My God, Ruth," James exclaimed, leaping to his feet.
"Where did you get this? Who wrote this? It's her, it must have
been her!"

"Let me continue," she said patiently. He nodded and slowly
sat back down.

"The men riding in the caravan were dressed in black
robes which covered their entire bodies including their
faces, except for a small slit opened for their eyes. I had
hoped the caravan would come closer but it did not. It was
traveling from somewhere far to the north and soon
turned, heading across the desert to the mountains.

"Later the Arab told me that these black-robed people
had the terrible custom of taking heads and they carried
them around much as one might do with trophies of war.
It was a most peculiar race, for he had seen them bury one
once, one of their dead, in Egyptian fashion, lying on their
backs with their arms across their chest.

"It was also rumored, though not observed by this man,
that the men of the tribe always carried a small blue stone
around their necks and when they died the stone was
placed inside their mouths as a token of passageway into
the hereafter. I thought at the time that this was a most
odd custom, though I have since learned that in ancient
Greece people often placed a coin inside the mouth of the
deceased as a token to pay Charon as he ferried the body
across the River Styx to the Land of the Underworld. This
custom may have been carried over from the early Egyp-
tians who buried their deceased on one side of the Nile in

the Valley of the Dead, but I do not know, and heard no more from the Arabs about this matter. Unfortunately, we left the next day and had no further contact or knowledge of this peculiar custom nor of the tribe which supposedly inhabited the area beyond the Devil's Tower. . . ."

"Ruth, that's it!" James was on his feet again. "My God, where did you get that? They must have seen her! Everything seems to fit. Then there's hope. Thank goodness there's hope. It must mean that she's still alive!"

Ruth Parker took off her glasses. Her green eyes bored deeply into James's.

"There is one small problem here," she answered softly. "The manuscript I am reading is a translation. It's part of a diary from a Portuguese explorer named Hernando Figuerez. It was written in the year *1735.*"

13

They were in the Arab mosque of El-Moshan. James and Jon Paul had taken off their shoes, as was the Moslem custom, and now they followed Ruth inside. They passed a small fountain and turned down an arched corridor into a section that had been marked, in Arabic, "ARCHIVES." It was here, Ruth told them, that nearly all of the early Arabic translations were kept. As they moved through the building, the faint sound of Islamic prayer drifted to their ears.

"Hernando Figuerez never made it back to Portugal," Ruth said. "He became ill and died in Mombasa during the year 1736, or, as the Moslems count it, the year of 1114 Hegira. His papers and diary were translated by Arab scholars along with a large number of other Portuguese manuscripts. Because he was a traveled scholar, the Arabs of the time held him in respect."

They came to a small arched doorway and followed the passageway into a dimly lighted room. The space smelled musty. As Ruth turned on the light, James noted the room formed a depository for hundreds of stacks of papers.

"In my own studies it was helpful to read accounts of early explorations. Since I know Arabic, they were easy for me to translate, and every now and then I would come across something of archaeological interest. When Lasiri mentioned that you had found the grave of a man buried Egyptian fashion, something seemed to click. About a year or so ago, I had read the diary of Hernando Figuerez. In fact, I talked to an Arab once who had visited the very same spot Figuerez describes when he saw the caravan."

"Then there is a city?"

"Nothing but ruins now," Ruth answered. "Overgrown with the jungle. But across from it is a great desert, just as he described. It may indeed be, based on the burial you found, that these people have come across the desert."

The implications of what Ruth was trying to tell them fogged James's mind. A diary two hundred years old. A Portuguese explorer. A captive woman with light complexion and long blond hair. He wondered what had ever happened to the poor woman. Had she been used as a slave, a concubine in a chieftain's harem? Or had she not been that lucky?

Ruth began to shuffle through a stack of papers. "Here they are," she said. She opened one of the manuscripts and began leafing through the pages, one by one. The script was in Arabic and completely unintelligible to James.

"And here is what we are looking for," she said.

She laid out a small map sketched in pen, the paper turned brown with age. There were six x's marked in an almost straight line leading inward from the coast. Then the rough shape of a Devil's Tower and then a seventh x beyond the mountains.

"Each x was a city or fortified stone outpost built around an oasis," Ruth said. "We know for a fact that the first of these is along the coast at Malindi and is quite well preserved. Most of the others have crumbled away to nothing except for the sixth city, which still has some of the walls and interior structure present. It's located near the oasis of al Jabbar.

"This small point on Figuerez's map is smudged but I believe it is the word for wadi," Ruth said, pointing.

"I remember seeing many of those when I first looked at a map of Ethiopia and the Sudan," James said. "What are they?"

"Usually depressions that become sinks or waterholes in the rainy season. But most of the year they're empty and dry. The x points marking the oasis should be springs, where one can find water any time of the year."

Ruth carefully folded the papers in front of her. "I think you have to make a choice, James. You can either continue to search around the area where she disappeared, hoping that it might have been Abyssinian raiders and that you might be able to lure some of the tribes down by bribing them to find out more information . . ."

"Or?"

"Or you head west, bypassing all of the areas in the Northern Frontier and going directly to the oasis of al Jabbar in the Sudan. I would suggest you start from there."

"You're assuming, of course, that she might still be alive."

"That is always the chance you have to take. You may spend the next two months looking for her and find nothing."

She paused, studying James closely. "It is my guess—and mind you, it's a guess and nothing more—but looking at all of the evidence, it seems possible that the raiders came to capture slaves. If this is true, then they might not have killed her."

A faint glimmer of hope seemed to flicker deep in James's mind.

"God, I pray that you're right, but how can you say that?"

"Because we know first of all that none of the cattle from the Turkana village were taken, so we have to assume that the raiders were not concerned with cattle. If they had come merely to make war on the Turkana, then there are a dozen other villages scattered in the vicinity that they surely would have razed. We know, too, from the description of the burial, the knife the man carried, the stone buried in his mouth, that they were not Abyssinians. *If* the description fits, *if* the story recorded by Hernando Figuerez is accurate, then it is my guess that she was captured by a nomadic desert tribe about which we know very little, a tribe that sounds almost like the Tuareg."

James shook his head. The name was meaningless to him.

"They were a very feared and hostile tribe that controlled the caravan routes in the old days. Wore dark robes. The men were always veiled."

"But why would they have come for her?" James frowned.

"I don't know." Ruth shrugged. "I don't think I can even venture a guess. But remember this. Your sister was an exceptional woman in both complexion and looks for the Northern Frontier. Word of her may have spread over many hundreds of miles."

James thought for a long time without speaking. "And what are your intentions?" he finally asked.

"If you decide to go to al Jabbar, then I'd like to go with you. Lasiri has already talked with me about it and he's willing to help us with the arrangements. I've never seen the other side of the desert. If there are rock drawings of archaeological interest or perhaps the remains of an old city, then I'd like to have a look at them. That is, of course, assuming we also find traces of your sister."

"Ruth . . ." James paused. A question had been bothering him ever since she had walked into the Thorn Tree Cafe that morning. "Why are you willing to help us like this?"

"Because I was very fond of Diana. We were great friends and I think she would do the same for me had the situation been reversed. If it is true that a tribe has come out of the Sudan, then we have a very long way to go. The point I showed you on the map is several hundred miles from the area where your sister disappeared. You will need someone to speak Arabic, and I can help you there.

"Second, if she was kidnapped, it will mean that no white woman is ever safe in the Northern Frontier again. Other tribes will hear of it and be encouraged to try similar tricks themselves. And last, if we find her and *if* she is alive, she might want some female companionship, someone to help from a woman's point of view."

Each of these arguments has merit, James thought. If Diana

was hurt or sick or injured, a woman like Ruth would be a tremendous help.

"And if we decide to stay up in the Northern Frontier to search out some word from the Abyssinians?"

"Then you can count me out," Ruth answered. "I don't have much interest in that place, and I think it would be a waste of time. Even to send a scouting party and wait for feeder information would take a month. It would be a month lost if your sister needs help."

"That bothers me too," James answered. "What do you think, Jon Paul?"

The youth nodded his head firmly. "I think Ruth is right. I think we should go."

A frown had worked its way across James's face. "Ruth, there's one thing I still don't understand. There was a gem—a sapphire—that Diana sent to New York about six weeks before she disappeared. The same type of jewel Lasiri found in the dead man's mouth. Lundstrom seemed to be familiar with the stone. It was stolen when he was speared."

Ruth nodded. "For a long time people have made reference to a large oasis out there in the desert somewhere, a city called Bogadez, which at one time was supposed to be one of the richest oases in the Sahara and a great center of trade. Harold Lundstrom and a hundred other hunter-adventurers have been looking for it for years. Occasionally a rumor emerges or someone finds a stone and the legends start up all over again. The stone, the blue-black sapphire with the palm tree etching upon the back, was originally thought to be from Bogadez. To my knowledge, no European has ever been there."

"But where did Diana find it?"

Ruth Parker smiled. "I gave it to her, James. We'd dug it up from a grave years ago. There are several in the museum."

"Ruth, I was almost killed for that stone," James exclaimed.

"You're not the first." She frowned. "And probably not the last. There is still one other alternative," Ruth said, eyeing James cautiously.

"And that is?"

"That you return to the States and forget about her. Perhaps with time, some news might turn up."

"I think we've already ruled that alternative out. There's no way I could go home and face my parents emptyhanded."

"You won't be," Ruth answered. "You've found where she was and you've discovered for yourself how incredibly difficult it will be to find her—*if* she is still alive. I can promise you nothing in the Sudan. We may spend two months up there and find nothing but hot desert and empty air."

James shook his head. "I know very little about traveling through the desert. Lasiri admitted it might be a very arduous trip, and that was only working up in the Northern Frontier. You're talking now about some fairly long distance traveling. What chance would we have?"

"In all honesty," Ruth answered, "if you really want to find your sister . . . I'm not sure that you have any other choice."

14

Two days later Lasiri called James and Jon Paul down to the lobby of the New Stanley Hotel. "The arrangements are complete," he said, presenting a list of their inventory and the estimated charges to assemble the caravan. James studied the items carefully. He wanted to be sure that his father would have no questions concerning the costs of the expedition. Should they be unsuccessful, he knew his father would want complete accountability for all monies spent.

"How many tents?" he asked.

"Three," Lasiri answered. "One for Dr. Parker, one for you and Jon Paul, and one for me." The Masai smiled. "I did not think you would want all of us to sleep together."

"And this item: five 'diggers,' one thousand dollars each?"

"These are the salaries for one month each for the five men who will come along as assistants with the dig."

When James had notified his architectural firm that he would have to take an indefinite leave, he'd watched a smile break out on Jon Paul's face. A month would put the boy well into the summer vacation. Well, it will have to be, James told himself. Finding his sister was his top priority and they would have to take as long as necessary to locate her—dead or alive. His attention turned back to Lasiri.

"Why do you use the term dig?"

"We will be going under the guise of an archaeological team supervised by Dr. Parker. She felt it would be easier to cross the borders, since she already has the permits for taking out a group such as this. Otherwise it might take months to apply for the proper papers."

"Five thousand is a lot of money for diggers."

"The men are specially trained," Lasiri answered.

James glanced further down the list. "And this item, *cook?*"

"We will need a cook, bwana," the Masai patiently replied. "Unless, of course, you would prefer to prepare the meals yourself?"

"Drivers, two men?"

"I will drive the first Land-Rover. Two men will drive the second and third Land-Rovers. They will also be responsible for the supplies, for breaking the tents and keeping everything in order."

"Why three Land-Rovers?" James frowned.

"Should one break down, we will need to transfer goods to one of the others. Transportation is the most important element and we cannot afford to lose mobility, especially if we're pursuing some camel caravan."

As Jon Paul listened, he could envision them hot on the heels of a pack of desert bandits, the nomads riding their camels like fury and the Land-Rovers charging after them, bouncing and lurching over the rough terrain. It all sounded terribly exciting. But what were they going to do when they caught them? Try to bargain? There were still some things the boy did not fully understand.

James suddenly stopped, his eyes fixing upon a four-digit figure. "Digging equipment: spades, shovels, and pickaxes, *seven thousand dollars!* Christ, man, that should buy enough equipment to dig all the way to China."

"I will bring the digging equipment to the hotel tomorrow so that you may inspect it."

"At that price we should be able to outfit the entire *National Geographic,*" James muttered.

"Yes, bwana," Lasiri replied. "We had to make some special arrangements."

James shook his head and did not comment further until he reached the end of the third page of the inventory. When he came to the final total charges, he looked at Lasiri cautiously.

"Nineteen thousand nine hundred dollars for a safari is a lot of money. Add ten thousand for your charges, and you're asking for thirty thousand dollars."

The Masai glared back at him. "That which we need to do is not cheap. You're asking for a fully outfitted caravan into the Sudan for a period of up to one month to search for your sister. If we cut back on the Land-Rovers or the men or supplies, we could be compromising our efforts."

The faintest flicker of impatience smoldered in Lasiri's eyes. "It would be foolish to go up into the desert unprepared. These are the best men, the best equipment I could find for the most reasonable price. Be thankful that you're not wiring home for a million dollars ransom."

James searched back through the list, rechecking the figures. If she had been kidnapped and there was a demand for ransom, at least they would know that Diana was alive. For a call back to his father maybe he could have her home. But what price was his sister worth? he wondered. A million dollars? Ten million dollars? And how many lives would it take to find her? When it came down to it, there was no monetary value that he could place on her safe return.

"All right." James finally nodded. "I'll have the money for you this afternoon."

The next morning Lasiri came into James's suite carrying a long wooden box over his shoulder. The top and sides were stamped ARCHAEOLOGICAL EXPEDITION. NORTHERN FRONTIER. With a grunt he rested it gently upon the floor.

"I thought you might want to see some of the equipment we're carrying, bwana." The Masai wiped his brow with a handkerchief. Pulling out a small penknife, he pried open the top of the box. Inside were three shovels, a pair of spades and two pickaxes, all neatly arranged.

James reached down and lifted out one of the spades.

"How many of these boxes do we have?"

"Four, bwana."

James removed the rest of the "digging" equipment, inspecting each item carefully. He could feel a surge of anger rising in him. Half of the items were not new. Some even bore rust-encrusted dirt from a previous dig. His eyes suddenly flashed with fury.

"Lasiri, what the hell is going on?"

"Now, bwana, if you would be so kind as to bring the box over here," the Masai responded.

James bent down to pick up the empty box. Grunting with surprise, he struggled to lift it. A flash of understanding began to spread across his face.

"Let's hope this works across the border," Lasiri said. He walked over to the box and pried loose a false bottom.

James's eyes opened wide with amazement. Hidden beneath the artificial bottom of the box was a rack of guns. Lasiri pulled one out, clicked the breach, and smacked a magazine into place. It was an M-14 automatic rifle. On the side of the barrel were etched the words: UNITED STATES, MILITARY ISSUE, 6554481.

He handed the weapon to James, who took the gun limply. "Sorry. I should have known."

"Your twenty thousand dollars will be put to good use," Lasiri replied. "We have all of the proper papers to verify that we are an archaeological expedition to the north. On the outside we have the equipment and the men required for a small research caravan, the type the museum often makes for a short three- or four-week dig. It is a perfect disguise for us to travel under. The five men who will accompany us as 'diggers' are professional soldiers. All have agreed to go with us for a period of one month. We have twelve automatic weapons, with one hundred rounds of ammunition each. Because of the black market running from Rhodesia to Uganda, they were easy enough to purchase. Seven thousand dollars was needed to cover the costs and make certain there would be no loose tongues. We've got three Land-Rovers, a cook, and two drivers. I would feel more comfortable if we had twelve soldiers, but if we are too many, we begin to arouse suspicion at the borders. Then there is a chance they might not let us pass. Granted, we could always blast our way through, but I'd just as soon remain on friendly terms with the Kenyan government, since this is my home."

James eased back into a chair, still holding on to the automatic rifle, trying to take in what Lasiri was telling him. He felt as if he had suddenly stepped into a maelstrom over which he had no control. For six days he had been fretting that everything was moving too slowly and now everything was going too fast. For the first time he saw that the stakes of the game they were playing were far more than a single human life.

"The tribes here listen to one thing, bwana," Lasiri said. "You're dealing with armed raiders who have burned down an entire Turkana village, killed a number of tribesmen and perhaps your sister with no more concern than if they were goats. What did you envision bargaining with—beads?"

"I'm not sure," James answered. "I guess I hadn't considered automatic weapons."

"Survival is measured in terms of firepower," Lasiri answered. "If you want to come back alive, we go prepared for war!"

15

At six o'clock on Friday morning, three Land-Rovers pulled up smartly in front of the New Stanley Hotel and braked to a stop. Ruth stepped out of the first Land-Rover and found James and Jon Paul waiting in the lobby. When they returned to the vehicles, Lasiri had all of the men standing in a line. The "diggers," as Lasiri had called them, were dressed in khaki shorts with long brown knee socks, heavy shoes, and dark shirts. Three of the men wore berets. All stood over six feet. Even the two drivers and the cook were impressive in their height.

James searched through the strong black faces towering above him, and he felt like a colonel starting inspection.

"Wadjo Mbili," Lasiri said, introducing the first man. "Digger."

"*Jambo*, bwana," the soldier answered, flashing a white-toothed smile. He shook James's hand firmly.

"Hamad Wadyuma. Digger."

"Good morning, bwana."

"Ferusa Surmari. Cook."

"Good day, sir."

"Umari Beda. Driver."

The man nodded.

"Mabruka Hassan. Digger."

"*Jambo*, sir."

As he finished introducing the last of the men, Lasiri gave a command in Swahili and they broke rank, returning to the Land-Rovers. The two drivers started the engines. Lasiri led James toward the lead vehicle. Fluttering from the antenna was the shield and crossed-spears insignia of the Kenyan flag.

"My apologies," Lasiri said. "I thought you might want to fly the American colors, but we would have trouble getting through the borders."

"I believe you've thought of everything," James said.

"I hope so," Lasiri replied. "I only regret that none of the men speak English well. I'm afraid they've exhausted their vocabulary with the introductions."

"Well, then, maybe we'll have to learn Swahili," James replied. Glancing into the lead Land-Rover, he saw the rear compartment neatly arranged with supplies: tents, cases of food, cooking utensils, water containers. More boxes covered with tarpaulin were strapped to the roof. Ruth Parker and Jon Paul were already comfortably seated in the backseat.

James paused, taking a deep breath, as if he were about to make an ocean plunge. "Well, let's hope we have good hunting," he said. Opening the door, he swung into the front seat. Lasiri started the engine and the three Land-Rovers pulled away from the hotel. As the morning sun began to rise in the east, the vehicles roared through the outskirts of Nairobi, like three ships moving out from port, heading for the vast region of uncharted desert beyond Kenya's Northern Frontier.

PART II

Africa is divided into four parts—the third part has no other name than Sahra, which means desert.

—Leo Africans, 1550

16

Driving north, the caravan soon left all evidence of civilization behind. Except for an occasional village, the country opened into gently rolling grassland. Small herds of gazelles grazed next to the road, rocketing off as they passed. Giraffes eyed them cautiously, then galloped away. Vultures, black-winged, with pink, featherless heads, soared low over the road.

As mile passed mile, the geography began to change. Broad umbrella-topped acacias disappeared, replaced by stunted desert shrub. Rivers became dry, dusty remnants of the seasonal floods. Gradually the greenery faded until everything became parched and burned and brown.

At five o'clock that afternoon they came to the small border town of Tula Gorda at the edge of the Northern Frontier. It was more of an outpost than a village, a few flimsy mud-baked houses, a general store, some scattered natives, a pack of mongrel dogs.

Ten miles outside the town Lasiri suddenly brought the Land-Rover to a stop. James had been daydreaming when he was almost thrown into the dashboard. A vicious-looking wooden barrier with sharp eight-inch spikes blocked their path. Half hidden on either side of the roadway were two military Land-Rovers.

"Border patrol," Lasiri muttered. He pulled the Land-Rover off to the side of the road, motioning for the two trailing vehicles to follow.

In an instant, a dozen armed soldiers surrounded them, demanding credentials and poking through their gear. James and Jon Paul filed out of the Land-Rover, waiting patiently, as one of the soldiers inspected their papers. For another ten minutes the soldiers searched through the boxes. Finally they stopped and waved them through.

"That was close," James commented, once they were safely past.

Ruth shook her head. "For an inspection, that was nothing. If they'd wanted to make it difficult, they would have forced us to unpack everything. But it's all a matter of having the right papers. The Kenyan government is interested in the development of science in all fields. They know we can't do our job if we're continually hassled by red tape."

"And what about photography?" James asked.

"An entirely different matter. When your sister wanted to go into the Northern Frontier, it took some doing to get her permits. The government is not keen on the exploitation of tribes by magazines that print pictures of half-naked natives."

"The Minister of Foreign Affairs suggested Diana's permits had been obtained by bribes," he scoffed.

"They were," Ruth answered.

They drove for another hour before Lasiri stopped to consult the maps. For most of the day they had traveled on a wide, smoothly graded road. Now they turned to the west and began following a barely perceptible trail. The sun had begun to sink when Lasiri finally brought the caravan to a halt.

They had just begun to pitch their tents when one of the "diggers" came hurrying back into camp. "Lasiri, bwana. Come!" he said excitedly.

They followed him out to the edge of a plateau. There looking down upon a valley they saw a herd of elephants. The animals were moving slowly, ears flapping, traveling in single file. As they walked a cloud of dust rose behind them, catching the last embers of the sun, and they looked as if they were bathed in gold. James watched for a long time, enthralled by the scene.

"It's not often you find them out here, this close to the desert," Ruth said.

"I almost wish I'd brought a camera," James replied.

Ruth looked at him with surprise. "Well, now you can understand why Diana came. . . ."

After dinner, with a full stomach and the weariness of the drive gradually dissipating, James walked out from the campfire, gazing up at the African sky. The stars dazzled above him with a clarity he had never seen before. He stood for a moment deep in thought, then returned to the fire. Ruth was sitting on a small campstool drinking coffee.

"Incredible night," James said. "I don't think I've ever seen the stars so bright."

Ruth smiled. "There's an African legend that says the stars are the holes in the blanket the gazelle threw over the earth in an attempt to trap her lover, the bustard. But he was too smart. He always left before dawn in order to avoid revealing his ugliness."

"Clever bird." James chuckled.

"This country can be like a narcotic," Ruth said. "Once it gets into your system, it's often very hard to get out. I think Diana felt that. She often said she was closer to the core of existence here. Less hindered by technological progress."

Across the campfire, Lasiri was showing Jon Paul how to work the loading mechanism of a small-bore rifle. A dozen feet away a second campfire burned. The two drivers, cook, and five soldiers squatted around it, talking quietly among themselves. James poured a cup of coffee, then pulled up a stool and sat down beside Ruth.

"Ruth, I never realized how tough Diana was until we saw the Turkana village where she lived. I mostly remember her as just a carefree girl, chased by dozens of young men who hung around the house all the time. What was she like over here?"

"A very dedicated professional photographer," Ruth answered. "Like many committed people, she was willing to put up with many hardships to achieve her goals. When I first saw some of her photographs in New York, I knew there was something special about her. The work she was completing here in the Northern Frontier was probably some of the best she'd ever done."

"But why here, Ruth? The country is so harsh, so primitive. My father suspected there was something in her home life that was deficient, something she was running away from."

Ruth glanced at James and she could see the confusion in his eyes. For the first time she realized that he still thought of his sister as a young girl. Somehow he and his family were living with an image of her in the past.

"I don't think there was anything wrong, James. She was obviously a very bright, creative woman. She wanted to explore some avenues of life she had never really tried. You've got to admire her for that."

"Diana was always difficult for me to understand," James answered. "I still remember an incident when we were growing up. Some older boys had locked her in a closet during a school recess with a belt fastened around a doorknob. She was screaming to get out. I came along and cut the belt. At the same time two of the older boys appeared. Being a protective brother, I challenged them to leave her alone. They just laughed at me, so I wound up and punched one as hard as I could. All it did was stun him. There was nothing else for me to do but run. The second one took out after me and just about caught me when I dodged. He slipped and broke his arm. Well, I thought I was a big hero for setting her free. She was furious. Told me never to meddle in her affairs again. I think it was the first time a girl really confused me. I've never really understood them since."

Ruth laughed. "Do you have a girl?"

James stared into the fire. "Married once. A French girl whom I met during a summer vacation in college. She was a stewardess for Air France. We dated for several years then got married. She never could adjust to the American way of life. One thing led to the next and we parted. Fortunately, there were no children."

"James, I'm sorry," Ruth said.

The muscles in his jaw tightened. "These things happen, Ruth. We were awfully young. Life has to go on. . . . And you?"

"Engaged once," she answered. "But I got scared and broke things off. He was an awfully nice man. Rich. A financier. It bothered me for months but I just didn't fit. I couldn't see myself back in London raising five children, giving afternoon teas, going to the theater. It would have been bloody awful." She frowned as a memory crossed her mind.

"I often think if my own parents had been anthropologists living out here in the bush, then maybe I would have gone the other way, married early, raised a huge family, and never left the city."

"What about the loneliness?" James asked.

He watched Ruth in the flickering light of the fire. The great display of the heavens shone above them. Somewhere off in the distance rose the melancholy cry of a night bird. Very slowly a film of moisture seemed to creep into her eyes.

"Loneliness?" Ruth said. Her voice fell as if she had trouble grasping the meaning of the word. She shivered once and stared into the fire.

A strange woman, James reflected. She was full of technological facts and anthropological data, yet suddenly the protective veil had been lifted, exposing a vulnerability that he hadn't noticed before. Too many days out here in the bush, he thought. Too many dreams unfulfilled, too many hopes lost and buried within her soul.

When she turned back to him the veil had returned and the softness was gone.

"There are times when I think about a family and wonder what it would have been like. But I've devoted my life to Africa, James. I no longer have a choice."

"If I were sure that was really what Diana wanted," James replied, "then maybe I would understand."

"She was happy," Ruth answered. "She was excited about her work. If she's gone, then at least you know that she died trying to seek out those things that she thought most significant. That's a lot more than most people do."

"And that's important enough to trade for one's life?"

Ruth looked at him sternly. "I think, to some people, not finding it is worse than death."

She sipped her coffee and stared at the fire, leaving James to brood on his thoughts. But what *were* the important things in life? he wondered. How many of his own dreams had been lost? How many times had he turned away from women since Nicole had left? And what was there about Page that made him so afraid? So, you don't need a desert and a hundred thousand miles of open country to lose yourself in. He, too, had his vulnerabilities and his protective veil. And maybe it wasn't a matter so much of losing himself as finding himself that counted. His mind flashed back to San Francisco, sailing beneath the Golden Gate, Page standing like some bow sprite with her breasts exposed, waving her bikini top at the crew of the freighter *Asperia*. He felt as if he had stepped through a time warp into another world a thousand light-years away. Page was beautiful and she loved him and he hadn't even called to say good-bye. But if there were things he couldn't explain about himself, how could he possibly expect her to understand?

When he looked up, Lasiri was standing behind him.

"Best turn in, bwana," the Masai said. "We've got a long day ahead of us tomorrow."

It was some time after midnight when James suddenly awoke. He'd been dreaming that he was in the Turkana village where his sister had lived. The old Turkana woman was describing the raid in her creaky voice, only this time Lasiri wasn't there and he couldn't understand the woman without a translator. In the dream people were running wildly through the camp and he heard Diana screaming. He was trying desperately to get out of bed to defend himself when he awoke with sweat pouring off his brow.

He lay for a long time without moving, listening to the sounds of the night. Very slowly he began to have an uneasy feeling that something was wrong, that some sixth sense had wakened him as a warning.

He searched through the darkness toward the cot next to him. Jon Paul was sleeping soundly. He heard a twig crack and then the faint noise of something stirring by the campfire. He got up slowly and fumbled for the rifle next to his bed. In the dark he couldn't see and he was unfamiliar with the loading mechanism. As he tried to ram a cartridge home he heard a long, low-pitched hissing sound as if air was escaping from some type of hollow chamber.

Where the hell are the soldiers? he wondered. The cartridge was in the rifle now and he closed the breach and grabbed for a flashlight. Jon Paul was stirring next to him when he moved silently out of the tent. He stood outside for a long moment listening.

He half imagined he would see strange black forms moving across the campground just as the Turkana woman had described them, but he found nothing. The fires were faint glows

of fading coals. No one was stirring. He shined a light down by
the fire and saw the soldiers and the cook and the two drivers
stretched out in the blankets asleep. Then he heard a slight
movement behind him, very faint, as if a tuft of grass had been
crushed beneath a heavy foot. He turned cautiously, staring
into the darkness. Something did not seem right. His eyes saw,
but his mind did not register, a gigantic shadow hovering beside
the tent. A long slender snakelike thing probed toward him in
the darkness.

He yelled and fired at the same time. There was a terrible
deafening shriek and then pandemonium broke loose. The huge
form charged past him, trumpeting wildly. The kitchen tent
was bowled over. Pots and pans clanged loudly. Men leaped
through the darkness, diving for safety. There was a loud crashing of brush and then the diminishing sounds of the elephants
as they stampeded off into the darkness.

Ruth and Jon Paul emerged from their tents. The soldiers,
cook, and the drivers collected themselves down by the second
fire. Miraculously no one had been hurt. James stood trembling,
trying to catch his breath when a firm hand grabbed him on the
shoulder.

"Welcome to Africa." Lasiri smiled.

17

It was ten o'clock in the morning in New York City. A small
desk radio in the executive tower of the TransOceanic Airlines
Building softly announced the news. The mayor, speaking from
Gracie Mansion, reported a major breakthrough in the garbage
workers' strike. The Dow-Jones was up three quarters of a
point. Rumors persisted that the city would have to float a bond
issue to avoid bankruptcy. For the weather: The sky was clear

with scattered clouds, the wind, southwest at seven miles per hour; the temperature, sixty-eight degrees.

Jacobson's secretary reached over and turned down the FM news to dial a telephone number. When the sound of a busy signal came on the line she hung up the phone in frustration. "I'm sorry, sir, but still no luck," she announced over the intercom.

"Keep dialing!" Michael Jacobson roared back at her. He had been trying to reach the American Embassy in Nairobi all morning. Sometimes "goddamned" international telephone calls were impossible.

The key was patience and persistence, and Jacobson was rapidly running out of both. He tried one time on his own, just for luck, and met with equal failure. Slamming down the receiver, he stood up and walked over to the large plate-glass window. From the seventy-second floor he stared out across the bustling face of Manhattan. His eyes scanned across tall, jutting skyscrapers, traveled past the open space of Central Park, now in spring bloom, and moved toward upper Manhattan and the George Washington Bridge, following the Hudson River until it disappeared in a gray impenetrable haze.

STARTING ON SAFARI FOR THE OASIS AL JABBAR IN THE SUDAN STOP JON PAUL WELL AND SENDS HIS LOVE STOP REGRET LITTLE HOPE DIANA IS STILL ALIVE

JAMES

Al Jabbar, he thought, reflecting upon his son's telegram. *Al Jabbar wasn't even on the charts!*

He'd spent half a day with William Simpson of the State Department going over some of the labeled satellite maps of Kenya and the Sudan, and they could find nothing resembling the name. Nothing up there but desert and a few scattered wadi. So, what the hell were they up to? And where had they gone? He had tried for three days to reach James without success. Jacobson's last telegram to the New Stanley had gone unanswered. When he was finally able to get through to the hotel by telephone, he discovered that James and Jon Paul had checked out, leaving no forwarding address, only a request that the hotel "hold all messages" until they returned.

He had finally managed to contact the Minister of Foreign Affairs. Wilson Tomboya advised him that he had met with his sons and recommended that they return to the States. Later, from the American Embassy, Jacobson learned that his son had been seen in a bar on the night a white man named Harold Lundstrom was speared. The details were unclear but worrisome. Worrisome enough for Jacobson to consider going over to Nairobi himself. It was bad enough having a daughter missing over there. Perhaps he had made a mistake in letting James and Jon Paul go. If it had been one of his older sons, Michael Junior or Donald, Jacobson knew that he would get a nightly telephone call with a complete report of the days' events. But checking in was not James's style.

Jacobson had first discovered this when James was in college. Both of his older sons had served as officers for four years in the navy. Following in his brothers' footsteps, James had been in the Naval Officers Training Corps throughout his four years at Princeton. Between semesters he told his father he wanted to try a special flight training course in Pensacola, where the navy tested young pilot applicants. Jacobson had been surprised for he knew the boy was talented in art and had never shown any particular interest in aviation. At the same time he was intrigued with the thought that one of his boys might become a pilot and follow him into the airline business.

James had written a couple of letters during the course telling him that everything was fine. Six weeks later he'd received a call from James stating he had decided against becoming a pilot, was returning to college, and then going on to architectural school. When James came home they had talked at some length about the navy program and James had merely said that he didn't fit. Although Jacobson had been disappointed, he had supported his son's decision.

It wasn't until months later that Jacobson's wife told him the entire story. James had hated flying in the small training aircraft, becoming so claustrophobic that he was constantly sick. Each morning for six weeks he had vomited after every flight. Then on the final day of their course one of his best friends had been killed in a midair collision. James had gone on and soloed but the next day he resigned from the school.

"Why the hell didn't he tell me this a long time ago?" Jacobson had asked his wife.

"Oh, Michael, don't you see?" she'd answered. "I think James was trying to please you. I don't think he was ever really interested in becoming a pilot."

It was like his marriage, Jacobson thought. James hadn't even intimated that he was having trouble at home until he called one day to say that his wife, Nicole, had decided to return to France. The girl had been beautiful, there was no question about it, and the elder Jacobson recalled when James first brought her home, he, too, was dazzled by her looks. She was tall, with black hair, green eyes, and an adorable French accent. But it was always difficult for a nineteen-year-old foreigner to adjust to life in a new country, and now James's marriage was just another statistic. Diana had guessed it wouldn't last. Jacobson thought if he'd had to bet on it, he probably would have agreed. He wasn't sure exactly why. Something was just not quite right. He remembered how upset James had been but, as everything else, his son had buried it deep in his mind and rarely spoken about it again.

But the boy has guts, Michael Jacobson thought. And he has determination and he's not a quitter. If he doesn't do something foolish, then maybe sending James and Jon Paul to Africa did make sense. James was single and in his prime. By virtue of his energy and youth, James could probably cover more territory than his father could have done.

Jon Paul was another matter. His grades were hardly good enough to get into one of the first-rate colleges. For Christmas a year before Jacobson had given him a dirt bike in the hopes that it might please him enough to try to work a little harder in school. A month later Jon Paul had wrecked it by playing "Evel Knievel," trying to jump over eight neighborhood children lying in a row. Jacobson shuddered at the thought. He'd almost been sued as it was. Now he was so frustrated with Jon Paul that he had leaped at any suggestion that might help straighten him out. So, there was some sense in sending the two of them over together. At the very least, Jon Paul might learn to assume some responsibility.

The only thing that bothered Jacobson was James's inexperience. He might go off half-cocked, do something heroic when he should have thought it over, been more cautious in his assessment of the situation. Despite all the information Jacobson had received, he couldn't for the life of him determine what James had found that would make him suddenly arrange an expedition costing thirty thousand dollars and take off for the Sudan.

As Jacobson paced back and forth in front of the window, he was interrupted momentarily by a telephone call. Vice-Chairman Miller was on the phone, worried about a detail concerning the sale of three of the company's 727s to Aerolineas Argentinas. Jacobson half listened, agreed with Miller's assessment, and told him to continue with the transaction. Clearly, his mind was not on company business.

He opened the State Department's map and spread it across his desk, searching through the southern region of the Sudan. Wherever his sons were, they were on their own. He no longer had any way to advise them what to do. So just be smart, Jacobson thought. Wherever you are, whatever you are doing . . . just be careful and be smart.

There was a click on the intercom.

"Sir, there is a woman calling from San Francisco," his secretary said. "I told her that you were busy but she insisted on speaking with you. It's her third call this morning."

"What does she want?" he said with irritation.

"She says she is a friend of James and her name is Page Sinclair."

18

James was sitting on a ridge, sweeping his binoculars across the terrain, when he began to realize the remarkable location of al Jabbar. Ahead, stretching as far as the eye could see, was the most inhospitable desert he had ever laid eyes upon. There was no blade of grass, no living thing, only a broad expanse of sand that melted into a mirage of heat waves at the farthest perimeter of his vision. Above this rose the distant peaks of desert mountains, stark and jagged, floating above the mirage with incredible ruggedness. Upon the sand nothing moved. The sun poured its heat upon the desert; it burned and glared like molten rock.

Yet, miraculously, at the very edge of this foreboding land, cool water ran. The spring that made up al Jabbar bubbled out of a carved limestone pool nearly fifty feet across. Pure and blue, the water rose from beneath the oasis like an artesian well, spilling onto the edge of the desert in a small stream that wandered for half a mile before it dissipated in a swamp. Wherever there was water, green vegetation grew. Flowers bloomed, vines wrapped themselves around tall trees, thick bushes rose upward, spreading in a canopy of leaves that practically obliterated the sun. Throughout these shadows, birds flitted, their colorful plumage flashing from one shaft of sunlight to the next. There everything proliferated in a wild frenzy of life. It was as if at any moment the wonderful flow of water might cease, and all might fade beneath the encroaching sands.

They had made the passage to al Jabbar in five days, just as Lasiri had predicted. Except for the elephants and a half-dozen flat tires, the trip had been accomplished without incident. Descending through a gap in a ridge of mountains, they had come out upon a broad plateau, and there, at the base of the desert,

they had found the oasis. Ruth explained that the spring was
the end passage of a long vein of porous rock that trapped the
water, probably somewhere high up in the mountains. In the
days of the Arab traders, the caravans had capitalized upon its
location and built a city there. "But we think there was a race
who inhabited these lands long before the Arabs came," she
added. "And it was probably these early people who dredged
out the quarry for the spring."

That afternoon Ruth showed James and Jon Paul the stone
ruins of the city, now almost completely overgrown with vegetation. Kicking away some brush, she exposed part of a wall.
Pacing out the boundary of the stone, James outlined a large
enclosure one hundred fifty feet across. In some places Ruth
pointed out openings that were apparently gates. In other areas
she identified stone blocks that resembled turrets. The foundations of the inner buildings were still present, and often the
three could recognize the outlines of streets.

"The city probably held two or three hundred Arabs at its
height," Ruth said. "At least, historical documents indicate this
was a main stopover for the caravans coming out of the interior.
It is still the best preserved. Most of the other oases, as you saw,
are scarcely more than a few scattered mudholes."

"What happens to a place like this?" James asked. "How
does it die?"

"Hard to say," Ruth answered. "In some areas, the springs
run dry and the people have to leave. From our dating esti-
mates, al Jabbar probably flourished around the year 1000,
reaching its peak in the mid-1700s. We know there have been
marked climatic changes in the past five hundred years. So
some of it may have been due to increasing droughts."

James walked through the stone foundations, moving from
one room to the next, sorting out the debris with his boot.
Occasionally they passed the outlines of a carved stone doorway
or the broken bowl of an Arab fountain.

"But I think what really happened here was the cessation of
trade," Ruth said. "Once the market for slaves and ivory began
to fail, there was no reason to keep the chain of oases going."

"Sad, in a way," James replied. He bent down, examining a
block of carved stone. "The sum effort in building such a city,

the amount of toil and sweat that went into putting up these walls, and then one day—nothing."

"Cities, civilizations, are like people," Ruth replied. "They decay and die for the same reasons as the people who inhabit them."

They had moved into an area almost completely covered by thick vegetation when James found the well. The shaft was composed of a circular wall of rocks ten feet across. As he peered over the edge, it took a moment for his eyes to become accustomed to the dim light at the bottom. Twenty feet below, a skull grinned up, staring from eyeless sockets. Scattered throughout the bottom of the shaft were more human remains. Leg bones, hands, ribs. As James stared down the shaft, he could feel a rising wave of horror. The entire pit was heaped with human bones.

Ruth and Jon Paul came forward and stared over his shoulder.

"God, what do you suppose happened?" he asked.

Ruth shrugged. "In the death throes of a city, there are often mass burials. Probably too few people left to dig the graves so they flung the bodies down the shaft."

Strange country, James thought. Death was never very far away. Life seemed to have a very precarious foothold here. And how little it took to tip the balance!

Half an hour later they were following the edge of the stream as it trickled down from the oasis and spilled out into the desert when Jon Paul let out a sudden shout.

"Ruth, James, over here!"

Next to a moist area where the water seeped grew a huge baobab tree. Its colossal stubby base was twenty feet in diameter. Rising from the massive trunk were odd, skeletallike branches with few leaves.

"There's writing!" Jon Paul exclaimed.

On the trunk of the tree a series of carvings had been etched into the bark.

Ruth Parker crouched at the base of the baobab, studying the writing. "Hard to make out much, but here"—she pointed to a group of markings that were much clearer than the others— "here is Arabic. That I can recognize for sure."

Peeling away the bark, she scraped at the tree with her fingers until she could see the signature clearly. "It looks like the name Abudullah Fadat. Followed by a date. A number: 278."

"Which means?"

"The year of the Arab calendar begins when Mohammed fled the city of Mecca in our Christian year of 622. Each year thereafter is related to that Hegira, thus they begin their count with 622 as zero. The year 278 Hegira would be"—she paused, trying to calculate the figure in her head.

"Nine hundred!" she exclaimed. "The initials must have been carved in A.D. 900."

"Incredible," James said. "That means that this tree dates back for more than a thousand years."

"Baobab trees are known to live for centuries," Ruth answered. "Even back then it must have been sizable enough to use as a landmark. From the number of different markings, I suppose members of every caravan that came through carved their initials upon it."

"Look, something's here in Spanish," Jon Paul said.

Ruth stepped forward and brushed away the bark, carefully studying the inscription. "No, not Spanish. Portuguese," she replied. "The date 1733. I can't quite read the name. Hernando . . . it looks like Hernando Figuerez."

"Figuerez!" James cried. "The man who wrote the diary!"

"Perhaps," Ruth answered cautiously. "The writing is blurred."

"And here," Jon Paul said. "English!" He read very slowly: "One hundred nineteen tusks, two hundred fifty slaves, Walter McKenzie, 1821."

"Well, there you have it," Ruth said. "Ivory, exploration, slaves. The route must have served its purpose well."

That afternoon James sat down upon a small knoll overlooking the ruins. Using a pad of paper and pencil, he sketched out what he thought the city at al Jabbar must have looked like three hundred years before. Ruth came up and peered over his shoulder.

"James, that's marvelous," she said. "You draw very well."

"Most of it is drafting." He shrugged. "I've spent a lot of

time studying the perspective of buildings and how certain structures were put together."

"You've got a good eye for detail."

"I'm not sure how accurate it is, but I get some idea of what the city must have looked like from the geometry of the foundations and the pieces of broken fragments scattered around."

"You should have gone into city planning."

James smiled. "The funny thing is, Ruth, based on what studying I've done, the city was probably as well planned as we might design it today. The original builders had a very good sense for utilization of space and efficiency of structure. We could learn a lot from those people. Look how they placed the buildings east of the oasis to gain shade from the trees in the hottest part of the afternoon; how the main streets all run north and south, probably to avoid the direction of the prevailing winds during seasonal storms; and there, the turrets at diagonal corners to take advantage of the terrain for maximum visibility. Today we use laser surveying equipment and sophisticated computers for siting. I doubt they had much more than some sticks and string."

"Well, that's progress." Ruth laughed.

"Yeah." James nodded. "Sometimes you wonder whether we've made much of an advance at all."

They had started back to camp when the ugly noise of automatic weapons fire broke the silence of the afternoon. A flock of guinea hen exploded out of the trees and flew past them cackling raucously. James froze, listening. In the distance he could hear yelling, followed by a second burst of rifle fire.

"I think we've got trouble," Ruth said.

James cocked his rifle and looked at Jon Paul. "I'd better get back to camp," he said. "Jon Paul, you stay with Ruth."

He broke into a fast-paced jog, moving cautiously toward the oasis. When he reached the tents he found the cook and two of the drivers staring off toward a series of brush-covered ridges to the east. They were armed and looked ready for war. A moment later one of the soldiers came running into camp.

"Memsaab Parker?" he cried. "Lasiri want memsaab."

Ruth and Jon Paul arrived in the camp a few minutes later. Ruth listened to the African speak rapidly in Swahili.

"They've got somebody pinned down out there," she translated. "Apparently Lasiri has been unable to communicate with them."

Following the soldier, Ruth, James, and Jon Paul came to a narrow canyon covered with thick underbrush. Lasiri was hidden behind a huge boulder at the mouth of the canyon. He waved for them to keep down, out of the line of fire. They darted across a narrow opening, then through a forested section of trees, working their way up behind him. In a moment they were crouched beside him.

"What do you have?" James asked.

"One of the soldiers found tracks this afternoon. He followed them up to the canyon and was fired upon. I've tried to converse with them in Swahili but get no response."

"Surely they understand," Ruth said.

"I think they're just playing around with us." Lasiri grunted.

"How many are there?" James whispered.

"Hard to tell. Eight, maybe ten."

Directly in front of them was a large clearing that ran into a steep-walled canyon. The ravine led for several hundred yards before it ended in a limestone cliff. The depression was choked with thick vegetation. Lasiri and three of the soldiers commanded a position at the entrance to the canyon. Two more of Lasiri's men had climbed up along the limestone cliffs and now peered down, weapons aimed into the underbrush.

James searched carefully through the vegetation, but whoever was hidden there was completely invisible to his eyes. He could see no movement, no sign of life.

"I'm going to ask them in Arabic to come out," Ruth said. "If there is no response, have someone fire down into the clearing. I think we'll be able to get their attention quickly."

She shouted in Arabic. A single grunt came from somewhere in the brush, then nothing. Silence.

Lasiri raised his hand and signaled one of the soldiers. There was a rapid volley of gunshots. A deafening echo rolled out of the ravine.

Deep in the canyon a bush moved. A moment later a white rag was thrust out tied to a branch. A man stepped into the clearing dressed in a tattered gray robe, with crossed cartridge

belts over his chest and a rifle in his right hand. Around his
waist a bright-red sash held a curved dagger. As he moved into
the opening he deliberately laid his rifle on the ground. Folding
his arms, he boldly faced them.

James studied him carefully. The man appeared to be in his
late thirties. He had a lightly tanned face, a wisp of beard, and
dark flowing hair. He raised his hand in a gesture of greeting
and began addressing them in Arabic.

"He says his name is Benghazi," Ruth translated. "He is the
leader of a small band of Abyssinians who have come into the
Sudan to trade. He is here on friendly terms. He only wants to
use the oasis tonight and will be gone in the morning."

"Ask him to bring everyone out," Lasiri commanded. "They
must throw all of their weapons on the ground—rifles, ammunition, daggers. Then we will talk."

Ruth translated the message. Benghazi shouted back into the
underbrush. To James's surprise the huge form of a camel
pushed out into the open. The beast was followed by a robed
man heavily armed with rifle, cartridge belt, and dagger. A
third man now came forward leading a camel, followed by another until a whole troop of them stood in the clearing. James
counted five men, seven camels, six women, and three children.
All of the men were armed to the hilt. The women were veiled
and dressed in brightly printed robes. The children ducked behind them and peered out shyly. Each of the camels was heavily
loaded with blankets, gourds, and bundles of cloth and skins.

"We are here in peace," the Abyssinian leader signaled.

"Why was one of our men fired upon?" Ruth asked.

"We thought he was trying to steal some of our supplies."

"Then why do you hide there in the brush?"

"We were not sure of your intentions," Benghazi replied.

"Probably better we know where they are than to have them
sneak up on us," Ruth answered. "What do you think, Lasiri?"

"We'll keep a couple of soldiers with them as guards," the
Masai replied. "I don't think they'll be too much of a risk if we
take their weapons. If they've been traveling long, we might be
able to learn something from them."

"Can we trust them?" James asked.

Lasiri scowled. "They're telling us only what they need to. You see those pieces of string hanging from the leader's sash?"

James counted a dozen eight-inch strands of braided rope.

"Each one stands for an enemy he's killed and castrated. Undoubtedly they planned to sneak into our camp tonight. I'm sure that's why they were hiding."

Lasiri now collected the pile of weapons and directed three of his men to escort the Abyssinians to the water. He spent the next half hour with the remaining men searching carefully through the underbrush. After a meticulous hunt, they routed out a single man far back in the canyon. The Abyssinian had been lying beneath a bush with a cache of another half-dozen rifles.

"It's an old trick," Lasiri said. "Raise a lot of commotion. Come out in peace. Make your enemy let down his guard. Hide someone off in the bush who can sneak into the camp at night, free the prisoners, and raid your tents."

James admitted he would have been completely fooled. "Trust no one out here," Ruth told him. "No matter what they say, or how they look to you. Never let down your guard."

From their campsite later that evening James watched the Abyssinians raise their tents on the opposite side of the water. Toward dusk the red-sashed leader walked over to their camp and sought out Ruth. "He wonders if we would join him for dinner," Ruth said. "They have some articles for trade."

"You've got me so worried, I'm afraid they'll poison us," James replied.

"They're not into such subtle methods." Ruth laughed. "Come on. You'll find it quite interesting. You might enjoy them."

"Well, why not?" James shrugged. "I guess I'd rather be invited to their dinner than be part of it."

The Abyssinians had pitched five small tents. The camels were hobbled a short distance away, and the women had spread out a series of blankets on which were now displayed various articles for trade. James and Jon Paul walked slowly back and forth among the blankets, inspecting the goods. Some held finely decorated knives, others pieces of pottery. One blanket displayed a number of sharp spear points and long wooden

shafts. The finest items, however, were delicately carved pieces
of ivory. One piece in particular caught Jon Paul's eye—a tiny
leaping gazelle. Two small reddish stones had been inserted for
the eyes. Jon Paul called Ruth over to look at it.

Seated behind the blanket was a veiled young woman. Jon
Paul had scarcely noticed her at first. When he lifted his head
from the ivory, he found himself gazing into the most beautiful
brown eyes. She caught his stare and turned shyly away.

"Ruth, ask her how much this is."

Ruth translated for him. The girl spoke back in a faint, musi-
cal voice.

"She says it is her best piece."

Jon Paul searched his pockets. He had a twenty-dollar American bill, some change, and a single house key.

"You think ten dollars is too much?" he asked.

Ruth laughed. "Not too many places over here that will take
a ten-dollar bill. Try something for trade. A knife, a package of
cigarettes, anything."

Jon Paul searched back through his pockets and finally shook
his head. "Tell her it is a magnificent piece but I'll have to pass.
She is very pretty. Can you ask her name?"

Ruth translated the message. The girl lowered her head, her
voice dropping to a whisper.

"She is called Faedra. She is fourteen years old and she is
sorry that you do not like her merchandise."

"Oh, no, I didn't mean that," Jon Paul said. "It's very beautiful. Tell her it's just that I don't have anything of equal value to
trade. I would be insulting her to give her something less."

Ruth smiled at him. "You're learning diplomacy fast."

"Is she afraid of me?" Jon Paul asked.

"Just respectful," Ruth answered. "She's been taught never
to challenge a man. It's the rule here."

James had walked up behind them and was now listening to
Jon Paul's conversation. He chuckled out loud. "Better take her
back with you." He winked. "She'll be in great demand."

"Only until she learns better," Jon Paul replied with a grin.
They left the ivory carvings and moved back toward the main
fire. When Jon Paul looked over his shoulder, the girl was staring after him.

They joined Lasiri and Benghazi by the fire. Despite the Abyssinians' initial hostility, their leader proved to be a most gracious host. He offered them all blanketed seats, then passed around a bowl of thick porridge, some chewing tobacco, and a beerlike liquid in a long slender gourd. James tried the beer and found it not half bad. Ruth drank the liquid and ate the porridge without hesitation. Jon Paul gingerly tested the soup. Finding the taste pleasing, he drank three-quarters of a bowl before he caught something small and gritty in his teeth. He pulled it out, stared at it for a moment, and almost choked. Ruth saw the look of horror on his face and began to laugh.

"It's a damned foot!" Jon Paul exclaimed.

"Let me see." James snorted. He took the object. To his surprise, he recognized the tiny foot of a lizard. He burst into a loud side-splitting guffaw.

Jon Paul brought his hand up over his mouth and darted out of the firelight. James could hear him gagging off behind the tents. The youth returned in a minute appearing very pale.

"Better look before you eat." James chortled.

"Very funny," Jon Paul shot back at him.

"Now, don't be too upset, boys," Ruth said in a motherly fashion. "Remember, meat is a scarcity over here. It was well cooked. If you hadn't found it, you'd have to admit the soup wasn't all that bad."

"That look on your face, Jon Paul," James cried, laughing. "I wish I'd had a picture."

"I bet you do," Jon Paul retorted, glowering. "They could start franchising this stuff."

"Yeah, Sheik Benghazi's African-fried lizards' feet." James laughed. "I think it would go over great in the States."

"I forgot to warn you about the beer," Ruth said.

"Oh, Christ, don't tell me, Ruth," James answered. His face began to blanch. "Probably something like goats' urine. Maybe I'd rather not know."

"Worse," Ruth said.

"Worse!"

"Supposedly, they season it with lion scat."

Benghazi asked what all the laughter was about and Ruth politely explained that the food had been a little rich for Jon

Paul. When they brought out a fresh hindquarter of gazelle,
however, everyone ate heartily; both James and Jon Paul
thought it ranked with the best steaks they'd ever had. After
dinner a strong Somali tea was served and Ruth began to question Benghazi about his travels.

The Abyssinian told them they were ten days' march from
their home. They were returning now after a month's visit into
the southlands, trading metal and ivory for skins and hides.
They planned to go out into the desert in the morning. From
there they would travel directly north for three days before
heading east again. Lasiri quizzed him at some length about the
land west of the desert, but Benghazi said he had only been
there once. He'd found some old ruins but everything else was
deserted. They'd come across no recent raiding parties of veiled
men and had heard of no reports of tribes taking white captives.

"It's really very hard to sort through what he's telling us,"
Ruth said. "The Abyssinians are notorious liars, and if he suspected some of his own people were involved in a raid, he would
cover up for them without question."

They talked for another hour, discussing the terrain, James's
safari, and the Land-Rovers. Benghazi then clapped his hands
to begin the evening's entertainment. Two women stepped forward and began to play stringed instruments that were plucked
like small hand-held harps. Another woman joined in with a
type of flute. Soon the oasis was filled with a wild, rhythmic
music. Several of the men got up and danced, twirling around
in a pattern of steps quite similar, Ruth said, to some of the
tribes in the northern Sudan, where the dancers were known as
whirling dervishes.

After the men had finished, the women started up the music
again and, to Jon Paul's surprise, Faedra suddenly appeared.
She had changed into a gossamer robe worn over a white undergarment. Swaying, her hips undulating, she began to dance. She
clapped her hands and snapped her fingers, picking up the
tempo until her hips were gyrating wildly to the sensuous, re-
lentless beat. As she danced it was obvious to everyone that her
attentions were directed toward Jon Paul. She would move
away and dance for short periods toward the other men but

always she returned to Jon Paul, her hands beckoning to him, her eyes flashing in the firelight.

"I think she likes you," Ruth whispered in Jon Paul's ear. He blushed furiously and watched, fascinated, as the music increased its tempo and her body abandoned itself to the frenzied dance. When it ended abruptly, she took a graceful bow. To a loud applause from the audience, she ran out of the firelight and disappeared behind one of the tents.

Benghazi began speaking quietly again. Another round of beer was passed. Jon Paul would not let James get away without taking a couple of swallows. The two brothers laughed at each other.

"Jon Paul," Ruth said. "Benghazi says his beautiful daughter is very interested in you. You should be honored. He says she is for sale. He wonders if you would take her as a wife."

"Tell him that she is very lovely," Jon Paul said.

"Wait until she gets her hands on your credit cards," James kidded.

"Butt out," Jon Paul answered with a grin. "Ask him what he would trade her for."

The message was translated and Benghazi thought for a moment before speaking. Finally he began talking with much gesticulating of his hands.

"He says in this country a young woman, fourteen, with no children, is the best bride that can possibly be offered. Under most circumstance, he says, he would want at least a dozen camels and several goats. He would be willing to give her up, however, for six of our automatic weapons."

"Ah ha," Lasiri interrupted. "Now we get to the crux of the matter."

"Tell him I'm honored for I have never seen a woman so beautiful as his daughter," Jon Paul said. "Maybe someday in the future, if we come back this way, I can visit his tribe and we can talk further."

"He says you are always welcome with him," Ruth translated. She turned to James. "I think we're spawning quite a statesman here."

James smiled. "When it comes to anything concerning sex, he'll warble like a canary."

"Sir, these are matters of great delicacy," Jon Paul quipped. "Not for a mind as crude as yours."

"I'm just jealous." James laughed. "She's a most fascinating girl."

"Well, let's propose a toast," Ruth said. "To the long life of his daughter and his good trade and our good fortune in finding him before he found us." She held up her gourd. "I'll change it a little bit in the translation, of course."

"Of course." They laughed.

When he went back to the tent that night, Jon Paul lay on the cot for a long time thinking about Faedra. He wasn't sure if it was the circumstances, being out in the bush a thousand miles from nowhere, or whether it was the veil or the pure raw beauty of her, but there was something about her that had definitely aroused his senses. Her body was so perfectly formed, yet wondering what her unveiled face looked like tantalized him.

He wondered what kind of a life she must lead wandering from one oasis to the next. He was amazed to consider how very different her life had to be from that of girls back home. Here women were considered marriageable at fourteen and some, he had learned, were pregnant soon after.

Girls his own age worried about perfume, hair styles, and makeup, and fussed over expensive clothes. Here, things were stripped down to the barest essentials. It was ludicrous to consider that he would fall in love with such a girl. He knew he could never possibly take her home, and yet, given the right circumstances . . .

When he finally fell asleep he dreamed that he was leading a caravan across the desert and she was his wife. But when it came time for them to sleep together, she explained that she was also the wife of Benghazi and three other Abyssinian traders, and somehow all of them wound up in his bed back in New York. He finally woke up, glad to be in control of his thoughts, then spent the rest of the night restlessly tossing and turning.

He rose at the crack of dawn and went down to the oasis to freshen up. The sun had just begun to illuminate the eastern horizon. There was still an hour before the rest of the camp would be rising. At the edge of the water he found the Abyssinian camels loaded and ready to travel. Faedra was standing

in the shallow end of the oasis up to her knees filling a gourd.
Jon Paul walked over to her. "You are very beautiful," he said,
holding out his hand. Though he realized that she could not
understand a word, he continued. "I want to wish you good
luck with your travels. I came to say good-bye."

She took his fingers and gripped them tightly, then motioned
for him to follow. Stepping out of the water, she walked to the
shoreline and placed her gourd on the ground. Reaching up into
her robe, she produced a small folded piece of cloth. Inside was
the delicately carved ivory gazelle. She held it out for him.

"Faedra, I couldn't . . ." he said, but her eyes searched him
imploringly. He reached into his pocket, looked frantically, and
found nothing but loose change and the key. He took the house
key and gave it to her. It's a dumb gift, he thought, but it was
the spirit of it that counted. God, how he wished that he'd
brought something valuable to give her in return.

She brought the key up to her veiled lips and touched it
softly. Her eyes stared at him longingly. A yell came from
across the water. Benghazi had loaded up the last of the camels
and was calling for her to come. She nodded toward Jon Paul,
picked up her gourd, and fled back to the rest of her people.

When Jon Paul saw them again he was sitting on a ridge
scanning the desert with his binoculars and they were a faint
line of dots moving across the desert toward the distant horizon.

19

She met him in a small bar just off Fifty-seventh Street, two
blocks west of the TransOceanic Airlines Building. Michael
Jacobson was already seated when she came into the room. He
looked up and saw the waiter talking with a tall, well-dressed

red-haired woman with incredibly long legs and he guessed in an instant it was she. He stood up and offered his hand as she slid into the booth beside him.

"Mr. Jacobson, I appreciate you meeting me like this."

"I'm delighted to speak with you," he answered.

She blushed slightly, trying to maintain her composure. The similarities between Michael Jacobson and James were faint but they were there, the same wrinkle at the corner of the eyes, the same firm line of the nose. She felt instantly attracted to this man, and because she was in love with his son, it made what she said all the more important. She faltered for a moment, searching carefully for the right words. She had practiced what she would say a dozen times, thinking she would begin with some nice social amenities, trying not to appear too forward. At a glance, however, she could see that Michael Jacobson was much too perceptive for idle chatter. Now all her planning seemed irrelevant.

"I—I managed to arrange a business trip to New York," she began. "I tried to reach James but his firm told me he had taken an indefinite leave. There was no forwarding address. I—I wanted to be sure that he was all right."

"As far as I know, he and his younger brother, Jon Paul, are safe. They left a few days ago for a small oasis in the southern Sudan."

"There have been a lot of wild stories in the news. . . ."

"Damned sensationalistic bastards." Jacobson grunted. "Most of them should be quartered and hung."

"Is there anything I can do?"

"No, but thanks for asking."

"Mr. Jacobson, I know how you must be feeling. I'm terribly sorry about your daughter."

Jacobson stared at her. "I appreciate your concern," he answered carefully. "But I don't think you came all this way just to tell me that."

"You're a very perceptive man."

"And I think you are probably a very courageous woman. Now what can I do for you?"

"I—I treated James very unfairly before he left. I wanted to tell him that I'm sorry. I hoped that he would give me . . . us, another chance."

"You're a very beautiful woman, Page. You must have other men in your life besides James."

"No one else that counts."

"How long have you been seeing him?"

"Almost a year."

"Are you very fond of him?"

"I think if something happens to him over there I could never forgive myself."

"He was determined to go. You can't blame yourself for that."

She frowned. "I'd like to believe that . . . but I was pressing him. I think he wanted to get away."

Jacobson shook his head. "I thought at first that it was Diana . . . but I think now it was more than that. James is sometimes very hard even for me to understand. I think he was looking for some test, some way to reassure himself. I think it was important for him to go alone, without me or any assistance from anyone else but Jon Paul. If I hadn't felt that way, I would never have let him go. You may have been a small part of it, Page, but I think it was much more. Since his marriage—" He stopped suddenly, realizing he was going to get into a subject he wasn't sure he should talk about.

Page bit her lip. Then she raised her head and her eyes were clear and probing. "You asked me why I came—why I really came. I need to learn what happened so that maybe I could understand, so that maybe I would be able to be more patient with him."

"I don't think a man ever gets over his first love very easily, Page. Not someone like James."

"Can you tell me about her?"

"What has he told you?"

She lowered her eyes. "Not very much."

"James was very young when he got married. He'd been traveling in Europe on a summer vacation when he fell in love. Nicole was nineteen. At the time she was working as a flight attendant for Air France. She was a lovely girl but she was one of those free spirits. If I had to guess, it was the isolation for her here in the States and their immaturity that finally defeated them. They'd been separated for almost a month before we even found out about it.

"Nicole went back to France. Her family was quite wealthy; her father an industrialist. I made several inquiries to see how she was doing. She spent some time in and out of one of the psychiatric hospitals in Paris, then was finally sent to Switzerland."

A deep frown etched its way across Jacobson's face.

"Yes, please go on," Page urged.

"A year ago I was notified by her family that she had died. It was an overdose. I think she had become very sick."

A tear worked its way into Page's eyes. "I . . . he never told me," she said.

"No, I don't think he ever would," Jacobson answered slowly. "I think he took it all personally. He never talks about her anymore."

She paused, searching in her purse for a handkerchief. Finding one, she lightly dabbed her eyes and stared back at Jacobson.

"If you receive any word from him, I hope you'll tell him that I stopped by, that I asked about him."

"Certainly," Jacobson answered.

"I'll only be in town for a couple of days. I'm staying at the Plaza. Please let me know if you hear anything at all."

"All right, of course," Jacobson replied. "If you have time, why don't you come out to the house?"

She shook her head, then slid out of the booth and stood up. "I know you're awfully busy. Thank you for asking. Maybe when James gets back. . . ."

Suddenly she reached forward and kissed Jacobson softly on the forehead. "God, what a fool I've been," she said.

As Jacobson watched her go, his eyes were drawn to the slender line of her figure, his nose still catching the faint smell of her perfume. He was reminded in a way of those tender, uncertain days when he had courted his own wife. Page is a remarkable and beautiful woman, he thought. If there was any fool in that relationship, it must be James.

20

At dawn Lasiri had driven one of the Land-Rovers out onto the desert to test the sand. Now the vehicle was stuck up to its axle, wheels spinning, a plume of dust rising behind it like smoke. Despite its four-wheel drive the Land-Rover had hit a soft section of sand and become hopelessly stuck less than two hundred yards from the oasis. James, Lasiri, and three of the soldiers pushed mightily against the rear frame, but it was no use. Finally Lasiri went back to camp and brought a second Land-Rover. Using a series of ropes, with all of the men pushing from the front, they were at last able to back it out.

When James arrived back in camp he fell heavily onto a chair, exhausted. "Christ, it's like quicksand out there," he muttered to Ruth.

"Can we detour?" Jon Paul asked.

Lasiri shook his head. "The maps indicate it's another four hundred miles north before we can cut across and then we would have to work our way back to the mountains to get our bearings. That might take us at least another week."

"Got any other ideas?" James asked.

"Perhaps we should try walking," Lasiri suggested.

James stared at him and scowled. The desert looked too impenetrable, too harsh. The mountains are at least fifty miles away, he thought. We'd be crazy to try to walk across.

"Any other options?"

"We could try the Land-Rovers again," Ruth replied. "There has to be some place the sand will hold."

For the rest of the day they devoted their efforts to testing the sand. They drove slowly, carefully easing out upon the soft spots, backing up whenever Lasiri felt the wheels begin to sink.

On occasion they still became stuck and had to use the second Land-Rover and sometimes the third to pull the first out. In places they were able to advance out into the desert for a quarter of a mile. But at each point, sooner or later the vehicles hit soft sand and bogged down.

"It's no use," Lasiri finally said. "We're going to have to figure out another way."

James stared toward the distant mountains with a rising sense of disappointment.

"Why not do like the Abyssinians?" Jon Paul asked. "Try camels."

"If we were lucky, we could buy a couple from some of the neighboring tribes," Lasiri answered. "But it might be days before another troop of Abyssinians comes through here. I think we would need at least twelve for a full caravan, and they don't part with their camels easily."

"So where does that leave us?"

"Not very well off," Lasiri answered. "We can stay here and hope to collect enough camels to get across but we lose more valuable time. The other alternative is that we go back to Nairobi."

"No," James said firmly. "We've come this far. Let's not consider that option until we've explored every other possibility. Not yet. . . ."

Before dinner that evening they gathered all of the maps and spread them out upon a flat place on the ground.

"There's a point here marked wadi," Ruth said. "Benghazi indicated they would go out into the desert for water then head north. Since the spring flows here, there's a good chance we might find some seepage of water there."

Lasiri nodded. "By my estimate the wadi is at the midpoint twenty-five, maybe thirty miles away. With luck, we could walk it in a day and a half."

"And if it's dry?" James asked. "How many days to cross the desert on foot?"

Lasiri stared off across the desert. He paused a long time before answering. "If we made good time, if we traveled only in the morning and evening when it is cool, if there is good light so that we can travel at night, too, then maybe we could make it in three days."

"What about the soldiers?"

"I would leave some of the men here at the oasis. If we did not return in a week, I would instruct them to go back and bring help."

James turned to Ruth. "It's a long way across," he said. "You know I don't expect you to come. Perhaps you should wait here for us to return."

Ruth glared at him. "If you mean because I have a limp and sometimes walk with a cane, I must tell you that thanks to a problem with my hip, I have limped since the age of six. I've already walked across half of Africa, James. I don't suppose a small desert and a little sweat will stop me now.

"Frankly," she continued with a grin, "I've been wanting to see the other side of this desert ever since I first heard of al Jabbar."

"And if we don't make it back?"

"This old body's seen a lot," Ruth answered. "I can think of a lot worse ways to bring it to an end."

"And you, Jon Paul?"

"I think the sooner we start the better," Jon Paul answered.

It was in the evening, with the sun squatting low upon the horizon, that they saw the silhouette of a man. He stood like a crane, resting on one foot, leaning upon a spear. Jon Paul saw him first and cried out in alarm. James instantly scrambled for a gun when Lasiri stopped him.

"It's all right, bwana," he said. "We've been watching him all day. He has come out now waiting for us to invite him into camp."

Lasiri walked toward the man and greeted him in Swahili. The figure immediately came down from his single-legged perch and moved in toward the fire. He was dressed in a thin red blanket that draped down in front, leaving his behind exposed. He carried a long spear and a knobbed wooden club. As he approached the campfire, James could see that he was wrinkled and old with few teeth and whitish grizzled hair. Two thin wire earrings, six inches in diameter, looped through to the tops of his ears.

"Probably a Somali," Ruth said in a whisper. "Undoubtedly he has come to dinner. It's the custom in the bush to offer a single man on foot something to eat."

Lasiri invited the old man into the camp. They talked for a few minutes in Swahili. He took the food Lasiri offered eagerly, squatting down by the fire. Smacking his lips, he devoured the meal noisily, then sat back, picking his remaining teeth with a pointed stick. When he spoke, his speech was slow and halting, punctuated with long pauses and occasional stops to spit into the fire.

"He says he is a Somali elder," Lasiri translated. "For two days he has been looking for some cattle that escaped from his village."

"Why have we seen no signs of the village or the rest of his tribe?" James asked.

Ruth shook her head. "Two days' travel to this man may mean a hundred miles."

"He says that he stopped here to meet us because he has seen only a dozen white men in his life and Ruth, here, is the second white woman he has ever seen. He is sure it will bring him evil luck, seeing two such women within a period of several weeks."

"Lasiri!" James leaped on the words. "Who was the other white woman? Who else did he see?"

"He says that he was passing here a full moon ago and saw a caravan going out across the desert. There were many men, all covered in black, and they looked like demons to him. They were riding camels and they had a white woman with them with a skin like Ruth's, only she was young and her hair was yellow like the lion."

"Good Lord!" James gasped. "Then she may still be alive!"

"He says he was quite close," Lasiri continued. "In fact, he was frightened because the sides of the camels were strung with human heads. He was afraid that if they saw him they would kill him, so he hid in the bush. He watched them replenish their water here at the oasis and then go out upon the desert. They stopped only long enough to get some water.

"He says they left, traveling in the direction of the sharp

mountain located directly across from the oasis—the mountain that curves up to a point like a horn."

"The Devil's Tower," Ruth exclaimed. "Then we're on the right track!"

"The woman," James said quickly. "Ask him if she was bound or tied up and how she looked. Did she seem wounded?" The questions rushed out of him so fast that Lasiri had to ask him to slow down.

"He thinks that the white woman was not bound. She rode a camel with the others. There were twelve or fourteen blacks tied around the neck who were made to walk like slaves. When he found us here at the oasis he was afraid we would capture him. But when he saw we held no prisoners, he finally decided that perhaps we might be peaceful. Only tonight did hunger get the best of him; he came forward to see if we might offer him some food. He apologizes for bothering us except that he has had little to eat over the past several days. The game here has been elusive, his walk tiring, and his hunting eye is no longer good."

"Ah, tell him it is good luck to see such a woman," James exclaimed. He reached into his pocket and pulled out a small Swiss knife with multiple blades. "Tell him I would like to give him this as a present."

The old man's eyes widened as he grasped the knife and rolled it over in his fingers. Lasiri showed him how to work the blades, and he clucked and shook his head as if it was the best present he had ever received.

"He wants to thank you," Lasiri told James. "He wants to give you something in return."

The wrinkled Somali reached into a pouch beneath his blanket and pulled out a ragged piece of cloth. Unwrapping it slowly, he grabbed something and dropped it into James's hand. When the American looked in his palm, he saw a small dark stone covered with a film of mud. James held it up to the fire and scraped away at the surface with a fingernail. Tiny blue needles began to dance and dazzle from its depths. With trembling fingers he chipped away at the layers of dirt until a familiar faint etching began to appear.

"The stone of the oasis!" James gasped.

"He says it came to him from his father and to his father

from his father's father," Lasiri translated. "He says it came from an oasis far across the desert. In a place which the Somali have always called the Land of No Return. . . ."

21

Dawn broke upon the desert in a flood of light that swept away the darkness like a fleeting shadow. A jackal called from somewhere out in the dunes as a small pack fled along the horizon until they blended with the first shimmering waves of a mirage.

The sun rose steadily. Degree by degree, heat began to pour into the desert, reflecting off the sand in a shifting restless glare. Lakes seemed to appear out of nowhere and drift across the void. Rocks a dozen miles away became magnified and distorted, dancing like boulders upon barren ridges. Small sticks, no larger than a hand, looked like trees in the distant sky, faded, then reappeared. Gradually the horizon began to melt until there was nothing visible except for a dull, impenetrable haze. Only the peak of the Devil's Tower hung like a beacon in the western sky. And it was this summit that the single line of humans used as their guide.

In order to travel light Lasiri had picked three of the fittest soldiers to accompany them. The cook, the two drivers, and the remaining two soldiers he had decided to leave in camp. A small group was less conspicuous and required less food and water. Here they needed to travel as quickly and efficiently as possible.

They had been walking for five hours when Lasiri finally called a halt. By eleven o'clock the heat was almost unbearable. He instructed them to cover their heads with cloth, to hide all exposed flesh under blankets. During the hottest hours of the afternoon even breathing became an effort.

At four in the afternoon they started up again, plodding steadily, always keeping the tall peaked mountain ahead. When they stopped in the evening James was surprised that the day had gone so easily, and he remarked to Ruth that he thought they were doing much better than he had expected.

"Don't be fooled," she answered. "Every day will be harder than the last. The heat has a way of sapping your strength until all of a sudden you discover there's nothing left. One of the early explorers found an entire caravan—a thousand camels, eight hundred people—mummified in the desert. God knows how long they had been dead. They were less than ten miles from the nearest water. Somehow they got lost. The slaves were all huddled together as if they were waiting for help. And if it's not thirst, or the heat, it's *le cafard*."

"I don't understand," James replied.

"There is a saying that the Arabs know two things about the desert: the sun and the sand," Ruth answered, "but the European knows three: the sun, the sand, and the madness. The French Foreign Legion called it *le cafard*, which means 'cockroach.' When you went mad staring day after day at a land in which there was no change, no visible living thing, no break in the monotony of the vision, they said that the cockroach had gotten loose inside your brain. Never underestimate the desert, James. What may seem easy today may be impossible tomorrow."

As they rested, Ruth showed them a small skinklike lizard that burrowed beneath the sand. When prodded, it wriggled underneath the surface particles as if it were swimming. Jon Paul followed a second set of tracks and dug up another lizard with his hands. Delighted with this amusement, he moved a short distance away toward a series of S-shaped ridges.

"No, Jon Paul, stop!" Ruth shouted suddenly.

James rushed over to him.

"Don't move!" she cried. She motioned for Lasiri to bring a gun. Very carefully they pulled Jon Paul back. Digging slowly, she made two small probes with her cane. On the third there was a sudden violent explosion of sand. A four-foot adder erupted from its resting spot and slithered away. Lasiri was on it in a second and dispatched it with a blow from his rifle.

Astonishment flooded across Jon Paul's face.

"You were saying how easy it was, James?" Ruth said wryly.

"Nice place." He grunted. "Remind me to bring the family here on a picnic sometime. . . ."

Just before dusk James turned and stared in the direction they had come. The oasis of al Jabbar was only a small smudge of green on the horizon. Then darkness descended upon them, the stars lighting up the blackness like a grand city in the sky.

"I've always liked the desert best at night," Ruth said. "The first explorers used the stars to guide them just like the sailors at sea. The Big Camel there"—she pointed up—"the Arabs' name for the Big Dipper, with its bottom two stars always pointing north. And there, the Little Swan flying to the east. And there, the Great Scorpion and the Mighty Warrior, Orion."

There was only the blackened desert below and the dazzling night sky. Now all landmarks were above them. A shooting star blazed across the heavens, leaving a long trailing afterglow.

"Some people prefer to travel here entirely at night," Ruth said. "In the daylight all direction may be lost. The land becomes totally devoid of distinguishing features. They say some of the best guides in the desert were blind, you know. They could smell water miles away. Knew the routes by heart."

A three-quarter moon rose slowly, lighting the way ahead. They traveled until midnight before Lasiri stopped the group. Then they drank a small amount of water and broke out the blankets. One of the soldiers carried a pack of wood, and they lit a fire and huddled together in a small knot—a single, fragile island of humanity.

In the wee hours of the morning, James awoke and wrapped part of his blanket protectively over Jon Paul. "You asleep?" he whispered.

Jon Paul shook his head. "Can't. I'm too tired and I'm too cold."

"Two more days," James said hopefully. "If it's all like this, we should make it easily."

"I was thinking, James," Jon Paul said. "You really stuck your neck out to have me along. I guess I've been sort of an ass back home."

"To put it mildly." James smiled.

"Well, whatever happens out here, I'm glad I came. No matter what."

"Me, too, boy," James answered.

"Maybe when we get back I'll take school a little more seriously. There's no reason why I can't get good grades."

"That's what everyone who knows you says," James replied. "You've got it all up there. It's just a matter of putting it together."

"You think Dad would be proud of me?"

"I think he would be tickled pink."

Ruth shivered behind him and mumbled something half in her sleep.

The three soldiers were resting next to them; Lasiri, a short distance away. James could see the glint of his eyes in the waning light of the moon. The Masai was sitting like a statue with his legs crossed underneath him. He had not lain down once during the night. James was sure that he had been awake the entire time, watching over them like a sentinel.

"Best sleep now," Lasiri said softly. "We must be up soon."

They'd been walking for two hours the next morning when they saw the vultures, wheeling and circling like small dots in the sky.

"Something dead," Lasiri said with a grunt.

"Must be hundreds of them," James said.

"Some kind of large kill," Lasiri answered. "Very fresh. The vultures come down off the mountains. I have seen them strip a zebra to bones in a matter of hours. They will not linger here for more than a day."

They moved west until the birds were circling directly overhead. Somewhere just beyond the horizon James could see them plummeting downward, dropping to feed. As they came to the top of a large barren ridge, Lasiri uttered a short cry. "The wadi!"

Two things now greeted James's vision, and they were so diametrically opposed that it took him a moment to fully comprehend what he saw.

Directly ahead in a shallow valley was a soft, moist depression in the sand. Surrounding it were a few scattered sentinel palms and some dried, scraggy trees. James knew at a glance that there was no free water, but the presence of trees and the damp spot indicated that there must be moisture below.

Next to the wadi, strewn out across the desert, were crumpled, darkened forms; and at each point of irregularity, the vultures swooped and churned.

James stared in wide-eyed astonishment. Slowly he began to recognize the shapes.

"Camels? Dead camels?"

"I am not sure," Lasiri answered grimly. Throwing a cartridge into the breech of his rifle, he took one of the soldiers and started down toward the wadi. In ten minutes they returned. There was a wild, unsteady look in their eyes.

"Six camels," Lasiri said slowly, "and five men. The men are nothing but skeletons; the camels still have some flesh left. From the looks of the remains, they must have been killed yesterday. Certainly no longer. The vultures do their clean-up well."

James glanced at Jon Paul and then at Ruth with horror.

"I found this," Lasiri said. He held up a large red sash.

"Benghazi!" James gasped as the stark reality of the situation exploded inside his brain. "The Abyssinian traders!"

"Faedra!" Jon Paul cried. He broke from the ridge, running down toward the nearest cluster of birds.

"Wait, stop!" Ruth shouted, but Jon Paul plunged toward the carcass. The vultures erupted in front of him, flapping wildly into the air. Finally the sight of a dead body and the smell overcame him and Jon Paul turned back.

"I had to see for myself," he said when he returned. His voice was trembling. "We killed them, Lasiri!" He grimaced. "We took their rifles. They had no means of defense."

"Jon Paul, no!" Ruth said. She grabbed him by the shoulders. "It's the law of survival here. We didn't kill them. We were only trying to protect ourselves. You saw those strings on Benghazi's belt. That could just as easily have been us lying back there at al Jabbar, the vultures picking our bones. I'm sorry, but we had no other choice. You've got to understand that."

He pushed away from her, staring off in the distance. "God, how did it happen?" he muttered. "How can it be?"

When he looked back the vultures were already dropping back, plummeting downward until the carcass was covered with fighting, squawking, feeding birds.

That evening there was a reddish ring around the moon and the sky was overcast and dark. When they awoke the following morning, a sand-colored haze surrounded them.

The soldiers were up at dawn, preparing some tea over a small fire. James stood up slowly, trying to ease the aching in his joints. Shaking his blanket, he saw two scorpions tumble out of the folds. He watched the insects scuttle away, shivered at the unpleasantness of them, then turned toward the fire. As he stepped up to get some tea, there was a faint booming noise that sounded like a distant explosion. The soldiers crouching around the fire heard it and stopped talking. Lasiri stood up, his senses acutely alert.

In a moment the sound occurred again. It was followed by a subtle trembling vibration that passed beneath their feet like a ripple. Ruth dropped a cup of tea and did not move.

"Lasiri? Ruth?" James said with alarm. "What is it?"

They had camped in a narrow valley between two enormous dunes at the edge of a long sand sea that spread for several miles. Lasiri bent down and picked up his rifle, staring up toward the crest of the dunes.

"Grab your gear," he said quietly. "Collect everything and be ready to move."

The deep resonating thunder came again. The noise built in intensity, rolling and reverberating, until suddenly it was upon them. A sharp ridge leading to the top of one of the dunes abruptly gave way and cascaded down like an avalanche. A dull explosion burst forth from the dune next to them. Its crest folded in a wall of sand.

"This way!" Lasiri shouted.

He ran down the valley, pulling Ruth behind him. The soldiers bolted after them followed by Jon Paul and James. The noise of the explosions was deafening. James looked back once; the very place where they had been camped was inundated with a flood of sand. The noise of the concussions roared and echoed around them and then suddenly it was gone, the booms fading farther and farther into the distance until all was quiet. The absence of sound, the total solitude of the desert that now surrounded them, was awesome. The soldiers glanced at one another with frightened looks.

"What in hell was that?" James asked.

"The dunes were shifting," Ruth said. "Caused by a type of harmonic boom that starts when there is a rapid change of the barometric pressure. We're lucky we didn't get buried back there."

"We're not out of trouble yet," Lasiri said. He pointed up to a long ridge where the faintest wisps of sand indicated that a slight breeze had begun to stir.

"Storm coming," he muttered. "We've got to make as much distance as we can."

At midday, the sun shone dimly through the haze in a pale yellow disk. Gusts of wind had begun to rise, sending the sand spinning past them, biting into their faces. As the velocity of the wind rose, the air became hotter and hotter until James felt as if they were moving through the vent of a blast furnace.

The sweat oozed off his temples and stung into his eyes, and he had to devote his total concentration to keeping his balance. The soldiers wrapped cloths around their faces and heads, trying to protect their eyes. Ruth staggered along beside them. By midafternoon, when the visibility had dropped until they could barely see a finger at the end of an outstretched hand, Lasiri brought the party to a halt. Even talking had become difficult.

They huddled together with their backs to the storm, wrapping their blankets around them as a protective shield. As evening approached the sky became incredibly dark, turning from a light brown to mud and finally black, without a sunset. It was midnight before there was a break in the clouds, and only then did the moon come out, in a pale-tan disk.

When morning arrived, there was no change. The wind roared and howled, and the brownness whipped at their faces in a cloud of stinging sand.

Lasiri was on his feet. "We cannot wait any longer," he shouted. "Another day and we will be out of water. We must go on."

They rose painfully and staggered into the wind. "Take off

your belts," he yelled. "Use them like rope so that each of you can hold onto the next. If you fall, stop immediately. Don't lose touch with the man in front of you."

Sometime in the afternoon James felt his legs give way beneath him. He was tired beyond measure, though the feeling of thirst had long passed. Ruth fell beside him. She seemed practically unconscious.

"Got to rest," she said, gasping as she turned to James. "It's best you go on. If the storm continues, it will finish us all. At least there's hope for you while you're still strong."

"We can't leave you." James shook his head.

"Then you're crazy and a fool," Ruth shouted. She fell back and covered her head and sank into the sand.

James pulled himself up and wrapped a blanket around her shoulders. "I can't go much farther," he said. "Neither can Jon Paul."

Lasiri moved toward them and sat down with his back to the wind to shield them from the blasting sand. "We'll stay," he answered.

Once during the middle of the night James dreamed that the storm was over and the air was clear and the moonlight was around him so that he could see the Devil's Tower shining directly ahead. It was not very far away and he was next to the dim outline of a cliff. And then he dreamed he was back with Nicole in France during a summer vacation on the Mediterranean. The colors of the dream were soft as a painting by Monet. He could visualize the warm flash of her eyes, the softness of her smile. He remembered now how beautiful she was and how much he loved her. There were bright red and yellow flowers in the cafe, and he picked one and placed it behind her ear. The waiter came over to serve them some drinks, and James was very insistent that they be served ice. In the dream the waiter kept trying to explain that the restaurant *never* served ice, and James was furious.

And then he dreamed they were arguing and he could hear himself shouting at her, only in the dream the woman was no longer Nicole but it was Page, and she was yelling that she was going to Seattle and she didn't give a damn what he thought and he wasn't sure exactly what had gone wrong. And then he remembered *that day*, the day he'd been living with for the past four years, the day he had never told anyone about—not anyone, ever.

It had happened a year after they'd arrived in San Francisco. They'd been arguing again and finally, out of frustration, James had said that he would consider a separation, if that's what Nicole really wanted. They hadn't made love in more than a month. He'd been down in L.A. for two days and he'd come home unexpectedly, wanting to apologize to her about all of the disagreements they'd had, wanting to tell her that he loved her and that he would move back to France if that's what it would take to keep the marriage together. He'd come home with flowers and slipped into the apartment to surprise her. When he'd found the bedroom door closed, he'd hesitated. Something had told him not to open that door and yet, drawn forward in some kind of an awful fascination, he'd quietly stepped into the room. "Nicole—" he started.

He'd turned and walked slowly out of the apartment, very much in physical control but his brain spinning like crazy, the hurt tearing into his mind until he thought he was going to explode. Not Nicole. Not his precious Nicole. Not his young and lovely wife.

He'd never found out who the man was other than that he was one of her old friends, a steward from Air France. The next day she was packed and gone. He'd never seen her again.

He realized now he was dreadfully tired. His dreams played tricks on his mind, obscuring the line between reality and hallucination. There were no flowers, no drinks, no ice. Nicole was gone. Page was gone. He tried to close his eyes and drift painfully off into semiconsciousness.

When he awoke again it was morning. His mind was confused and his senses dulled so that at first he could not remember where he was. He could tell there was no wind and the sky was clear. They were only a few hundred feet from a tall cliff that ran for several miles along the edge of the desert, but his eyes refused to focus. Faintly he could hear the cries of swallowlike birds wheeling in the air above him. He closed his eyes and for another hour he slept until he felt a gentle touch.

As he opened his eyes, he saw a strange hand with thick fur

and black fingers reach out for him. He recoiled from the smell of something awful breathing in his face.

He blinked trying to clear his vision, then heard an odd grunt that did not sound human to his ears. When he opened his eyes again, he saw a shape staring down at him only a few inches away. It was a head with fierce brown eyes and sharp, vicious teeth. He tried to yell but only a faint gasp escaped his lips. He couldn't sort out in his own mind whether the image was real or still some part of his terrible dreams.

22

The sharp explosion of a rifle shattered the morning stillness as thousands of birds hurtled from the face of the cliffs, filling the air with their cries. On the desert floor the troop of baboons scampered for the safety of the rocks. They had been out foraging when they came across the party of humans buried in the sand. The young males, bolder than the rest, had advanced and one primate, filled with curiosity, had reached forward to touch a face, different from yet remotely like his own. Now they fled in terror, the noise from their screams adding to the reverberating echo of the gun.

With the greatest effort Lasiri pulled himself to his feet. Smoke still issued from the end of his rifle. The three soldiers, half hidden in the sand, began to emerge, shaking themselves free. Jon Paul's eyes were open but he did not move, and James lay on his side breathing heavily. Ruth was so covered by sand that only the side of her face showed. She didn't appear to be breathing and she looked dead.

Staggering forward, Lasiri helped James to his feet, then turned to aid Jon Paul. When the boy was up they hunched over Ruth, wiping the sand away.

"Is she all right?" Jon Paul asked. The faintest twitch of Ruth's nostrils blew out a speck of sand.

"She's breathing," Lasiri said. "Let's get her uncovered."

Gingerly they cleared the sand until Ruth was free, then they pulled her to her feet. But she could not stand. Her legs crumpled under her and she fell back moaning softly.

"Got to find water," Lasiri muttered. He checked the soldiers to be sure they were all right, then stumbled off leaving James and Jon Paul to assist Ruth. But even as the Masai began to walk, he could feel his strength fade. How many hours since water? he wondered. Ruth was already half dead. How long could the rest of them last?

He paused for a moment studying the myriad patterns across the desert floor. He knew primates drank in the morning before they began to explore. But where were the tracks? The cursed storm had hidden everything.

He had moved a hundred yards along the cliff face when a dark smudge of sand caught his eye. The sand was damp. He crouched down to study the footprints. A small antelope, two desert hares, and a number of baboons. Very carefully he sifted through the signs. There were sets of baboon tracks moving in both directions. So they drank this morning and returned after they saw us, he thought. A flock of sand grouse flew past him, moving along the face of the cliff. He watched them for a moment and saw the birds descend, and a broad grin spread across his face. Sand grouse always flew to water every morning. Their flights were as reliable as clockwork.

He began moving swiftly now, jogging at a steady trot. From the top of a low ridge he scanned across the base of the cliffs. His gaze stopped at a sheltered area in the shadow of the rocks. Three small palm trees grew in a cluster. A printed sign couldn't have announced the spring more clearly.

"Water!" he yelled. "Water here!"

Dragging Ruth across the sand, they rushed to the shallow spring and plunged into the water, feeling the precious liquid flow over their skin. They drank like animals, greedily, and when they finally staggered out of the water, they lay down upon a soft mat of green grass next to the water's edge.

Jon Paul seemed to have survived the desert heat the best of all. Once his thirst was quenched, his eyes brightened and his strength returned. James, too, had endured the heat surprisingly well, for the brief period in the spring had rejuvenated him considerably. Likewise, Lasiri and the three soldiers had fared well. Only Ruth seemed to have lost resilience; now her face took on the appearance of old age. Despite her immersion, her mouth was dry and coated. When she tried to speak her voice was only the barest whisper. She lay in the grass for a long time, scarcely moving.

In the evening, Lasiri took Jon Paul and went hunting. Just before dusk James heard the rolling echo of a shot. Moments later, Lasiri returned carrying a small desert antelope. That night, with meat cooking over a fire of dried palms, James thought he had never smelled anything so good. He gorged like a wild man. As his strength began to return, he could feel a new surge of enthusiasm.

"A little Rothschild 1964 and some flaming crepes for dessert and you would have made a four-star rating," he told Lasiri. "But the silverware leaves a little to be desired," he added, licking his fingers.

Lasiri smiled back at him. "Glad you're feeling better."

"Amazing what a little food and water can do," James answered. He turned to Ruth. "How you doing?"

"A little sore in the joints, but otherwise improving."

"Jon Paul?"

"Good," the younger Jacobson replied.

"Tomorrow morning, I'll take one of the soldiers and follow the cliffs north. We found some signs of camels up there," Lasiri said.

"Fresh?" James asked.

"Past week," Lasiri answered. "But the storm has hidden practically everything. If they're coming across the desert here, we should be able to find their access into the mountains."

"You want me to stand watch?" James offered.

"No, bwana." Lasiri shook his head. "You've had a tough day. Tonight you need to sleep."

But no matter how much he wanted to rest that night, James found that he could not sleep. Either he was too tired or he had already slept too much, for when midnight came he was tossing and turning in his blanket, his mind racing like a runaway wheel. He finally stood up and moved in toward the warmth of the fire. Ruth, Jon Paul, and Lasiri were tucked into their blankets, sleeping soundly. One of the soldiers was taking the watch, sitting cross-legged with a blanket wrapped around his shoulders. The tip of the barrel of his rifle stuck out from a corner of the blanket and James felt reassured at the sight of it. The other two soldiers were curled in their blankets close by his side.

Lasiri had introduced this man as Mbili—"Billy," as Jon Paul called him. At six foot four, with a thick neck and broad shoulders, he was the largest of the soldiers. Like the other Africans, he spoke practically no English.

Their eyes met and James stared at him, reflecting on the man's massive size.

"Okay, bwana?" the African said.

James nodded and motioned that he would take over the watch if Billy wanted to go to sleep, but the African shook his head.

James lingered for a moment, wishing that there was some way that he could communicate with him other than through sign language or the few Swahili words he had learned. He wrapped his arms around himself to signify that it was cold and Billy smiled, offering him his blanket. Feeling awkward now that there was little more he could say, he motioned that he was going out for a short walk and then started to leave the fire.

He heard the word bwana and turned around. Billy pointed toward a small-bore rifle and motioned for him to take it.

"Thanks," James said. He grasped the gun, feeling the cold touch of steel in his hands, then checking the breech to be sure it was loaded, he turned and walked out of camp.

In a minute he was clear of the palms and the shadows of the cliff and moving in the soft desert sand. The moon had risen and was nearly full, shining brilliant and white. James walked until he could barely see the light of the fire. The sand swept away from him in a gentle series of waves that reflected the moon like an ocean.

A slight breeze worked its way along the edge of the cliffs, and he took a deep breath, marveling at how good he was beginning to feel, when a peculiar odor came to him. It was an odd, musky smell and it made him feel extremely uneasy.

He searched the face of the cliffs but the shadows were dark and ominous, crowding the edge of the desert in a blackness that hid everything from view. For a long moment he did not move, testing the wind as if he were an animal, staring into the darkness as if he could somehow penetrate the veil of the night. Suddenly there was the clatter of a rock, followed by a grunt, then all was quiet.

He squinted, cursing the inadequacy of his vision. Something is there, he thought. He could feel a shiver steadily work its way up his spine. He pulled the rifle into the ready position, clicked the safety with his finger, and waited. A minute passed and he heard nothing. His senses were acutely alert, his eyes straining, looking for anything that seemed out of place.

Must have been some wild animal, he thought. He reminded himself that he was in Africa, not Central Park. It was night, and there was a good chance there might be some large animals about. He searched for the reassuring glare of the fire, found it, and slowly retreated, moving quietly back toward the camp. It was then that the smell came to him again, nauseating in its intensity. There was an unconscious familiarity about it that was associated in his mind with something extremely repugnant. He found that his heart had begun to race.

Jesus, I'm shaking, he thought. He remembered his encounter with the elephants. Just calm down, he told himself. Nothing out here but some animals and hundreds of miles of desert.

When he reached the small fire, Billy was sitting solid and immobile, just as he had been before. His glance followed James into the camp.

"Okay?" he whispered.

James nodded and moved in closer to the fire, trying to stop the trembling of his body. Warmth and safety here, he thought, and he crouched down and slowly began to catch his breath. He wondered about telling Billy what he had heard and smelled but there was no way he could communicate the idea in Swahili so he just laid the rifle across his lap and rubbed his hands in front of the fire, welcoming the surge of reassuring warmth.

He had been squatting like that for five minutes, beginning to steadily relax, when the smell came to him yet again. It roused him like an alarm. There in the farthest periphery of his vision were two small glowing dots reflecting the light of the fire. He could not judge how far away they were, nor was there any absolute means by which he could measure their height. He saw them for a minute, then they were gone and he was left staring into the blackness wondering what he had seen. Glowworms? Some type of fireflies? Christ, they were eyes!

He turned, determined to communicate to the African that he was sure something was wrong when he gasped in surprise.

Standing behind the soldier, half hidden by the shadows, was a huge figure covered in black. James could see a slit for its glowing eyes and the outline of broad dark robes, practically invisible in the darkness. He had just opened his mouth to shout a warning when a sword flashed in the firelight. The next moment Billy's squatting figure tipped forward as if it had been a statue someone had pushed from behind. Tumbling toward James, bouncing like a ball across the fire, was a large round object that could only be a human head.

James scarcely had time to raise his rifle and shout an alarm when they were upon him. Dark, devillike men leaped across the camp, their eyes reflecting the fire. He saw Lasiri trying to struggle madly out from beneath his blankets, heard Ruth's shrill scream, saw a figure in dark robes bend over the position where the soldiers were sleeping and begin hacking wildly with his sword when one of the demons leaped at him, a blade crashing down toward his chest. James rammed his rifle across its path and felt a sudden collision of steel as his gun was ripped from his hands. He had an instant to realize that he was helpless when a thundering blow hit him from behind, and the sleep that had eluded him earlier in the night suddenly flooded upon him with paralyzing numbness. . . .

23

The tent was made of black muslin, a canvaslike material strung out for a hundred feet on either side of a central pole. A number of lesser struts buoyed up the cloth so that it could be divided into compartments, each separated by hanging blankets. Within this structure were chambers for eating, sleeping, prayer, and a ceremonial meeting room. Although massive in size, the tent was designed for the life of the nomad. Four camels carried the cloth of the tent, two camels its wooden supports, and a dozen camels the furniture, rugs, and various trappings of comfort. The structure itself was erected only during the seasonal stops, which lasted three to four months. While on the road following the winter and spring migrations, much smaller shelters were used. Marked by a yellow banner flying from its crest, the large black tent was the winter home of Sheik Ahmed Rassam, leader of the Tuareg Confederation, an assemblage of people some two thousand strong.

For centuries his people had lived a nomadic life on the desert. Their existence was relatively simple. They followed Koranic law, herded goats and camels, guarded the mountain passes, and traded with the Arabs for salt. In the fourteenth and fifteenth centuries, when the Tuaregs numbered over one hundred thousand, the tribes were divided into three main confederations. Each subgroup controlled a certain section of the Sahara and had one additional, extremely lucrative source of commerce—the plundering and looting of merchant caravans.

Over countless generations the Tuaregs had controlled routes between the oases. For the proper bribes, they would escort a party safely across hostile territory. If the payment proved too little or their assessment of the wealth of a caravan was too tempting, they might suddenly disappear in the night, leaving the victims waterless, their goatskins severed. Then they would follow such a hapless group like jackals, waiting for the merchants to die. They were known to be incredibly cruel, and dealing with them was always treacherous. Small caravans often tried to avoid them entirely by slipping through their routes at night. Large parties, if sufficiently armed, might try to bluff their way past. In either case, the abrupt disappearances of merchants traveling across the Sahara were too numerous to count. It was little wonder the chief produce of the desert—salt, gold and ivory, ostrich feathers, and slaves—came highly priced.

But in recent times a change had come upon the desert. With the discovery of oil, great nations began to plumb the empty quarters of sand. Gradually the Tuaregs had seen their pastures ruined, their good wells contaminated, their special oases plundered by foreigners in large, gas-drinking machines. Once, years before, the nomads had openly tried to fight such progress. Charging down upon a French battalion, they were massacred. It took no great intelligence to understand that flintlock guns and simple swords were no match for machineguns. When dealing with Europeans, they learned to attack mostly at night. To survive, they retreated into the depths of the Sahara, back into a hundred thousand square miles of nothingness where a man could wander for days without ever seeing another living thing.

Sheik Rassam thought about these changes as he sat inside his ceremonial tent and waited for his warriors to bring the woman in. For two days he'd heard advance news that one of his caravans had captured a blond woman, and he looked forward to this encounter with no small sense of excitement. Folding his legs beneath his long black robe, or *gandurah,* he rested upon a soft cushion and surveyed the room before him. The furnishings were few but rich. A thick red Oriental rug covered the floor. To one side a low table was set with a metal vase containing scented water. Next to it another table held a plate of desert fruit. Behind the sheik stood a chest of silks and gems locked with a single key, always worn beneath his robe. To the side, next to the blanketed entrance, rested a large hemispheric drum. This calling instrument was the one traditional insignia that marked his station as the head of the confederation. Here his word was absolute law. Here disobedience meant death.

Rassam heard the blankets rustle. A moment later two veiled warriors came into the room dragging a fair-skinned woman. They stopped in the middle of the floor and released her. She appeared hollow-eyed and exhausted. How far had they brought her? he wondered. Six hundred miles? Her blond hair was matted with dust and her shirt torn in several places. She stood now in the dim illumination of oil lamps and faced him, rubbing her arms where the guards had roughly gripped her.

He was surprised at her reaction. He'd thought at first she would throw herself at his feet and tremble as others had done. Instead she met the fierceness of his stare, unflinching.

She was in her late twenties, he judged. Despite the disorder of her appearance he saw at once her great beauty. Her eyes were blue and clear, her facial features strong. And her skin. *Her skin was white!* He thought back now on the first white woman he'd ever been with, a half-caste French-Egyptian who plied her trade in the brothels of Al Quatran. A young man then, he'd gone into town with his brothers and for two nights they'd drunk and debauched. The only thing that had stuck with him for all these years was the coolness of her skin. It was testimony to what his father and his father's uncle had passed down to him in the traditions of Tuareg lore: "Add a white woman to your harem and your sleep will always be refreshed."

He sat now in silence, his eyes staring outward through his headdress. His veil and turban were made of a single cloth of blue indigo called a *litham,* wrapped many times around his head, leaving only a small slit for the eyes. He traveled, ate, and slept in this veil. For all his adult life few human beings had ever seen his face. When he drank, even in the presence of other elders, he lifted the bottom of the *litham* with his left hand, bringing the cup into his mouth with his right. It was intensely bad luck to ever let a stranger see his face. Centuries ago, tribal legends said, the Tuaregs had lost a great battle. When they returned to their villages the women had thrown down their veils and told the men that from that time forward *they* would have to hide their faces to be reminded of their cowardice. Now they fought like devils. Yet there were Tuareg warriors, he

knew, who had abandoned the old traditions, taken off their
lithams, and gone to work in the cities. A few had staggered
back to the nomad life, broken in spirit and riddled with disease. Were not the old sayings true—show a stranger your face
and evil spirits will invade your body through the nose and
mouth? He'd seen it happen too often to deny it.

Rassam stood up slowly, pulling his *gandurah* around his
legs. Although slight, at his full height he was six feet two, the
dark turban adding another half foot to his impressive size.
With a motion of his hand he excused the two warriors. So this
was the prisoner the entire camp was buzzing about. Walking
across the room, he moved to a low table and poured out a cup
of scented water. Reaching forward, he offered the woman a
drink.

Without taking her eyes off him, she raised the cup and drank
thirstily. Finished, she handed it back. Her eyes now ran across
the chamber, resting for a brief moment on the table holding
the fruit. Sure she was hungry after coming so long a distance,
he offered her a small desert pear. She accepted the food and
began to eat. At the same moment he placed his hand upon her
shoulder.

Although no word had been spoken between them, the meaning was unmistakably clear. He would give her comfort, safety,
and shelter. She must offer him physical affection in return.

She froze. Very deliberately, she removed his hand from her
shoulder. Taking the fruit from her mouth, she handed it back
to him, half eaten.

He looked at her incredulously. She had denied him! She was
refusing his protection, his riches, the power of his heritage.
How incredibly stupid, he thought. Did she not know that she
was totally within his power? He'd killed women for less. Her
action was ludicrous. He threw back his head and began to
laugh a loud deep-throated guffaw.

Her eyes suddenly flared with anger. With a quick motion
she grabbed the cloth around his chin and yanked down his
veil. His forehead was triangularly shaped leading down to a
thin pointed chin stained with blue dye from the cloth. His
teeth were well formed; his nose and lips almost delicate in their
proportions.

He stared at her in shock. His first reaction was that of fear and vulnerability followed immediately by overwhelming fury. He struck forward with an open-handed slap that landed squarely on the side of her face. She staggered from the impact. Regaining her balance, she swung now with her right fist in a blow that caught him completely by surprise. He was knocked to the ground. By the time he could get himself untangled from his robe, she had fled through the curtained passage. There were shouts from his men as she ran outside the tent, then the sound of scrambling feet as they pursued her.

Collecting himself, he replaced his veil, rearranged his turban, and sat back down on his soft cushion, crossing his legs beneath him. He was trembling with rage. The warriors had told him that she had already tried to escape twice. If another person had been in the room when she had pulled down his veil, he would have been forced to execute them both. Perhaps it was better to kill her outright. Even if she was placed in his harem, if she was uncooperative and hostile, she could cause more trouble than she was worth. Yet still, there was something about her that greatly intrigued him. If there was some way he could subdue her, make an example of her, then perhaps it might be worth his while.

Fifteen minutes later they brought her struggling back into the room. He glared at her for a moment in silence. Again she met the ferocity of his stare. There is absolutely no fear in her, he thought. Abruptly he waved his hand to have her removed. He would have her tied up in one of the side tents until he decided what to do with her. He would confer with his priest, who spoke many languages. Perhaps between them they could find a common tongue. But he needed some way to force absolute submission on her. She had subjected him to an act that defied all Tuareg dignity. *She had pulled down his veil!*

Slowly the thin margins of a smile spread across his lips. He'd only heard it used once before, mentioned by his father as a penalty for a young woman who had run off from a harem several times and refused to obey. It was called the "kiss of a thousand suns." It would place her forever at his mercy. He thought carefully, weighing the consequences. Short of death it was the only other realistic option he had. But the teaching of

Mohammed was clear. God had made two things for man's pleasure, woman and perfume. "A woman is like a field," the Scriptures said. "Go and plow it as often as you like."

Rassam could not know that the abduction of this woman would raise alarms on another continent ten thousand miles away. And indeed, it would be an entire month before James or Jon Paul first heard the news of their sister's disappearance.

24

Far across the desert, dawn broke upon the oasis of al Jabbar just as it always had for the past thousand years. Small green wrens, orange and black warblers, tiny rust-colored weavers darted back and forth across the water, fluttering noisily between the trees. A dik-dik, the smallest of the African antelope, scarcely bigger than a hare, tiptoed from the shadows, took a cautious drink, then fled into hidden pathways in the thickest portion of the vines. Ancestors of this antelope had seen the great caravans come and go, stopping at al Jabbar with their trains of slaves, their camels loaded with bags of gold and jewels destined for ports thousands of miles away. Before that the great-great-ancestors of this antelope had seen mighty kingdoms rise and fall. Black nations with men who rode horses and wore armor had charged across the country enslaving all. And before that, a white-skinned tribe who quarried wells and rode chariots and forged metal into hunting spears and knives and arrows.

Yet there was a time once when the only men who visited the oasis were primitive, wandering nomads, and strangely, now it was as if it all had come back—a return to the beginning. Gone were the great nations, vanished were the caravans, abandoned were the cities; the only victors, time and the desert—both unyielding, interminable, and harsh.

For seven days the remnants of James's caravan—the two soldiers, the cook, and the two drivers—had camped on the ridge overlooking the oasis and waited. They were faithful men, dedicated to their job. Every day they were up at sunrise, brewing a strong Somali tea. For the next three hours, they would take turns scanning across the desert with a pair of binoculars, looking for some signs of life. At noon they would start the Land-Rovers and be sure each was in working order and ready to go. Then for an hour they would polish the windows and clean the sides of the vehicles until each was spic and span. During the hottest hours of the day they would rest, returning to their watch in the afternoon, and there they would remain until dark. For diversion, they would go hunting in the mornings or scout along the desert, but always they left one man upon the ridge as a lookout and one armed man in camp to defend their goods. Once when a small band of Somali herders came wandering into the oasis to water their cattle, the men had broken out the guns and sounded an alarm. But the Somali proved peaceful and eventually they sat around the fire, the black mercenaries in their khaki shirts, their tan knee socks and their berets and the Somali herdsmen in their tattered, flimsy blankets. They spoke Swahili, exchanging stories about their tribes, and traded four single bullets for four small delicately carved pieces of ivory, each destined to be an ornament worn on a bracelet or around the neck.

Yet as day passed day there was a restlessness about them. Even though the site was good and the water from the oasis rose with unequaled purity, there was a certain uneasiness in their minds that they had camped next to a haunted ground. The ruins of an ancient city undoubtedly contained the spirits of a thousand men. It took only one look down the well James had discovered to note that it was filled with human bones, bones whose owners undoubtedly roamed through the night. Lasiri had asked them to wait for seven days before going for help, and they had waited these days with increasing apprehension and concern.

In the evening on the seventh day, Ferusa Surmari, the cook, who had been sitting out upon the ridge, scanning the desert, sounded out the alarm. "Camels! Camels upon the horizon!" He rushed back into camp, telling the others that Bwana James and his brother and Lasiri and Memsaab Ruth had returned.

They hurried to the ridge with great excitement. There upon the desert they saw a distant caravan making its way across the sands. But, by the time darkness fell, they realized that it was moving not toward them but in the opposite direction, toward the tall peaked mountain called the Devil's Tower. The caravan was too far for them to see clearly in the fading light, but they could make out the outlines of camels, dark-robed riders, and what appeared to be a number of men on foot. "All men in this country are enemies until proven different," one of them said, and they wisely kept their rifles ready that night and stood a double watch. But when the eighth morning came and the sun rose upon the eastern horizon, spreading its glare across the desert, the caravan was gone.

They waited an extra day, then drew straws. Two men were chosen, a driver and a soldier, to go for help. That morning, they loaded up one of the Land-Rovers with some supplies and started on the long drive back to Nairobi. If no help came in another week, the remaining three men would pack up the rest of the gear and follow, assuming that the first Land-Rover had broken down.

The driver of the first Land-Rover had explicit instructions from Dr. Ruth Parker to go directly to the Nairobi Museum and give the following message to the curator, Ian Anderson:

Dear Ian:

On May 15 we departed from the oasis of al Jabbar following the old Sudan-Jabbar-Malindi trade route in search of James Jacobson's sister. I have instructed the men who remained in camp to return to you after seven days if we have not come back. By this time we may be in serious need of assistance. If there is no word from us by telephone or wire from one of the desert outposts when you receive this letter, I would urge a search party be gathered at the earliest opportunity. Notification should be sent to Mr. Michael Jacobson at 145 Ridgeway Drive, in Bedford, New York, USA, and also to the village of Lasiri Jamba Mzonbili in Naivasha. This letter is not to cause undue alarm but merely to alert you that we may have run into difficulty and would appreciate any assistance you can give.

Sincerely Yours,
Ruth Parker

PART III

"There in Abyssinia they slept near a thousand years, forgetful of the world by whom they were forgotten."

—Gibbon

25

Four hours had passed since the ambush of James's small caravan upon the desert. The first blush of dawn glowed upon the horizon. Next to the cliffs, adjacent to the spring of water where they had camped, everything was still as death. Two sand grouse called plaintively in the distance. As the shadows of night receded, a vulture soared above the cliffs, then circled, drifting lower. Motionless forms lay upon the sand.

The sun began to edge above the horizon. From one of the forms came a moan. Lasiri was wedged against a shrub lying in a pool of blood. With a grunt he rolled over on his side. He tried to rise to his feet, then collapsed. Minutes passed. Finally he shuddered. With great effort he pulled himself to a sitting position and examined his wound. A twelve-inch gash cut across the left side of his chest down to the bone. By some miracle the blanket must have caught the main force of the blow. Yet even if he did not succumb from loss of blood, a wound like this left open and unclean would fester and he would die. Time was against him, he thought. Time, and the rising sun.

Fighting a surge of dizziness, he struggled to his feet and stumbled across the remnants of their camp. A quick check told him that Mbili and the two soldiers were dead. He staggered forward and fell into the water. The bodies of James, Ruth, and Jon Paul were missing. Where were they? he wondered. Dead or captured? He tried to reconstruct the night in his mind. They must have been watched. Probably the shooting of the gazelle had alerted others to their presence. If he hadn't let down his guard, they might have been able to defend themselves. Their lives had been his responsibility. He did not consider that he'd been practically without sleep during their three-day crossing of the desert. He'd been careless and his mistake had cost them dearly.

When he pulled himself out of the water he was still oozing blood. He had to close the wound. Another hour and he might be too weak to walk. Forcing himself up, he lunged toward the cliffs, searching the ground. He found a small one-quarter-inch trail in the dust and bent over, following it. The track was smooth and cleared of debris, as if someone had taken his finger and drawn a wavering line. It ran for a hundred feet, then came to a series of secondary trails which radiated like spokes from a low mound.

Here he stopped. Urinating in his cupped hands, he carefully cleaned and irrigated his wound. Then he took a small twig and fished into the hole at the top of the mound. When he pulled the stick out a huge black ant was clinging to the wood. He deftly grabbed it by the back of its thorax and held it up, watching it open and close its pincers. Slowly he brought the ant up to his chest and held it to the upper end of his wound. The ant gripped angrily into his skin. Lasiri squeezed its thorax and it closed its pincers tighter. He then twisted off the back of the insect, leaving the mandibles of the ant imbedded in his skin, holding the top of the laceration together like a staple. One by one, he fished out twenty more of the ants and repeated the process, advancing from both ends toward the middle until his wound was completely closed.

The sun was up. Nearly seven o'clock, he thought. He started back toward the dead soldiers. He doubted he had enough strength to try to bury them. He needed to rest. He was afraid he was going to pass out again.

He'd just reached the campsite when he heard the cough of a camel. Using all his remaining strength, he retreated back to the cliffs. Climbing a low shelf of rocks, he found a small crevice and rolled in, gasping for breath. A moment later a veiled rider appeared, moving slowly toward the water.

Lasiri had no fear of death. *Fear* was not a word in the Masai vocabulary. Only after associating with Europeans and some of the less stoic tribes had he fully begun to understand the meaning of the word. As he lay in the shelter of the rocks, his heartbeat surging, then fading, he knew death was very near. He'd only been this close to death once before. And he remembered it now as his body struggled against the growing waves of shock.

He'd been a young boy then, guarding a herd of twenty-five cattle. That night they'd become very restless and he'd heard the grunt of lions. Somewhere in the shadows big cats were stalking his herd. A Masai boy's duty was to guard his cattle and it was expected that he would guard them with his life. To do less would have been a disgrace. He knew there was no way he could defend all the cattle against the lions, so he picked out one of the old and diseased cows and hobbled it next to a ridge of tall grass, the most likely spot where he thought the lions might approach. Then he'd taken his spear and crouched behind the cow and waited. The moonlight was bright enough for him to watch the stalk, and when they charged he'd moved forward to greet them. The first lion, a male, he'd taken head-on with his spear, thrusting with all his might. Throwing at the last instant, he'd buried the weapon up to its hilt into the lion's chest. He fell back under the momentum of the lion's charge and was raked terribly across the shoulder.

The second lion, a female, had leaped on the old cow and pulled it over when he struggled out from beneath the first lion and caught the lioness just behind the shoulder with his long stabbing knife. When morning came he was found unconscious, lying in a pool of blood next to the two dead lions. The herd had run off but none of the good cattle had been injured. Lasiri had been marked by the elders then as a youth of tremendous bravery.

For a time they had thought he was going to die. He'd lain in camp for a week, delirious from loss of blood and infection. Yet, by some miracle of magic herbs and a witch doctor's incantations, he'd made it through. After he'd been nursed back to health they held a great ceremony for him. He'd been taken into the hut for a private audience with old Lapingi, one of the last great chiefs of the Masai. Lapingi had no teeth, was practically blind, and the legends said he was nearly a hundred seasons old. "Not since our ancestors has anyone demonstrated such courage, Lasiri," the old man said. "We are very proud."

"I was doing my duty," Lasiri answered simply.

"The Masai gods have looked kindly upon you," Lapingi added. "You have been chosen for a great future."

"I will serve the tribe the best I can." Lasiri replied. "I will devote my life to helping this village."

"No," the old man answered. He placed a trembling arm upon Lasiri's shoulder. "You have good intelligence. You are still young and you are very strong. There is a white man's school in Naivasha. I want you to go there."

"But why?" Lasiri argued. "The Masai works for no man but his tribe."

"That is true," the old man said. "But the Europeans are very clever. Learn from them what you can. Bring this knowledge back to the Masai. You have bravery and courage but you lack one thing to be a leader. You do not have wisdom. A great chief must learn that above all else. Go to the school and learn everything that you can."

In the ceremony they gave him a young maiden for the night, the tails and claws of the lions, plus the mane of the male. He could now wear the mane as a headdress in any hunt. He had killed two lions. He was now a *moran,* a full-fledged warrior of his tribe.

He had started school late. At age twelve he began the first grade. But he was quick to learn so that by the time he was sixteen he had mastered the first seven years of grade school. From sixteen to nineteen he completed the equivalent of four years of high school, and it was here that his studies came to the attention of Dr. Ruth Parker. Ruth had heard about him and recognized him as a particularly gifted student. Through her contacts in England she had arranged for him to begin a two-year scholarship to Cambridge.

He remembered now how incredibly different the world was than he had imagined. No amount of studying or reading could help him grasp the significance of a city like London with its modern buildings, its crowds of people, its trolleys, airplanes, and great ships. Yet of all the experience which he came away with during this period of education he could really boil it down to three things.

First, he learned that no matter how proud he was of his Masai inheritance, there were multitudes of people across the world, incredibly different from him, and many just as proud and prejudiced against other tribes and races as he had been. He was Masai, of that he was sure, but now he had incorporated a feeling of tolerance for other peoples. Like the animals of the Serengeti, the zebras and the wildebeests and the gazelles, each race seemed to have its respective place in the great scheme of things.

Second, he learned he could run faster than almost any European. He'd been in Cambridge for only a couple of months when he'd been invited to a track meet by a fellow African from Nigeria. He'd watched the first heat of the one-hundred-yard dash with great interest. At the beginning of the second heat he'd been standing near the starting line when the starter's gun went off. Out of curiosity he'd run after the contestants to see how he matched up. To the astonishment of all he'd beaten them by ten yards. And he was in his street clothes and shoes.

Despite vigorous encouragement from members of the track team, he'd decided not to run. Competing with others, especially Europeans, seemed somewhat beneath him. He'd come to Cambridge to study and he didn't want to disappoint Dr. Parker. Running would take time away from his studies. Besides, he already knew that he could run. Why did he need to prove it to others?

The few times they persuaded him to race he'd never been beaten, and his best time, if the Cambridge watches were correct, was not far from the fastest time ever recorded at the university.

The third thing he'd brought back from England was a son, and the bittersweet memory of a woman he'd fallen in love with. He'd been introduced to her one night after a study group, at a local pub. She was from Jamaica and she was majoring in drama. She was everything he was not. Where he was often silent, brooding, and quiet, she was flashy, vibrant, and talkative. They'd talked during that first encounter only long enough to make him furious.

"Well, how do you like Cambridge, Jungle Boy," she said.

He was not used to being addressed quite so disrespectfully, especially by a woman.

"You may call me Lasiri, miss," he answered.

"Where do you come from?"

"I am Masai," he said proudly. "I come from a village in Kenya."

"They say the Masai can kill a lion."

"On occasion, when they have to."

"Some day I would like to see your spear." She had chuckled.

Her words shocked him. Yet there was a twinkle of mischief in her eye. She had turned away from him then and without waiting for him to answer spent the rest of the evening conversing with her other friends, hardly taking any further notice of him at all. When she finally got up to leave she said, "Good night, Jungle Boy."

He'd scowled and not answered.

Two weeks later he saw her walking across the campus. She'd come up to him and invited him to a play she was in. He'd watched the performance with amazement. On stage she was beautiful and very much in command, and he thought how different she was from the women he was used to. Here she talked and acted almost like a man. She was a first-rate actress. Even in his naiveté he knew she had a great future on the stage.

That night they'd gone back to her small flat and after several beers she'd taken off her clothes. She had good, firm breasts, thin legs, and a fine pair of humped buttocks. When she'd undressed him and he stood before her naked she'd stared at his manliness with astonishment.

"My God, Jungle Man," she exclaimed. "You carry a harpoon!"

He could look back at the night with some satisfaction, for from that time on she referred to him only as Lasiri. They went together for more than a year and she became pregnant by him. Their son was only six months old when his scholarship ran out. He knew he would have to return to Africa. He wanted her to go with him, but she refused. "There is no life for an actress back there," she said.

In his heart he knew she was right. She was too proud to come back as a subservient wife in his tribe, just as he was too dignified to linger on in England and work at some menial task, being a waiter or a bellhop, as other blacks from Africa had done.

They both realized that a child would only get in the way of her acting career. But when she had suggested they put the boy up for adoption, Lasiri had refused. There were no orphans among the Masai. He would bring his son back to Kenya, where he could be raised.

By the time Lasiri returned to his village, old Lapingi and many of the elders had died and the Masai had split up into a number of small feudal groups. No one particularly cared about Lasiri's education or his return. He tried working in the tribe for a while, but it was no use. He'd gone too far, seen too much to be satisfied, so he'd gone to work for the white hunters. Now six years had passed and he needed money to educate his son. When he heard James's offer to go up to the Northern Frontier, he had jumped at the chance. Ten thousand dollars was far more than he could earn in Kenya in several years.

As he lay in the rock crevice, hidden among the cliffs, fighting through waves of dizziness, he thought it was funny that he'd come back from Cambridge with only three things. Not his studies in Latin or history or math. But his ability to tolerate people, his speed, and his son.

Lesser men would have died. Yet the sinew of Lasiri's life, passed through a hundred generations of Masai, was incredibly strong. If he had a chance at all, it would be this one significant factor that would keep him alive.

Sometime during the morning he awoke to hear the shouts of men. He rolled toward the edge of the crevice and saw three veiled riders moving down among the rocks, searching for him. He shrank back toward the darkest recesses of the cave. Once they came so close that he had to hold his breath to avoid making any sound. Then, finally, their noises began to fade away.

He lay there panting in the growing heat. If he could just make it through this first day. He was close to water. Even weakened he was sure he could snare small animals that came to the pool to drink. But the hardest hours were still to come. Time and the sun were against him.

He closed his eyes, not sure he would wake up again. His pulse beats became faint, like the feeble fluttering of a dying moth. He'd done everything that he could. The rest was up to the *shauri,* the Will of God.

The sun was an orb of molten ore, the wind like the tongue of a branding iron. And Jon Paul thought if there was ever a hell in this life, he had found it. His mouth was parched, his body drenched with sweat. When he closed his eyes, he dreamed of a land with moist breezes and tall green trees. Here there were none, only sheer slabs of barren rock. The walls of the cliffs reflected the sun like an incandescent oven and he staggered in its glare.

The previous night would be confused in his memory forever. He had a vague recollection of a kaleidoscope of images as dawn broke upon the desert. He could remember being awakened by James's yell, the sound of gunshots, then the tall veiled shadows charging through the camp. Before he could untangle himself from his blanket, they had been overrun. Ruth had lunged on top of him yelling something in Arabic. By the time he could get to his feet, he had a sword blade at his chest. Now it was noon and he was walking along the floor of the desert next to steep-walled cliffs.

A group of black prisoners staggered ahead of him, each fastened to a line of rope that circled around their necks. Six camels moved at the front of the procession ridden by tall men covered in black robes. Their heads were hidden by a swathe of cloth that wrapped around their faces, leaving little visible except for fierce, probing eyes. All were armed with swords sheathed in scabbards at their waists. Two of the men held rifles while the rest carried long, pointed lances.

Dangling from the sides of the camels were strings of rounded objects that at first glance appeared to be gourds. It had taken Jon Paul a moment to recognize the shapes. They were human heads. Some were dry and shriveled with tongues hanging out between purplish lips; others seemed fresh, one still oozing a bluish fluid, its eyes rolled white and vacant.

Swallowing hard, Jon Paul managed to repress a shudder as a shift of wind brought the odor of death to his nostrils. He twisted around and glanced at Ruth. "Is James all right?" he asked. His brother staggered along behind them followed by three more of the veiled riders at the rear of the caravan.

"Don't slow down," Ruth answered. "He's still with us."

Jon Paul quickened his pace, looping the rope around his hand to take the tension off his neck. For another five minutes he walked without speaking, sorting the events of the previous night in his mind. James had been knocked unconscious. Even now his brother seemed dazed. Had they not been able to get James to his feet, Jon Paul was sure the raiders would have killed him. All the soldiers were dead. Lasiri was not accounted for but it was unlikely that he survived. As they walked now Jon Paul could hear James mumbling to himself. Half the time his brother made no sense at all. Always he kept asking the same questions over and over again.

"Ruth, where are we?" James whispered.

"It's all right, James, you're all right," she answered. "Just keep walking."

"But the soldiers—where the hell are the soldiers?"

"They surprised us, James," Ruth answered patiently. "Swept over the camp. Caught everyone asleep. I don't know if it was because we were white or because they realized I was a woman, but for some reason they spared us. You were on the ground. Mbili was murdered. The two soldiers were slain where they lay. I saw Lasiri leap up and knock one of the men down but after that I lost him in the darkness."

"Lasiri gone?" James cried. "Lasiri gone?" He repeated the statement as if he didn't believe it. "Goddamn them," he cried. "Goddamn the murdering bastards." Suddenly he charged forward but the rope caught him by the neck and flipped him over. Disoriented and confused, he fell in the sand, struggling wildly.

Jon Paul yanked up the slack and rushed over to James's side.

"Jesus, James, get up!" he cried. "Don't go crazy. They'll kill you in a second."

The procession halted abruptly. One of the veiled men turned his camel and came galloping back.

James floundered on the ground, swinging weakly at Jon Paul.

Ruth pushed her way in between them. "James, damn you,"

she shouted. She slapped him across the face as hard as she
could. The blow stunned him and he stared at her numbly. At
the same moment the veiled rider stopped his camel next to
James and pulled a long sword from his sash.

Jon Paul leaped forward, blocking the camelman's way.

"He's all right, leave him be!" Ruth shouted in Arabic. Pulling at James's belt, she slowly brought him to his feet.

"Come on, James, keep cool, just walk, do what they want,
and stay alive!"

As James gathered his feet beneath him, the veiled rider lowered his sword, glared ferociously at them, then swung back to
the front of the procession. They started up again, James staggering after them. Blessed Christ, Jon Paul thought. They
would be lucky to make it through the day alive.

They had been following the base of the cliffs along the edge
of the desert when the precipice suddenly opened into a steep-
walled canyon nearly twenty yards across. From a distance, the
passage was practically invisible, hidden among a series of rock
outcroppings. Turning through this entrance, they followed the
canyon inward toward the mountains. There on the sand floor,
protected from the desert storms, were tracks and droppings
from dozens of previous caravans. Squares, circles, weird geo-
metric designs began to appear along the walls of the canyon.
As the caravan penetrated deeper into the cliffs, the drawings
became more common until the walls were entirely filled with
them. Mixed among figures of animals were crude stick drawings of humans, sometimes hunters pulling at bows or men
fighting or simple outlines of women identified by breasts.

Jon Paul could feel Ruth pull on the ropes to slow the procession down. She moved tentatively now, studying the drawings
along the cliff walls.

"God, what I would give to study them," she said. "This pass
must have been used since the very earliest of times."

"Sorry we got you into this," Jon Paul replied.

"Keep the faith." She mustered a faint smile. "I think they
would have killed us last night if they'd wanted us dead."

"Ruth, who are these people?" he asked.

"Probably Tuaregs," she answered. "The Arabs call them the

Abandoned of God. Most of them are nomads who inhabit the
mountain ranges of the Hoggar and the Air, a thousand miles
from here. But why they are here escapes me. They speak little
Arabic. Earlier this morning I tried to get through to them but
they've preferred not to talk."

"And the blacks?" Jon Paul motioned toward the line of
captives.

"They look like Somali or Samburu. I suspect they've been
gathered as slaves."

Jon Paul walked for some moments in silence. As thirsty and
tired as he felt, he knew it was nothing compared to the prisoners who shuffled along in front of him. Most were women. Some
were young and in the prime of health, though others appeared
older, looking haggard and bent. Two of the girls had firm,
erect breasts that jutted out in the fullness of pregnancy. All
were barefoot and were garbed in little more than small pieces
of cloth around their loins. They moved in a slow, staggering
gait. Several appeared so exhausted Jon Paul was not sure how
much farther they could go on. One strapping youth among the
captives seemed about his age. Though he had a large sword cut
across his back, the boy walked without flinching, sweat oozing
down across the wound. Jon Paul marveled at his courage. The
youth had obviously not been captured without a fight.

Hardly an hour had passed before one of the older women
fell. The nomads stopped and cut her loose. As Jon Paul
watched her crawl off into the rocks to die, he almost charged
at them, trying to muster some superhuman strength to break
the ropes. But the presence of James and Ruth behind him
sobered his thoughts. There was nothing he could do. When
they finally brought him some water he refused it, pointing in
the direction of the young wounded man in front of him. The
youth took it, swallowing deeply until the Tuaregs ripped the
goatskin from his hands. His eyes seemed hollow, vacant. He
stared back at Jon Paul with an expressionless face, then turned
toward the front of the procession again. The water was now
passed back to Ruth and finally James. James took a couple of
swallows, then poured some of the water into his hands and
wiped the moisture across his forehead. It was obvious to Jon
Paul that his brother was becoming stronger. James had been

quiet for the last hour but his confusion seemed gone. He drank again, then wiped his mouth with his wrist, nodding toward Jon Paul.

"You'd better drink it while you can," he said.

"I'm all right, James," Jon Paul answered. "How are you feeling?"

"Somebody switched off the lights," James answered in half a grin. "I think I was on a little vacation."

"Glad to have you back," Jon Paul replied.

"I'm not sure." James frowned. He glanced around, motioning to the line of slaves and the veiled men. "I can think of a lot of places I'd rather be. How long have we been walking?"

"Since dawn," he answered.

"Any idea which way we were going?"

"Mostly west," Ruth replied.

"Well, let's hope we get to where we're going soon. I don't think I can take much more of this."

"I don't think any of us can," Ruth answered.

As the camels started up again, Jon Paul felt exceedingly relieved. A glint of determination was back in his brother's eyes again. At least for the moment, he thought, James is his old self again.

They traveled for the rest of the day. By midafternoon the caravan moved out onto a long plateau. There, for the first time, the ridges opened so they could look down on the terrain ahead. At the base of the mountains was a flat stretch of sand that spread out toward the north. Beyond that, mirages, heat waves, dust devils, and all of the familiar signs of the desert. At the edge of this great sand sea, mountains rose up, each peak higher than the last, culminating in a singular pointed crest that Jon Paul recognized as the Devil's Tower. This unique landmark was visible in all directions. Below it, just at the junction of the desert with the mountains, they first saw the city.

Exhausted as they were, still the sight took their breath away. From a distance it appeared to be a sprawling metropolis complete with walls, towers, and complex buildings.

"So the diary was true!" Jon Paul exclaimed. "The seventh city exists!"

"Ruth, it's huge," James murmured.

"Perfectly located." Ruth nodded. "Surrounded on three sides by mountains and on the fourth by an inhospitable desert. It must have stood here for a thousand years."

"But why isn't it on the maps?" Jon Paul puzzled.

"Because it's dead," Ruth answered. "The oasis existed once as a great center for trade. Now there's nothing but ruins."

For the rest of the afternoon the caravan progressed steadily toward the ancient city. With a goal in sight, Jon Paul found an inner reserve he didn't know he had. The ropes chafed his neck and his feet felt like stumps of wood, yet he staggered forward, refusing to be overcome by fatigue. The only chance any of them had was to keep walking. Whoever fell was cut loose to die.

At one point they made a sharp turn and entered another canyon. There along one wall of the cliffs was the carved facade of an elaborate tomb. A central doorway led back into the rocks surrounded by large stone columns several stories high. Centuries of weather had begun to obliterate the details, yet the structure was remarkable in both its size and architecture. Next to the columns at various levels on the face of the cliffs, running for a quarter of a mile, was a series of cavelike tombs. These tunnels were connected by a latticeway of paths.

As the caravan reached the narrowest part of the canyon, three of the veiled riders drew their swords. With a cry they charged forward, stabbing and slashing the air. The caravan halted for several minutes until this display was completed. Jon Paul glanced at Ruth with surprise. A troop of brown monkeys scampered along the cliff walls, but there was no visible enemy there.

"Probably a ritual," Ruth said. "They're ridding the area of evil spirits. To the nomads a necropolis like this has many demons. The Tuaregs must show they are powerful and not to be dominated."

Suddenly a stone whizzed past Jon Paul's head. A second bounced on the ground just in front of James. The camels began to groan and shuffle nervously. Searching along the cliff wall, Jon Paul thought he saw a figure dart back into one of the caves. A small avalanche of loose rock abruptly crashed down into the valley. The Tuaregs began whistling to one another as

the caravan lurched ahead at a quickened pace. In a moment
they had crossed the narrowest part of the canyon. When Jon
Paul looked back the caves seemed silent and uninhabited.
Whoever had thrown the rocks had disappeared, and there was
no further evidence of life. Yet there was an eerie, uneasy feeling
about the canyon. Spirits? he wondered. And if alive, who were
they? And why do they hide? And why are the Tuaregs afraid
of them?

In another hundred yards the canyon opened up, the cliffs
ended, and they moved onto a gradually descending plateau
that led toward the walls of the city. If Ruth had thought the
oasis was city without life, she was wrong. For everywhere
along the ruins were scattered tents.

At the entrance to the city was a large pool of water surrounded by palms. As the caravan worked its way along the
oasis, they passed scores of women filling gourds. Donkeys,
goats, and small groups of sheep milled in the shallow water.
The caravan detoured around a large herd of camels, then
moved upward following a well-trodden pathway toward the
main gates of the city.

At the outer perimeter of the ruins they came to a row of
posts to which were tied a series of decaying remains. Three
vultures rose before them, flapping wildly. Jon Paul felt a rush
of uneasiness. Passing close by, he could see the birds had been
feeding upon human carrion.

"Probably criminals," Ruth remarked. "Murderers, sex of-
fenders, insurgents. Moslem law has always been strict and un-
forgiving."

Next to the posts was a tall slab of wood. Jon Paul glanced at
it, then paled as his mind slowly registered the sight. Hands
severed at the wrist had been staked to the wood through the
palms. The fingers, twisted and gnarled, reached out gro-
tesquely. A long green lizard dashed across the top of the slab,
its back a flash of iridescence.

"That is the penalty for thievery," Ruth commented. "An
eye for an eye. Left here as a reminder to the rest of the popu-
lace that the law is to be upheld."

Once inside the walls, they were split off from the other prisoners. The blacks were led by a second group of Tuaregs along a side alleyway.

Jon Paul watched the black youth with the sword wound follow the line of captives off into the ruins. The youth looked back once as if to say something, then he disappeared. God, I wish him luck, Jon Paul thought.

They were being taken straight into the heart of the city. They traveled for another ten minutes until they came to a large open market that was packed with booths and crowded with people.

Along the ground were round, open baskets containing dates, dried apricots, and desert melons. Stacked cages held small fluttering birds. One booth exhibited swords and knives from Germany; another, vases and china from England; a third, scarves and silk from the Orient. As the cries of hawkers filled the air, a plucked, bald chicken darted through the crowd in front of them. Everywhere they moved, people stopped and stared. Some of the crowd appeared similar to their nomad captors, their faces hidden by black headdresses. Others looked Arabic, with brown eyes and hooked noses. Many wore fezes or turbans and a variety of desert robes. Most of the women were veiled and dressed in brightly colored fabrics. Here and there, the more affluent women carried parasols.

"Ruth, look," Jon Paul exclaimed, his eyes suddenly caught by an open booth. There, half hidden on a table, buried between a large copper pan and an old oil lantern, was the dusty screen of a Sony television set.

"What the hell do you suppose they'll do with it?"

"Lord knows." Ruth shrugged. "And there—*perfume!*"

They passed a table with a series of glass containers all neatly laid out just as one might find in the cosmetics section of a modern department store. The labels read *Joy, Chanel, Revlon.*

"Goods from every country," James marveled. "It's as if this were a grand market of the desert."

"The people, too, are a mixed lot," Ruth answered. "Tuaregs, Ethiopians, Berbers, Nubians, and a hundred mixtures from God knows where. The oasis is alive again. But how? Why? I can't explain it."

"And there." Jon Paul pointed. "What is that?"

A roped-off area at the corner of the market contained a dozen camels. Large slabs of white material were being unloaded from their backs and placed in neat stacks upon the ground. A group of Arabs hovered around them.

"Salt, Jon Paul," Ruth answered. "Here in the desert, it's as precious as gold."

They came to a standstill as they struggled to pass through the thickest portion of the crowd. The throng pressed forward and the camels were unable to break through. One of the veiled men dismounted, shouting at the people to get out of his way. They waited impatiently, feeling the oppressive heat and the surge of the crowd, wishing desperately to start moving again.

A beggar with a crutch, covered in tattered black robes, moved toward them. A moment later he was tugging at James's leg, bowing and rocking, his hand held out for some token gratuity. As James reflexively pushed the man away their eyes locked. The man's skin was tanned almost bronze, his face covered by a snow-white beard. Blue eyes stared out at James from under the shadow of a hood. The man reached up and grabbed James's arm, gripped solidly, then released as he moved back into the crowd.

Hours later the incongruity of that contact would come to James. The blue eyes had seemed to want to tell him something, the urgently gripping hand, to give some message. But what? And how was it to be interpreted? Or was it, as Ruth later suggested, some Berber, demented and confused, searching for sympathy and human compassion?

For twenty minutes they moved, stopped, then moved again, working their way slowly past the crowd. As they traveled through the market, Ruth's gaze jumped from one person to the next, her mind trying to sort out the pieces of a puzzle that had been growing steadily in her mind. *An ancient city alive!* A marketplace filled with goods, not just simple native crops but items from ports around the world. A tribe of Tuaregs gathering human slaves. And then her mind flashed back to a passage she had read in the archives of al Moshan months before.

In 900 Hegira (Sixteenth century) there existed a magnificent oasis called Bogadez through which all roads led.

It was a city like an ocean port, the great caravans stopping here before embarking on the long stretch of sand that would lead them north to Fez or Cairo or Marrakesh, and it was said that all forms of commerce were paid for in solid gold. . . .

A shiver of excitement surged through her. A lost oasis hidden from the rush of modern times. An oasis never touched by an archaeologist's spade. What grand discoveries! What hidden treasures still to be found! She smiled at the absurdity. She had dreamed of such an opportunity all her life. And now she was tethered at the end of a rope, dragged like a goat by a group of camel men who could hardly care if she lived or died.

Searching through the crowd, the thoughts rushing through her mind in volleys, Ruth noted a large framed palanquin carried by four men moving along the outer perimeter of the market. She watched attentively as the litter swung out of a back alleyway. A curtain covered the sides of the structure but from the reflection of the light, Ruth could see that there was a figure inside.

The palanquin stopped and a graceful hand opened the curtain. The head of a woman stared out across the market, then turned up toward the sun. For a fleeting instant Ruth saw a veiled face with a lock of blond hair. Then the curtain closed, and the men picked up the litter and disappeared into the crowd.

"Diana!" Ruth gasped with astonishment. "Diana Jacobson!" But something was wrong. Something about the way the woman had stared out and moved her head seemed very strange.

"What was it?" James asked.

Ruth turned and saw that James had been staring in the opposite direction. He hadn't seen the woman at all.

"Nothing," she murmured. "I . . . it was nothing at all."

26

In a small roofless room in a remote section of the ruins, they were cut free. James stumbled to the floor, an exhausted wreck. Every fiber of his system seemed to cry for rest. Jon Paul fell against the window, staring down across the ruins, studying the scattered tents. Ruth had never felt so tired in her life. Her hip hurt beyond measure. She limped to the doorway and called to one of the guards.

"We must have food and water," she said in Arabic.

"You will be fed," came the answer.

"And what is to happen to us?"

"You will wait."

"For what?"

"To see what they will do with you."

"And who makes that decision?"

"His Excellency, the noble Tuareg, Sheik Rassam."

"When will he meet with us?"

"*Hazzah,*" the man answered, his eyes flashing. "Do not ask the ways of a hawk!"

Ruth sighed, then lowered herself wearily to the stone floor and tried to rub the soreness from her hip. Always the same answers. The Tuaregs were playing with them as if it were a game. She closed her eyes and thought about the blond woman in the marketplace. She had not mentioned what she had seen to either James or Jon Paul. For too many years her scientific mind had trained her not to jump to conclusions. Some Tuareg women, like the men, were known to be light-skinned. Such a woman might well resemble Diana Jacobson. So we wait, and we pray, she thought, and she wondered if there was really any hope for them at all.

As Ruth fell into a restless sleep, Jon Paul stood by the window watching for activity in the ruins below. There was one black tent not far from their room that was far larger than the others. On top of its crest flew a yellow banner. Next to the tent was an area that had been cordoned off. Kneeling here were a half a dozen snow-white camels, decorated with colorful bridles and saddled with huge leather seats. Two veiled Tuaregs crouched next to them, arms folded, rifles across their laps.

In front of the opening to the tent a huge black man paced back and forth. From where Jon Paul could see into the entrance, the space inside was divided into compartments. Occasionally someone drifted past the opening but the interior was largely hidden from view.

He was thus surprised to see a procession of men emerge from the doorway and begin to wend their way up through the ruins, gradually approaching the small room in which he stood. The leader of these men was a dark, balding man with an unkempt beard, dressed in a flowing red and black striped robe. At a distance he looked like an Arab, though his gait and general carriage were different from the five men in brown robes who followed. He wore three pouches around his neck along with a foot-long object that looked green and leathery. It wasn't until they were a hundred feet away that Jon Paul recognized this latter article as the mummified body of a lizard.

"Ruth, I think we've got company," Jon Paul said.

Ruth pulled herself to her feet and stared out of the window alongside him.

"I wonder what they want?" she murmured. "The man in the striped robe is a marabout, one of the religious men, and the others must be his disciples. The small red pouches around his neck contain verses of the Koran."

She waited until the procession had disappeared around the corner of the building, then bent down and shook James by the shoulder. "Better get up," she said. "Welcoming party's here."

There was a sudden commotion outside the doorway. Suddenly the figure of the man in the flowing striped robe filled the arched passage.

Up close the priest's face seemed ageless, his cheeks and forehead burned to a reddish brown. His eyes were black yet his eyebrows and the lower portions of his beard had been so bleached by the sun that the tips were nearly blond. He strode boldly into the room and placed his hands on his hips, scrutinizing the prisoners before him.

"Parlez-vous français?" he suddenly asked.

James glanced at him with astonishment.

"Sprechen Sie Deutsch?"

"English," Ruth answered.

"Then you are British?" the priest said.

"Good Lord, you speak English?" James cried.

"I have learned a little as a boy." The bearded man nodded. His eyes shifted toward James. "Why are you here?"

James stared at him incredulously. "My God, man, we had no choice. We were brought here as prisoners."

The priest smiled. "Ah, yes." He nodded. "My apologies for the inconvenience. You see, Tuareg nobles are warriors. Their knowledge of the Koran is limited, their women unveiled, their prayer clumsy." He paused, muttering something in Arabic that James could not understand. A small piece of spittle gathered at the corner of his mouth. His voice rose. "But in the eyes of God, the most merciful, and Mohammed, His Prophet, all men are people of the desert." He smiled a wide-toothed grin. "In his divine wisdom each must be forgiven. . . ."

"We've got no war with these men," James shot back at him. "Why are we being held captive here?"

"Surely to have been captured by the Tuaregs you must have been wandering in their territory."

"Yes, we were looking for—" James started, but before he could finish Ruth had pushed in front of him.

"We had a small caravan," she said quickly. "We were at the oasis of al Jabbar, searching for ruins, evidence of the ancient people, when we were taken prisoner."

"There must be some mistake," James added.

"Mistake?" The priest snorted. "There is no mistake in the ways of Allah, the most compassionate."

"My God, Ruth," James muttered under his breath. "I think the man is mad."

The priest's eyes rolled toward James. "I am Ibrahim Razouli Mohammed el Bin, grand sharif of Bogadez, related to

Mohammed the Prophet by my father and my father's father and sixty-three fathers before. I am advisor to the Tuareg noble Sheik Rassam, and I am to tell you that he has generously offered twenty gold coins for you. The Tuareg warriors have accepted."

"Then we are to be free," Jon Paul cried.

Ibrahim wagged a cautioning finger. "That decision must be up to Rassam. He has ordered the warriors to keep you under guard until he has had a chance to interview you before the Council of Elders."

"And when might that be?" Ruth asked.

Ibrahim shrugged. "Perhaps tonight. Perhaps next week."

"Next week!" James roared. "Goddamn it man, you've no reason to hold us captive."

"My friend, be thankful that you still have tongues to speak, hands to feel, eyes to see . . ."

James glared at him angrily.

"And what might the sheik decide to do with us?" Ruth asked.

"It is not my place to even guess," Ibrahim replied. "Much will depend upon what you tell him. But I must warn you that Europeans are not welcome here. Of course, things will go better for you if you are followers of the Prophet."

"Of course." James scowled.

"Ah, then you know the Koran?"

"No, not exactly," Ruth said. She glanced at James with a frown.

Ibrahim's eye suddenly stopped at the small gold cross dangling from Ruth's neck. It was as if he had seen it for the first time. "Christians?" he said with horror. He backed slowly away. "You are Christians?"

He brought his hands up to his nose to pinch off his nostrils. "I thought I smelled a strange smell here!" he cried. Turning, he spat ferociously at them, then was gone, the air crackling with the swish of his robes.

27

With nightfall, the ruins were marked by a hundred scattered fires. The Tuaregs offered their prisoners some tasteless gruel and a skin of water. After they had eaten, James studied the open roof and eyed the veiled men crouched outside the doorway. "You know, Ruth, we could be over these walls and off in a second," he said.

Ruth reached up, tested the crumbling stone, then slowly shook her head.

"I could never make it, James. I don't think I could climb the walls easily and even if I could, I can't walk much faster than a hobble. We could hide out somewhere in the darkness but we have no weapons. In the morning they would track us down and catch us, and then we would find ourselves tied to one of those posts outside the city walls, left for the vultures. None of us is in any condition to travel now. If Diana is here we must try to find her and wait until the timing is right before we escape."

"I don't think it will make any difference," James replied. "I've got a strange feeling that we're doomed here. That no matter what they do with us, it's not going to be good."

"Wait until we've had an audience with this Sheik Rassam."

James frowned. "If you ask me, we should make it out tonight. While we've still got a chance."

"Let's try to negotiate with Rassam," Ruth argued. "See what options we have. If you and Jon Paul want to escape, I can't stop you, but I think you're foolish. You don't know where Diana is, and if she is here and alive, I don't think you want to do anything to jeopardize her safety."

James thought for a long time, staring out of the window,

inhaling the cool night air. He longed for freedom, longed to be out from beneath the harness of the Tuaregs, but he knew that what Ruth said was true. If there was any hope for them they would have to play along with the whims of their captors.

"How do you think we should approach them?" he asked.

"At this stage, I would mention nothing of Diana," Ruth answered. "We don't know if she is here or what their response to her might be if they knew you were her brother. Tell him we have come across the desert to study the ancient ruins. Historically, these desert tribes have always considered Europeans as meddlers who pry into all sorts of crazy things that do not have much importance in life. Remember, their economy is not too far above the basic essence of survival."

"And the Christianity?"

"Just play it down," Ruth answered. "Unless you can recite a couple of verses of the Koran, they would have found out sooner or later."

"James, Ruth," Jon Paul suddenly said. "Someone is coming."

There was a sound of shuffling feet and scattered voices outside the doorway. Ibrahim suddenly walked into the room. He held a flare in one hand and shone it across their faces, glaring at them.

"You are lucky, infidels," he hissed. "Rassam has called a meeting of the Council of Elders. He has requested that I bring you. May Allah be merciful."

The marabout's mission was now one of official business. Scuttling quickly, he moved along the roadway lighting the way with his flare. James, Ruth, and Jon Paul hurried after him, the three Tuareg guards bringing up the rear.

After a short walk, they came to the huge black tent that Jon Paul had noticed earlier in the day. They moved through a curtained corridor to a large compartment. At one side a fire leaped, casting the surrounding walls in flickering shadows. In these shadows sat an audience of veiled men. An aisle had been cleared between them, and Ibrahim led the prisoners forward toward a tall man resting cross-legged on a cushion in the middle of the room. He was dressed in Tuareg fashion, his head covered by a white turban and veil. He held the stem of a long curved waterpipe in one hand, huge rings sparkling from his fingers. Around his neck was a delicate gold chain that ended in a magnificent blue stone. James's eyes were immediately drawn to the luster of the gem, and he stared at it for a moment in surprise. He turned and started to whisper something to Ruth but she raised her finger to her lips for silence.

A minute passed and no one said a thing. The sheik tugged occasionally at the tip of the waterpipe, somehow managing to keep his face hidden, and watched the three prisoners reflectively. Once he turned to the side and whispered something to a comrade behind, then stared back at James, the smoke drifting out from beneath his veil.

As the minutes passed perspiration began to ooze from James's brow. He felt suddenly uncomfortable and hot, and he fought off an urge to change position. The sheik stared at him with cold, calculating eyes.

Another minute passed and still no one spoke. Abruptly, as if tired of this game, Rassam waved a finger for Ibrahim to proceed.

"Rassam is the leader of the Council of Elders," the priest said quickly. "I have explained to him that you are from lands far away and he has asked that you come here now so that the council may judge you for themselves. You may speak."

James stepped forward, glancing across the veiled faces of the audience. He had thought carefully what he would say. He knew that the council could not understand English yet he wanted to talk boldly, to present his case with dignity and firmness so that they might be impressed with his voice as well as his manner. Now, in his most articulate fashion, he began.

"I am called Jacobson," he said. "And I have been traveling in the desert with my younger brother and my good friend Dr. Parker. We have come to study the ancient ruins. There are drawings on the cliffs next to the desert that were made many hundreds of years ago, and it was near there that we were attacked by your warriors. Three of our best men were murdered in the night while they slept. We have been told that the Tuaregs fight like lions, that you are brave and noble men, not murderers. We have come to meet you, to share our ideas, to talk of the ruins and the people who inhabited these lands centuries ago.

We come from places very far away, from countries named England and America where there are people like ourselves who believe in peace and freedom. We have heard legends about how fair and great the Tuaregs are. Yet you kill our men and treat us like prisoners. We have brought no harm to you. We have come in peace and we wish to go in freedom."

As Ibrahim translated the message, Sheik Rassam leaned back and whispered with other members of the council. A wave of murmurs passed back and forth among the elders.

"His Excellency says we have experienced the Europeans before," Ibrahim translated. "Sonteg, of this council, states that his father was killed in Timbuctu by white men and Rassam has two relatives who were murdered by them. Seasons ago the Europeans brought guns to the desert, and with them a coward could kill a man with the pressure of one finger. Rassam says it is not good. There is no longer room for bravery or courage or the skill of the sword. In the past many Tuaregs have been slaughtered by European guns. And always the Europeans have come to the desert. At first they came searching for jewels and gold. Now it is oil."

"Perhaps that has been true in the past," James replied, "by the Germans or the Italians or the French. But I assure you that we are not interested in such matters now. In my country, I am like a prince. My father runs a large organization of people and has great wealth. We have no need for your jewels or your oil."

There was a moment's pause as the message was translated first to Rassam and then through whispers to the rest of the Council. The sound of faint chuckles began to surge back and forth among the veiled men.

"Why are they laughing?" Jon Paul murmured.

Ruth clenched her jaw and did not answer. A frown had worked its way across her face as Rassam spoke and Ibrahim translated.

"If it is true what you say, O son of Jacob, that you have great wealth and that you are like a prince, then where are your jewels? And why are you traveling like a vassal with few servants, an old woman, and a boy?"

"We travel alone, without pretense, because it is easier for us to study the lands of people who once lived here," James answered carefully.

A buzz of whispers flowed through the Council of Elders. Rassam turned back to James. "Our ancestors came to this city a thousand seasons ago and we traded for many winters in prosperity. Now droughts have killed our cattle. New settlements have interrupted our trade. Many of our own young men have left their families to work in the cities of the west. The Tuareg's land is gone, his life changed. Even his camels are no longer used, replaced by machines that travel across the desert with great speed. These ways are not good. In days past, we collected slaves and ruled the desert. It is to this life we have returned."

"We ask only that we be permitted to go free, to go back across the desert to our own lands," James said. "Surely, with the sheik's wisdom, he is a fair man."

"We do not want any interference from the outside," Rassam replied.

"I assure you," James answered, "if you do not let us go, my father will bring hundreds of men looking for us. You have my word that we will not interfere, if you set us free."

"Ah, son of Jacob." Rassam laughed. "See how the bird sings when faced with the fangs of a snake. No," he added slowly. "No matter what you promise, we could never trust you to keep your word. If you are telling the truth, your fate must be decided by the Council of Elders."

"There is no lie," James answered firmly.

Rassam nodded to Ibrahim. The priest rose and clapped his hands. At the sound a small boy rushed into the room carrying a woven basket. He bowed deeply toward the sheik, then turned toward the prisoners. Reaching into the basket, he pushed the lid aside and grabbed something in his fingers.

"Hold out your hand," Ibrahim commanded to Jon Paul.

"What the hell is this?" James growled.

"If there is truth among you it will be in the youngest," Ibrahim answered.

"Jon Paul—no," Ruth whispered. "Don't let him, James."

James tried to step in front of him. "I will do it," he said angrily. "I am the leader here."

"No, it's all right," Jon Paul answered firmly. "Let me show them we're telling the truth."

"Step back, infidel." Ibrahim pushed James out of the way.

"Now open your hand," he told Jon Paul. The Arab boy placed something in Jon Paul's palm then closed his fingers around it. The youth bowed to Rassam and backed a short distance away.

Jon Paul could feel a slight weight, something irregular and large. Suddenly there was a movement in his fingers that sent a primitive rush of fear up into the pit of his spine. Good God, he thought. What was it? Something alive?

He tried not to move his fingers but he could feel something burrow into his palm. Very steadily the hair began to prickle on the back of his neck. His stomach tightened into a knot and he fought off a reflex to release his bowels.

"Allah have mercy upon you." Ibrahim smiled. "You may open your hand."

Jon Paul's eyes dilated. A surge of fluid rushed up into the back of his throat. He swallowed hard and stared at his hand in horror.

In the flickering light was the largest scorpion any of them had ever seen, poised on the edge of Jon Paul's palm, stinger up, ready to drive its venom into the soft fleshy portion of his hand.

Thick beads of moisture began to pour off his brow. The scorpion turned and waddled across his palm. When it reached his fingers it stopped, backed up, and rotated again, working its way around the islands of flesh. With every movement of its feet, Jon Paul could feel a shock of repulsion. He watched with growing terror as the scorpion found the bridge of his wrist and began to crawl up his arm. He calculated in his mind what he would have to do to flick it off but he knew there was no way he could move fast enough. Sweat stung into his eyes and his heart fluttered inside his chest.

"You're all right," Ruth whispered in his ear. "Be cool, try to stay as still as you can."

As the scorpion reached the midportion of his wrist, it stopped and made a complete circle probing the fine hairs on his skin. Moving slowly, it waddled toward his forearm. A shiver ran through his body. The scorpion froze, sensing movement. Its tail raised, its stinger cocked like a harpoon.

"Steady, Jon Paul. For God's sake, steady," James said between clenched teeth.

Beads of perspiration rolled down across Jon Paul's eyes and past his nose, working their way toward the corners of his lips. With all his will, he concentrated on his hand. Slowly the tremor stopped. Moving cautiously, the scorpion sidled, crablike, back to his palm.

"You got him," James whispered. "By God, you got him!" He looked up triumphantly at Rassam. "See, we have told the truth. There is no lie."

James heard the faintest *whiff* out of the side of his ear, like a gentle tuft of wind spit out between pursed lips. Ibrahim had maneuvered himself in between Rassam and Jon Paul. The priest was bent slightly forward. The tiniest bit of moisture shot out of his mouth. The scorpion was now poised on the base of Jon Paul's palm. A drop of spittle landed on its back. With a sudden whipping motion, the insect raised on its hind legs and drove its stinger home.

James was so surprised at first he could not move. Jon Paul stared at his hand in disbelief. A moment passed before a sharp burning fire ran like electricity up his forearm. Twisting violently, he shook the insect from his arm, his voice raising in an agonizing cry. At the same instant James launched across the space towards Ibrahim. "You scum-sucking bastard," he roared. His hands were at the priest's throat, his fingers choking him to the ground.

28

As had been his custom for the past forty years, Ian Anderson, Director of the Nairobi Museum, rose at 6 A.M. that fine Tuesday morning and spent the first twenty minutes of daylight sitting at a table, glancing through the front page of a day-old London *Times*. His breakfast consisted of a single soft-boiled egg, two pieces of toast buttered lightly, and a cup of strong Darjeeling tea. This menu had never varied as long as Mbuta, his houseboy, had known him. Other than a customary good morning in Swahili, there had been little verbal communication between them and now Mbuta hovered attentively, waiting for a nod or a motion from the bwana to bring him another cup of tea.

The director was a tall, thin man with white hair and a thick mustache that he stroked from time to time, whenever he was deep in thought. His face, well tanned from countless hours in the sun, looked considerably younger than his sixty-nine years.

Once satisfied that he had gleaned all the significant news from *The Times*, he turned to a large folder and began to shift through a stack of correspondence. A letter from the University of Rome inviting him to give a guest lecture caught his eye. Rome was marvelous in the springtime, he reflected, and then he remembered that the new chief of the University's Anthropology Division was an opinionated Italian who had argued with him for years about the dating of early man in East Africa. On the one hand, it would be a vacation in a city rich in the world's greatest art. On the other, he would have to constantly defend his theories against the rapier-sharp tongue of Dr. Pietro Iaconetti. No, he thought, Rome is for travel and relaxation,

not for work. He scratched "reject" on the side of the letter and
placed it in a pile destined for negative replies.

He next read a letter from London. One of his old colleagues
had written inviting him back to a class reunion. He reminisced
briefly about his days of study at Cambridge. Without particular emotion he wondered what distinction there would be in
becoming the last living member of the class of Twenty-nine. A
grim smile broke across his lips. Maybe then he could invite
himself to his own bloody reunion.

Reading quickly, he scanned through half a dozen other letters, some requests for speaking engagements, others inquiring
about various aspects of his research. This finished, he turned
his attention to a sheaf of papers that made up a chapter of a
book he was writing on the migration of Nilo-Hamitic tribes
into East Africa. For the next hour he went over the chapter
making small notations in the margins until the wording met
with his approval. He then dressed, collected his dog, and left
the house for his usual morning walk.

Anderson lived on fifteen acres of beautiful grassland just
outside the city of Nairobi. Occasionally small groups of antelope still wandered through his property, and on this particular
morning he saw a herd of six Thomson's gazelles. He approached them carefully, trying to keep his dog close at heel,
but they picked up his scent and bounded away, their smooth
brown shapes leaping through the grasses like a school of
porpoises.

As he followed the narrow path he breathed in the fresh
morning air and thought about what he had read in the paper.
How difficult it must be to live in a place like London, where
one had to worry about the daily fluctuation of the pound, or
the latest parliamentary scandal, or the most recent strike of
factory workers. There was a time when such news made him
angry but now, with age, he had slowly come to realize that the
cities with all their evil still brought forth a considerable
amount of good. That was why, he guessed, he had never quite
been able to give up reading the *Times*. Just find yourself a
niche and stick to it. At least, that was what Ruth Parker had
always said, and he smiled at the thought of her, "the feisty old
wench." How in the hell she thought she could leap into a

Land-Rover with some Americans and go into the Sudan looking for a lost girl and a legendary oasis was beyond him. She'd
left a desk full of work, half of which he had been forced to
complete for her. He'd scolded her sharply before she left, but
as usual, she wouldn't listen to him at all.

It reminded him of the time she'd gone on a camel safari with
two German rock hunters down in Tanzania, then called Tan-
ganyika. She'd been rather naive and the Germans had approached her with all kinds of crazy stories about diamonds
that were so plentiful they could be plucked like hen's eggs from
the ground.

They'd come back in a month, half dead with malaria and
dysentery, and they hadn't found a single gem; and what had
she done? She'd discovered an old stone fortress that nobody
had known existed. She promptly wrote a report that she later
presented to the Royal Geographic Society with proof that the
early African civilizations were much more advanced than anyone had imagined. But then she'd been young and strong and
bold. Now she was just plain crazy.

He was returning on the homeward leg of his walk, the
springer spaniel out in front, lunging across the path, when he
heard Mbuta honking the horn of his Land-Rover. Damn it, he
thought. He had been daydreaming and had slipped behind on
his morning schedule. Moving quickly, he hurried to the house,
locked the dog in its kennel, and joined his servant in the Land-
Rover.

"You'll be late, bwana," the black man said, patting the side
of his watch.

"You're right. Thanks for reminding me."

They turned down the long driveway that ran for half a mile
before it joined a two-lane Tarmac road. From there it was
twenty-two miles to Nairobi.

"*Swala uji,*" Anderson said. "Antelope today."

"Oh, how many?" came the reply in Swahili.

"Three big ones and three small."

"Ah, maybe they're coming out onto the plains with the
spring rain. Remember, bwana, when the herds used to be here
all the time, not so long ago? And before that, when I was a

boy, my father used to say there were hundreds there where you have your house."

Anderson did not answer. A man's lifetime was not so long in the geological time of things, but Africa was changing fast and certain things were disappearing quickly. Like the elephants, he thought. Herds measuring fifteen thousand twenty years ago, down to a thousand now and in some places nearly gone. The price of civilization again. The biggest animals in the oceans practically extinct. Now maybe the same fate for the biggest animals on the land.

Half an hour later, they were stalled at an intersection along the outskirts of Nairobi. For fifteen minutes they waited for the morning traffic to clear.

"There's progress," Anderson cursed. "That's the trade. A herd of a dozen gazelle for a traffic jam of a hundred cars."

"Not getting better, bwana," Mbuta answered. "Maybe you should do like Memsaab Parker. Memsaab says that she never drives these roads during the traffic hour. She says she would rather be late than have to drive in heavy traffic."

Anderson's eyebrows rose at the mention of his colleague. "And when did she tell you that?"

"Two, three weeks ago. Shortly before Lasiri took them on safari."

"That's why she's always late?"

"Memsaab says that many times she beat you to the museum."

"Ha!" Anderson snorted, winking at Mbuta. "Memsaab's memory gone. Her brain addled."

"Black or white, women all the same." Mbuta laughed.

When they pulled into the museum at eight thirty, there was another Land-Rover in the driveway.

"Hello, what's this?" Anderson exclaimed.

"Visitors, bwana," Mbuta answered.

"Look, isn't that one of the expedition trucks? By Christ, are they back already?"

As Anderson got out of his vehicle, two of the expedition men were waiting for him.

"Yes, what is it? What's happened?" Anderson cried.

Mabruka Hassan, a tall angular man hired by Lasiri as one of the "diggers," handed Anderson a sealed letter. "This from Memsaab Parker," he said in Swahili. "Memsaab say they no return in seven days, we come to you for help."

Anderson took the envelope, opened the letter, and read it quickly. He then sat the two men from the expedition down and made them tell him exactly what had happened. When they repeated the story for the second time he paused, stroking his mustache, deep in concentration. Fools, he thought. Damned, stupid, bloody fools. Trying to cross the desert on foot. The whole thing sounded insane. It was as if they had been struck with *le cafard,* the desert madness.

It would take him at least two to three days to outfit a caravan and then five days of steady driving to reach al Jabbar. Another week lost. Not to mention the fact that the museum had little funds for this type of expedition. . . . No, that wasn't smart, he thought. There was only one way to adequately search the area. He moved quickly to the telephone, his fingers trembling.

29

It was the beginning of the third hour of sunlight that morning when Ruth Parker looked out of the small stone window of their prison and saw Ibrahim and his retinue of priests emerge from the great tent of Sheik Rassam. In addition to his usual disciples, the marabout was accompanied by half a dozen armed Tuareg warriors. They advanced at a steady pace toward the room in which Ruth and the others were held captive. Had she much of a sense of humor, Ruth might have thought that Ibrahim and his robed followers resembled sheep, scurrying along the pathway while the taller, veiled nomads looked like shepherds ambling leisurely along. As it was, however, she was most displeased to see the priest. Undoubtedly he was bringing them the final verdict of the Council of Elders, and the armed procession that followed did not promise good news.

She turned back into the room. "Ibrahim's coming," she said to James. Jon Paul was lying in the corner feverish and delirious. Once during the night when the youth's pulse had shot up to one hundred eighty and his forehead felt hot enough to explode, Ruth had been afraid they were going to lose him. She had gone outside and persuaded one of the Tuareg guards to give her a moistened cloth. For the rest of the night she and James had taken turns wiping water across Jon Paul's brow. As morning approached he seemed to be resting more comfortably, the periods of unconsciousness briefer. Yet he still was extremely sick. His arm was swollen and only occasionally was he coherent enough to recognize his surroundings.

"Allah akbar, akbar Allah!" Ibrahim announced with a bow. "God is great, great is God. My apologies for an uncomfortable night, but you must understand in the court of Sheik Rassam the only reaction to lies is punishment."

James stared at him from the corner of the room. "Go fuck yourself," he growled.

If Ibrahim heard this, he disregarded it entirely. "I have good news, my friends. The council has judged and Rassam's recommendations have been approved."

"Good news?" James grunted at him. "I doubt there is such a word in your vocabulary."

"Ah, yes, his Excellency has been most merciful. Your lives have been spared. Think of it, my friends. There is hope for you. The council has decreed that you be sold as slaves."

"Slaves?" The words came to James like the pounding of a judge's gavel. Only it was the sentence of a crazed and insane jury for a crime they did not commit.

"Good Lord, man, can't you see my brother is sick? He needs medical attention. Are you going to let him die?"

Ibrahim shook his head. "He will live. The test of truth is to determine the lie, not the punishment." Ibrahim paused to smile. "The punishment is left up to the Council of Elders."

James edged toward the priest, his eyes flaring. "What kind of bullshit is this?"

"You'll not get away with this," Ruth added. "There will be people coming to search for us."

Ibrahim backed carefully away. "Ah, it is always difficult to teach old dogs," he said. "Even now the taint of the barbarians comes through. The Prophet has said: 'Beware of the savage for one virtue may hide a thousand sins.'"

"You're lucky I didn't kill you last night." James scowled at him.

Ibrahim waved a cautioning finger. "Take care, infidel. One more outburst like that and you will all be killed. When they pulled you off me, Rassam could have had you executed. I would advise you to follow the orders of the Council of Elders."

He turned briskly to Jon Paul.

"You, young man, if you have not learned too many ill manners from the infidel, should bring a good price at the market. Once you recover there is much good fortune for a strong boy like you."

"And you, old woman," the priest said, moving up to Ruth and eyeing her as if she were a goat. "I would hope you might find a master in need of carrying water or bringing supplies from the market. But I fear you would not be such a good purchase for one wanting children, eh?" He laughed.

Ruth glared at him, her eyes filled with disgust.

"And you, infidel," Ibrahim said, regarding James cautiously. "You say you are like a prince in your country yet you act like a barbarian. Perhaps there is still some hard work left in you, eh? Rassam has ordered that you be sold to one of the salt caravans. There at least, in your last days, you might see the light of the Prophet. Be thankful and embrace Allah into your heart."

"Bastard," James hissed at him.

"Come, come," Ibrahim said. "You've been given your lives. What fairer sentence could you ask? Had it been me, I assure you the outcome would have been much different."

He stood for a moment sneering triumphantly at the captives. After intoning *"Allah akbar, el Hamid Allah!* God the greatest, praise be to God!" He bowed and then disappeared.

As they were led to the marketplace that morning, Jon Paul had never felt so sick in his life. Ruth had fashioned a crude sling for his arm from a piece of cloth and he staggered after them as if in a drunken stupor. He smelled the tightness of the air, choked with dust and flooded with the pungent odors of dried and decaying foods, and he gasped for air. James walked next to him, trying to keep his brother on his feet. Ruth studied the hundreds of different faces—Arabs, Moors, Berbers, veiled Tuaregs—and she heard the sound of a dozen guttural tongues. Jon Paul half dead. The three of them taken to the market to be sold as slaves. She felt like a sleepwalker going through the motions of a surrealistic dream.

They were brought up to a low platform in the center of the market and placed in a roped enclosure. A huge crowd had already gathered in front of the platform, where a group of young black girls were being auctioned off. Stripped to the waist, some barely showing more than the first blush of puberty, they looked no more than twelve or thirteen years old.

The girls stood like sheep, their wide dark eyes shifting fearfully through the crowd. Amid hoots and catcalls from the audience, they were sold one by one until the platform was empty.

James watched the auction with revulsion. The audience's display of inhumanity was something he had never witnessed before. Arabs at the front of the crowd stepped forward and poked the girls' private parts with sticks or fingered their small nipples. Some grabbed their mouths and opened their lips to assess their teeth. The young girls whimpered or cried at these examinations, yet the greater the indignity, the more the crowd shouted and cheered.

As the last young girl was led from the platform sobbing, James was startled by motion beside him. One of the Tuaregs singled out Jon Paul and began to push him forward with his lance. There was a sudden commotion and then a loud yell. The sound of a slap was followed by Jon Paul's voice in a moan.

"Let him be!" James roared. He leaped forward only to find his path blocked by three of the Tuaregs.

Ibrahim pushed in next to him. "The infidel has bitten a man."

"I hope he drew blood!" James cried, but the next thing that happened made his pulse leap wildly and a rush of panic surge into his mind.

Jon Paul emerged between two of the warriors, pushed up onto the platform. A short rope had been twisted around the boy's neck and was now held by one of the Tuaregs.

James looked around wildly, searching for a gun, a spear, anything he could grab. As he tried to clear a pathway around himself, the guards moved in closer and held him back.

There came a shout again from one of the Tuaregs. Jon Paul had kicked him in the leg. The second Tuareg squeezed the rope around Jon Paul's neck until he doubled forward, his face turning blue.

"You're going to kill him!" James yelled. "By God, give him air!" He struggled forward only to be knocked back again by one of the guards.

A strange silence came over the crowd: The Tuareg behind Jon Paul carefully loosened the rope and let him inhale, yet kept a grip on the line so the instant Jon Paul tried to fight he could tighten the noose. The boy gasped for breath. Very slowly the color began to return to his face. Two Tuaregs now climbed up on the platform and stripped his clothes away so that he was standing completely naked. He pulled himself upright, trying to hide the manliness of his penis with his good arm.

A dozen robed Arabs came forward and felt Jon Paul's legs. Others pinched his biceps and tested the muscles of his neck. One man pulled away his hand so that he could view the genitalia. Jon Paul stood passively through this inspection without flinching.

A bald Arab in a dusty robe leaped upon the platform and rattled off an introduction to the crowd. James looked to Ruth for a translation, but before she could begin, the bidding had commenced. Members of the crowd moved forward, inspected his brother, called a price, then argued back and forth among themselves. In ten minutes the auction of Jon Paul Jacobson was over. A tall man with a heavy beard won the bidding. The new owner clapped his hands and three of his men scurried up the platform and pulled Jon Paul down.

"A fair price," Ibrahim exclaimed. "Eight blocks of salt. The boy is lucky. He has been bought by a rich trader with a harem."

A terrible frown pushed its way across James's face. I've got to do something, he thought. I can't let this happen to us. He watched Jon Paul being pulled off the platform then heard a cry of pain as someone hit him across the cheek.

Suddenly Jon Paul pushed one of the Tuaregs away, freed his injured arm, and struck another in the jaw. For a moment he was free. "James, help me!" he yelled. "They're splitting us up!"

The words echoed in James's mind like an explosion. Moving quickly, he kicked one of the nomads in the groin. Ramming his right fist into another's face, he could feel teeth splinter beneath his knuckles. He threw Ibrahim aside with a glancing blow and rushed through the crowd toward Jon Paul.

But there were too many of them. Before he could reach Jon Paul they had pulled him down and knocked him senseless with their rifles.

As consciousness returned to James for the last time, he had no idea where he was or how much time had passed. He knew that he'd been badly beaten, for every fiber in his body seemed to ache. A terrible aroma of rotting meat came up to his nostrils. When he tried to move his hand, he found he was tied securely. The pain in his body was replaced by a growing, pounding ache in his neck. He stared wildly around trying to see where he was. Each time he opened his eyes, stinging beads of sweat trickled into the corners of his lids. Very slowly, he began to understand. He was fastened to a pole on the outskirts of the walls of the city and he was hanging *upside down.*

A herd of camels passed down the roadway in front of him. Far in the distance he could see the shallow waters of the oasis. Two women walked toward him, water gourds balanced on their heads. They peered at him, halting momentarily, then fearfully hurried on.

An hour passed. Flies buzzed around his head, lit on his face, dug into the corners of his eyes, and drove him practically insane. Spasms of fever racked his body, carrying his mind into a realm of bizarre and hideous dreams that left him weak and exhausted.

Sometime later, whether in a dream or awake, he could not remember, Ibrahim and his retinue of priests came down and stood in a semicircle, studying him carefully.

"May your last moment be in comfort," Ibrahim said. "Remember that the Prophet has said that only through suffering may one find the Promised Land."

"May you rot in hell," James snarled back at him.

The religious men stood watching him for a time, whispering among themselves. Finally they turned and hurried back toward the city.

Time passed slowly, ten minutes like an hour. During the hottest part of the afternoon, when the temperature soared to one hundred twenty degrees, when the perspiration evaporated off his body before it could even form as beads of sweat, an old beggar covered in a black robe came up to him. As he peered over at him to determine if he was alive, James could see that his eyes were blue and his hair a silvery white. Then—or was he dreaming?—the beggar very gently poured some water onto his lips. There was some shouting, and he heard the sound of hoofs as a caravan of camels approached. The beggar quickly turned and scurried off down the pathway.

When James opened his eyes again the man was gone and there was another caravan of slaves coming up past the oasis toward the city. He could remember when they were brought in like these prisoners, with ropes strung around their necks. He had stared at the bodies fastened to the stakes on the outskirts of the city with horror. And now? Good God, he thought. Now I'm one of them.

The shadow of a huge bird swept over him, circled once, then drifted lower. A second shadow glided past and then a third. He heard the sharp rasping cry of a vulture somewhere overhead. Behind him was the soft flutter of huge wings, and he knew they had come for him.

He could remember everything clearly now. He knew where he was and who he was and what had happened and he realized, finally, that this was the end of the line.

A Tuareg on a camel broke away from the caravan and rode toward him. The camel stopped a few feet away and the man stared down at James, surprised to find a white man tied to a

stake usually reserved for murderers and thieves. But such were
the laws of Bogadez. He shrugged, turned his camel back, and
trotted to join the rest of the caravan.

James watched him go and felt a rush of dizziness. This time
he knew consciousness would not return. It was as if he were
floating on the edge of a maelstrom, drawn steadily inward,
each rotation carrying him faster and faster toward a swirling
bottomless abyss. "Well, this is it," he told himself. "Just close
your eyes and hope the end will come quickly. . . ."

At dusk the hyenas began to cackle and gurgle at the outskirts of the city. Soon they were moving in their ugly, sloping
gait, following the edge of the wall toward the area where they
had often found something to eat. One of them gave a yelp as it
discovered a body tied to a stake. The others slunk in behind it,
approaching cautiously, for the smell of the humans was still
strong there.

The largest of the hyenas moved away from the pack and
approached the man, advancing one foot at a time, until its
thick, tearing jaws were only inches away. As the hyena
watched, it could see no sign of life. With a surge of hunger, it
started for the man, its jaws reaching for the soft open portion
of the neck when a sudden movement caught its eye. The animal spun around, saw a dark figure dart out of the shadows and
glide along the stone wall leading up from the oasis. A second
figure moved without a sound, drifting and blending with the
darkness, and now a fresh scent came to the hyena. A rock
zinged across the waning evening sky, catching the hyena in the
flank and sending it howling away. The rest of the pack backed
off, retreating into the shadows.

Since dusk these two figures had moved cautiously. At times
they had stopped for five minutes, sometimes ten, gliding from
one dark spot to the next, each time halting to listen. Their
approach was so stealthy that once a group of women coming
up from the waterhole had passed within a few feet of them
without noticing their presence. Just before dark a camel carrying a Tuareg rider had smelled them and, for a moment, as they
hid in the shadows, they thought they would have to leap out

and kill the rider. But the Tuareg had pulled his camel back and continued on the pathway toward the ancient city.

Shadows of the night flooded steadily into the oasis. Now they moved quickly, gliding out from the wall to the pole onto which James was tied. Strong hands cut the ropes that bound his hands and feet. Gentle fingers caught him as he slumped to the ground. There was a quick feeling for a pulse at the neck and an audible sigh.

"Thank God! He's still alive."

With a grunt one of the men, a giant, picked up the unconscious form and slung it over his shoulders. Then, crouching with their heavy burden, they slipped off into the shadows and were gone.

30

Earlier that same afternoon, Ruth Parker, age fifty-seven, Caucasian female with a Ph.D. from Cambridge University, was sold in the market of Bogadez as a slave. She was purchased with little bidding by an elderly Arab who lived with his brother and half a dozen wives in a modest tent on the outskirts of the ruins. (The actual price was bid at half a camel, though no one was exactly sure how this would be paid.) During the first night of slavery she was ordered to undress in front of these two men. They poked and examined her body, laughing at the recklessness of their purchase, but from that time on she suffered no further indignities at their hands. In twenty-four hours she had cast off her civilized clothes, and now, wearing a desert robe, she had become an integral member of the Arab's family.

The duties expected of her were simple. At the light of dawn, she was to accompany two older women down to the oasis to collect water. This was brought back to the tent in a large gourd, which she had to learn to balance on her head. In the evening she repeated this task. On the following day she was permitted to go into the market to help carry back some of the brothers' supplies. She was never allowed to travel alone. Whenever she left the tent she was accompanied by at least two other women. Although she constantly thought about escape, she began to realize it would be nearly impossible for her to get away.

Yet the beginning of slavery was much easier for Ruth than she had expected. There was water for bathing, ample food for the evening meal, and as long as she performed her duties she was left pretty much to herself. Her fate could have been much worse. She could have been treated like one of the young black girls the brothers had purchased. Throughout the night Ruth had listened to her pitiful moans as the two men took their pleasures, and for the first time in her life Ruth was glad that she was no longer young and attractive. Once, when she heard the girl cry out in pain, then sob hysterically, she had longed for a knife, to try to kill these men. Yet her common sense was too strong. To live, she realized, she must follow the rules and learn the habits of her captors. She might hate them, but no matter what happened, she must be patient and survive.

And then something happened that placed a new urgency upon her escape. During the second night she was curled up beneath a blanket in the back of the tent, trying to sleep, when an old woman shuffled into the room. "You will come with me," she said in Arabic.

Ruth got up and followed obediently. The woman moved outside the tent and out across the ruins so quickly that Ruth almost had to run to keep up with her.

They passed a huge tent that Ruth thought might be Sheik Rassam's, then stopped at a smaller adjacent enclosure. Ruth was ushered into a chamber blocked off by hanging carpets, illuminated by a dim oil light.

"You will wait here," the old woman whispered. She turned and quickly disappeared.

As the minutes passed Ruth's fears mounted. Had she been brought there for some special retribution? There was no way of knowing what to expect from Rassam or Ibrahim. The Moslems never had much tolerance for other faiths, especially Christianity. It would be like them, she thought, to devise some devilish torture for her.

Nearly half an hour passed before Ruth heard a rustle from the blanketed passage. She turned to find a slender figure had stepped into the chamber behind her. She could see in the dim light the glint of a woman's blond hair.

"Ruth? Ruth, can that be you?" the woman whispered tentatively.

"Diana . . . Diana Jacobson!" Ruth exclaimed. "Thank God you're still alive."

There was a sudden noise from somewhere in the hidden confines of the tent. Diana placed her finger to her lips and froze. A moment passed and there was no further sound.

"We don't have much time," she said quickly. "If you're caught here, you'll be killed."

"How did you ever find me?" Ruth asked.

"They said three Caucasians were brought down to the slave market. One was described as an older woman with red hair. I had to take a chance."

"Is the Arab woman safe?"

"She's a slave," Diana replied. "I told her to bring you here on the orders of Rassam."

Ruth pulled back and stared at Diana with concern. Something's wrong, she thought. Something's odd in the way she looks at me and turns her head. "Have they been treating you well?" she asked.

"I've been kept in the harem of Sheik Rassam. It's safe here. But how did they capture you?"

"We came across the desert searching for you."

"*We?*"

"Then you don't know!" Ruth exclaimed. "I came with your brothers, James and Jon Paul."

"My brothers . . . here?" Diana gasped. She was visibly shaken. Tears suddenly welled up in her eyes.

"We've come to take you home," Ruth said firmly. "To help you escape."

Diana shook her head. "When they first captured me I knew I could never leave alive. No one has. The Tuaregs patrol every mountain pass, survey every route across the desert. They sweep down at night in raiding parties and murder or enslave everyone in sight.

"On the outskirts of Bogadez there is a tribe of people who live in caves. I'm told the nomads are afraid of them. If you could make it there, perhaps you could find safety."

"Then you will come with me," Ruth replied. "We could get away."

"No," Diana answered slowly. "I can never go back."

"What are you saying?" Ruth cried.

"It is because . . . because of this," Diana answered. She leaned forward toward the light so that Ruth could see her face. Reaching upward, she unfastened her veil. As the thin cloth dropped away, her long golden hair fell down around her shoulders.

Ruth stared at her incredulously. A sudden gush of emotion clouded over the anthropologist's eyes.

"Oh, Diana . . . oh, no!" She gasped. Moving forward, she took the younger woman in her arms. They stood for a moment, embraced, both quietly sobbing.

"How could they do this to you?" Ruth murmured softly. "God, tell me how it happened."

31

It was eleven o'clock at night. Michael Jacobson was sitting in the plush Golden Carpet executive waiting room in the International Terminal of Kennedy Airport in New York. Next to him were businessmen, one German couple, and an assortment of others waiting for European flights. He glanced impatiently at his watch, then finished the remains of his third cup of coffee. He hadn't smoked in nearly twenty years, yet at times like this, he could still feel that nervous edge that made his fingers twitch for the comfort of a cigarette. A steward approached him.

"Mr. Jacobson, your flight is ready, sir."

He nodded and stood up. The flight had been delayed for half an hour because of an engine problem. As usual, he had insisted that he be the last to board. The night operations officer for TransOceanic Airlines held out his hand.

"Here's for good luck, Mr. Jacobson."

Michael Jacobson managed a grim smile and turned toward the door. The steward pressed up beside him.

"Sir, I must warn you that there are some reporters outside."

Jacobson frowned. "Is there any way to avoid them?"

"I'm afraid not, sir. You'll have to cross about a hundred and fifty feet of the main concourse before entering the restricted passenger zone."

"Well, let's get it over with," Jacobson said. He lowered his head like a bull and plunged out the door.

In an instant he was surrounded, flashbulbs exploding in his eyes, his ears bombarded with a myriad of questions, all asked at the same time. He cursed under his breath and held up his hand, realizing there was no way to escape them.

"Gentlemen, I have a plane to catch!" he shouted, but his voice was lost in a cacophony of interrogations.

"Is there any word on your daughter? Is it true that your two sons have disappeared? Are you leaving for Nairobi tonight? We understand there have been some new border skirmishes along the Sudan. Have they any relationship to your sons' disappearance?"

"Gentlemen! Gentlemen, please!" Jacobson yelled. "One at a time."

He started down the concourse. He would have to put up with several minutes of questioning before he could exit through the special boarding gate to the waiting aircraft. Six and a half hours to Paris, another four to Athens. A change of planes and then seven hours to Nairobi. With a little luck, a refueling stop, he should be on the ground in East Africa within twenty-four hours.

He began walking briskly forward, the reporters hovering around him.

A man in a trenchcoat pushed in front of him. "Mr. Jacobson, what was the reaction of your family to your sons' disappearance?"

"We were, of course, very concerned."

"Has there been any recent news?" another reporter asked.

"No, nothing of significant value."

"Has the State Department offered any assistance?"

"Yes, they've been extremely helpful."

"And what are your plans, sir?"

"A lot of it will depend upon the situation in Nairobi."

"But certainly you will be organizing a search party?"

"I'm not sure yet. We've been kept apprised daily by the American Embassy. I plan to go and offer what assistance I can. The embassy has been working with the director of the Nairobi Museum, who helped coordinate a portion of my sons' expedition."

"Do you have any idea where they are?"

"Yes, we think we have a good approximation."

"Will the American government be involved?"

"Well, let me say at this point I'm not sure my sons are lost. They had a checkpoint designated in the Sudan and a certain time frame in which they were supposed to return. There has been no word. I hope to cover every possibility in the event that they may have run into trouble. Other than that, there is nothing else I can tell you."

"And your daughter, Mr. Jacobson? Do you feel there is any chance she is still alive?"

"Yes, of course, there is always hope." Jacobson stared at the newsman with a frown. Why were some of the press so tasteless, so insensitive, in their search for a story? He felt like a rabbit pursued by a pack of hounds.

At last he was at the gate. He turned and slipped through a narrow opening. An official from the airport wrapped a chain behind him blocking the press from going further. There was a parting flurry of questions and then all of the noise and commotion seemed to fade in the background. Ahead, the sleek white fuselage of the 747 loomed in the darkness. The beam from the airport tower flashed across the plane, reflecting off the cockpit windshield.

The pilot glanced down, recognized Jacobson, and waved him a salute. They were ready to launch. The high-pitched whine of electrical power started up. The lights on the plane dimmed, then surged brightly. Far out on the runway came the thunder of an airliner as it lifted off the ground.

He looked back once, as if to be sure he was safely away from his pursuers, then turned and disappeared up the ramp onto the waiting plane. In twenty minutes the *Golden Eagle,* flagship for TransOceanic Airlines, was taxiing down the runway, its engines roaring.

32

Shortly before dawn the old woman escorted Ruth Parker back to her tent. When morning came she accompanied the two Arab women on their usual trip to the oasis, her mind spinning with what she had seen. Steadily she began to give up all hope that any of them would ever get out alive. Though she did not mention it to Diana, she was sure James was dead. Jon Paul might be healthy, wherever he was, but he was certainly unable to help Ruth escape. And Diana? What she had seen made Ruth bite her lip to keep back the tears. It was far better that James never knew. No, she thought. If she meant to escape, she would have to make it on her own.

She was pondering these thoughts, filling her gourd in the shallow water, when she heard one of the Arab women speak about a caravan to the north.

"What?" Ruth interrupted with alarm.

The two women stared at her and laughed. "Of course," one answered. "We will be leaving soon."

"But where?" Ruth asked cautiously.

"To the summer pastures."

"And is that far?"

They laughed at her again, realizing how naive she was.

"Two moons' travel," one answered.

"When will you go?"

"You mean when will *we* go?" the woman corrected her. "Soon, very soon."

As she walked back from the oasis, Ruth mentally calculated the distance of two moons' travel. If they went by camel and they averaged twenty miles a day, in two moons' travel they could cover a thousand miles. And now a fact that she had somehow overlooked came upon her with sudden clarity. All of the nomads gathered in Bogadez would be leaving soon. It was time for the seasonal change. The current inhabitants lived in tents, traveling back and forth between points widely scattered across the desert. In a matter of days they would all be gone.

Sixty days across the desert! Ruth was not sure she could survive such a trip. But what was worse was the fact that they would be split up. Jon Paul might be taken in one direction and Diana in another. Ruth knew she could not afford to wait any longer. But how could she escape? And which way to run? And alone, what were her chances for success?

During the afternoon Ruth found a large blanket in the Arabs' tent and hid it away. That evening she accompanied the two older women back to the oasis, this time carrying the blanket beneath her robes. If she could get away that night, she would need warmth. The blanket at least could offer some protection.

Stepping into the shallow water, she searched desperately around the oasis. Two herders were watering a flock of sheep. Beyond that a single man covered in a hooded robe lounged next to one of the palms where a herd of camels knelt down to drink. Further still, a group of nomads huddled around a fire. A quarter of a mile away a caravan was wending its way in toward the city.

She waited until the two women had filled their gourds and then started back toward the ruins after them. If she waited much longer she might lose her chance forever.

Just inside the city walls, she found her opportunity. As the women turned a corner, a stone foundation blocked them from

view. Ruth suddenly dropped her gourd and fled. She heard
angry cries and shouts behind her. She tried to run faster, picking her way through a section of the crumbling ramparts, but
her hip began to hurt terribly and the best she could manage
was an awkward hobble.

A mile ahead she could see a field of jagged irregular boulders. Beyond that the canyon stretched out toward the mountains. Safety in the caves, she thought. If she could only make it
to the canyon.

Suddenly her heart leaped into her throat. A Tuareg mounted
on a camel, his sword drawn, was advancing toward her,
searching through the ruins. She shrank back against the stone,
crouching down, not daring to move. His shadow slid across
the wall behind her. The camel stopped. For a moment there
was no sound.

No way out, she thought. If they catch me now, I'm dead.
She ducked around a corner and started across the ruins when
her hip gave way. She fell head over heels, her legs skidding out
from beneath her on the loose rock. Somehow she managed to
regain her feet, then found the safety of a crevice and darted for
shelter.

She heard a noise behind her, turned and let out a startled
scream as the blade of a sword smashed against the rock next to
her head. She groped backward, trying to get out of the way of
the camel. The Tuareg spun around, raising his sword in a wide
curving arc. Ruth tried desperately to run. The camel lurched
forward, almost trampling her in its turn. She saw the sword
flash and raised her arms protectively, waiting helplessly for the
blow. There was a solid thump then a moan. She looked up
with surprise to see the Tuareg sink past her, falling to the
ground. A huge stone bounced away between her feet.

The camel reared, snorted, then backed away as a hooded
figure moved forward from behind a thick section of wall. He
had intense blue eyes and silvery hair and was dressed in the
tattered rags of a beggar.

"Better put some wind in yer sail, sister," he said. "We've got
some rough waters to cross."

PART IV

Those who are dead are dead, those who have left have left. A few have managed to escape and never returned. Those who stay have been forgotten by God.

Dawda saying

33

The sun had begun its final descent, sinking rapidly behind the desert mountains, as Ruth Parker hurried across the last open section of sand. The ruins were behind them. Ahead was a narrow pathway that led toward the canyon walls. Ruth had traveled this distance breathing heavily, trying desperately to keep up with the ragged figure in front of her. Moving with amazing agility, the man darted around scattered boulders, using his crutch like an extra leg.

Finally she halted, gasping for breath. "I must stop to rest."

The beggar nodded, shinnied up to the top of a huge rock, and searched the area behind them.

"It's all right, sister. I think we're clear of them now."

He turned, scanning up along the steep rock walls. Bringing his fingers to his lips, he made a sharp whistle. Ruth saw a movement high upon the cliffs as a small brown monkey scampered down the face of the rock and disappeared behind a ledge. Abruptly it reappeared with a flying leap to the beggar's shoulder.

"Evening, Alabaster," the man said.

"Who are *you?*" Ruth gasped.

He leaned forward on his wooden crutch and gave a little bow. "I, sister, am Isaiah. Shipwrecked on this godforsaken desert for the last seven years, and this is me monk, Alabaster."

"But why did you help me?"

"Ah, now that's a captain's secret—eh?" He winked. "Come along now, we've got to get moving before they think to follow you here."

He climbed down from the boulder, the monkey clinging to his shoulder, and started along the pathway. Ruth hobbled after him, trying not to fall behind.

"We're a fine pair, sister." He laughed. "Look like two sailors out of sick bay, me with my crutch and you with your limp, and all."

"You look strong enough to me."

"Oh, I get around okay," Isaiah said. He reached up and scratched Alabaster on the chin and was rewarded with a series of chirping sounds. "Actually, we was planning to break you out in a couple of days but the opportunity looked pretty good back there, so I thought I'd better help."

"You saved my life!"

"Couldn't pass up the chance to lay out one of these devils. Been wanting to do that for a long time."

"Well, I'm glad you did."

"Me, too, sister. There's some people here who'll be pleased to see you."

They climbed a narrow trail that snaked up along the wall of the canyon toward a series of cavelike holes cut into the face of the rocks. A quarter of a mile away Ruth could see the magnificently carved facade of the necropolis.

"There are more of you?"

Isaiah nodded. "Mostly runaway slaves. People like yourself who've escaped the city. Then there's some people that've been living in the caves for years. They work the mines and trade with the Tuaregs from time to time."

"But where do you come from?"

"You mean, before here, sister? I was a merchant sailor, born and raised in Capetown. Rode the seas for nearly thirty years. Shipwrecked off the coast of Mauritania on the HMS *Trinidad,* God rest her stacks. Seven years ago almost to the day, I figure. We were carrying ore at the time and she went down like a ton of rocks. I was picked up a month later wandering in the desert, starving and half insane. Rescued by a band of Tuaregs.

"I thought they were the funniest-looking people I'd ever seen. I mean, who ever heard of men wearing veils? Thought they were funny until I saw what they could do to a man. Then I just kept acting crazy and they carried me along. . . . You Christian?" He paused.

Ruth nodded.

"Try Jewish." He smiled, thumping his chest. "They love infidels about as much as dogs love cats. I been bowing and

nodding toward Mecca ever since they found me. Guess it was
the only way I could keep alive. Seen a man out here in the
desert once. He had no hands, no feet, no ears and no eyelids
and he spouted German. Wore a cross around his neck. God
knows where he came from or what he was doing. They used to
bring him out from time to time to show him off. Probably a
good thing I couldn't understand German or I might have tried
to kill them all. Ah, looky there. . . ."

They were a hundred feet above the canyon floor, walking
carefully along a precipitous ledge, when Isaiah pointed back
toward the oasis. A small caravan of mounted Tuaregs worked
its way along the boulder field.

"Better duck in here," he said.

He turned, moving into the darkened recesses of one of the
caves. The tunnel was a narrow orifice carved directly into the
sides of the rock. Pausing at the entrance, he watched the
Tuaregs search the area below, then held out his crutch.

"Grab hold, sister. I ain't going to win no popularity contest
if they see you up here."

They moved into the rear of the cavern following a narrow
shaft that led back into the rock. The cave was pitch-black and
Ruth stumbled after him, trying to maintain her balance.

At first the space smelled musty and pungent. Then the air
became fresh again and the passage opened into a wide, spa-
cious corridor. As her eyes became accustomed to the dark,
Ruth noted they were moving through a large shaft perpendicular to the cliffs. They passed side rooms in which Ruth saw
dark, hooded figures huddled around small fires. In one place a
man was working with the metallic point of a spear, stoking it
red-hot in a crude furnace. He looked up, watched them pass,
and said nothing. In the weird illumination of the flames, his
face appeared scarred and distorted.

At last they came to a large cathedrallike chamber where a
fire blazed on the hearth and a dozen robed figures sat gathered
at a long wooden table. They looked up from their meal in
surprise as Isaiah entered the room.

"Mates, will you looky what I found!"

Confused and bewildered, Ruth stumbled toward the table.

Halfway there she saw a familiar face staring at her from beneath the corners of a hooded robe.

"Oh, my God . . ." she cried.

The figure leaped from his seat, embracing her affectionately.

"I can't believe it." She gasped. "I thought . . . I thought
you were dead." Moisture welled up in her eyes.

"Nice of you to drop in for dinner." James grinned. "Someone else here you might want to say hello to."

A second figure stood up and pulled his hood away.

"Lasiri!" Ruth cried. "But I thought . . . ?"

"Thought my head was rolling on the side of one of those
Tuareg camels? Not yet, memsaab, not yet."

Ruth stared from Lasiri to James and then back to Lasiri,
shaking her head in astonishment. "Maybe I'd better sit down,"
she finally said.

"Have some food, sister," Isaiah offered. He walked over to
the fire and cut a portion of meat from the hindquarters of a
roasting lamb. Then, to Ruth's surprise, he handed her a small
silver goblet, filling it with a dark reddish fluid from a goatskin.

Ruth brought the container to her lips and smelled the liquid.
"But it's wine," she said, amazed. "Where did this come from?"

"Many strange and wonderful things back here." James
laughed. "Sit down. There will be plenty of time to talk after
dinner."

"Brothers, this is Memsaab Parker," Lasiri announced to the
gathering in Swahili. "She will be sharing meals with us for a
while."

Ruth glanced around the table, nodding to the others. In the
flickering light she counted ten men. Some were bearded with
dark faces and Arab characteristics. Others were blacks from
tribes in the Northern Frontier and the Sudan. One man was a
giant, towering above the others, his black head bald and glistening. A small golden ring pierced his right nostril.

So many questions, Ruth thought, and everything moving so
fast. But there was one undeniable fact, and her spirits leaped at
the thought. She was free! And James and Lasiri were alive!

Across the table Isaiah held Alabaster in his arms. The monkey had taken hold of one of the wine goblets. Sniffing curiously, he poked a hairy finger into the liquid, then brought it up

to his mouth. At the first taste, he spat wildly, his lips puckered back in an expression of disgust.

"Careful there, monk." Isaiah grunted. "That'll run you aground for sure."

Then the smell of food and wine overcame Ruth. James was right, she thought. There would be plenty of time for questions later on.

The men were scattered throughout the cavern, some talking to one another in quiet whispers. Isaiah sat against the wall, his head back, snoring lightly, with Alabaster cradled beneath one arm. Lasiri crouched before the fire and probed a small stick into the flames. James pulled up a stool next to the Masai and motioned for Ruth to do the same.

"James, you don't know how good it is to see you alive. And Lasiri. . . ." She threw up her hands with a shrug. "I saw them strike you with my own eyes."

"The *shauri.*" Lasiri smiled. "The Will of God. The blanket must have caught the main force of the blow. It knocked me out and left a sizable wound." He opened up his robe and showed Ruth a fresh twelve-inch scar that ran from the left side of his chest down to the top of his stomach.

"They must have thought I was dead. By the time I came around in the morning the soldiers were dead and you, James, and Jon Paul were gone. I managed to get the wound closed and hid up in the cliffs. I was able to snare a few small antelope and I was close enough to the water to come down and quench my thirst at night. After about a week I was strong enough to walk. Since all three of you were on foot, I was able to track the direction of your caravan. I realized then I might be able to follow you all the way to the oasis. Fortunately, you traveled direct enough so that it was easy for me to follow. In those places I lost your track, the routes were well marked by a dozen other caravans."

"All roads lead to Rome." Ruth smiled.

"Once I reached the ruins I saw it was useless to go farther, so I turned back. I hoped I might be able to find safety in the caves until I could determine your exact location. As it turned out, there were a number of people before me here."

"But why do they stay?" Ruth asked.

"For most of the escaped slaves there is no way out. They may try to cross the desert but alone there is little chance of success. If caught, they're usually beheaded or tied to the poles outside the city and left for the hyenas. So mostly they run here to the caves and hide. A few can travel into the city without being recognized and the Tuaregs leave Isaiah pretty much alone. He goes into the market practically every day.

"I passed the word around that I was interested in any information regarding Europeans," Lasiri continued. "Isaiah found James tied to one of the posts and was able to cut him down before it was too late. They had seen you, Ruth, either going down to the oasis for water or walking through the market. We'd been following you for several days trying to figure out the best time to help you get away. As it is, it's probably better that you tried to escape on your own. For the time being, Isaiah would like to keep as low a profile as possible."

"Surely the Tuaregs know that there are people living here."

"They do, but they're afraid. They think they are inhabited by spirits, ghosts of the old city, so they leave the caves pretty much alone."

"Thank goodness for that," Ruth answered. "And what about you, James?"

"I'm too tough." He grinned. "Nothing a little rest couldn't solve."

"And Jon Paul?"

A sudden frown worked its way across James's face. "We've heard nothing of him."

"Nothing?" Ruth said with surprise.

"No one has seen him," Lasiri answered.

"That's very strange," Ruth answered. She had thought somehow Jon Paul would be used outdoors, to collect wood or tend to camels. "You don't suppose they've taken him out?"

"No, I don't think so," Lasiri answered. "We keep a pretty close watch on the major caravans moving in and out of Bogadez. There have been a couple of salt caravans and the usual Tuareg slave-gathering parties, but nothing more."

"We don't have much time," James said. "Isaiah says they'll

be leaving for their summer pastures soon. We may have a week or ten days, but no more."

Ruth nodded. "I didn't understand it at first, but now it all makes sense. During the winter there's enough rain in the mountains to keep the springs full. With the summer everything dries up. That's why we found no water at the wadi. In another couple of months there won't be enough water here to support more than a handful of people."

"Ruth, they've seen a woman here," James said. "She first appeared about six weeks ago and she's been described as blonde and Caucasian. Isaiah thinks it might be Diana."

"She's here," Ruth said slowly. "I've talked with her, James, and she's alive."

"Good lord." James leaped to his feet. "Is she all right? Have they harmed her?"

Ruth hesitated. God, how could she tell James what she'd found? It would enrage him beyond all measure. But what was done was done. There was nothing they could do to change things now. No, Ruth thought, not now. But as she thought of Diana Jacobson, she had to fight back her tears.

"Your sister is alive and well," Ruth answered. When she looked at James there was courage and hope in his eyes so she added what she knew he most wanted to hear.

"She needs our help, James. She knows that you and Jon Paul have come for her and she wants desperately to go home."

34

One hundred miles to the square inch, the contour map covered an area that included all of the Sudan and the sub-Sahara region from Ethiopia to Lake Chad. Ian Anderson had circled al Jabbar with a pencil and now he made a faint mark westward, across the region labeled "desert" to a point where the elevation contours of five thin lines indicated cliffs. He was sitting at a table in the Thorn Tree Cafe in Nairobi, the map spread out before him. Michael Jacobson sat next to him. Across the table were two East African bush pilots, William Collins and Jackson Tate. Collins was a thick burly man with a broad chest and hairy, muscular arms; Tate was smaller, his face thin and angular. Both men studied the map intently as he spoke.

"It was Ruth Parker's theory that there was originally a string of oases running all the way out to the coast, and the caravans used these routes to carry ivory, jewels, and slaves. She believed that al Jabbar was the first stop for the caravans coming out of the interior from a large trading center somewhere to the west." He spread his hand across an area of some five hundred square miles. "We know only that James's party left from al Jabbar and headed toward a peaked mountain that the Arabs call the Devil's Tower." He tapped on the approximate location with a pencil.

"We would like to search this area as quickly and expeditiously as possible. The biggest question is, What's the best way to proceed?"

"Usually, sir," Collins answered, "we can pick a section and fly over a specific area. For instance, we could probably cover a hundred square miles, the size of one of these contour blocks, in about half a day. Then we'd need to come back and refuel."

"So that means one plane could cover an area of five hundred square miles in five days?"

"Roughly." The pilot nodded. "Figure Tate here could take the southern section and I'll take the north."

"It would be my thought to go first to al Jabbar then follow the directions to the Devil's Tower as far as we could," Anderson said. "If we found nothing, we could split up and cover the northern and southern sections independently."

"Exactly what do you expect to find?"

A frown slowly worked its way across Anderson's face. "I'm not sure. To be honest with you, if we could locate their camp, that would be our luckiest shot. Short of that, I guess we search for any evidence of what might have been their campsite. In addition, we look for anything that resembles a collection of tribes or nomads where they might have disappeared. I don't know what else to tell you. You both know what the hell the bloody desert looks like. We're just searching for evidence that they're alive."

"And what do we do if we spot them?"

"Note their coordinates on the map. Give them some signal that you've seen them and come back. Then we'll try to figure out some way to get out to them and make sure everything is all right."

"One other thing," Jacobson added. "If it comes to a point where we actually have to go up there with Land-Rovers, we'll need a fairly accurate idea of what to expect, what concentrations of people are where. . . ."

"What's the date of this map?" Tate asked.

Anderson searched along the lower border of the chart. "British, 1943, Civil Engineers. Probably done for the war. Why do you ask?"

"Because a desert can change a lot in thirty years. Waterholes dry up, dunes move across a section and cover everything. We may find some surprises."

Tate looked up. "Company coming," he said. "Isn't that the Minister of Foreign Affairs?"

A thick black man in a dark suit approached the table and stopped next to Ian Anderson.

"Sir, might we speak?" he asked politely.

"Certainly." Anderson patted a napkin across his mustache. "You've met Mr. Michael Jacobson?" The American stood up. There was a brief handshake.

"We've had the opportunity to talk several times on the phone," Jacobson said.

"I heard from the embassy that you were in town, Mr. Jacobson. It is unfortunate about the news. I wish there was some way my government could help."

"Thank you, I appreciate all you've done already," Jacobson answered.

"If I could interrupt you, Dr. Anderson, I would like to speak in private," Tomboya said.

"Oh, yes, all right," Anderson replied. "I'll be with you in a moment."

Tomboya nodded to the American and two pilots. "My apologies, gentlemen. I'll take a table across the cafe. Perhaps Dr. Anderson can join me when you're through."

"Strange bloke," Collins said as he watched the minister cross the room. "I get the feeling that behind that smile lurks the mind of a snake."

"You've been flying too long, William," the other answered. "He's just like a politician. There's a hundred like him back home. Different color maybe, but cut from the same mold. On the surface a lot of white teeth and soft handshakes, but you know damn well that they've got something slippery on their minds."

Anderson grunted. "Maybe I'd better not keep him waiting too long." He stood up from the table. "I'll be back in a few minutes."

Jacobson turned to the map and began discussing the topography with the two pilots. Anderson ambled across the cafe and took a seat across from the Minister of Foreign Affairs. As he sat down, he thought the pilot was not far from wrong. Wilson Tomboya *did* look like a snake. A black snake with thick, widespread fangs. Danger here, he sensed. Something about the way the minister watched him made him extremely uneasy.

"To what do I owe the pleasure of this unexpected visit?" Anderson began.

"I contacted the museum. They told me I might find you here."

"I'm always available to speak with you at any time, Mr. Minister. What can I do for you?"

"Let me get to the point." Tomboya stared coldly into Anderson's eyes. "There has been a considerable amount of money transferred to Barclay's Bank here in Nairobi under a special account for the Jacobson family. I'm told that it is a sum well over a million dollars."

Anderson shrugged. "What does that have to do with me?"

"There is further news that you outfitted one of your colleagues with several vehicles to go up and look for Jacobson's daughter in the Sudan."

"That's not exactly true," Anderson replied. "Dr. Ruth Parker, one of my associates, led a research team up to the

Sudan to do some collecting as part of her work. James Jacobson and his brother chose to go along."

"Do you know who went with them?"

"You mean as a hired crew? It was my understanding that they took a cook and two drivers and a number of assistants. That's all."

"Did you know that some of them were mercenaries, professional soldiers?"

"No, I was unaware of that," Anderson said with surprise. He listened to the minister, carefully trying to sift through the facts that were being laid down before him. But what was Tomboya really driving at?

"Did you know, Dr. Anderson, that they carried automatic weapons across the border?"

Anderson's eyebrows rose. "I would be very surprised if that were true." Yet, silently, he reviewed what Ruth Parker had told him: *some shovels, pickaxes, spades—specially crated.* Bloody hell, maybe they did take automatic weapons. It would not be above Ruth Parker to try a stunt like that. And also not beyond her to keep it a secret from him all along.

"Let me make it clearer," Tomboya said. "We were tipped off that a certain payment of seven thousand dollars was made to a group in Rhodesia for a number of automatic weapons. Do you know the penalty for transporting arms across the border, Dr. Anderson? Five years in jail and suspension from ever working in this country again."

"You have an excellent border patrol, Mr. Minister. I doubt that they could possibly have gotten arms through even if they wanted to. Besides, what in the world would she use the weapons for on an archaeological mission? It just doesn't make sense."

"That's just the point," the minister replied. "I'm beginning to doubt that your archaeological team, as you call it, had much to do with research at all. This young man, James Jacobson, was most disturbed when he came to my office looking for help. It was just a thought, mind you, but I wondered if perhaps you might have outfitted them with guns and vehicles and mercenaries in exchange for some type of donation to the museum."

"Your mind works in devious ways, Mr. Minister," Anderson

answered. "I don't know what you are talking about. If you want, I can lead an inquiry when they return. . . ."

"I can only draw certain conclusions." Tomboya grunted. "But the facts are it was *your vehicles, your associate, your museum cartons,* that were used to smuggle illegal arms across the border. There is even talk that the border patrol might have been bribed."

"Come on." Anderson snorted. "Dr. Parker would never do such a thing!" But in his mind he was now thinking: Damn the wench. She did bribe them. Sure as hell she orchestrated the entire matter.

Tomboya's eyes drilled into Anderson's face. "It seems that the Jacobson family is fairly important back in the States. We've been getting an increasing number of inquiries about them. The American Embassy is quite concerned. I need to give them some assurance that the boys are all right and that you and Mr. Jacobson are not about to do something foolish."

"Perhaps, Mr. Minister, you should have thought of that when the two Jacobson boys first came to you asking for help."

Their eyes locked.

"If I were Michael Jacobson and I sent my two sons to Kenya looking for help to find my kidnapped daughter and you gave them none, I think I might feel a little angry about your lack of courtesy," Anderson said.

"And if I were the Kenyan government," Tomboya retorted, "and if I found out that the director of the Nairobi Museum helped outfit a foreigner to cross the border with automatic weapons, I think I would feel more than a little angry about the infraction of the law."

"Well, it sounds like a stalemate, doesn't it?" Anderson smiled. He stood up from the table. Across the restaurant Jacobson was still engrossed in conversation with the two pilots.

"If there is nothing else, Mr. Minister, I have a busy afternoon."

Tomboya rose from his chair. "I would hope you will let me know if there is any word on them."

"You'll be the first," Anderson replied. "Dead or alive."

35

In the black recesses of the caves time seemed to have no meaning. Here there was neither night nor day; the inhabitants slept
and ate and moved at hours governed by neither the rising nor
the setting of the sun. It was perhaps sometime the following
day in this realm of perpetual darkness that Isaiah led his guests
through a series of corridors that tunneled deep within the cliffs
of Bogadez. Carrying a flare at the front of the procession was
the huge bald black man whom Isaiah called Solomon.

"He's the only man I know who likes the Tuaregs less than I
do," Isaiah said as they followed a long, empty shaft hollowed
out of the rock. "Two seasons ago the Tuaregs cut out his
tongue. I found him dying out in the desert, brought him to the
caves, and nursed him back to life. Never knew his name or
what tribe he came from or how they caught him, 'cause when I
found him, he couldn't talk. But somehow 'Solomon' seemed to
fit."

"His tattooing looks like Zwala," Lasiri remarked, pointing
to a series of scars on the side of his right cheek. Next to the
giant, the Masai seemed as thin as a rail and James felt dwarfed.

For half an hour they followed the tunnel, bypassing innu-
merable side chambers. From time to time beams of light penetrated the darkness from hidden entranceways or small win-
dowlike openings that looked out over the ancient city.

"Whoever the city planners were, they built a tunnel system
better than the Paris métro," Isaiah said. "There are catacombs
down here that rival the ones in Rome."

They entered a small room with smooth walls, its floor covered with several inches of soft dust. Stacks of clay gourds lined
the walls. Bone-white in color, each two and a half to three feet

in height, they reminded Ruth of the Greek amphora she had studied in the ruins of Cyprus and Rhodes.

"This here is the wine cellar, sister," Isaiah said. "I broke one of these open two seasons ago. It smelled like rotten vinegar. Tried another and it was as fresh as the Queen's Bordeaux."

He raised his flare so that Ruth could see and she sucked in her breath.

"They must be centuries old."

"Could be, sister. All I know is that this is where I found them. Found Alabaster down here, too, in a room full of marble vases. Must have gotten lost or somehow deserted by her mother. Heard her crying and I thought it was a bloody kid. Been a pretty good friend since then—eh, monk?" He reached up and tugged affectionately at the monkey's tail.

"But there's a lot here, sister. Seen some rooms full of furniture, benches, chairs, tables. The kind like you ate on back there in the main cavern. Some rooms are filled with chariots, helmets, swords, and armor. Others even got paintings across the walls. Lasiri says you can read some of that old writing—eh?"

"Some of it," Ruth answered. "Most of it was Arabic after the seventh century. Mainly because the Koran was written in the language and all of the scholars were priests."

Isaiah turned and started down a tortuous tunnel. There was a flutter of excitement in Ruth's chest. Secrets, she thought. Great secrets hidden away beneath this ancient city and now she had her own guide.

Deep beneath the plateau of Bogadez, Isaiah now led them through a labyrinth of connecting corridors. Some looked well traveled and indeed, they passed people from time to time moving in the opposite direction. Robed, their faces obscured by hoods, they moved silently through the darkness, slipping past with little more than a sidelong glance, shielding their eyes from the brightness of the flares.

"Who are these people?" Ruth whispered.

"I'm not sure I know," Isaiah answered. "They speak a little Arabic but mostly a dialect of their own. My suspicion is that they've been here for generations. Maybe some of the original descendants of the city. All of 'em are riddled with leprosy.

Except for times of trade, they're pretty reclusive. Mostly they just stick to themselves and leave everybody else alone."

Once they came around a corner and two women suddenly appeared. They were covered in black robes, their heads wrapped in dark shawls. Before they could turn away, Isaiah's flare illuminated their faces. The nose of one was a twisted scar, her lips gone, her eyes dull and opaque. The other's face was a mass of open sores. James had to fight himself to keep from crying out in horror. He had never seen faces so hideously deformed and wondered now if some of the strange inhabitants of these caves lived their entire lives without ever seeing the light of day.

They traveled for another thirty minutes in silence, passing through caverns with roofs no higher than a man's head, moving through huge chambers that rose so high above them that they couldn't see the ceilings even with the light of the flares. Bats flew from one room to another, breaking the tomblike silence with a flutter of wings.

At the end of a long shaft, they came to a huge vaulted cavern with an arched ceiling that disappeared in the darkness above. Isaiah held his flare up and painted murals leaped to life on the walls.

Here were drawings of elaborate banquet tables spread with abundant food, hunters on horseback driving wild beasts, and gentle, shapely women with ample breasts bathing in an oasis surrounded by palms.

"How did you ever find this place?" Ruth asked.

"There are people here who know these tunnels far better than I," Isaiah answered. "But I've been here a couple of seasons now and I'm beginning to find my way around."

He led them up a series of steps following a chiseled passage. At one junction they took an abrupt turn and entered a cavernous room. Two chariots stood in its center. One of the wheels was off and lying on the floor; breastplates, helmets, and swords were stacked neatly in one corner.

"Ah, look at this, James!" Ruth exclaimed. "A Latin inscription, *'Lux et Veritas.'* These may be the weapons of the legionnaires. There's a story that one of Caesar's battalions disappeared searching for the source of the Nile. Could they have ended up here?"

They moved down a long, empty passageway with small corridors leading off to either side. At the end of this shaft they climbed a flight of stairs and came to a large open room. As the light from the flare illuminated the chamber, James's eyes widened in amazement. They had entered a library. Parchment volumes were arranged neatly on the shelves. At a long wooden table, arms folded over a parchment, head down as if the person had fallen asleep at work, a skeleton sat. A second skeleton lay on the floor beside it. The clothing had fragmented and fallen away, but decaying leather sandals still clung to the bones of the feet.

Ruth stepped forward, her heart pounding. The parchment, several pages long and scrawled in black ink, had obviously been written by the seated individual for the pen was still gripped tightly in the bones of his hand.

"Arabic!" she exclaimed.

Gently she pulled the parchment from under the skeletal fingers and began to read, slowly at first, then, as her eyes became accustomed to the script, faster, until it was as if the departed figure were speaking the words. James listened, stared at the fleshless bones, and shuddered.

"I, Tobiah Arzad Tabul, treasurer and scribe of the great city of Bogadez, do write these last words on this blackest day of death. There is nothing left. Myself perhaps the last citizen alive to witness the glories of a great civilization gone. Even as I write the Tuareg nation has devastated the last of our people. Our youths' blood flows through the streets. Our leaders' heads hang from poles, our women are dismembered and thrown to the hyenas. Blackness has overcome us all.

As a child I saw this oasis as a great city. There was Timbuctu to the west and Bogadez to the east and all trading routes passed in between. For a thousand years the city was run by great kings. There was a mixture of all peoples. All faiths and religions were tolerated. There was a time when the oasis flowed out into a broad river which ran

down past the mountains into a wide valley. Christians
came from the kingdom of Prestor John. Moslems from
Cairo and Fez. There was a great slave trade and men
carried ivory tusks so long that three boys could not reach
their points standing on each other's shoulders. Here with
my own eyes have I seen a caravan bound for Cairo laden
with precious stones three thousand camels long.

But the richness of Bogadez came from the mines hidden beneath the city. From the caves came an abundance
of blue gems, and it was this stone, which looked like the
sparkling water, that was a trademark of the city. It was
called the stone of the oasis, and if you had ever been to
Bogadez, you wore it. When men died the stone was placed
in their mouths so that they might always taste the sweet-
ness of an eternal spring.

People came from all over the desert to carry on their
trade. The king controlled an army of ten thousand men
and his land was bounded in every direction by ten days'
camel ride.

Now the Tuaregs have burned everything. The water of
the oasis turns red. A month has passed and the spring is
drying—water which has flowed for a thousand years and
a thousand years before, flows no longer, and without
water there is only death.

A few of us were able to escape by going into the caves,
and here we have hidden what remains of the treasury of
Bogadez. Thank God they have not followed us here.
There is nothing left. I write this note after we have been
four days without food and water. The Tuaregs still scour
the streets. I have given my last flare to my slave so that he
may attempt to escape alive. In the name of the Father and
the Son and the Holy Ghost, God save our souls."

"So there were Christians here," James exclaimed.

"There were isolated enclaves of Christianity in the desert,"
Ruth answered. "Bogadez may have been one."

"And the slave?"

"The second skeleton," Ruth answered. She pushed the flame

over to illuminate the pile of bones on the floor. The right hand still clutched to an unlit flare.

"Look!" she said. "It was never burned. The slave never left his side."

As James listened he could feel a growing sense of loss. The figure in front of him was no longer a fleshless skeleton but the last dying member of a race that had built an incredible city, now gone.

"Alabaster!" Isaiah suddenly cried. The monkey had crawled up along a ridge at the corner of the cavern and was chattering from a tiny peephole at the top of the cave.

As Isaiah shinnied up the side of the cave trying to retrieve the monkey, something caught his eye.

"Mates, bring the flares," he shouted. "There's another passage here!"

Working quickly, he began to clear away the rubble, tossing stones down, one after another, until he could wedge his body through the opening.

James could see the faint semblance of stairs. He ascended carefully, holding on to the wall as he helped Ruth up toward the crevice.

When the light from the flare fell upon the room, James paused in astonishment. Carefully carved into the sides of the walls was a series of vaultlike tombs, each pointing outward like the arms of a star. Within each of the tombs was an open stone sarcophagus.

Isaiah illuminated one of these vaults with his flare. Resting in the sarcophagus were the skeletal remains of a human covered with jewels. Emeralds, diamonds, rubies, sparkled in the light. People of great importance, a dynasty of royalty, buried here, James thought. As he leaned over to study a skull, he noted a thin gold chain that disappeared inside a viselike grip of ivory teeth. Lasiri reached forward and pried open the mouth, pulling out a small blue stone that glinted by the light of the fire. He looked up, caught James's eye, and nodded.

"Mates, it's enough to make you cry," Isaiah exclaimed.

Ruth sucked in her breath, her body trembling.

"You all right?" James asked.

She stared at the gems glittering from the skeletons. "This

must be only a small portion of the jewels," she murmured.
"The main treasury must be hidden beyond, somewhere back in
the tunnels. I've waited all my life to find a burial like this. It's
everything I think I've dreamed it would be. So the maps were
all true, James. The oasis really did exist. Oh, my . . . oh, my.
. . ."

How much treasure was back there in the darkness? James
wondered. Ten million dollars? Twenty million? Yet as he
glanced through the room, he could feel an increasing sense of
claustrophobia. It was a dead tomb from a dead city, the treasury of those who could never buy back what they had lost:
their youth, their health, their lives.

For a moment, as he gazed at the riches, he wondered how a
man might penetrate the labyrinth and take the treasure out.
Without a guide like Isaiah, it would be practically impossible.
The tunnels leading to the treasury were a dizzying series of
corridors and blind alleyways. There were hundreds of miles of
passages. Maybe with a map and years to work it out, a man
might unravel the secrets of the catacombs. But not now, he
thought.

He reached out, put his arm around Ruth's shoulders, and
slowly pulled her away. "If we ever get out of this, I promise
you I'll get my family to finance an expedition back here for as
long as it takes and with as many men as you'll ever need. I've
seen enough. I've still got a brother and sister out there somewhere. All the treasures of Bogadez are useless to me unless
there is someway we can get them out."

"Oh, James," Ruth said suddenly. "There's something I must
tell you. You're not going to like what I have to say."

"Nothing could be worse than what we've already been
through," he answered.

"Yes." She nodded grimly. "There are some things that are
worse."

A dark frown pushed its way across James's face.

"You have to understand the history of these people, James.
The desert tribes have always been brutal beyond measure. The
worst punishments are often for disobedience. What I'm going
to tell you is very typical of the things nomads will do. I'm
sorry, James. Sorry for Diana. I wish it wasn't so."

"Good God, woman, what is it? Tell me what is wrong!"

"Diana killed one of the Tuaregs in the Turkana village—the man whose grave you and Lasiri found. Since her capture she's struggled with them continually. She told me she tried to escape three times. At first she refused to be enslaved, refused to be Rassam's mistress, refused to follow any of their requests. Even when they threatened to kill her she told them she didn't care and would rather be dead. I suppose if Rassam hadn't taken an interest in her they would have killed her long ago."

"That sounds like Diana." James nodded. "She was always a fighter."

"James, they did the one thing that would make her dependent upon them forever."

"What the hell are you saying?" James roared.

"They blinded her, James. Rassam had them put out her eyes."

36

It was the flowers she missed the most, the vibrant brilliance of red and yellow and orange. In her mind she would often go back to those Impressionistic canvases she had studied in college and paint them over as if she was the artist, starting afresh. She would mix her imaginary palette with exotic oils—alizarine red, Naples yellow, cobalt blue. She remembered the paintings well. Monet's *Poppies*, Cezanne's *Delftware Vase*, Renoir's *Bouquet in Front of Mirror*. They were like old friends to her now, and God, how she missed them.

Then, when she wasn't painting, she would imagine she was walking down the corridor of one of the great museums pausing at each canvas, studying the greens of the forest at Fontaine-bleau or the reflection of the water at La Grenouille. For in the

world of semidarkness in which Diana Jacobson existed there
was no longer any color. It was as if someone had suddenly
fogged her vision, as if the camera of her eye had not only lost
its focus but the exposure had been closed down ten stops so
that what light did come through was dim and blurred.

Yet as she moved through the moors of darkness she had
never given up hope. Someday, somehow, she was determined
she would have her vision again. Couldn't she recognize the
light of the sun? Couldn't she tell if a flare was burning across
the tent at night? If there was some reception of light, wasn't
there a chance that her eyes could one day be restored? Clinging
to this thought, she persisted, waited, and dreamed.

Despite her blindness, parts of her life at Bogadez were not
totally unpleasant. As Sheik Rassam's mistress she was treated
like a queen, and although she had an inkling that Rassam had
other wives, she could hardly care that she was one of twelve.
Because she was his favorite consort, she was constantly bathed
and perfumed. In the confines of the harem tent, slaves spent
long hours combing her hair and working over the texture of
her skin with oils and soft creams that the sheik insisted all his
women use.

If she wanted to eat, an aide was ever ready to bring her
anything she desired. If she needed to make her toilette, two or
three slaves might assist her with a bath and perfume. If she
wished to go to the market, there were four huge men to act as
litter bearers, available to take her practically anywhere she
wanted to go. In short, she hardly had to move her finger to do
anything at all. With her eyesight intact, perhaps she might
have enjoyed such a pampered existence for a time. Without it,
her life was a form of idle hell that she desperately prayed to
escape.

Now the market was her greatest pleasure, for there a multi-
tude of smells assaulted her senses. She learned to recognize the
sharp spice scents of cumin and coriander, the fragrance of
cinnamon, the sweet smell of sandalwood. Often she would pull
the curtains of the palanquin aside and stare up toward the sun,
trying to visualize the source of the smells. It was at just such a
time that Ruth Parker had first spotted her at the back of the
market.

Through some of the slaves who spoke Swahili, Diana had learned that three Europeans had been brought into the oasis by the Tuareg warriors.

"There are people of your race in the city, memsaab," Tanaku, her harem attendant, had said. "Brought in this morning. A white man, a woman, and a boy."

"What does the woman look like?" Diana had asked.

"I'm told she is older, stout, and with red hair."

"Red hair? Are you sure?" There was no other woman she knew who was more likely to make an expedition to the Sudan than Ruth Parker.

She had asked the slave to go fetch the red-haired woman and then she had hidden in the shadows of the tent, almost afraid to find that it was Ruth, for what could she tell her? What hope could she possibly offer?

When she learned that James and Jon Paul were in Bogadez, she was terrified. They could never escape. If Rassam knew that the two were even remotely connected to her, she was sure he would have them murdered on the spot. She thought of trying to bribe some of her attendants to help them, but without her eyesight, even this would be difficult. No, she thought. Escape would be impossible. But what could she do? How could she possibly help?

She knew that next to the oasis was a series of tombs and caves of which the Tuaregs were desperately afraid. Through her informants she had learned that a handful of people lived there who were riddled with disease. From time to time a slave would vanish, and it was rumored that he took refuge in the caves. Usually they were never seen again, so among the Tuareg servants there was both fear and wonder about their disappearance. It was rumored that the people living in the caves had leprosy. The desert tribes believed that to touch a leper was to receive the kiss of death, for in a month or two even the strongest person would be covered with the most horrible sores. The end result: loss of all fingers and toes, collapse of the nose, blindness, and finally, gratefully, death.

A slave in Bogadez had only two choices. If he remained a slave, he had a predictable life; he could usually rely on being fed and clothed. If he fled, he might be caught and decapitated;

if he escaped to the caves, he would eventually succumb to disease. For most of the captives, remaining a slave seemed the better alternative.

On this particular morning Diana Jacobson had finished her bath; the attendants had completed grooming her and left her alone. She had started across the harem chamber when she heard a swirl of fabric from one of the partitioned curtains and sensed the presence of someone else in the room.

She stopped for a moment and waited for the person to address her, thinking it might be one of the slaves.

"Tanaku?" There was no answer. She paused, listening, then heard a movement behind her. A hand reached up and firmly grasped her breast.

"*Allah akbar, akbar Allah,*" a voice said.

"Ibrahim!" she cried. "You're not supposed to be here."

"It is so, my beauty," the priest answered. "But Rassam is out running the racing camels and he has asked that I be sure you are comfortable."

"You know that to touch a harem woman means loss of a hand!" she said angrily.

The priest gazed absently across the room. Even if the servants heard their conversation, he knew none of them could understand English.

"I'm afraid, my beauty, that you would present Rassam with a most awkward dilemma," he answered boldly. "For you to so much as suggest such a thing of a holy man would imply sacrilege. I would have to tell Rassam that you were merely trying to cause trouble—again."

"You bastard!" she spat at him.

He bowed and then politely said, "You know, it would give me great pleasure if you would try to learn even the first chapter of the Koran."

"*Merde!*" she answered.

"People have been killed for less."

"Ha!" She snorted. "Why do you think Rassam did not kill me long ago? You know he would never consider such a thing. As long as I have his interest, I have that one power over you, don't I?"

"There are many fates worse than death," Ibrahim answered.

"Don't you think that giving in might make life a little more pleasant for you?"

"You have taken away my eyes and my freedom and now you want to take away my spirit. Go to hell!"

"The Europeans that were sold in the market fought like you and do you know what happened?"

Diana flushed, quickly trying to gain her composure.

"No, tell me about them," she bluffed.

Ibrahim studied her shrewdly. "I think there is perhaps some connection with the Europeans and you."

"I can't imagine anything more absurd," she answered, trying to hide her emotion. But her thoughts ran wildly. God, did he know? she wondered. And how in the world did he find out?

"Their fate is of no particular interest to me," she stated calmly. "I only hope that Rassam will be fair in whatever his decisions are. I am told there is a man, an older woman, and a boy."

"You hear well, my beauty. But the man is dead. He was strung up on a pole and left to die outside Bogadez."

James! She could feel her knees buckle beneath her. She tried to support herself. For a moment she felt as if she were going to faint.

"And the boy?" She gasped.

"He has been sold to an Arab, Tmazzari. They plan to make him into a harem guard."

"And the older woman?"

"Suppose I could somehow arrange to help her get away. What might it be worth to you?" he bluffed.

Diana bit her lip. "Little," she answered flatly. "I would only like to hear that she is treated with dignity, especially since I understand she is somewhat crippled."

"If certain favors were extended, I might be able to help to arrange their escape," he replied cunningly.

"What favors could I possibly give to you?" she hissed back.

"Be obedient, learn the Koran. I'm only suggesting, of course, but there might be a time when Rassam is away that we could spend together in one of the side tents. It is merely a thought, you understand, but it might benefit her."

"I would rather rot in hell!"

"Well, then, maybe you will get that chance," Ibrahim murmured.

Diana Jacobson heard the priest depart. Finally alone, she sank to her knees, tears flowing down her face, her body shaking in a spasm of despair. My brother dead? No. It can't be true. She would have to hear it from someone else beside the treacherous Ibrahim. And Ruth? Did Ibrahim really know where she was and what had happened to her, or was he merely lying? And Jon Paul? Oh, no, oh, God! She shuddered. How could it have happened? What had she gotten them into?

37

A small single-engine plane darted north, no larger than a gnat above the shrub-pocked land, ten thousand square miles of arid brush and dust and scattered acacia trees. To the east the parched terrain ended in a desert, an *erg,* or great sand sea, that spread out in a series of dunes contoured by the wind. Beyond that, a purple haze of mountains, vast and inhospitable, and, from the perspective of the occupants of the plane, seemingly unapproachable by land.

Clouds clung upon the horizon like cathedrals, white, sculptured, and unmoving. Just where the sky met ground was a small patch of green, a dot of color barely distinguishable from the monotony of the desert brown.

"There it is," the pilot said. He pointed to the small discoloration ahead and swung the nose of the aircraft north and ten degrees east. A herd of desert gazelle broke out from a fringe of bush and scattered below the plane, dust rising from their hoofs like small explosions.

"Al Jabbar?" Ian Anderson asked. He consulted a crude map

laid out before him, dots and circles drawn in pencil. Michael Jacobson stared over his shoulder.

"Yes, bwana," Mabruka Hassan replied from the rear seat. "That is where we were camped."

Jacobson tried to search through a pair of binoculars but the air turbulence was too great and the bouncing only made him dizzy. In fifteen minutes the small patch of green had become an oasis, a brilliant sapphire of blue surrounded by lush vegetation on all sides. The pilot swung low toward the spring. They could see the glint of white stone composing the ruins and the huge skeletal branches of the baobab tree. They were almost on top of the oasis when they spotted the Land-Rovers. Three men ran out from a flat plateau of rocks. One of the men was waving a white flag.

"There, that's them!" Mabruka cried in Swahili.

They circled a second time passing low over the oasis, dipping their wings at the three men below. Then the plane turned west across the broad sea of sand.

"My God, this desert is formidable," Jacobson marveled. "They must have been crazy. On foot, it was insane!

"Do you remember their exact direction?" he asked Mabruka.

The soldier nodded and pointed to the west, toward the faint purple mountains rising in the distance.

For half an hour the plane flew over barren, lifeless sand. In thirty minutes they crossed a distance that had taken James's party three days to walk. In places the desert was flat and barren, like the surface of a tranquil sea; in others, the dunes rose upward in great waves, turbulent and hostile, erupting as if in an angry storm.

The wadi was hardly more than a small dot upon the sand. They were searching toward the edge of the mountains as they approached, moving so quickly that they almost missed it.

"There, something!" Anderson cried.

The pilot banked the plane and they came back, skimming over the wadi at an altitude of a hundred feet. They could see the lifeless branches of a few trees surrounding a damp spot in the sand. Spread out around the wadi five or six feet in diameter were half a dozen dark spots. A vulture flapped up from one of

these spots and rose cumbersomely away. Small white objects
lay in haphazard piles within the dark smudges.

"Christ, what's that?" Jacobson suddenly shouted. "A skull?
I thought I saw a skull!"

The pilot turned the plane again and they made a second run
over the wadi. This time they studied the area, watching the
dark spots as they passed beneath them.

"Bones! They're bones all right."

Jacobson looked at Anderson. "What do you make of it?"

"Probably some animals, ran out of water."

"Don't you think they're humans?"

"They look too big. More like a horse or camels."

"But out here . . . ?"

"Can't tell without dropping down, and here there's no place
to land."

"Let's make one more circle," Anderson said.

On the third run, they watched carefully again.

To experienced observers, it was obvious that the stains in the
sand were places where something had died. The porous ground
sucked up the body fluids and bird droppings, leaving small
telltale stains that would remain for weeks after the bodies were
gone.

"I guess it could be them," Anderson said slowly. "But we'd
have to come back here and investigate it thoroughly. Doesn't
make sense though. They had no camels, and why would the
sites be spread out like that—twenty-five or thirty yards apart?"

"Digging there, bwana," Mabruka said. He pointed to small
holes that had been tunneled into the base of the wadi in a
search for water.

"Might have been anyone coming across the desert," Anderson answered. "Let's look further. Maybe they made it past
here and those belong to something else."

"We couldn't cover this land with a dozen search planes," the
pilot said.

"I know," Anderson answered. "But let's keep going west,
toward the mountains, and see what we find. How's the fuel?"

"Not great, but we've got enough for a look."

Ahead the broad purple cliffs rose abruptly from the edge of the desert, ascending in a series of mountains that ultimately ended in jagged peaks.

The plane passed over the edge of the cliffs and across the foothills.

"Nothing here," the pilot said. "The land looks inhospitable, no water, no vegetation, nothing but dry, barren ridges."

"Try back along the cliffs," Anderson answered. "Maybe there's a passage or trail leading into the mountains."

They turned the plane and ran down along the cliffs skimming low over the desert, the rock walls rising almost to their wing tips a hundred yards away.

"No way for anyone on foot to get over the cliffs in the first place," the pilot said. "If they got this far, they must have found some kind of passage."

They flew for another fifteen minutes.

Finally Anderson shook his head. "Let's try the other direction."

The plane banked and turned north flying just above the edge of the cliffs. Two ostriches darted out from the shade of the rock and galloped across the sand.

"At least there's life," Anderson exclaimed, and he almost missed the canyon. They were by it in a flash, a narrow crack of an opening that led back into the tall rock walls.

"Wait, there's an opening!" he cried. "Swing her around."

The plane banked sharply and reversed direction, then rose up over the top of the cliffs.

"Look, there! Drawings!"

They turned again, running perpendicular to the cliff walls, and there upon the face of the narrow crevice were primitive stick figures. Because of the shadows, they had been invisible from the opposite direction. Now, running back, they could see them clearly.

"What the hell are they?" Jacobson asked.

"Petroglyphs," Anderson answered. "Drawings of some of the desert tribes."

"Recent?"

"They could be at least ten thousand years old."

"Bwana, look!" Mabruka cried.

Down below, along the narrow canyon they saw three camels

scurrying into the safety of the overhanging rock. The plane passed over them in a second. When they turned back the animals were gone.

"Three camels with riders, I'm sure I saw them!" Jacobson cried. "But why would they hide?"

"Possibly some of the desert tribes. Often they're superstitious and don't want to be seen. Can we head farther west?"

"Fuel getting too low," the pilot said. "Sorry, but I think we'd better go back."

Anderson frowned. Leaning forward, he searched the desert below. As they came over the cliffs and headed back across the desert toward al Jabbar, he thought he saw two more men on camels shrink back into hidden crevices in the rock.

"There's people down there, all right. But, boy, are they shy. Let's get a little height before we head home."

They climbed steadily to an altitude of one thousand feet then turned and ran north, parallel to the cliffs. They traveled for another ten miles, studying the edge of the mountains, before they banked to the east and started across the desert.

"What's beyond the mountains?" Jacobson asked.

"Never been up there," Anderson answered. "According to the maps just more desert for another half a continent. Two more mountain ranges, one a hundred miles north and then a second two hundred miles west. The rest, nothing but sand. A few tracks, roadways for oil companies, but nothing more."

"Got any suggestions?"

"Not without more gas."

"I've seen enough to want to come back," Jacobson replied.

Ian Anderson glanced out of the window, watching the mountains fade gradually behind him. His colleague, Ruth Parker; Lasiri; and Michael Jacobson's two sons—swallowed up out there somewhere, he thought. And the chances of finding them not much greater than looking for a pebble in an ocean of sand.

38

Nightmares. They came to Jon Paul in salvos. Horrible images of huge insects crawling on his arms and legs. Then softness. Someone bending over him, wiping his cheek with a moist cloth. A veil. Beautiful brown eyes. The face was somehow familiar but he couldn't quite place it. He was lying on a thick folded blanket in a tent. But where? How? In the flickering light of a flare a young woman was bending forward, gently rubbing the cloth across his forehead.

He rolled over on his side. His right hand was still throbbing. He felt the girl raise his hand and anoint it with some kind of cool greaselike salve. The substance worked its way into his skin, easing the pain. He moaned again. The dreams were coming back.

He was a young boy and he was standing on one side of a stream across which a tree had fallen, making a natural bridge. Michael and Donald were on the opposite side of the stream and they were yelling to him. "Come on, Jon Paul. Don't be afraid." He took a faltering step onto the log. The surface was still slippery from the rain. Eight feet below a shallow stream rushed through a narrow gorge.

The diameter of the trunk was not more than a foot. The surface was precarious at best for there was a mossy cover on the top side of the log. Yet Donald and Michael had made it easily. It was his turn to follow. James was standing behind him trying to push him out.

"Just be cool," James said. "Take it one step at a time."

He started. One foot ahead of the next. Holding his arms out, he tried to maintain his balance. If he could only make it to the middle of the log he could stumble across to the other side.

Another step, his right foot hit a slippery piece of bark. He began to fall.

"Help me!" he shouted. He tried to reverse himself, but his feet slipped out beneath him. Gripping wildly, he threw his arms around the trunk and caught himself, dangling precariously. There. On the bark. A scorpion. Waddling forward. Crablike. Moving toward his face. He screamed and let go. He was falling . . . falling . . . falling . . .

He could feel gentle hands push him back onto the blanket. A girl's voice spoke to him in murmuring tones. Somehow he knew he had been yelling. His neck was lifted and a cup of warm broth placed into his lips. He swallowed slowly. The brown soft eyes were there again, the beautifully featured face, hidden behind the mask of a veil. "I know you," he said in a daze. "I know you. . . ." He tried to rise but she gently pushed him down. She was rubbing his hand again with the cool, soothing cream.

She stopped now and pulled from around her neck a small string to which had been attached a key. *"Faedra!"* Jon Paul gasped. "Faedra!" He fell back on the blanket. His eyes rolled and he drifted off into unconsciousness again.

She came to him four times a day. Often alone, sometimes with one or two other women, and each time she gave him a little to eat and gently rubbed the potion into his arm. In the mornings she visited him each day just at dawn. Then she would gently wake him up and give him the cup of warm broth and murmur to him in a language he couldn't understand. He slept mostly. For a while he was too weak to walk, but gradually as the cream began to work and Faedra nursed him back to health he began to feel stronger. He got up one afternoon and walked around the space and discovered that he was held in the small compartment of a much larger tent that had been cordoned off by hanging blankets. The door was slit between two large partitions of cloth. When he pushed through he discovered an armed Tuareg standing guard outside the doorway. Inside the compartment he found a small area of the tent that was worn enough for him to rip a tiny peephole. From there he could see the ruins below, scattered with tents. His eyes followed the pathways, down to the walls of the city, and then out

to the palm trees of the oasis. Even a glimpse of the outside
world excited him.

How many days have I been like this? he wondered. Three,
maybe four. And James? What had happened to James, and
where was Ruth? He remembered dimly that James had been in
some kind of a fight but he was confused, and in his own mind
the scuffle that occurred during the night of the council between
James and Ibrahim and the battle in the slave market were the
same. Ruth, he could remember during their meeting with the
Council of Elders, but no more. And then he remembered the
scorpion creeping up his arm and the triumphant, grinning face
of Ibrahim the priest.

He was feeling stronger daily. The sting mark was now a
small red patch on the surface of his palm and his hand pained
him only occasionally. He began to think about escape. If he
was isolated and by himself he would need to discover the lay of
the land. To leap up and try to take off now, he realized, would
be fatal. But as long as Faedra was there, he thought there was
hope.

Just at dusk she came to him again, bathed his arm, and gave
him a large plate of meat. He ate hungrily. There was a moment
after dinner when all seemed quiet. She had brought a folded
robe into the room and now she opened it up for him to wear.
He still had on his pants but his shirt was shredded in a hundred places. He took off the shirt and put the robe over his head
and smiled at her, gripping her hand. She gently kissed his
forehead. Unable to control himself any longer, he drew her
next to him and pressed his lips to her mouth over the veil. For
a moment they stood, embracing. There was a noise from outside the tent. She pushed away, disappearing quietly through a
slit in the doorway.

A minute later two Arabs with rifles stepped into the room.
They motioned for Jon Paul to stand up and made him take off
his robe. As he stood bare-chested, the nomads went over his
skin very carefully, inspecting his arm where the scorpion had
stung him. They studied his eyes, then examined his mouth.
Seemingly satisfied, they nodded to each other and left.

Jon Paul slept restlessly that night. He didn't like the way
they had approached him. He was becoming fearful that he

would be moved. Obviously he could not remain where he was, nursed daily by Faedra forever. How he wished he could communicate with her. He wanted to know what had happened to her father. Had Benghazi been killed at the wadi with the rest of the Abyssinian traders? He wanted to tell her how sorry he was, that he had felt somehow responsible. And what about James and Ruth? Where were they? What had she heard? And how had she been brought to Bogadez? Was she a servant or a slave? A hundred questions he wanted to ask. Instead he could only look at her and feel the reassurance of those soft brown eyes and try to smile to let her know he greatly appreciated her care.

It was sometime shortly before dawn when he heard a rustle of the tent and sensed another person in the room. He started to rise but felt hands gently push him down. Faedra moved in beside him, lying on the blanket. He could smell her perfume and feel the closeness of her and his heart began to patter steadily inside his chest. He kissed her now, first on the neck and then on the cheek moving slowly toward her mouth. She pulled her veil aside, and this time their lips embraced in a long, sensuous, open-mouthed kiss. She reached underneath his robe and began to rub his chest, her fingers moving in soft tantalizing circles. Slipping off his pants, he pulled her robe up and tucked her into him, gradually pushing his way inside her. They made love this first time lying on their sides, her buttocks pressed up against his groin. Later she pulled him on top and he took her softly at first, building into a wild crescendo until she began to call out in a breathless cry. He brought his arm up to her lips to muffle the sound and she grasped the flesh in her teeth and bit down, lost in the ecstasy of love.

Afterward he lay with her, feeling the soft rise and fall of her breasts. Dawn was approaching. Faint orange streamers began to edge up in the east. The bray of a donkey sounded. From a tent nearby a child cried. God, how I want her, he thought. Not there but away from this, away from the captivity of the Tuaregs, someplace where he could teach her his language, somewhere that he could show her what his world was like. Somewhere they could be together for as long as they wanted.

Half an hour passed and then she arranged her robe and readjusted her veil and stood up. She kissed him softly on the lips and then silently left. A few minutes later his food was brought, but not by a woman. This time it was a man. As soon as he had finished eating, the two Arabs came back into the room and at gunpoint escorted him outside the tent. He was taken to a second chamber, much smaller than the first. A blanket was pulled aside and he was thrust into a compartment with a young black man. The youth was naked except for a cloth around his waist. Jon Paul noted a long healing wound across his back and recognized him as the youth who had been brought across the desert with the slave caravan. But what had the Tuaregs done to him? Before he had walked proudly and tirelessly. Now he looked anxious and fearful. He reminded Jon Paul of a wild animal that had been caged and broken in spirit.

Jon Paul searched his mind for some way to communicate with him. He wanted to tell him what he had learned, to explain that their captors would not harm them as long as they remained cooperative, yet now the smallest sense of distrust began to creep its way into Jon Paul's mind. If he'd been moved away from Faedra, it meant that they had some purpose for him and he did not like the thought. And why had he been placed in here under guard with the second youth?

For the first day the two did little more than glance at each other, eat their evening meal, and lie down in their respective corners and sleep. The next morning Jon Paul thought of a game. Moving across the enclosure, he tried to show the African that by throwing a stone closest to a line drawn on the ground they could have a contest. The boy soon saw the trick of it. In a moment they were throwing pebbles against each other.

"Kamani," the young man said, pointing to his chest. When he repeated the word several times, Jon Paul realized he was trying to tell him his name.

"Jon Paul," the American answered. Kamani mouthed the words. "Lon Ball," he repeated.

That afternoon Kamani taught Jon Paul to play a game of stones in which each found a round stone and thumped it across the floor like marbles. From there they graduated to thumb wrestling, then arm wrestling, and finally to a contest to see

who could pull the other off a line without losing position.
Through these games Jon Paul held his own. Kamani was
slightly bigger and could sometimes get better leverage, but
they were surprisingly well matched.

That evening Kamani began to draw figures in the dirt.
Through a series of pictures he tried to tell Jon Paul the legends
of his own people. Though Jon Paul could not understand the
tales, he had a vague idea that the stories were about lions and
elephants and great feats of bravery that the men of Kamani's
tribe had performed in the past.

At night they could hear music from one of the neighboring
tents and the twitter of young women's voices. Later they heard
the sound of girls laughing and occasionally gasping noises.
Kamani looked at Jon Paul and poked him in the ribs when he
recognized the sound of couples making love. Jon Paul thought
of Faedra. It had now been three days since he had been removed from her tent. Where was she and why hadn't she come
to see him again? Perhaps now that he had recovered, she might
not be allowed to speak with him. He thought again of escape.
He could follow the days by making a mark in the dirt floor. He
would give it another week. If nothing happened by the seventh
day, he would try to flee with Kamani.

He awoke in the morning lying on his side next to the walls
of the tent. He could see that it was daylight, and he had the
vague perception that something was buzzing in his ear. At first
he thought it was a fly, but the noise continued droning onward.
An engine coughed and sputtered somewhere off in the distance. Jon Paul leaped to his feet. Good God, he thought. It's a
plane! Someone was searching for them.

He awoke Kamani in a frenzy, pointing to his ear, urging the
African to listen. He had to get outside. It was a risk but he
would have to take it. The plane might only make one pass.
There might not be a second chance.

Moving quickly, he eased up to the curtained doorway and
peered out. A Tuareg with a gun resting in his arms was sitting
across from the doorway. In a flash Jon Paul darted past the
guard. Just at the main entrance he ran into two more of the
veiled nomads. He knocked one over, kicked the other in the
leg, and managed to reach the doorway. For an instant he was

free. Sprinting quickly, he raced outside. His heart leaped up into his throat.

"Here, over here!" he shouted.

A mile away, coming rapidly over the tops of the cliffs, was a small single-engine aircraft.

On the third day of their search, covering the northern sector of the contour map, the plane had followed the steep-walled canyon in toward the Devil's Tower. Now from a height of fifteen hundred feet and a distance of one mile the ruins of Bogadez spread out upon the desert like a metropolis.

"City there, *look!*" the pilot exclaimed.

"Must be ruins, one of the ancient cities," Anderson replied.

"Anything on the map?" Jacobson asked.

Anderson pulled the chart from between his legs, searching across the contour squares, but there was only a wide brown area marked *reg,* the Arabic word for "desolate plains."

"There, caves!" The pilot pointed. They banked over the canyon where tomb sites had been cut into the rocks.

"And up ahead. An oasis. Water!"

"Jesus, this is no dead city!" Jacobson cried.

As they came in low over the oasis people stopped what they were doing and stared up at them. They saw a herd of camels and a flock of sheep, then noted a man with goats dash for a hiding spot within the palms.

"What the hell are they running for? They must know we've already seen them."

"Just scared," Anderson answered. "Superstitious and scared."

The plane circled out over the desert, then flew back directly above the oasis. Jacobson surveyed the tents dotting the stone foundations below. He counted at least fifty large tents and nearly a hundred small ones. He saw the marketplace, watched the crowd stop and stare up at them before it scattered. Below them, people were running in every direction, trying to hide.

They passed over what looked to Jacobson like the remnants of a mosque then a cluster of tents at the upper edge of the ruins. There Jacobson thought he saw a boy or man running and waving at them. This figure was followed by three others, and a moment later all were lost in a struggling mass. He tried to follow the action beneath the right wing. He thought he saw the figure being dragged back into a tent and then he lost them.

He saw all this and he did not speak. None of them did—not he, the pilot, or Ian Anderson.

A dozen thoughts flashed through their minds. Anderson was astounded at the existence of the ruins and even more surprised at the presence of numerous tents. An entire nomadic society lived there. Michael Jacobson could still visualize the figure running out below them. A rising sensation of uneasiness began to grip the pit of his stomach. He swung around in his seat searching desperately for some further sign but there was nothing.

They were just over the beginning of the mountains when the pilot finally spoke. "Wow! I've never seen anything quite like it. Did you see the man running back there? Did you see him? It looked as if he was trying to signal us."

The pilot started to bank for another run.

"Don't turn back," Anderson said. "Keep going straight."

"Good lord, man. My sons may be down there!" Jacobson cried.

"Too dangerous," Anderson replied. "We've seen that there is an entire city here and the presence of this plane disrupts them significantly. If they're in trouble, I don't want to endanger their lives. Let's see what else is up here for another couple of miles, then go back and get some help."

"What did you have in mind?"

"A dozen Land-Rovers. Fifty or sixty soldiers. We'll need to bring some power in here."

Already Anderson was calculating how to arrange the expedition. Their biggest problem would be crossing the border. The Minister of Foreign Affairs would have to be called in for help. Hell, with Jacobson's backing they might be able to get half the Kenyan army.

They passed over a low plain leading up into the mountains and then the pilot banked in a slow, lazy turn. Two desert oryx streaked across the flat land below, gray with black socks and

black skull-like faces, their rapier horns forty inches from base
to tip. Then the plane swung north, disappearing into the hot,
suffocating African sky.

39

He was dressed in silk trousers tied at the waist with a leather
cord. Over a cotton shirt he wore his indigo *gandurah,* or outer
robe. A white turban and veil were now wrapped around his
head. He sat cross-legged on a cushion in the prayer chamber, a
curved, bejeweled knife attached to his waist. His fingers were
bare of rings. The large blue sapphire that he wore on special
occasions was locked safely inside his chest. The oil lamp flickered softly. On a small pedestal was a thin sheet of wood on
which was painted the Arabic inscription "There is only one
God and Mohammed is his prophet." Except for a small prayer
rug the room was bare. It was an hour before sunset. Time to
think and rest. Sucking in the sweet smoke from the waterpipe,
Sheik Ahmed Rassam drifted into a euphoric semiconsciousness, his mind wandering back to his youth.

Those were good days, he thought. Days when a man's life
was spiked with plundering and war and treasure. A Tuareg
was bred for such a life. In the old days he had held court; his
women had made poems and sung him songs of bravery, and he
had ruled all of the sands. Yet steadily the world had begun to
close in on him. Bogadez was one of the last safe refuges for his
people. But this morning had changed all that. A plane over the
oasis! Now their sanctuary was jeopardized. It meant more
Europeans might be coming soon. If they came here and
erected their tall oil derricks and hired away his people, he was
not sure where he would go. There were not many good winter-
ing places left. Tibetsi, maybe. Maybe west to Chad. Over the

years other tribes—Berbers, Arabs, Gallas, Felonis—had heard
of the Tuaregs migrations here and they, too, had come to
trade. Each year the Tuaregs had returned, they'd found more
people. A handful at first, then several dozen, now a population
numbering over a thousand, all followers of Mohammed. Someday, Rassam thought, I will make my pilgrimage to Mecca.
Maybe it was getting time. Next year everything might be
changed.

In a way Ibrahim was right. The priest was clever and cun-
ning and often a liar, but about the woman he'd been correct.
He'd predicted Rassam would have nothing but trouble with
the blonde. Rassam had thought by blinding her he would gain
her submission. Instead she had become passive and cold, cold
as her skin. Making love to her was like making love to a stone.
She neither grunted nor moved. She just lay there and accepted
him. It was hardly the fantasy he had envisioned. He loved her
beauty and the features of her face, and he struggled with himself on how to best befriend her. She had been by far the most
frustrating woman he had ever known.

He remembered now his first conversation with Ibrahim. It
was two days after she'd been brought into the encampment,
after she had pulled down his veil and she'd tried to escape. Yet
he'd procrastinated about her fate. He'd asked the priest to
speak with her so that he might learn something about her past.

"She speaks English, Italian, and French," the priest had
said. "But English is her best language."

"Good, let us talk with her," Rassam replied.

They'd kept her in a side compartment of the harem tent,
bound both hand and foot.

"What is your name?" he'd asked, with Ibrahim acting as an
interpreter.

"Diana," she answered. "Who are you?"

"Rassam. Sheik of the Tuareg confederation."

"Why are you holding me captive?"

"Because you are my slave."

"I am no man's slave."

"You know it is futile for you to fight."

"What kind of a man are you to hold someone against their
will?"

"I could offer you your freedom."

"For what?"

"To be a member of my harem."

"I would rather be dead," she muttered.

"Where is your husband?"

"I have no husband."

("Undoubtedly she is lying," Ibrahim had whispered to him.)

"Where are your children?"

"There are none."

"What kind of a woman are you?" he asked incredulously. "You are not married and you have no children. What possible use could you have."

"I am a photographer."

There was a pause here as Rassam held a side conversation with Ibrahim to try to determine the meaning of the word. Years ago he had seen magazines in some of the markets of Algiers, and Ibrahim said she was the type of person who made pictures like those he had seen there.

"Is she some type of sorceress?" Rassam asked. Now some of her actions seemed to make sense.

"No," Ibrahim had answered, "she is *European.*" As if the word explained it all.

"What were you doing when you were captured?" Rassam asked.

"Working with a tribe of Turkana," she replied.

There was a pause again as Rassam and Ibrahim discussed her answer. They spoke in the language of the Tuaregs, a rare, little-understood tongue called Tamajegh that was not related to Arabic or Swahili. But this answer made no sense to Rassam at all. The only conclusion he could come up with was that she was a concubine for the men of the tribe and because she had magical powers and the ability to take their images and put them down on paper, they were afraid of her. "But why?" Rassam had asked Ibrahim. "I don't understand it. The woman is lovely. Her place is at home. Even the grossest of Tuareg women take care of their men. She knows no poetry. It is unlikely she can sing any songs, nor does she have any ability to make music on the *amzad*. Except for raising children, I would say she is completely useless."

"Worse," Ibrahim replied. "Where there is one European there will be others. Mark my words. You have not seen the last of them by this woman. I would advise she be killed. Keeping her in the oasis is extremely dangerous. Others may come to look for her. You have migrated here so far in peace."

"And if I do not kill her, what then, O priest?"

"She has seen your face." Ibrahim said.

Rassam blanched underneath his veil. "She has told you that?"

"I don't think she has lied." Ibrahim answered sternly.

"I demand to be freed," she said suddenly, and began struggling with her ropes.

"You have tried to escape three times," Rassam answered harshly. "And you will not escape again. The priest thinks you should be killed."

"Then kill me," she retorted harshly.

Ibrahim spat on the ground. The two moved out of the room. "She is European, undoubtedly she is an infidel, and she has no business in this encampment," the priest argued.

"There are ways, O holy one," Rassam answered quietly.

"I would rather embrace a snake."

"We shall see," Rassam answered.

Determined for success, the next day he ordered his men to inflict upon her the "kiss of a thousand suns." Yet, even blinded, she was a strange woman. All European women were strange. Some, like this woman, had absolutely no fear of death. In this respect they were like men. They were tough and strong, they spoke their minds and had absolutely none of the social graces of the Tuareg women. So why did he keep her?

He knew. Deep down inside he knew only too well. It was the year before he'd become the leader of the confederation. He remembered the incident clearly. His older brother, Ajjatel, was the natural heir. How long ago had it been, thirty years? They had been following a caravan through the lesser Tobaz. Two of his men had volunteered to escort the travelers through the *reg* to the next oasis. It had been a sizable caravan: twenty tents, two dozen soldiers, and a score of merchants including two young European women. Rassam, his brother, and another thirty bandits had carefully followed the camels at a distance, watching them closely each night. They'd observed the girls with great interest. Both were escorted by an older woman whom they judged to be in her late fifties and by three Caucasian men. What was most peculiar was that the three women slept in a large orange and red striped tent, the men in a separate tent entirely. For five days Rassam and his brother had followed closely behind, until they decided they would have these women. If they got nothing else from the caravan, this would be their prize.

On the sixth day the two Tuareg guides deliberately led the caravan in the wrong direction. Instead of turning toward water, they moved along a tall steep-walled cliff. The going was slow and arduous; perfect for an ambush. That night one of them slipped back to his comrades. "They are ready for plunder," he said. "The soldiers are careless; they have been drinking frequently. They have set few guards. I think we can wait until they are all asleep. When the constellation of the Big Camel is overhead it should be easy."

As planned, they'd waited until after midnight. Slipping into camp, they were already through the tents before the first alarm was sounded. Rassam and Ajjatel moved up to the orange and yellow canvas. With a sudden slash of a blade Rassam ripped through the cloth. They leaped into the room. Lying upon cots, two forms were immediately visible. Rassam took one. When she struggled and screamed, he knew it was one of the girls. Pulling his arm around her throat, he tightened his grip while the other hand raised up his robe. She fought furiously until he was inside her and then she began to moan. He heard Ajjatel laughing next to him as he struggled with the other. From outside the tent came volleys of gunshots and shrieks of death as the Tuaregs massacred the unsuspecting traders. While the rest of the caravan fought for its life, Rassam took his pleasure, spurred on by the girl's grunts, her panting, her screams. He'd just finished when one of the warriors came into the room and held up a torch. Rassam collected himself and stood up. He looked at his brother hunched over on top of the other struggling form. But it was not the other girl. It was the old woman. At first Rassam had thought it was hysterical and he began to laugh out loud. Ajjatel had jumped up, horrified at his mistake, then both of them started laughing, as did the Tuareg warrior at the door.

They'd been so distracted that they'd not seen the movement. Across the room hung a closetlike affair made of blankets. Someone had been hiding behind it. A gun pushed through the blankets and fired. Rassam saw his brother clutch his chest and pitch forward. He swung his sword, catching the figure broadside. When they pulled away the blanket he saw he'd killed the second girl. There was another gunshot and he'd spun around in fury, shocked to find that the girl he'd wanted as a prize had killed herself. She'd had a gun that she'd obviously been unable to get free earlier. Now she'd ended her own life rather than be taken alive by the Tuaregs.

They'd found no gold and jewels. There were several black boxes. "Cameras," they were called, and a score of books with European writing. They had not believed it when the guides told them that there was little evidence of riches. They couldn't understand that these people would come to the desert just to record their travels.

He'd buried his brother at the base of a massive outcropping of rock, and had become the natural heir of the Tuareg Confederation. When he'd returned home with the sad news, his father had told him that such things were the *shauri,* the will of Allah. That it was destined to happen and that his own fate must be fulfilled. He'd wondered then if the girls had not died, or if his brother had not been killed or if somehow he could have stopped the European from killing herself, what might have happened. But they were strange; all Europeans were strange. And now he was left with this blond woman whom he had blinded and who was still as uncooperative and as puzzling to him as every other European had been.

Why did he put up with her? The answer was simple. In a way she represented everything he could not understand. She was the white skin in the brothel and the European girl who had killed herself to avenge her honor and the race of men who came to the desert to build great oil derricks and kill his men with their automatic guns. She was progress and modernization and everything else the Europeans stood for. But mostly she was beautiful, her skin was cool, and he would master her. If it was the last thing he did, she would surrender to his will.

As he was smoking his waterpipe, sorting through his thoughts, Ibrahim came hesitantly into the prayer room.

"I'm sorry to bother your Excellency but I thought this was news of importance. The European woman has demanded to speak with you."

Rassam slowly withdrew the waterpipe from his mouth and stared at Ibrahim. "Ha, so she is beginning to soften. I told you it would happen."

Ibrahim frowned. "Let us first hear what she has to say."

"I will talk with her in the outer room," Rassam replied.

The priest met Diana Jacobson in the large ceremonial meeting chamber and told her that he had spoken with Rassam. Diana was accompanied by her harem attendant, Tanaku.

"She must wait here," Ibrahim said, pointing to the slave.

"She speaks neither English or Tamajegh. She will not betray what she cannot understand."

"Then follow me," Ibrahim said. He led the two of them into a small blanketed chamber. They waited for ten minutes. Rassam appeared suddenly. He had replaced his rings and was now dressed totally in black. He took a cushion across from them and sat down.

"I would like to talk," Diana said as Ibrahim translated.

By now Rassam was somewhat used to her forthright manner. "I am listening," he answered.

She searched toward him with gray, visionless eyes. "There is a young boy here in the ruins. A European, I'm told. He has been sold to the Arab Tmazzari as a slave."

Rassam looked at Ibrahim. "Yes, that is true," he said.

"What is to happen to him?"

"The boy is to be made into a harem guard."

"Has this been done?" she asked, trembling.

"If it has not, it will be," Rassam answered. "Tmazzari will be leaving the oasis soon. Already I have seen his camels packed."

"I would like to offer my cooperation in exchange for his freedom."

"How?" Rassam asked.

"If you would set him free, I would come with your harem and be your loving wife for the rest of my life."

"I'm not sure Rassam can do that," Ibrahim answered. "The boy is owned by Tmazzari. He is an Arab, not a Tuareg."

"You said the boy is a slave. He was purchased for a price. There must be a price to sell him again. Double Tmazzari's money. Whatever it takes, buy him. Give him an escort across the desert. Once I learn he is free, I will never fight you again."

Rassam's interest had been piqued. "Why are you interested in this boy?"

"Because he is my brother," Diana answered.

Rassam stared at her for a long time without answering.

"Well?" she finally said.

"That would explain it," Rassam answered. "The brother looking for the sister. The ritual of the scorpion proved true."

"I had warned you they would come looking for her." Ibrahim scowled. "Undoubtedly the plane today brought more of them."

"And the two others, the older white man and the woman?" Rassam asked. "Who were they?"

"The older man was also my brother, the woman a good friend."

"So now it is all explained," Rassam replied. "You know the older man has been killed."

"Yes, I understand that," Diana said. There was the slightest tremble to her voice. "For him I would have made a bargain too. I'm only sorry it is too late."

"You must understand the rules of the Koranic law," Rassam replied sternly. "Your older brother attacked the priest here in these very chambers. The next morning he charged a number of Tuaregs in the market. I tried to spare their lives. He gave me no other choice."

"But surely," Diana pleaded, "the young boy has done you no wrong. Please, for me. If there is any possibility of honor and dignity to your name, please set him free."

"I will think about it," he replied.

"There is no time," she answered quickly. "Even now it may be too late."

"I will give you my answer first thing in the morning," Rassam replied. "You may go."

She stood up slowly, led by her servant Tanaku, and walked out of the room. Just as she reached the blanket she turned back. "You must promise me if we do this that you'll never tell him I am here. Promise me that and give him his freedom and I will always do as you wish."

"How do you know that I will not go back on my word?"

"Because you are a noble and a sheik and I don't believe you would," she answered. Then the blanket closed and she was gone.

Rassam turned to Ibrahim. "Well, priest, if that is her price, the conquest is easy."

"I would not trust her," Ibrahim said. "She will tell you this and as soon as he is freed she will go back to her old ways. It is better to tell her that you have freed him and let her think that he is gone. Tmazzari leaves in two days. She will not know if he is on the caravan or free. They go on toward Hajjarro."

"Of one thing she is right, O holy one. I could make no such bargain and not fulfill my side."

"Then wait a day and tell her it is too late, that they have already performed the ceremony. You can tell her then that you have paid Tmazzari good money to take care of the boy. She would believe that and if it is better for your heart, you should do so. But turn him free, never! The boy will just go back and bring more Europeans to hunt you down. There is no place in the desert they cannot go with their planes, and there is no place you will be able to hide. Sooner or later they will find you. Perhaps she wants to turn him loose so that he will go for help. There is no telling what word might have already passed between them."

"You are a shrewd man, Ibrahim," Rassam said thoughtfully.

"Only wise in the manners of Europeans." Ibrahim bowed humbly. "It is the will of Allah that he is here, your highness. Don't change that now. Let the fates have their way."

It was dusk by the time the priest made his way back to his tent adjacent to the ruins of the mosque. As he moved through the growing darkness, his mind was increasingly disturbed by the day's events. First, a camel's moan had interrupted the morning prayer; then their solitude had been violated by the aircraft. Two bad omens, and now the confession of the blond woman that her brothers had come. It foretold much difficulty. He was intensely glad they would be leaving soon.

As his mind churned through these events he heard the call of the muzzein for evening prayer. He fell to his knees, bowing in the direction of the approaching darkness. *"Laa illaha illa llaah,"* His own words matched the hoarse chant of the muzzein. Standing up, he wiped the dust from his robes and started for his tent when an old beggar moved out of the shadows toward him. The man looked gnarled and bent, and he crawled through the street, reaching out with a pleading hand.

"Help me. Give me the blessings of the Koran."

"Out of my way, you cur," Ibrahim replied, snarling. "Do not clutter the street like so much offal."

"But my legs are paralyzed," the man groaned.

"Then all the more reason to work. Find some use for yourself. Even the dung of the camel can be burned on a cold night to bring warmth."

"But, holy one . . ." the man persisted.

"Be gone, you sore of the leper!" the priest shouted. He kicked out at the man in a blow calculated to send him rolling backward. But as his foot struck the beggar's side, a strong hand reached out. With a sudden twist Ibrahim was thrown to the ground. Two figures lurched forward from the shadows. The priest tried to yell, but his voice was muffled by a rag stuffed into his open mouth. Before he could struggle further, he was twirled tightly in a blanket and immobilized.

As this human bundle was hoisted by the two men and carried off into the night, the crippled beggar leaped up, gathered a crutch beneath his arm, and hobbled quickly after them.

In less than an hour, the kicking, cursing form of Ibrahim Razouli Mohammed el Bin was deposited by a large fire in one of the back chambers of the caves of Bogadez.

40

The flames leaped brightly from a stack of burning wood as Lasiri and Solomon the Mute lowered the writhing blanket onto the floor. In a moment Ibrahim was out, struggling to his feet. Standing defiantly, arms folded, his eyes darted from one face to the next. He recognized Ruth and stared at James with surprise, but the others—the tall Masai, the silver-haired, blue-eyed beggar, the assorted mixed faces of escaped slaves, Arabs, Turkanas, and Somalis—he had never seen before.

"What is the meaning of this?" he hissed. "You dare take a holy man from the city of Bogadez?"

"There are many questions to be answered, my friend," James said.

"I am the sixty-fifth generation of the Holy Prophet, son of a grand sharif whose family goes all the way back to Mohammed. I demand to be freed this instant."

"In time, if you answer the questions put to you properly," James replied. "Then perhaps we will let you go."

"Rassam will never tolerate this. He will have your heads."

"Well, then, let's say that our heads will have good company, eh?" Ruth retorted.

"What do you want to know?" the priest growled.

"Where is my brother?"

"I don't know."

"Bull crap!" James roared. "You knew who bought him when we were in the market. Now, where is he?"

"I answer to Allah alone," Ibrahim retorted, snarling. "And no barbarian shall ever force words from my tongue."

"Wait a minute," Ruth said. "That accent. Something's wrong."

Ibrahim glowered at her.

"Where did you learn your English?"

"In Fez, during the British occupation."

"And your French?"

"From the garrison at Marrakesh."

"And your German?"

"From the Germans during the war."

"And your Arabic?"

"From the—" Ibrahim suddenly caught himself. "I was raised speaking Arabic," he replied quickly.

"Then how do you explain that the French were never in Marrakesh and the British had no occupation in Fez? You don't speak English right for an Arabic dialect, my friend," Ruth said. "I thought something was funny from the first but I couldn't quite put my finger on it. The rolling of the *r*'s, the use of the tongue in the *d* and the *g* sounds. English may be your second language but Arabic is certainly not your first. What is it? Italian? Relative to Mohammed, my ass!"

"I am a holy man, devoted servant to Allah!" Ibrahim screamed. "I carry a single hair from the beard of the Prophet to prove it."

"That I would like to see," Ruth replied, scoffing.

With trembling fingers Ibrahim pulled one of the small red pouches from around his neck. After some fumbling, he produced a piece of cloth and unwrapped it, unveiling a tiny curled hair.

"There!" he exclaimed.

"That is absurd and you are a phony!"

"I tell the truth!" Ibrahim screamed.

"Oh, balls," Ruth snapped back at him. "Your accent sounds Italian and that fucking piece of hair most likely came out of your ass."

James watched her with astonishment. She was cursing like a sailor.

"He lies blatantly and we'd be fools to try to elicit information in any civil way." Folding her arms, Ruth Parker stared fiercely at the priest. "I'm tired of such useless chatter and we're getting nowhere."

"You are right," Lasiri answered. He took a knife and

plunged the blade into the fire until it turned red hot. Nodding, he motioned for Solomon the Mute to grab the priest by the arms.

"Ha, infidels," Ibrahim cried. "I tell the truth. Touch the blade here, as hot as you can. The story will not change." He stuck his tongue out defiantly, challenging Lasiri to bring the knife to his lips.

When the blade was red hot, Lasiri took it from the fire, watching the vapor of heat rise from the metal.

The priest's eyes widened as the knife approached his neck. He tried to shake his head but he was held too tightly to move. There was a sudden hiss followed by a sharp scream, then the pungent aroma of burning flesh began to fill the room.

James turned away. God, could he really bring himself to watch the torture of a man, even if he hated him?

"No, no! You cannot do that!" the priest shrieked.

Lasiri pulled the knife back, holding on to a piece of the mummified lizard that hung around Ibrahim's neck. The heated blade had severed the dried body of the reptile, dividing it into two neat parts. James had to suppress a snort of laughter. The knife had not touched the priest at all.

The knife was back in the fire heating again. Lasiri waited until it was orange and steaming before he pulled it out and moved it toward Ibrahim.

The priest tried to struggle, but the strong hands of Solomon held him firmly.

"Wait!" Ruth suddenly exclaimed. "There's a mark. There, on his right arm."

Ibrahim shook his hand and tried to slide the corners of his robe down across his forearms.

James leaped forward and grabbed the priest's arm. With the assistance of Lasiri they twisted his hand until they could see it clearly. There in the flickering light was a small tattoo shaped in the form of an armed cross.

"So!" Ruth cried. "Grand sharif, are you? Devoted servant to Allah, are you? Sixty-fifth generation, related by your father and your father's father all the way back to the Prophet, are you?" She stared furiously at the priest, her eyes glowing red in the light of the fire.

"Gentlemen," she said slowly, "behold the cross of Agamore."

Perspiration oozed out on Ibrahim's brow. He looked down at his forearm and across toward Ruth. A shudder seemed to pass through him. "Oh, God," he muttered, and his arms and legs began to shiver.

"Give him the blade," Ruth cried. "We're wasting time. What kind of fools does he think we are?"

Lasiri reached back into the fire and began heating the knife again, but before he could move back to the priest, Ibrahim raised a trembling hand.

"No, no, I will talk," he muttered. "Don't touch me with that. Tell me what you want to know. . . ."

41

Jon Paul was standing in front of his Arab master, a huge man with a heavy beard, wearing a bracelet of pure gold, when he thought: Something's wrong, there's something about the way they're looking at us that tells me they're up to no good. He'd been stripped down to a single undergarment and he stood next to Kamani feeling awkward and angry. The Arab was accompanied by two women, both veiled, one older, heavier, her body hidden by a loose gray robe, the other perhaps in her late teens, dressed in pantaloonlike bottoms and a thin, transparent top. For ten minutes they had poked and inspected the two youths, once opening Jon Paul's mouth and closely examining his teeth. He felt like some kind of animal and he did not like the indignity of it.

He thought at first they were going to punish him for trying to escape, yet the hour and a half of unconsciousness that followed the blow to his skull was probably enough. It didn't make sense that two women would be brought in to decide upon some disciplinary measure. So what are they up to? he wondered. Are we going to be sold or are they merely looking us over in preparation for some hideous task?

When the inspection was finished the young men were escorted back to their enclosure. As they passed the main opening of the tent, Jon Paul was able to look outside. It was evening. Next to the tent stood a long line of camels heavily loaded for travel.

Back in the enclosure, he thought about the scene for a long time. He remembered distinctly that no camels had been strung up outside the tents when they were first brought into the city. He began to consider the possibilities. What if the nomads were getting ready to leave? What if he had been traded to some caravan and was about to be taken out of Bogadez? What if he and Kamani were to be split up? And what had happened to Faedra? The thoughts sent a surge of uneasiness through his mind. He had no idea if James or Ruth were still alive or where Diana might be. If they took him on a caravan away from the oasis, he would never find them again. But no caravan will ever take me away, he told himself. They'd have to escape that night.

Sitting in the confines of the small enclosure, he thought about how he could tell Kamani of his plans. He had no way to communicate "escape," so he would have to draw a picture of the tent and show Kamani he meant to slip out beneath the canvas. They could wait until after midnight when everyone was asleep. Then they'd make their break. It was comforting to think that Kamani would be with him. The African would know much more about survival in the desert than Jon Paul. He wanted to bring Faedra with them, too, but where was she? Could he find her in time? He realized now that he couldn't afford to wait. He'd have to come back for her later. But first he must get free. He was sure if Faedra had been able she would have visited him before now. So coming to me must bring her danger, he thought. The one thing he didn't want to do was get her into trouble. He and Kamani would have to try it on their own.

Shortly after dark the music began; the singing was louder than it had ever been before. The intensity of the clapping convinced Jon Paul that the nomads were having one last grand banquet before they departed.

An hour passed. Jon Paul could feel a growing tension. Suddenly there was a rustling of blankets and Faedra appeared. She was covered in a veil with a hood draped over her head, so well hidden beneath her robe that Jon Paul did not recognize her at first. She was out of breath as if she had been running. Her eyes looked wide and frightened. As soon as she saw Jon Paul she threw her arms around him.

Reaching beneath her robe, she produced a small curved knife. With a gesture she indicated that Jon Paul should roll it underneath his pants and hide it. Then she motioned for him to slit the canvas and escape. She repeated her gesture several times. "You must come with us," Jon Paul answered. But Faedra shook her head. She reached forward, kissed him quickly on the forehead, then turned and fled. Jon Paul followed her to the curtained doorway. For the moment the guard was gone and he wondered how Faedra could have gotten through. A second later, however, a procession of three men came along the corridor of the tent. Jon Paul ducked back with Kamani.

He held out the knife for Kamani to see. *"Kisu,"* the African whispered. It was the Swahili word for "knife." Jon Paul signaled with his hand. They would cut the canvas and escape. He pointed to himself and then Kamani. They would flee together. A broad grin spread across Kamani's lips. He understood. He was eager to go.

A moment later there was a noise outside the doorway. Jon Paul quickly palmed the knife. Two Arabs entered the room and motioned for Kamani to follow them. Jon Paul tried to intervene but they pushed him back.

As Kamani walked toward the door Jon Paul squeezed his arm. "Hang in there." The African grimaced bravely, yet Jon Paul could see fear in his eyes. Maybe they were going to take him out for another inspection. Jon Paul tried to smile reassuringly. "Tonight," he said softly. "When you come back, we're gone."

An hour passed and Kamani did not return. Jon Paul began to worry. At one point the music became louder, accompanied by a chorus of chanting. Then Jon Paul heard a cry that the chanting could not drown out. It was a desperate roar of fear and pain and horror, and it sounded to Jon Paul as if someone were being tortured. A minute later he heard a hoarse scream and then there was only the music, droning on, repeating itself. As he listened a sinking feeling began to work its way up into his stomach. Something awful had happened. Abruptly the curtained doorway parted and the African was thrust into the enclosure. He staggered to the middle of the room and sank into a heap on the ground.

"Kamani!" Jon Paul cried. He rushed over to help but the African only moaned and rolled his head. As he stared at Jon Paul there were tears in his eyes. His voice came out in the barest croaking sound. "Lon Ball." He moaned. "Lon Ball . . ."

"What happened to you?" Jon Paul roared. "What the hell did they do to you?" He tried to shake Kamani into wakefulness.

He thought at first that the young man must have been whipped or severely beaten. He felt across his chest and abdomen to see if he could detect some sign of injury, but there was nothing there. Suddenly he realized his hand, which had been holding onto Kamani's leg, was warm and damp. He pulled his fingers away, horrified to find they were covered in blood.

Kamani's eyes opened again and there was a faroff, glazed expression in them. "*Kisu . . . kisu . . .*" He gasped, pointing for the knife. Jon Paul gave him the dagger and Kamani ran his finger slowly across the blade, feeling the sharpness of it. A tear worked its way down the side of the African's face.

"Oh, Lon Ball," he said in a whisper. Then with a sudden powerful thrust, he rammed the knife into his heart.

Jon Paul watched in stunned horror. He felt Kamani begin to ease in his arms, felt the tenseness of his muscles soften as the knife pulled away in his hand. The African reached forward, clutching wildly for Jon Paul, and then the grip eased, the fingers began to relax.

Jon Paul laid the black youth on the ground, so shocked he could barely think. He pulled Kamani's waistcloth aside searching for the wound. When he found it, the horror cut through his

mind as if he'd plunged the knife directly into his own heart.
There between Kamani's legs was a fresh jagged laceration.
Where the penis and scrotum had been was now only a cauter-
ized mass of raw flesh.

Jon Paul heard movement behind him and looked up. The
two Arabs who had taken Kamani from the room stood in the
doorway motioning for Jon Paul to come. Now he understood
what Faedra had been trying so desperately to tell him. So this
is their game, he thought. It was *his* turn to follow. Palming the
knife in his hand, he stood up slowly. Fire ignited in his eyes.
They would never do that to him. Not while he was still alive.

42

The black man came out of the night like a shadow. One moment the cave entrance was empty and the next he was there,
soaked with sweat, his body trembling. He staggered into the
main chamber, found Lasiri, and fell back against the side of
the cave breathing heavily.

Bursts of Swahili erupted from him like the hammering of
drums, and James could tell in an instant that something was
wrong. The black was a Somali who lived with Isaiah in the
caves. He had been sent down with two others to steal some
camels during the night. Now he had raced back from Bogadez
without stopping.

Lasiri quizzed him for a moment then turned to James. A
terrible frown worked its way across his face.

"We're too late," he said.

James stared at him in horror. "Good God, man, what do
you mean, too late? What's wrong? What's happening?"

"Your brother, Jon Paul."

James's heart fell. Oh, God, he thought. What's happened to

him? Either he's been killed or he's gone, disappeared with some caravan or maybe something worse. . . .

"They stole the camels," Lasiri translated. "All five of them, and the Somali was coming back through the ruins when he saw figures running through the city. People dashing everywhere. 'A slave has escaped!' they shouted. They said it was the barbarian boy. They said he killed one of his master's servants and then slit the tent and escaped."

"How long has he been gone?" James cried.

"Only minutes," Lasiri answered. "The man ran here to us as soon as he heard the news."

"Good Lord!" James exclaimed. "Ruth, does he know how to get to the caves?"

Ruth Parker shook her head. "I don't know. We've never been able to get any word to him."

"We must find him before the Arabs get him!"

"But how?"

"To the city. He may be hiding out there."

"Quickly!" Lasiri shouted. "Isaiah, bring the guns. Ruth, stay here in case he tries to find the caves. Hurry, now. There may not be much time!"

At the cave entrance, James searched down across the ruins of Bogadez. Not long before, the city had appeared peaceful, the scattered fires like pinpoints of warmth in the chill of the night. Now the ruins seemed alive. Everywhere he looked he could see flares. Suddenly the sound of distant shouts reached his ears. He bent down, pulling a hood over his head, and plunged into the night. My brother is out there somewhere, he thought, running for his life.

They moved through the darkness of the ruins in silence, rarely speaking to one another and then only in whispered tones. Lasiri led the way. Isaiah hobbled along quickly to his left. Behind him hovered the giant, Solomon the Mute. Disguised in hooded robes, they lowered their heads or turned sideways to hide their faces as others passed. Groups of nomads carrying flares dashed past them in the darkness. Suddenly, ahead, came the chorus of a hundred voices.

As they came around a corner, James's heart leaped into his

throat. Moving toward them was a mob of several hundred men. Some held flares, others had fists bared and were yelling curses. Pushed in front of the mob, his hands tied behind his back, his chest bared and bleeding from a dozen scattered wounds, was Jon Paul Jacobson. He staggered once, then was pulled back on his feet and dragged along. Bystanders lunged forward and spit at him. Others darted out and gouged his chest or kicked at his legs.

In a flash of rage, James pulled out his rifle, but Lasiri grabbed him.

"Hold, bwana, they will kill you in a second. Not now."

James watched in horror. The boy hardly looked like his brother. His eyes were wide and dilated, blazing with a hatred he had never seen before. There was a glint of fierceness, of wild desperation that made the youth look like an animal captured and held at bay. Quickly the mob surged past, pushing Jon Paul in front of them.

"We'll follow!" Lasiri whispered. They turned and joined the tail end of the crowd. The mob surged through the streets like an angry snake, growing steadily in size until it came to the marketplace. There they dragged their captive forward until he fell at the base of one of the auction platforms. More Arabs, Gallas, and Tuaregs poured into the market until practically the entire city was there.

A sudden hush came over the crowd as Sheik Rassam stepped up to the center of the platform. He stood between two men who were holding flares. Glancing down at the boy, sprawled in the dust below, his voice rose in a stern proclamation. Others whispered his words in an echoing murmur of translations. Isaiah listened carefully, interpreting the message so that James could understand.

"For those crimes committed against the people of Bogadez . . . for slaying the servant of his Arab master and then trying to escape, there can be no quarter. No crime is worse than disobedience. As leader of the Tuareg nation, I hereby sentence the infidel to be executed tomorrow during the first hour of the sun. His head shall be cut off with one stroke of the sword."

Fists hammered at the blackened sky. Raised spears flashed in the reflection of flares. Then all words were lost as a thousand voices took up the cheer, the chorus rising into a deafening, thundering roar.

PART V

There is no God but God and Mohammed is his prophet.

Moslem prayer

43

In a blackened chamber lit by a small dwindling fire, James Jacobson paced back and forth, a rising knot of tension in his stomach. If Lasiri's plan worked, they had a chance to save them both. If, if, if, he thought. Too many ifs. Too many damned ifs and nothing to count on, nothing for sure. There were two points in their favor, surprise and timing, and a thousand against. Even if the plan was only partially successful, there was a chance that they might still be able to save his sister. But he was beyond the point of settling for any consolation. There would be no compromise. He had to win it all or nothing. He would do his best and if it didn't work, then it was his life as well. But what did it matter now? He'd come there to get Diana and he wasn't about to leave without Jon Paul. Given the right amount of persuasion, Ibrahim had confessed everything they wanted to know. Ruth's suspicions had been correct. The marabout had been born and raised in Italy. He'd developed an early interest in languages and gone to a college in Naples where he'd studied Arabic, Latin, and Greek. During the war he'd been drafted into the Italian army and sent with a company to fight in Northern Africa with the Germans. Because of his language background, he'd become an interpreter. But he hated the war, hated the Germans, and resented ever having to leave his studies. When the war turned against the Axis forces and Rommel was forced to flee across the Libyan desert, Ibrahim had deserted. The Germans caught him and shipped him off to a concentration camp in the middle of the Sahara. There he'd been branded by his Arab guards with a swastika, but the Arabs had copied it wrong and reversed the direction of the arms. Ibrahim and a dozen others had been able to escape. Two years later (and Ruth had filled in this part of the history) one of the survivors surfaced with an incredible story of wandering through the desert, living off camel urine and cannibalism to keep alive. After the war the reverse swastika, or the cross of Agamore, as it was called, became known as the cross of hell. The men tattooed with the insignia had lived in one of the most horrible concentration camps. Those few who had escaped had gone through an even worse hell trying to survive.

Somewhere off in the Sahara, Ibrahim had cast off his civilian clothes, grown a beard, and submerged himself in the Arab culture. He'd traveled for a while with a small band of nomads. During a Tuareg raid he'd saved his life by posing as a religious man, and there in the far reaches of Northern Africa he'd shed his old identity forever. Now thirty years had passed and he was an important advisor to Sheik Rassam. The movement of civilization back into the desert had threatened his disguise. Things were going too well for him as it was. He wanted no interference from outside.

During the night Lasiri had forced Ibrahim down into Bogadez. At knifepoint the priest had shown them the harem tent where Diana was being held. But no one was sure where Rassam was keeping Jon Paul. And the main tent was too well guarded to attempt a rescue at night. They would have to wait until morning. Ruth, Isaiah, and Solomon would go to the harem tent at the first light of dawn. At the same time James and two Somalis would work their way through the crowd at the market and try to free Jon Paul. Lasiri would stampede the camels. Surprise would be to their advantage, but timing would be critical, and much of the success would depend on Lasiri. They had no other choice. If it didn't work, James was determined to fight his way onto the platform with guns blazing until he was out of ammunition. Rassam first, and then anyone else who got in the way until they killed him. Winner take all. There would be nothing in between.

Home, James thought. God, what sweet music to that word. In his mind he was ringing the doorbell to his parents' Westchester estate. He could hear his mother's footsteps hurrying down the hall. As she opened the door he could visualize her face, and he watched her expression change from shock to surprise, to euphoria, then emotional exhaustion as tears streamed down her cheeks. He could hear his father and his brothers rushing down the hallway toward the open door, shouting and yelling. "They're home! They're here!" But something was wrong. In James's fantasy someone was missing. Was it Jon Paul? Diana? Maybe himself? The image had turned into a nightmarish vision of failure and grief.

He trembled once and wondered if perhaps he should pray for help. It's been a long time since I've done that, he reflected. How would he say it? "Dear Lord, if you help me get my family out safe, I promise to always believe in you and devote my life to the church forever after. Hail Mary and amen . . . ?"

No, he thought. If there was a God who looked over the affairs of men, such a God would never fall for such hollow promises. Better make it all come out all right and then, when it was all over, offer thanks.

His thoughts were suddenly interrupted by a firm hand on his shoulder.

"The guns are ready, bwana," Lasiri said.

They were in a small side cave, a flare stuck into a crevice on the wall. On the floor, Lasiri had arranged the rifles and ammunition into neat columns.

"Not the most modern of weapons," the Masai announced. "From time to time Isaiah's men have been able to make off with some of the nomad's guns. Five Italian carbines, one 235 English army rifle, two pistols, and six medium-sized hunting guns were the best I could find. There are others back in the caves, but they look rusty to me and there isn't enough ammunition for them other than a few rounds. I wanted to leave some for Isaiah and the others."

"He's not coming?" James asked in surprise.

Lasiri shook his head. "Ruth is talking with him now, but I don't think so."

James crouched down and surveyed the arms. "Man, what I would give for our automatic weapons."

Lasiri nodded. "I tried to find our guns the night we were ambushed, but the Tuaregs must have taken them. Once they discovered they didn't know how to use them, they probably threw them away."

James picked up one of the Italian carbines. "How much ammunition do we have?"

"Roughly twelve rounds for each rifle."

"Not a lot," James answered.

"Isaiah has arranged for his men to meet us with camels tomorrow. We'll have blankets and water and limited supplies."

"And then?"

"Once we have your brother and sister safely, we go for al Jabbar. It shouldn't take us more than two days if we really push it."

"You don't think it is best to stay here?"

Lasiri shook his head. "The Tuaregs might come in here after your sister, once they found she was gone. If the priest is right and she's Rassam's favorite, there is no telling what he might do. It could mean he'd massacre all the cave people, looking for her. Remember, the people here depend on trading with the nomads for their supplies. We'd be jeopardizing their safety. They've no quarrel with anyone. Best not put them in a position where they have to fight."

"Why not just hide here in the caves and wait for help?"

"Help, bwana? What help? The plane might have had nothing to do with us at all."

"And what do you think our chances are of getting out?"

Lasiri looked at James and smiled. "Probably one hell of a lot better than they were coming in."

Isaiah was in the big cave crouched by the fire. He'd propped Alabaster up on one shoulder and was gently scratching the monkey under the chin. Ruth sat next to him on a small stool drinking broth from a metal cup. Solomon stood next to a second fire, working with the shaft of a spear. His muscles flexed and bulged as he hammered at the metal, trying to forge it straight. Sweat glistened off his brow, his nose ring a flash of gold in the darkness. Half a dozen other ex-slaves lounged in the shadows.

"Well, sister, I'm wishing us much good luck tomorrow," Isaiah said.

"And you won't be returning with us?"

"It's tempting, but I think I'd better pass. I figure there might be a man or two needing my help before they all leave the oasis. It'll probably take a month or so before everyone is gone. The Tuaregs first, then the Arabs and Berbers, and finally the Moors. There's always a few stragglers who linger until the very end."

"And what about the men here?"

"They'll make it out all right. They'll just wait things out and then when everyone is gone, they can slip back across the desert to their homes."

"And you, Isaiah, what will you do?"

"Been living here for a couple of seasons now, sister. Figure this is pretty much my home. Next year if the Tuaregs come again and the city springs to life, well, then, maybe I'll have some more rescuing to do. But not much for me back there in Capetown. Work in a factory maybe, or on the docks, punching a time clock, making seven dollars an hour. I've had enough of that. It's time I settled down. Surviving the shipwreck was lesson enough. Alabaster here is a pretty good companion and Solomon will take care of me. No, sister, thanks for the offer but I think I'll be staying on."

"You know you could take some of the jewels, Isaiah, and go back to civilization. You'd be rich for life."

"Thought about that, too, but what the hell would I do? Sit on a beach somewhere and retire? Maybe if things get too hot for me here, trying to break James's family out, I'll join in with one of those caravans out of the city. But go back to civilization? No thanks. At least here I got some purpose.

"Besides"—he winked—"what would I do with me monk?"

"Well, whatever happens, I want to thank you first for helping us and second for showing me the chambers beneath Bogadez."

"Don't mention it. You'd have done the same for me."

"I want to come back someday, Isaiah, and bring a full archaeological team to excavate this place from top to bottom. Much of the history of the desert is buried back in these caves."

"You do that, sister, and I'll be delighted to show you around."

He paused, placing a cup of broth to heat in the coals.

"I've got to hand it to you, sister. You were right about kidnapping the priest."

"What's to happen to him after we leave?" Ruth asked.

Isaiah chuckled. "Figure the one thing he could use is a little humility. Maybe after you and James get out of here safely and the Tuaregs have gone, we'll turn him over to the cave people. Let them work on him for a while. Maybe there he will find grace—eh?"

"And what about the cave people?"

Isaiah shrugged. "Figure they've been living back here since the beginning of Bogadez. They leave everyone pretty much alone and mostly, with the leprosy and all, everyone leaves them alone as well.

"Awful disease . . ." He shuddered. "Thing I don't understand is how they could live with it, one generation after the next."

"It works on the body very slowly," Ruth answered. "The caves may be ideal for these people, but they're perfect for the transmission of the disease as well."

"How long you figure someone lasts when he gets it?"

"Sometimes years," Ruth replied.

"And what are the first symptoms?"

"Usually nothing too noticeable," Ruth answered. "Often a patch of numbness in the fingers or the toes. Might go on like this for several months, maybe even a year. Then something happens, an injury occurs and a finger is gone. You see, it's the loss of the nerve endings that often results in the damage. With the numbness one can't feel the danger."

She paused at the smell of burning flesh. Isaiah had reached into the fire to withdraw his cup. Smoke rose from his fingertips.

"Isaiah, careful, you'll burn—" Ruth started to say and then she stopped, suddenly understanding it all. Understanding why Isaiah remained there in the caves, understanding why he was reluctant to go back, understanding what he had been trying to tell her. In his own mind the disease had been too terrible for him to acknowledge. He could only show her.

"How long . . . ?" she asked.

He stared at the fire without looking up. "Maybe a couple of months," he answered.

44

Dawn. The first rays of light like glowing streamers. Colors dissolved, brightened, then changed as peaks of the desert mountains became violet, then orange. A falcon launched from its craggy roost and soared across the sky, its cry echoing through the canyon. Below, shadows fled across the ruins as new rays of the sun caught the tops of ancient buildings reflecting from the sandstone in sparks of fire. Camels moaned. A herd of goats pushed impatiently toward parched clumps of brownish grass. Inside the vast city of tents people began to stir. The women first, chattering with one another; then the children, their high-pitched cries mixed with the brays of goats. Finally the men, cantankerous and insolent, grumbling as they rose. By the time the sun had begun to edge above the horizon in a fiery globe, the transformation was complete. The city was alive. And on this particular morning a steady stream of nomads began to flow toward the marketplace until nearly a thousand were there. The disorder that had reigned the night before was absent. The crowd patiently watched and waited, all eyes fixed on the central platform. But the crude wooden structure was empty. Rassam was gone. And the young infidel, Jon Paul Jacobson, was nowhere to be seen.

From the top of an ancient watchtower a muzzein called out the morning prayer, his voice wavering in a melancholy chant: *"Laa illaha illa llaah . . ."* Everyone in the market fell to his knees. Hidden among them, his face covered by a hooded robe, James Jacobson bowed with them, touching his forehead to the

ground. The last words of the third prayer echoed across the
market and then all was silent.

As the sun arched up another degree, faint whispers began to
ripple through the crowd. Suddenly a cheer, growing, building
in a chorus of voices. At the corner of the market an aisle
formed. Six Tuaregs strode forward at a steady march. Between
them, his hands bound behind his back, his chest bare, came
Jon Paul Jacobson. Behind him was Sheik Rassam, followed by
a dozen Tuaregs. Moving like a living phalanx, they pushed
through the mob toward the platform. A steady, high-pitched
cry began to rise from the women, a piercing noise, shrill and
grating in its intensity.

When the party reached the platform, Jon Paul was led up to
the front of the structure. He stood there, gazing out upon the
throng, his eyes vacant. Rassam stepped onto the platform and
raised his hands for silence.

James fingered the rifle beneath his robe and pushed steadily
forward, nudging his way around one person, past the next,
working toward the front of the crowd. Carefully he undid the
string holding the rifle to his leg. He slid his finger along the
side of the chamber, releasing the safety. The silence was un-
canny. A moment before he wanted to put his hands over his
ears to avoid the shrill sound of the women's voices. Now all he
could hear was the pounding of his heart. His mouth was dry;
the knot at the pit of his stomach steadily tightening.

What if Lasiri is caught? he wondered. What if Rassam has
moved Diana? What if Ruth and Isaiah run into trouble? Better
cross that bridge when you come to it, he told himself. There
was no time for a faint heart now.

For a moment as Jon Paul stood upon the platform, James
thought his brother had seen him. The boy's eyes stopped and
stared in his direction, but there was no hint, no sign of recogni-
tion. Then James realized that his hooded face, bearded and
rubbed with dirt, would be indistinguishable from a hundred
others who watched from the crowd. He feels he is by himself,
James thought, alone, abandoned, and about to be executed.

Jon Paul's hair was matted with dried blood. His face and
chest carried open sores where they had struck him. How brave
he is, James thought. How amazing that he stepped into this

country with no fear and it was I who wasn't sure of myself.
Now, in the face of death, he's still stronger than I've ever been.
Well, we're in this together, Jon Paul, he thought. And if you go
down, so do I. He moved his hand tighter around the breech of
the rifle.

His thoughts were suddenly interrupted as Rassam nodded to
a huge Arab standing at the right of the platform. The man
bowed and unsheathed a long, curving sword. The sight of the
blade sent James's pulse thundering like a sledgehammer.

Can't wait much longer, he thought. He eased the rifle from
his robe and shifted it to his right hand. Moving slowly, he
nudged his way into a position in front of the platform where he
had a clear and unobstructed view of Jon Paul. Come on,
Lasiri, his mind screamed. Where the hell are you? Don't fail
me now.

As the first rays of light had broken over the ruins of
Bogadez, Isaiah, Ruth, and Solomon the Mute crept along the
outskirts of the city toward the harem tent of Sheik Rassam.
Solomon carried a spear and Isaiah a knife, but they had no
other weapons.

They paused from time to time to duck behind a wall of rocks
or step back into the recesses of the ruins as others passed them,
hurrying to the market. The monkey, Alabaster, was perched
upon Isaiah's shoulder. Moving cautiously, they advanced from
one stone foundation to the next.

In twenty minutes they were crouched behind a low wall,
surveying the great tent of Sheik Rassam. Next to the structure
was a corral containing half a dozen camels. Two Tuaregs stood
adjacent to the enclosure, guarding. Behind the main tent was
the smaller tent of Rassam's harem.

As the distant wavering voice of the muzzein reached them,
both Tuaregs dropped to their knees, bowing to the east. Isaiah
nodded to Solomon. "Now!" he whispered.

In an instant Solomon slipped over the wall. Moving like a
cat, he darted across a narrow opening, then crept in behind the
corners of Rassam's tent. Without a sound, he maneuvered
himself behind the Tuaregs. Isaiah heard a low thud followed
by a moan. As the prayer finished, he peered over the stone

wall. Solomon was waving to them. Both Tuaregs were out cold
on the ground.

As soon as they reached the corral, Isaiah cut the ropes and
set the camels free. Moving quickly, they crept around the perimeter of Rassam's tent toward the smaller harem tent. Everyone is down at the market, Isaiah reflected. Maybe they'd be
luckier than he had imagined.

At the back of the harem tent, he slashed the canvas with a
quick downward thrust of his knife. Ducking over, they entered
the opening, moving into the interior.

Dim oil lamps illuminated the chamber. Ahead was a corridor partitioned off by blankets. A shadow passed in front of one
of the lamps and they crouched back in the darkness. From
somewhere in the tent they could hear the splashes of someone
bathing. Ruth reached up and tightened a veil that hid her face,
then pulled the robe up around her shoulders. The disguise was
not perfect, but if she was discovered, there was a good chance
she might be taken for one of the harem servants.

"We'll wait here," Isaiah whispered. He pulled Solomon back
into the shadows.

Ruth started carefully down the corridor. She'd taken only
three steps when her foot caught a group of pans, which clattered away from her in the darkness. There was a sound of
scurrying feet as two women rushed down the hallway toward
them.

"Huzza, who's there?" cried a voice in Arabic.

Ruth bent over as if to rearrange the pans, hiding her face
and muffling her voice. "Desert rats," she muttered back in
Arabic. "They've been in the pans again."

"Ah, we thought it was an intruder."

"It was," Ruth answered harshly. "And when I catch him,
we will serve him up for dinner."

The women laughed and turned back, talking quietly to
themselves. In a moment the passageway was cleared and Ruth
let out a sigh of relief.

She advanced cautiously now. Halfway down the hallway,
she heard a noise behind a curtained chamber. She pushed the
curtain aside and peeked into the room. Two nude women were
being bathed by three black servants. No blond woman there,

she thought. She closed the curtain and moved another ten feet
down the hall. Opening a second curtain, she saw two veiled
women combing the hair of a third. It was not Diana. She let
the curtain fall. For a fleeting moment she felt her nerve begin
to fail. Then, ahead, she heard the sound of splashing water.
She moved swiftly to the chamber and pulled the curtain aside,
mentally calculating how she could retreat if she found trouble.
But a glance told her that she was momentarily safe.

In the soft illumination of an oil lamp she saw the bare back
of a beautiful, curvaceous woman. She was seated, a robe
loosely wrapped around her waist, her long golden hair falling
across her shoulders. A black slave girl crouched next to her,
washing her feet in a pan of water.

"That will be all, Tanaku," the blond woman said in Swahili.
The slave looked up, saw Ruth, and uttered a gasp of surprise.

"*Shalom,*" Ruth said in Arabic. She bowed as if she'd made a
mistake and quickly dropped the curtain. Stepping out into the
corridor, she waved to Isaiah and Solomon. She'd found her!

The two men had started up the corridor when a harem servant unexpectedly came out of one of the side doorways and
almost ran into them. There was an instant of surprise as the
woman faced the intruders. Then she let out an ear-piercing
shriek and fled back into the chamber. The alarm echoed down
the corridor as the tent erupted in a chorus of frightened
screams. . . .

In the crowded market all eyes were fixed on the young
American standing on the platform. Two of the Tuaregs came
forward and forced him to his knees, pulling him forward so
that his neck was extended, his head pointing toward the
crowd. The executioner walked toward him, brandishing the
sword in his right hand.

Hidden in the crowd, James could feel his muscles tense. He
pushed his hand down around the rifle and gripped the trigger.
Isaiah's two men were somewhere lost in the crowd, but he
hadn't seen them since he entered the market. And Lasiri? Time
was running out.

The Arab with the sword positioned himself directly next to
Jon Paul. Gripping the handle with both hands, he widened his

stance to stabilize the blow. The cry of the women started up
again, rising in intensity until it became deafening. Rassam nodded to the executioner. The Arab raised his sword, the long,
curving blade flashing in the morning sun.

James watched for a second, paralyzed. Christ, what's happened? Lasiri was late. He would have to go it alone. It was the
moment he most feared. He brought his rifle up in one swing of
his arm and sighted on the swordsman's chest. As the executioner rocked back to begin the blow, James held his breath and
pulled the trigger. All this happened in an instant, time enough
for one fear to blaze across James's mind and imprint itself
indelibly on his brain. They had lost. The plan had failed.

Inside the harem tent all bedlam had broken loose. Isaiah
pulled Solomon behind a curtain as one of the harem guards
came running down the corridor. When the man went lumber-
ing by, Isaiah reached out with his crutch and tripped him. The
guard sprawled to the ground, tried to struggle to his feet only
to meet a single blow from Solomon's fist, aimed directly between the eyes. From the noise, it sounded as if the man had
been struck with a club. He crumpled into a senseless heap and
did not move.

Isaiah and Solomon charged down the corridor. Ruth had
already wrapped a blanket around Diana.

"Diana, come on, we're taking you home," Ruth said.

"But I—" she started to answer when Solomon lifted her up
and threw her over his shoulder with no more effort than if she
were a bag of straw. The giant turned, following Isaiah and
Ruth back down the corridor toward the opening in the back of
the tent.

They had just reached the end of the chamber when the un-
mistakable report of a rifle echoed across the ruins, followed by
a volley of gunfire.

Ruth's eyes darted toward Isaiah. "James . . . ?" she asked.

"Sounds like they've started," Isaiah whispered.

James heard the crack of the rifle, felt the recoil dig into his
right shoulder. Sword suspended in midair, the executioner
froze, then toppled forward, a blossom of red springing from his

chest. The blade fell from his hands and clattered onto the platform. Then James heard the explosions of rifle fire behind him. God, let it be Isaiah's men, he thought.

Working in a frenzy, he ejected the cartridge and rammed another bullet into place. Shooting rapidly, he fired at one of the Tuaregs standing on the platform, saw the man fall, then fired a second shot at Rassam. Blood spurted from the sheik's robe just below his left shoulder. James's third shot caught a Tuareg directly in the chest, and the man dropped. In an instant, James was rushing the platform. Out of the corner of his eye he caught a glimpse of two wiry black forms leaping up on either side of the structure, firing wildly. A bullet whizzed by his head. He loaded his rifle, looked hastily for Rassam, but couldn't find him. He turned and fired suddenly point-blank at a Tuareg with a sword, charging toward his brother. The man slumped away from the boy and James rushed to him. With the sound of gunfire ringing in his ears, he drew a knife and cut Jon Paul loose.

"Boy, am I glad to see you!" Jon Paul cried.

"Just thought we'd drop by," James answered.

In the background James was conscious of the discordant voices of the women changing to cries and screams of alarm. Then he heard the deep-throated bellow of camels accompanied by the growing sound of trampling hoofs.

"Lasiri," he murmured. "Thank God."

They were coming out of the harem tent when Isaiah suddenly pulled Ruth and Solomon back inside. "Tuaregs." He cursed.

Outside the tent, inspecting the slit in the canvas, were six armed guards. One of them drew a sword and started cautiously into the opening. The rest followed him through the rent until all six were standing in the narrow confines of the room.

Reaching up, Isaiah took Alabaster off his shoulder and set the monkey on the ground. They crouched back in the shadows.

"Sister, take Diana to the caves," he whispered. "Don't wait for us."

He crept toward the guards, holding his crutch like a club. Solomon put Diana down and moved in behind him. Isaiah waited a moment to give Ruth a chance to start down the hall-way, then he charged.

He met the first Tuareg with a broadside, the crutch striking his opponent's sword halfway in the air. The Tuareg parried once, swung with a ferocious blow, then tried a savage over-the-head chop that Isaiah barely had time to block. The crutch caved in on top of him, the wood splintering. Solomon swung, jabbed, slashed with his spear, keeping the other Tuaregs at bay. When he saw Isaiah lose his crutch, he let out an angry roar and hurled the spear across the room, impaling two of the Tuaregs at once.

Isaiah glanced around in time to see Ruth and Diana disappear at the far end of the corridor. Then he yelled to Solomon, pointing toward a tent post the size of a man's arm. Using his fist like an axe, the giant smashed the wood in two, the canvas section of the tent collapsing in on top of them.

"Go with them!" Isaiah shouted just before he was buried beneath the falling canvas.

The stampeding camels thundered through the crowded marketplace like a herd of wild bulls. There were a hundred of them and Lasiri was riding the lead, yelling and firing his gun. The animals churned forward, heading directly for the platform, splitting the crowd as Arabs, Tuaregs, Berbers dashed wildly for safety. At the platform, Lasiri leaped down, running toward James and Jon Paul.

"Quickly!" he yelled. "Pull yourself up on a strap." He motioned to two camels that had been saddled and were running closest to the platform. James scarcely had time to jump off the structure onto the sides of one of the beasts. He almost lost his grip, but, gritting his teeth, he managed to pull himself up onto its back. When he looked around he saw Jon Paul on top of the camel behind him. Lasiri had leaped onto a third. Isaiah's two men darted off the platform and were lost in the confusion of the crowd.

The camels charged forward, racing out of the market toward a broad thoroughfare. Tents were knocked down, people barely able to lunge out of the way without being trampled. The beasts surged down the streets in a full stampede.

They'd come around a sharp corner moving at a gallop when they passed a group of women. Jon Paul happened to look up and saw a veiled face staring toward him. Her hand was up to her lips, moisture welling in her eyes. "Faedra! *Faedra!*" he screamed. He tried to stop the camel, tried somehow to slow the charging animals, but they were going too fast. He looked back once, saw her wave to him in a silent kiss, and then she was gone as the wild rush of the animals forced him past. In another minute they were plunging down toward the oasis.

At the outskirts of the city Lasiri was able to lead the three camels away from the herd, and James and Jon Paul followed at a gallop toward the canyon. The rest of the animals continued running to the water until they finally disappeared in a massive cloud of rising dust.

When they reached the base of the cliffs, they found Solomon waiting for them with five fresh camels. Ruth and Diana were perched on one of the animals.

"Hallelujah!" James shouted. "We made it! Everybody all right?"

Lasiri glanced around. "Where's Isaiah?"

"He said not to wait for him," Ruth answered. "He got temporarily detained by a band of Tuaregs."

"Is he all right?"

"He'll make it." Ruth nodded.

"We wait for five minutes and then we go," Lasiri said. "We have about a half-hour head start on Rassam. If we wait any longer, we'll be in trouble."

Lasiri looked at Diana. "Come on, my friend. Come down and say hello to your brothers." He reached up and pulled her gently off the camel.

Diana turned her head in James's direction and for the first time James realized he hadn't even said hello. He hadn't seen her in more than a year. He studied her briefly, noting the gray opacifications of her eyes. Taking her in his arms, he hugged her with all his might.

"God, am I glad to see you," he whispered, and then all three —James, Jon Paul, and Diana—were kissing and embracing.

"Sis, are you all right?" Jon Paul asked.

"Of course," she snapped. "I was worried about *you.*"

"Well, I was worried about you too," Jon Paul answered.

Ruth Parker watched with tears in her eyes.

"Better go," Lasiri said. "We'll have to leave without telling Isaiah good-bye."

"James, I've got to go back," Jon Paul said.

"You bloody crazy?" James stared at him in astonishment.

"Faedra's back there. I can't leave her behind."

Lasiri came forward and gripped Jon Paul firmly by the shoulder. "Too dangerous, bwana." He firmly shook his head. "If it was meant to be, you will find her again."

Jon Paul frowned, started to say something, then bit his lip and turned away to climb onto his camel. In his mind he knew they were right. But some small piece of his heart would remain in Bogadez forever.

"Let's go," James said. He mounted one of the camels. Lasiri helped Diana onto Ruth's camel and then swung into the lead.

"They'll follow the leader," he said with a grin. "Hang on!"

James reached down and grabbed Solomon's arm. "Thanks to Isaiah," he said, and then they were off galloping down the canyon, the echo of their hoofbeats clattering off the steep rock walls.

Isaiah pulled himself out from under the collapsed tent, wriggling like a snake.

"Come on, monk!" he shouted. He darted through the tent, ducking down a side passage, then through a curtained doorway. He entered a chamber, heard a sudden scream, and turned around to face two women lunging for their robes.

"Pardon me, sisters," he said, bowing.

He spun around and bolted out again as a harem guard came running down the corridor. Isaiah started in the opposite direction in time to see two of the Tuaregs come out from beneath the collapsed tent. He reversed again, drew his knife, and slit through the sides of the tent, then leaped outside.

He hadn't gone a hundred feet when a dozen Tuaregs came running around the corner of Rassam's great tent. Isaiah changed direction, hobbling quickly toward a smaller tent another hundred feet away. The Tuaregs split into two groups, running around the tent on either side. With a slash of his knife,

Isaiah slit the canvas and disappeared inside, the monkey dashing in behind him.

The Tuaregs surrounded the tent. Two rushed through the front entrance, while another two charged the slit in the back. But Isaiah was not there. A moment later they heard a whistle from outside the tent down by a low stone wall. Spinning around, they were surprised to find Isaiah leaning next to the wall, the monkey on his shoulder.

"Up here, mates!" he shouted. He turned and vaulted over the wall, Alabaster scampering after him. The Tuaregs pursued him, running past a column of rocks, through the empty foundations of an old building, and then they lost him. Before they saw him again, Isaiah had darted down a long alleyway, leaped through a narrow crevice, and was outside the city gates.

In twenty minutes he was scampering up the cliffs, with Alabaster hanging on to his shoulder. When he reached the ledge near the top of the cliff, he looked down in time to see Lasiri's party start through the canyon. He squinted, noting that one of the camels had two riders. "By God, they made it!" he cried. He placed his fingers between his teeth and gave a sharp, shrill whistle, saw the figures wave up toward him, and then he turned, smiling to himself. A moment later he'd disappeared inside one of the caves leading into the bowels of Bogadez.

45

They were halfway through the canyon, charging past the magnificent columned facade, when the horns started up. The signals came in low-pitched blasts, echoing off the rock walls, as unseen observers blared out the alarm.

Lasiri brought the lead camel to a halt. "Damn," he said. "They'll be looking for us all the way to al Jabbar."

"What do we do?" Ruth asked.

"No way back now," he answered.

A tiny puff came from the top of the rocks followed an instant later by the faint crack of a rifle. There was a second explosion, then a third. A zinging sound whizzed past James's ear as a bullet dug into the sand next to him. His camel wheeled, moaned, and almost dislodged him.

"Keep moving!" Lasiri cried.

They started up again, fleeing down the canyon. In a hour they had galloped through the cliffs and now were moving out onto the open plateau. The desert spread out to the north in an impenetrable, desolate grave of monotonous sand. To the south, the mountains rose in a series of peaks leading up to the Devil's Tower. Ahead stood a long line of cliffs. After a moment's search, Lasiri spotted the narrow pass and led the party toward it. Just as they entered the opening, a cloud of dust rose to their right, moving along the edge of the cliffs. Six Tuaregs wheeled out of hiding and churned toward them.

"James, Ruth, go on ahead!" Lasiri shouted. "Jon Paul and I can hold them off."

He brought his camel to a halt just at the edge of the cliffs and dismounted. Jon Paul swung in beside him. Crouching behind a line of boulders, they waited until the Tuaregs were less than a hundred yards away before they opened fire. Two Tuaregs fell with the first volley of shots. Jon Paul reloaded and fired again. A third fell. The remaining Tuaregs stopped, turned their camels, and galloped off.

"Good shooting!" Lasiri cried.

He swung back on his camel, Jon Paul following close behind. In another ten minutes they had caught up with the rest of the party moving through the steep-walled pass.

For the rest of the day they traveled through the narrow canyon, the walls hovering above them like a tunnel. The sun reached its peak, then gradually began to descend. They stopped once and rested, trying to find some solace in the shade of an outcropping of rocks. James poured a small goatskin of water over his hands and rubbed the cool, refreshing liquid into his hair. Giving some to Diana, he gently held the container so that she could drink. Her face was coated with dust, her beautiful blond hair matted and soaked with perspiration.

"How you feeling?" he questioned.

"All right," she answered.

"Couple of more hours," he said. He stared at Diana's eyes. There were gray scars over the surface of the corneas. "Wires red hot, brought up to the eyes," Ruth had told him. "It only takes a touch." He cringed at the thought of the pain.

"Can you see at all?" he asked softly.

"Yes, I can tell there's light."

"We'll get you back to New York, to a specialist. There's got to be some way."

"Oh, James," she said, placing her arms around him and hugging him. "I didn't give up back there, never. Somehow I knew you would come."

"We'll be all right," James murmured. "Everything will turn out okay."

Lasiri moved up next to him. "Best keep moving," he said.

They had been traveling for two hours, moving at a steady pace, when suddenly the canyon began to open up into broad, wide walls. Stick figures appeared along the rocks.

"The drawings!" Ruth exclaimed. "We're almost out."

"Keep low, trouble ahead," Lasiri murmured.

Five dark forms hovered above the edge of the cliffs, staring down into the canyon. James could see the remnants of an old watchtower high up on the edge of the cliffs. Adjacent to it rose a tiny tuft of smoke. A bullet sang by overhead. Scattered flashes ignited from the rocks. A second bullet struck a corner of a boulder and ricocheted near them in a high-pitched whine.

"Keep moving!" Lasiri yelled. "Jon Paul, hold your fire until we're directly beneath them."

As they galloped around a bend in the canyon, the mountains opened up. Broad daylight ahead. The desert stretched out before them in a wide expanse of sand. Beyond that the wadi and then al Jabbar. Almost safe, James thought.

More gunshots came from the cliffs. Lasiri halted his camel and fired up at the Tuaregs. Jon Paul pulled up beside him, took aim, and fired. A small dark figure straightened up and plummeted off the edge of the cliffs.

"Good shot, Jon Paul!" James cried.

Lasiri fired twice more. Jon Paul aimed, pulled the trigger, and his gun clicked. "Damn it. Out of ammunition," he said.

"I've only got a couple of rounds left too." Lasiri grunted. He glanced toward the desert ahead. "Looks like we made it just in time."

He fired once more, saw a dark figure roll forward and cascade down the side of the cliffs with an avalanche of rocks. Turning his camel, he led the party at a full gallop out through the cliffs toward the desert. "Go for it!" he shouted.

Behind them came a desperate fusillade of shots as the Tuaregs tried one last volley of gunfire. James could hear the shots whiz by overhead. "Ha, catch us now, you bastards!" he cried. And then he heard a gasp from behind. Swinging around, he saw Ruth clutch her chest and slump sideways, off the camel.

"Oh, Christ," he yelled. "Lasiri! Ruth's hit. She's down."

Lasiri pulled the camels to a halt, dismounted, and ran back to her. James and Jon Paul quickly joined him. Ruth lay in the sand, a pool of crimson spreading out across her robe.

"I'm all right," she muttered, but there was a deep-throated gurgle to her voice. "Just help me up."

"We'll have to double up," Lasiri said.

Jon Paul and James helped Lasiri hoist Ruth onto Lasiri's camel. The Masai mounted behind her. James rode with Diana now and Jon Paul rode alone. They started up again, driving the camels forward. Steadily the cliffs began to fall away behind them.

"Keep going. Don't lose strength," Lasiri commanded. "They'll not be letting us go that easy."

For an hour they moved rapidly onto the desert. The camels were soaked with perspiration, a greenish-white froth exuding from their mouths. Finally Lasiri slowed the party to a trot.

As the mountains sank behind them, James could feel the tightness in his stomach begin to ease. Every now and then he would look back, relieved to see the steady distance grow between them and the mountain pass. But there was a cloud, there, hanging low on the horizon, and it rose ominously as if it were dust.

"Lasiri," James said, "something moving back there."

The Masai pulled the caravan to a halt and studied the cloud. "More Tuaregs." He grunted. "I'm afraid they've started after us." He searched toward Jon Paul and Diana. "You two all right?"

They nodded.

"How much ammunition do we have left?"

"Three rounds here," James said.

"Empty," answered Jon Paul.

"I've got three rounds," Lasiri murmured. "And one handgun with six bullets. Not much to fend off the entire Tuareg nation."

He shook Ruth gently. "You all right?"

"Still here," she whispered. But her face was white and her arms hung limply at her sides.

"We keep going," Lasiri said. "Even if we have to drive these camels into the ground. If we can last until dark, they'll never catch us."

They traveled for another hour. For a while James thought they were holding their distance, but as he studied the cloud he realized it was growing closer.

By six in the evening they reached the wadi. The sun had already begun to drift down behind the distant mountains, the western sky turning a brilliant orange. There was nothing for them at the wadi but a damp, moist depression, a few scattered dig holes, and some skeletal branches of desert shrub. The Abyssinians' remains were completely gone.

Lasiri brought the procession to a halt. Ruth had been riding in front of him, between his arms. As he let her go, she slumped forward.

He dismounted and pulled her gently down, cradling her in his arms. She smiled bravely, but her hands could not grip and her eyes rolled back in her head. Lasiri loosened her robe and felt down across her chest. A damp ooze of blood seeped out from her breast. She coughed once in a deep, racking spasm that brought blood-tinged spittle from her lips. "Sorry. . . ." She tried to smile.

The Masai swung back on top of his camel and galloped to a ridge of sand. Here he stood motionless, studying their pursuers.

"I count nearly thirty of them," he said when he returned. "We've got another hour or so of light. Even if we were in good shape and the camels were fresh, they would catch us before dark."

There was a long, grim moment of silence.

"I've got a plan," he said slowly. "I want you to gather some sticks. Get branches five and six feet long. We can take the blankets and rig them over the wood and tie them in a bundle so they look like riders. I'll take off for al Jabbar. From a distance they'll think we're trying to race them to the oasis. If they follow me, stay here until nightfall. Then head north. Follow the constellations. You can circle back to al Jabbar tomorrow."

"Lasiri—" James began, but the Masai cut him short.

"No arguments," he replied. "Find me branches as long as you can. The longer the better. Hurry. We don't have much time."

In twenty minutes Jon Paul and James had gathered a dozen long branches. Working deftly, Lasiri tied them together in clumps. They fastened these bundles to the backs of the camels, then draped the blankets over each bundle and tied them on with a length of line taken from the camels' bridles.

When they had finished, Lasiri rode back out to the ridge and studied the approaching caravan. He returned quickly and dismounted, fastening all of the camels together in a line.

"We've only got fifteen to twenty minutes before they reach us," he said. "Bury yourself beneath one of the sand ridges and wait until dark."

He bent down and kissed Ruth Parker on the forehead. "That's for Cambridge and all the other things you've done for me. Good luck, memsaab."

Ruth's eyes fluttered. She moaned, then fell back, breathing heavily.

Lasiri turned to Diana. "Sorry we didn't get you out sooner."

"Oh, Lasiri," she replied, holding him in her arms. "How can we thank you?" There was moisture in her eyes. "Go carefully."

Lasiri reached out and shook Jon Paul's hands. "Take care of yourself." He grinned. "No more C's in school."

"I'm coming with you," Jon Paul said firmly.

"Not this time," he answered. He threw his rifle to Jon Paul. "You've got a family to defend. Take good care of them."

He turned to James. The American met his stare and for a long, silent moment they looked into each other's eyes.

"Good luck, bwana," he said.

"Lasiri, what can I say?" James's voice was choked.

The Masai turned and mounted his camel. Reaching inside his robe, he pulled a thin gold chain over his head. On one end of the chain was a small blue stone.

"If anything happens out there and you make it back, I would appreciate it if you would give this to my son. He's only six now and he lives in Naivasha. He's a smart young lad. Tell him that I loved him."

"Lasiri!" James wanted to shout. "Don't go. Christ, stay here and we'll fend them off. If we had the automatic weapons, we could shoot them by the hundreds." But he looked at his defenseless family and realized that Lasiri was right, that they had no other options. They were fighting time and the fading light. It was their only chance.

James held out his hand and Lasiri pressed the stone of the oasis in his palm.

"God bless you," James said, and then Lasiri swung the lead camel around. He glanced back at the line of stick figures covered in blankets behind him.

"It's a noble crew." He laughed loudly. "Let them catch us if they can. Hiyyyaa!" And then he was off, waving his revolver, the blanketed stick figures bobbing and weaving behind him.

Crouched on top of a hidden ridge, James and Jon Paul watched Lasiri until he was hardly more than a trail of dust heading for al Jabbar. From a distance the camels looked like a small caravan, the blankets like riders, and James thought, Maybe, just maybe, it would work. He turned and searched for the rising cloud coming toward them. Their pursuers were no more than half a mile away, bearing down on the wadi at a tremendous pace. He could see their black headdresses and the glint of their rifles. As he listened he thought he could hear them yelling to one another, urging their camels on. The line fanned out in either direction as the camels galloped toward them. In the middle of the group, James saw a figure dressed in white.

"Rassam!" He gasped. So he had only wounded him. Lasiri had been right. Rassam had gathered his best men and come after them, following them all the way from the Bogadez. And now a new worry began to creep into James's mind. If Rassam was pursuing them, there was no telling what lengths he would go in order to get Diana back. Well, he won't get her, James thought. We've got two rifles and six shots left, and sure as hell one of these bullets is going to be for Rassam.

He pulled Jon Paul down and they lay along the sand ridge and waited. A lump worked its way up into his throat. "Get ready, Jon Paul," he whispered. Jon Paul cocked his rifle. "Wait until they're right on top of us so that we can make every shot count."

James could see the froth on the camels' mouths, and the sweat glistening from their sides. Wait until you see their eyes, he thought. He tightened his finger around the trigger and still the Tuaregs came.

They were less than a hundred yards away when there arose a sudden series of shouts and the entire band turned east. In the distance Lasiri was a cloud of dust, moving rapidly away, and the Tuaregs bolted after him.

James eased the safety back on his rifle and let out a quiet sigh. His jaw hurt where he had been gritting his teeth. Turning, he followed Jon Paul back down the ridge to Diana.

Half an hour passed before they heard the first shot, a single faint clap as if from a pistol, followed by the scattered booms of rifle fire.

"There's one," James said quietly, counting Lasiri's shots. There was a moment of silence, then more rifle fire and then a second and third faint pop. "There's two and three," he said to himself.

Silence again. Nothing more for five minutes and then two more faint explosions in the distance.

"There's four and five."

There was a long quiet period. God, he must be giving them a

merry chase, James thought, and then he heard the last shot of
Lasiri's revolver. The noise had barely reached his ears when he
heard the distant thunder of a volley of shots echoing off the
desert. When he heard no more shooting, he knew the chase
was over.

James stood up slowly. Already the sun had disappeared below the horizon. Faint light bands flickered, changed, then
faded in the western sky. He walked over to where Diana was
holding Ruth.

"James, she's gone," Diana said.

He looked down and saw Ruth's peaceful resting features and
a great silent hurt leaped up inside his chest, a pain of frustration and loss.

"Come on, Jon Paul," he said quietly. They dug a small grave
next to the wadi and carefully laid Ruth to rest. Taking two
sticks, James fastened a crude cross and pushed it down into the
sand. Once finished, he helped Diana to her feet. The moon was
far above them, its pale light dancing on the sand ahead.

James picked up his rifle and checked his remaining ammunition—three cartridges, bullets he hoped he would never have to
use. Taking his sister by the hand, he searched up into the night
sky until he found the polar star.

"Which way now?" Jon Paul asked.

"What's your preference?" James answered. "Paris or
Rome?"

46

By ten P.M. the brightest lights in the parliamentary building in
Nairobi blazed from the chandelier of the seventh-floor conference room. Michael Jacobson stood next to the long mahogany
table and looked as if he were about to explode. His face was

red and angry, that same furious expression he wore whenever he was told something he neither accepted nor thought made any practical sense. His eyes glared, his lips tightened, and his fingers tightly gripped the table. Now, aware that if he spoke more he might say something that would further inflame the issue, he shook his head in disgust and sat back down. What he wanted to say and what he knew he should were diametrically opposed.

"Then you might as well issue them a death knell," he muttered.

Next to him was the ambassador of the United States, dressed in a sports coat and tie. To his left, Dr. Ian Anderson from the Nairobi Museum. At the opposite side of the table sat three of Kenya's government officials. One of them was Wilson Tomboya, the Minister of Foreign Affairs. Tomboya rolled his eyes toward Jacobson and frowned.

"You want me to ask the president of Kenya to send troops into the Sudan, Mr. Jacobson? An armed convoy across the border to look for a crazed expedition that already may be dead? That's what's insane. You've no idea where your sons are. You've seen a collection of desert nomads occupying the ruins of an ancient city. What proof is that? Did you find Dr. Anderson's associate Dr. Parker? Did anyone send up a distress signal for help? What evidence do you have that your sons or your daughter are there? I can't ask the president to send out troops because you *think* that is where they are. An armed force of any kind moving across the border would be considered an act of aggression. Do you want to start a war?"

The two black men in three-piece suits sitting on either side of the Minister of Foreign Affairs nodded firmly. One, an Under-Secretary to the Council of State, was an older man with gray matted hair; the other, younger, with a broad nose and thick lips, represented the President's Special Advisory Committee. Jacobson had managed to gain an audience with them under the pretext of an international crisis. All three men were clearly annoyed to have been detained for such a trivial matter so late at night.

"I'm not asking for an entire army, Mr. Minister. We saw some roads up there. There's got to be some access into the area. All I'm asking for is a couple of Land-Rovers and some armed men to see what's going on."

Tomboya shook his head. "The Sudan is a country, sir, governed by an independent political entity. I have no responsibility nor authority to send any kind of force across the border. Why don't you contact the Sudanese government yourself?"

"I've already tried," Jacobson answered angrily. "Their government is too involved in its own internal revolution to be bothered. I could get no help from them at all."

"Your son knew the best way to get across the border, Mr. Jacobson. Have you considered arranging another expedition to follow the same route?"

"Christ, it would take us a week to outfit a safari and another week to drive up into the Sudan."

"Well, then why don't you do it? Under these circumstances I think I could arrange for the proper permits."

"Because, damn it, man, by then it will be too late!" Jacobson roared.

He turned toward the United States ambassador. His pulse was pounding in his temples so hard he thought he was going to have a stroke. Well, that's it, he thought. The last hope to help my family, like a fading sun, going, going, gone. And then he did the one thing his better judgment had warned him not to do, the one thing that would prevent any further cooperation from the Kenyan government.

Unable to hold himself back any longer, he slammed his fist down upon the table.

"Mr. Ambassador, I'm sorry that I've wasted so much of your time," he said. "How the hell are we supposed to deal with the braying of these asses?"

47

It was long past midnight. The desert sky was black and cold, the stars like a blizzard of snow. The Big Camel had begun to sink to the west while The Great Scorpion rolled over on its back, its heavenly barb now poised directly above them. For six hours they had stumbled through the sand until they finally fell, exhausted. Directly ahead, even in the dull reflection of a quarter moon, James could see a great sand sea, dunes a hundred feet in height, poised at the edge of a *reg* like mighty ocean combers.

Time and direction against us now, he thought. Four hours until light and then the burning desert sun. Little water, no food, no protection. No caravan ever started out more ill-prepared. I'm like the captain of a ship with no sails, in a dinghy—adrift on an angry sea. My crew, a brother and a blind sister and I with no compass other than the stars. But which way to go? he wondered. We can't go west because that's the way we've come. Nothing there but nomads and the inhospitable desert mountains. And east? Maybe. Maybe the soldiers and Land-Rovers are still at al Jabbar. Or maybe they've given up and left. Or maybe Rassam's men are already there waiting for us. So north, he thought. You keep going north and you hope and pray by some miracle that you'll find safety there.

He fingered the carbine and felt for the remaining bullets. Could he ever use the rifle on his brother, sister, and himself? he wondered. Probably should do it now, he thought, before the sun wipes our last strength. Diana and Jon Paul would suffer less. Take them while they think there's still hope before they know what's in store for them. He reached out and placed his arms around his brother and sister. No, not that way, he told himself. Never.

"James, where are we?" Diana asked.

"Hard to tell," he answered. "Big dunes ahead. We'll try to work our way along the edge of them in the morning."

"Not much chance of us making it out, you know."

"We've got a rough day or two ahead," he answered. "We've been through worse before."

"No, I mean it," she replied. "I know the desert. There's a hundred thousand square miles of nothing up here."

"That's what I thought when I first looked at the maps of Africa." He laughed.

"The born pessimist," Jon Paul chided.

"You don't know what the word means," she shot back at him. "How long do you think we can last out here when the sun comes up, Jon Paul? Eight hours, twelve hours? God." She shuddered. "What did I get you into?"

"You got us into nothing," James answered. "We came to find you and bring you home. It was Jon Paul's idea as much as mine. We thought you might be in trouble and we came to help."

There was a long moment of silence.

"You know it's funny," Diana said. "After they . . . after I lost my vision . . . I used to dream that somehow, some way, someone would come for me. I thought maybe Dad, or Michael . . ."

". . . or Donald." James finished the sentence for her.

"Oh, James," she said. "Never in a million years did I dream that it would be you and Jon Paul." She laughed suddenly. "You two, the runts of the family. . . ."

"That's gratitude for you," Jon Paul said. "She's not even thankful."

"Oh, shut up," she snapped. A tear broke free and ran slowly down her face. "I just felt so bad, so powerless, when Ruth told me that you were in Bogadez." She began to cry silently.

"Wouldn't have traded it for the world," James said softly. He bent over and tried to kiss her tears away.

"Well, if we don't make it, at least there's a paper on the

election of 1860 that I won't have to worry about," Jon Paul said.

"I guess there are some advantages—eh, Jon Paul?" James replied.

"There's an Arab proverb," Jon Paul said. " 'From the bush that makes the thorn so comes the rose.' "

"Where the hell did you learn that?"

"Lasiri taught me," Jon Paul answered. He paused, reflectively. "Do you think he made it, James?"

"I'd like to think that," James said. "I'd like to think they'd never catch him, that he's out there now giving them a hell of a chase."

He pulled Jon Paul and Diana in close to him. There's got to be some way to get out of this, he told himself. But what could he do? What was there anyone could do? Rassam churning after them in the morning. It would be a miracle if they were still alive by noon.

Funny, he thought. Surprising that now that he could see the end of his life, everything seemed to fall into place. The important things had sorted themselves out and the lesser things dropped by the wayside. If he ever got back to San Francisco, he would break off from the architectural firm and try to do something meaningful with his life—not work for somebody. Never again for that. Find Page, raise a family, use his talents to cut his own career. Those were the important things in life. Nothing else seemed to really matter. Strange that all of this was so clear now that he was twelve thousand miles from home and surrounded on all sides by the desert.

An hour passed and they huddled together shivering in the cold. Now that James realized there was no hope for them, he began to think about how he might die. He'd heard somewhere that a man exited the world in the same way in which he lived, and he remembered a short story of Thomas Wolfe's that he'd read once. It involved an old black soldier who was chased down for murdering his girlfriend's lover. Just before the horsemen caught him, the man took off his shoes and turned to face them, standing stiffly at attention, chin up, eyes straight ahead, his shoes tucked under his left arm, as if he were making ready for inspection. And then James thought about dying out in the desert, crawling over the sand, crazed and weak from thirst and exposure. If he had a choice, he would rather have it end with Rassam. The Tuaregs would come charging over the horizon, camels racing toward them, and James would stand to meet them. He would wait until they were right on top of them and then he would fire. And when there were no bullets left he would fight them with his hands.

If you lived your life with some dignity and ended it with the same, then maybe death wouldn't be so bad after all, he thought. He was surprised that he no longer felt any fear. He'd been through a lot since they'd come to Africa. He'd seen Harold Lundstrom speared and he'd faced the Tuareg Council of Elders. He'd survived a midnight ambush, and he was still alive after being tied to a pole and left to die hanging upside down. Now he wasn't concerned with death so much as how he should die. With courage and dignity, he prayed. So let tomorrow come. He'd found his sister and he had his brother and they were all together. No one could ask for more. In a way, if there was any consolation, he had won. . . .

He felt Diana shift underneath his arm. Thinking she was trembling from the cold, he started to pull her toward him.

"No, wait," she said, listening.

"What is it?"

"Shhh," she whispered.

No one spoke.

"Listen, hear it?"

James listened but he could hear nothing.

"It's an engine, hear it?"

"Yeah," Jon Paul said.

"Shhh."

Very faint at first came the steady droning, high-pitched sound of a diesel engine. They heard a shift of gears far off in the distance, then another, as if some truck were struggling up an incline. There was a flash of light beyond the first ridge of dunes, a brief flicker, like a torch, then nothing. Then a pair of headlights, two beams coming toward them, probing the blackened sky. . . .

48

It was four A.M. and Smiling Tex Redding was half asleep, the
droning of the huge eighteen-wheeler singing like a lullaby to
his ears. Hauling a rig full of drilling pipe, he could cover six
hundred fifty miles from El-Obeid to Zarh in two nights' travel.
A thousand bucks for the drive, across to the oil fields and back.
Then off to the Riviera for a little ass and relaxation. Shifting
gears was so mechanical to him now that he could detect a
subtle change in the pitch of the engines long before the diesel
began to strain. Downshifting, he went through five gears so
smoothly, the big rig barely slowed down.

   He had been on the road for eight hours, through some of the
most desolate country in the world. But who was he to argue if
the Italian oil company AGIP paid him for hauling pipe? He'd
made the run a dozen times before. Twelve hours' driving at a
time, nothing to break up the monotony except some bloody
Arab music and a few good dreams. It was too hot to travel
during the day; one hundred fifty degrees sent the diesel engines
running too hot. The trucks always traveled better at night, and
he liked the roads best anyway when there was just him and the
night. Not much to see in the day. A lot of sand and desolate
stretches of monotony. Nothing more.

   He slowed the truck, his bladder full, and pulled off to the
edge of the sand to urinate. Then he swung back into the cab.
Once comfortably seated, he twisted his thick frame around and
looked at a small map. His face was round, his cheeks puffed as
if he'd been made from dough. He brought a thick finger up and
scratched his chin, then spat out of the cab window. Ahead was
the Tibetsi sand sea, one hundred miles of the bloody awfullest

dunes he had ever seen. He would have to travel slowly to be
sure sand hadn't rolled across the road or blocked his path.

He picked up his C.B. radio and called back to a companion
rig a mile behind. By company rule, they always traveled in
pairs so that if something happened, like an engine breaking
down, there was someone else to help. No fucking place to
spend a day, he thought, frowning.

"Hey, Tennessee, this is Tex, you reading me? Over."

"Yeah," the voice drawled back. "You've been so quiet, I
thought you'd fallen asleep. How's the road?"

"Clear so far. Been keeping her at forty-five and no slow-
downs."

"Well, I'm on your ass, boy. You open your mouth and you'll
find my headlights shining through your teeth."

"Har." The big trucker guffawed. "I thought for sure you'd
stopped back there at some oasis and was having a good
woman."

"Shiiit. Only woman out here's camels."

"Well, you gotta get a hump where you can." The transmission was interrupted by a grunt of laughter.

"Where you spending the night?"

"Holiday Inn."

"You jest, boy," the other answered. "It won't take long.
Probably another year or two and there'll be Motel 6's and
McDonald's lining this fucking highway from Khartoum to
Timbuctu."

"Well, keep your eyes open, buddy, I don't want to find you
in some sand dune taking a snooze."

"Fat chance," Smiling Tex answered. "Just keep her floored
and see if you catch my ass. . . ."

He laughed to himself at the use of their language. They took
great liberties out here. Nobody monitored the air and even if
they did, no one could understand English. He smiled at the
thought of doing such a thing back in the States. The slightest
hint of four-letter words when he was driving the Houston–
Alaska route and they would have yanked his license.

He shifted now, watching the road spread out evenly in front
of him. The dunes rose up, like mountains, on his right. As he
kept the speedometer at a steady forty-five, his mind began to

wander—back to the Riviera, back to the bikini-bottomed girls
he loved to watch. By Christ, he thought. No rib-eye steak in
Houston tasted better than one of those girls.

A movement flashed across his vision, something cascading
down one of the dunes, like a skier coming out of the gates on a
downhill slalom. His voice suddenly over the C.B. radio.

"Holy Christ!"

"What's up, Tex?"

"Jeezus, some goddamned Arab stumbled off the top of a
dune and fell half down the side of it, almost ran into my
beams. I thought it was a bloody animal. I still see him in the
tail light. He's waving after me. Better slow down. You should
be coming up onto him in a mile."

"You think it's some kind of trick?" Tennessee carried a
30/06 rifle, which he loosened from a rack behind his head.

"Hard to tell. I'll keep the channel open. Let me know when
you see him."

Five minutes passed.

"I see him, Tex. He's waving at me in the middle of the
road."

"Christ, drive by him. There's nothing out here but a bunch
of goddamned nomads."

"Son of a bitch's right in the center of the road. Can't get
around him. He's shouting something. Shouting and waving his
hands like a madman."

Silence.

Tex Redding loosened the pistol strapped to his belt and
gently applied the brakes. With the weight of two tons of oil
pipe, it took him a quarter of a mile to bring the rig to a stop.

"Come in, Tennessee, what's happening back there, over?"

"Tex. You've never going to believe this."

"What is it, man?"

"It's a goddamned kid. And he's jumping and waving and
. . . Christ, he speaks English! Wait a minute. Jesus Christ. He
speaks English and there's two more of 'em coming out of the
dunes. . . ."

49

In New York City a large crowd was gathered in the west wing
of the Wentworth Museum of Fine Arts. It was ten o'clock at
night and many of the guests were dressed in tuxedos and evening gowns. A small bar had been set up in one corner of the
room, serving French and German wines. Next to the bar a
table had been arranged with elaborate trays of hors d'oeuvres,
caviar, smoked salmon, and goose liver pâté. Across the room a
television crew had just finished an interview and now were
disassembling their lights.

Along the walls were perhaps a hundred photographs of
varying sizes. Many were in color and depicted a wide variety of
scenes. A model in a studio, nude, a soft throw of blue light
across her breast; a church in Paris in the evening, the shadows
long, the lighting muted and pastel. A young Masai woman, her
face smeared with reddish ocher, her head shaved, her neck
covered with multicolored beads.

Yet of all the images the most striking were three huge blow-
ups illuminated along one wall. The prints were in black and
white, the figures harsh, the contrasts stark. One photograph
was of a caravan of camels moving along the crest of a dune.
Behind it, the desert undulated like an ocean, spreading off in
an interminable sea of sand. The second was of a tent, tiny and
seemingly insignificant, pitched in a desolate quarter of rocks.
The photograph had been taken at dusk. The one bright spot
was a small fire burning next to the tent, over which was cooking some kind of pot. Next to the fire a small prayer rug had
been thrown. Two men dressed in robes were kneeling there,
praying toward Mecca. The scene was one of loneliness and
desolation, the precarious position of man.

The third photograph was perhaps the most dramatic. It was a large blowup of the head of a man swathed in black cloth, his eyes probing out through a slit. The man's eyes reflected the glare of the sun and were terrifying in their intensity.

Across from these photographs was a desk. Seated there surrounded by a crowd of people was Diana Jacobson. She wore a pair of tinted glasses; her long, shoulder-length hair fell radiantly across her shoulders. She was dressed in an attractive blue dress, with a yellow scarf around her neck.

She had just finished a television interview and now had returned to autograph copies of her third book, *Reflections of a Golden Sun*. A number of people pressed forward to purchase copies, then politely asked if she would sign them. Next to her on the desk were her two earlier books, one a thick, elegantly bound, finely printed volume called *Sand Shadows*.

"I'll take two copies, please," a man said. He was tall, slightly bald, in his middle fifties. "I—I want to send one to my daughter," he added almost apologetically. "She's always been interested in photography. You're one of her idols, you know."

"I'm delighted," Diana answered with a broad smile. "Tell me her name and I'll sign it for her."

"Marcia," the man said.

Diana opened the book and signed across the front cover. "To Marcia, with best wishes for a long and successful career."

"And you, sir?" She looked up at the man.

"Markus Walters," he said. "I'm a stockbroker. I've always admired your work. Very adventuresome spirit for such an attractive woman."

"It's not always been easy," Diana answered. She smiled politely and signed the book. Her father came forward, pushing gently through the crowd. Jacobson was dressed in a black tuxedo with a red plaid vest and a white carnation in his lapel. Fifteen years had passed since he had lost his daughter in the Northern Frontier. Now, approaching seventy-two, he was thinner than he'd been before, his hair gray. Yet there was still an athletic bounce to his walk and he looked in superb shape. Retirement had suited him well.

He reached forward and kissed Diana on the forehead. She

looked up at him and smiled. "I think we're almost out of books," she said. "We started with a hundred."

"Well, that's good news," he answered. "I thought it went beautifully."

A woman came forward and asked for an autographed copy of the book and then a small man, dressed in a sports coat and tie, his attire seemingly out of place at so formal an occasion.

"Miss Jacobson." He held out his hand. "I'm from the *Times.* I wanted to talk with you for a few minutes if you don't mind. We're doing a story for the Sunday magazine section. If you have a moment. Maybe a couple of photographs. I won't keep you very long."

"Yes, yes, of course," she said.

He paused, taking out a small notepad. A photographer moved in behind him, snapping several shots.

"I wonder if Miss Jacobson wouldn't mind standing next to one of her pictures," the photographer said. "Perhaps the man there with the cloth around his face."

"You mean the *litham.*" Diana corrected him. "It's part of the headdress."

She stood up and the reporter led her over to the wall, where she posed beneath the black-and-white print. The photographer took several flash shots, then nodded he was finished. "That's perfect," he said.

"I've always been intrigued by your work," the *Times* writer said. He escorted Diana back to her desk. "The first book, *Sand Shadows,* I think will always be my favorite. Did—?" He paused, trying to determine the best way to ask the question. "Did the injury to your eyes cause any permanent damage?"

Diana nodded. "I was lucky. We went to the Johns Hopkins Eye Institute. There's a surgeon there who has perfected a technique for corneal transplants. You see, the outer layer of the eye is like a glass window. With scarring it becomes opaqued. They were able to take donor corneas and replace the injured portion with a clear surface. Without my glasses my vision is twenty-one hundred but I can put up with that."

"It must . . . I mean, the actual injury . . . It must have been extremely painful."

"It was not one of life's more pleasurable experiences," she answered.

"And then you went back, to take these photographs." He raised his hand and pointed over his shoulder. "Why? After what they had done to you, how could you possibly go back?"

"There were many things unanswered in my mind," Diana said. "I wanted to meet Rassam on my own terms, to study his people. You see, they were a dying race. A people of the past. I knew they wouldn't last."

"And you held no ill feelings?"

"Not really," Diana answered. "They ruled as they always had. I was no more acceptable to him than a modern machine. I held no grudge. I wanted to learn more. To meet them again. To say, look, here is the type of woman you were dealing with. You see, women are very subjugated there. They're almost like furniture or cattle. Traded and sold, articles of pleasure for the harem. Nothing more."

"And, if I recall, you were never able to find him?"

Diana shook her head. "We followed the migrations north. That winter was the beginning of a terrible drought that lasted two years. Ninety-five percent of the Tauregs' camels died. The confederation was divided up and forced into refugee camps. Many of them disappeared. I was able to trace Rassam back to a camp at al Qatram on the Niger. Everyone there was placed in small Quonset huts. They lived four or five families under one roof. Terribly crowded, terribly oppressed. They told me Rassam lasted about a week. One day he just stood up and walked out into the desert. He was never seen again. That was the closest I ever got to him."

"Then the picture is not of Rassam, there on the wall."

"No," Diana replied. "I'd give a lot for a photograph of him, but I don't think it will ever come to pass."

"And this fellow Isaiah, or whatever his name was, the man you wrote about who helped your brothers in the caves."

Diana shrugged. "The desert is very large, Mr. . . ."

"Robert Altos," the reporter answered. "Yes, I understand. I wondered if we could use one or two of your photographs in the article. Would that be all right?"

"Certainly," Diana answered. "Look through the ones on the

wall. I can arrange to have my secretary send you several prints."

"I wanted to say your photographs are marvelous," Altos said. "They have a touch of Impressionism to them. Especially the color. The church in Paris, for instance."

Diana laughed. "I studied French Impressionism in college. I'm told many of the old masters had trouble with their vision. By the time Claude Monet reached *Giverny* he could barely see. There was a certain softness to his painting that I've tried to capture here on film.

"Maybe it's because I still have difficulty getting things in focus," she added with a smile.

A man came out of the crowd and put his arm around her. "Diana, they're on," he whispered. He was tall and dark with a thin mustache and a broad smile. "Hi," he said to the writer, holding out his hand. "I'm Peter Townsend, Diana's husband."

"Where's Dad?" she asked.

"Somebody brought a television set in. He's watching the Olympics, over there, behind the bar."

The stadium was filled to overflowing. Spectators from all over the world had poured into this ancient city to witness the XXV Olympiad. Newspaper accounts said there wasn't a vacant hotel within 100 miles of Rome. Late arrivals were sleeping in parks, in bars, in vehicles, anywhere they could find a place to rest. And on this warm Italian morning an audience of eighty thousand from fifty-two nations began to shift restlessly in their seats in anticipation of the one-hundred-meter dash, the event that would designate the world's fastest man.

Along the northern side of the stadium in seat 43, row K, James Jacobson shielded his eyes from the sun and glanced impatiently at the track. At forty-four he looked older now, more mature. Specks of gray had worked their way into his hair. At the corners of his eyes were the beginnings of tiny wrinkles. Yet age had treated him well. If anything, he had a certain rugged handsomeness that had not been present before.

Shortly after returning from Africa, he'd left his architectural firm and started out on his own. For five years he'd struggled, earning little. But eventually his perseverance had paid off.

Now the Jacobson-style home was known throughout the west.
White stucco walls with open courtyards, stylish fountains, and
solar heating. People unfamiliar with his work said it reminded
them of a Spanish or Mexican theme. Those who knew him
better were sure it had more of an Arabic flavor. The arched
doorways, the use of blue tile to suggest water, on occasion the
curve of a chimney, almost like a minaret. The style was
unique, exciting, and exclusive, and his homes sold throughout
California, New Mexico, and Arizona by the dozens. James had
been heralded as a new Frank Lloyd Wright, bringing to architecture the first revolutionary ideas for home building in more
than a decade. Modestly, James had laughed; his ideas were
nothing new. The general floor plan and style had worked suc-
cessfully in the Sahara for centuries. He'd merely modernized
the plan.

He'd married Page and had three children now, and for the
past year and a half he'd been working on the plans for a new
symphony hall in San Francisco. At men's clubs throughout
California he was a popular speaker on such topics as architecture, the building industry, and the hazards and pitfalls of designing homes. He'd even been offered an honorary degree and
had spoken once to the graduating class of a large midwestern
university.

On occasion when addressing smaller groups, he would relate
some of his personal experiences. Often someone familiar with
his past would ask him to tell about his adventures in the
deserts of the Sudan. Usually he would politely reject such requests, though rarely, if the mood struck him, he might begin
the tale of the search for his missing sister.

Frequently at the end of his story the audience would ask him
what happened to the desert nomads, the Tuaregs, the Berbers,
the Gallas. After his sister's operation, he reported, they'd gone
back with his father and flown over the ruins, but there was no
one there. The vast encampments of tents were gone, the thriv-
ing population of Africans, numbering at its height more than a
thousand, had migrated back across the desert, following myriad caravan trails north. All that was left of the oasis was a
damp, stagnant pool of sand and the massive stone foundations.

The marketplace, once filled with the cries and jabbers of a dozen guttural tongues, was empty.

A year later the World Health Organization had sent out a medical team. The cave people, mostly blind and riddled with leprosy, had refused all outside help. At best, James thought, they might last another generation, perhaps two, before the disease finally took its toll. Then they, too, would join the skeletal remains. And Isaiah and Alabaster and Solomon the Mute? He'd never seen or heard of them again.

"And what about the treasure?" someone invariably asked.

"Still there." James would laugh, his eyes glistening. The political situation at the borders had deteriorated so that few permits were given to allow passage into the Sudan. Maybe someday that would change. Maybe someday someone else would carve his initials in the baobab tree and trek across the desert, following the pathway of the old caravans toward the Devil's Tower and the seventh oasis at Bogadez.

"But I wish him luck," James would say. "God, I wish him luck."

Out on the Olympic track, the athletes participating in the one-hundred-meter dash had begun to warm up, stretching and jogging, trying to loosen their muscles for that tremendous burst of speed that would be required to win. James scanned across the sprinters until his eyes came to rest upon a tall youth wearing the colors of the United States. He was well over six feet tall; his body that of a runner, muscular and sleek. Although he was black, there was a certain height to his cheekbones and angularity to his nose that marked him as being of Nilo-Hamitic origin and set him apart from the other black athletes representing Africa to the South or West.

An announcement echoed across the stadium, first in Italian and then in English: "Ladies and gentlemen, in the finals of the one-hundred-meter dash, in lane one representing East Germany, Gernot Rinehart, in lane two representing The Union of Soviet Socialist Republics, Vladimir Slavorka. . . ."

James searched nervously around the stadium. Christ, he'll be late, he thought. And then he sat back, relieved, as he saw a young, distinguished, well-dressed man begin to work his way down the aisle toward him. The man was a professor of tropical diseases at the prestigious Albert Einstein Medical Center in New York. He had only been in practice for five years and already was world-known for his research on the *mycobacterium* that causes leprosy.

"I was afraid you were going to miss it." James smiled as the younger man took his seat.

"Not for all the world," the physician answered. "Tried to get hold of Diana, but all the circuits are jammed."

"Well, they'll be watching on TV," James replied.

"The boy looks good," Jon Paul said.

James nodded. "I feel as if I were running out there."

"Maybe in a way you are," Jon Paul answered.

As he sat in the Olympic stadium James could feel his heart begin to thump. He hadn't felt so excited since he had left the deserts of the Sudan. Well, what did you learn? he asked himself. Now that fifteen years had passed, would you do it over again?

Like all things in life, whenever considering such a question, he always weighed the pros with the cons. The fact of the matter was that Diana Jacobson was alive and well. That was on the good side of the ledger.

Two years after their return to the States, James's father had suffered a mild heart attack. Shortly thereafter he'd sold all of his stock and stepped down from the executive leadership of TransOceanic Airlines forever. Since then the elder Jacobson had dabbled in a number of enterprises. The family had donated two million dollars to the establishment of the Ruth Parker Memorial Fund to refurbish and maintain several projects at the Nairobi Museum, and now no less than three eastern universities had special chairs endowed by the Jacobson family for faculty members interested in the fields of anthropology and archaeology.

Jon Paul is destined to be a success in whatever field he chooses, James thought. The boy had it in him from the beginning. It was just a matter of getting him on the right track.

So what did you learn from such things? James wondered. What do you ever learn? Probably nothing. He had known all the options, all the risks, even before he went. In a way he had made no significant choices at all. If a member of the family is missing, somebody goes to help, It was the type of action that human beings had been taking for centuries. And if the same crisis came up now, would he go again? Yes, he told himself. Yes, a thousand times, yes!

When he looked up, the runners had moved into the starting blocks. A sudden hush came across the stadium. James could feel his breath quicken as his pulse began to crawl up until it was working like a piston in his throat.

Eighty thousand spectators rose from their seats, their eyes glued to the track.

"Runners, take your mark," the starter barked.

The tall black youth in the American uniform crouched down in the blocks, his muscles straining.

"Come on, boy," James murmured. "Push it now. Push it like you've done in all those hours of practice. Run like the wind."

There was a long, tense second, then the sound of the starter's gun cracked like a whip.

The runners exploded out of the blocks. For the first twenty meters, the East German took an early lead. As the rest of the pack caught up with him, James was yelling with all his might, his voice lost in the tremendous roar of the crowd.

At the fifty-meter mark, the Russian broke ahead, setting a blistering pace. While television cameras flashed the race across the world, everyone watching the transmission, wherever they were, whatever else they were doing, must have stopped to witness the finish.

The digital timer raced like fury, the microseconds flashing past in a blur of numbers. There was hardly time for the announcer to make more than a passing remark that a world record was in progress when out of nowhere came the American, striding like a gazelle, his legs thundering beneath him. At the seventy-five meter mark he caught everyone. With an astonishing burst of speed, he was suddenly in the lead, pulling away from the pack, and then he was across the finish tape, his arms up, waving triumphantly.

It took the officials five minutes to unanimously agree upon the final time of the race. The announcement over the loudspeakers—"A world record for the one-hundred-meter dash has just been set by the United States in a time of nine point eight seconds"—was followed by a deafening cheer.

"He did it!" Jon Paul Jacobson yelled. "Christ, by Christ, he did it!" He grabbed his brother and hugged him, noting for the first time the moisture that had welled up in James's eyes.

The tall American jogged around the track now, making his victory circle, waving to the crowd. James could feel such a swell of pride that he had to bite his lips to keep the tears from flowing.

"We'll have to take him out after this and get him stone drunk," Jon Paul shouted hoarsely.

"Yeah, except he doesn't touch the stuff," James answered. His voice was gone, he could only speak in a whisper.

Across the world, a hundred million viewers watched the satellite transmission. On television sets in Australia and Canada and Japan, the American stepped up onto the winners' box. On his left was the Russian, who had come in second. On his right, the East German, who had placed third. The band began playing the United States National Anthem and he stood straight and firm, his strong, intelligent face gazing off across the crowd.

As the officials lowered the gold medal over his head, the blue ribbon seemed to catch on a thin gold chain that hung around his neck. The young athlete reached up and pulled the chain loose. As he did this, a small blue stone rolled out from underneath his sweat-soaked shirt. It was visible for only a second before it was covered by the Olympic Gold.

From the north side of the stadium, James watched, choked with emotion. Two firsts for the Jacobson family, he thought. The first Olympic gold and the first adopted black son.

"If only the boy's father could see him now," he murmured. "By Christ, how proud Lasiri would have been. . . ."

On that same afternoon fifteen hundred miles across the Mediterranean, along the northwest coast of Africa, was a man oblivious to the Olympic games and scornful of the decadent influence of television. He was dressed in a brown cassock, his portly abdomen trussed by a white cord, knotted at the waist.

He hurried through the Djemma-el-Fna square in Marrakesh, accompanied by an old woman covered in a black shawl. As he walked, she hung on to his left arm as if she were blind.

Moving through the pulsing crowd, he wove back and forth, hesitating from time to time to catch his breath or wipe the perspiration from his brow. The air was choked with dust, the North African sun unbearably fierce in its intensity. Scattered voices cried out in a cacophony of shouts. *"Balek! Balek!* Make way! Make way!" as porters carrying raw goods darted through the throng. He passed a group of street barbers shaving the heads of mountain people, leaving a single lock of hair (should they die in battle) so that Allah might pull them up to Paradise.

The scream from a patient of an itinerant dentist reached his ears and he muttered a silent prayer. Pressing forward, he hurried down a long aisle between baskets of dates and ripe fruit as the strong aroma reached his nostrils. Ahead, troupes of dancers flowed through the crowd, the noise of their music mixed with the shouts and yells of hawkers. "Blessed Mary!" he muttered, stopping abruptly. He had almost run into a snake charmer, the cobra rising from a wicker basket to the coaxing of a flute. Next to the snake two young urchins probed a pair of scorpions in the dust. The man paled, detouring widely around them.

At noon the midday prayer rang out from the Koutoubia Mosque and the man stopped, waiting uncomfortably until the completion of the chant. He had never been inside the structure. It was off-limits to all non-Moslems, and he felt a rush of distrust. Even in peace the Christian-Moslem conflict was a never-ending battle in his mind. His eyes rose once, beyond the great mosque, beyond the minarets to the vast Atlas Mountains. Camel caravans still moved across those ridges, carrying goods from oasis to oasis, treading across the great Sahara. He reflected how little Africa had changed—the mosques, the markets, the people—over the past thousand years. Secretly he wondered if civilization should leave, if the airports closed, if the radio stations ceased, if the tourists stopped, would Africa return to the ways of the past? Progress was no more than a feather, he thought, precariously anchored on the edge of the continent—lost with the next revolutionary breeze.

The prayer over, he hurried down a cramped side road, past a crowded square, and into the medina, or old section, of the city. He walked with care, placing his sandaled feet around the scattered offal that lined the street. Two rats scurried across the narrow alley, scuttling between piles of donkey dung. Coming around a corner, he stiffened at the smell of death. A dog was lying in the street, its legs up, its body terribly bloated. As he escorted his companion around the carcass a thousand flies buzzed up past him. Hurrying forward, he made the sign of the cross.

Three blocks away he found the small wooden doorway of a white sun-baked house. The residence was little different from a dozen other impoverished houses that lined the street. He knocked twice at the door.

A moment passed, then a voice in Arabic. *"Shalom.* Who is it?"

The reply in English. "Father Dominick. I have a woman for you."

The door opened and an elderly man with a crutch under one arm stood in the doorway. Dressed in an Arab robe, he had silvery hair and a short white beard. He was blind in one eye; from the other, barely open, shone a deep blue sphere. Where an ear had been was now only a twisted piece of skin.

"She has the mark," the priest said. "She will be needing food and shelter."

The silver-haired man studied the woman. "Where is she from?"

"The mountains, abandoned by a gypsy family, I'm told. She speaks no language I can understand."

The man turned his good eye toward Father Dominick. "We will take her, Father. Thank you."

"I am to tell you that there is a medical team coming from the United States. A team that studies leprosy. They will want to examine all the people here. Can you bring them to the mission next week?"

"Yes, that is good."

"There is a young doctor. Does the name Jacobson mean anything to you?"

The old man searched his memory. Jacobson? Jacobson?

There was something vaguely familiar about the name but he could not quite place it. Finally he shook his head. "No, Father," he answered. "But I will bring them."

"God be with you," the Catholic priest said. The door closed and Father Dominick hurried back down the street, relieved to leave this terrible sector of the city, eager to be past the crowded market and back in the cool shade of his mission where he could breathe fresh air again.

Strange old man, he reflected. He'd seen many surprises in his life but nothing more baffling than the day this silver-haired, half-blind leper had brought a gift of gems to his mission. They had been valued at over three hundred thousand dollars. Why, the man must be a millionaire, he thought. But how? Why?

Placing his fingers over his nose, he shook his head and hurried around the dead dog lying in the road. They were answers he would never know. One did not question the ways of God.

Inside the house the blind woman was led to a long table where another dozen individuals sat. Some were terribly crippled and bent, others blind. One man had a gnarled scar where his nose had been.

A huge, bald black man brought out a bowl of porridge and set it down before the woman, then helped her into a chair. A gold ring glistened from the side of his nose.

The silver-haired man moved painfully to the end of the table and sat down. His hand was a claw, his fingers little more than stumps. Twisting his one remaining digit around a spoon, he dipped the utensil carefully into the thick soup. As he brought it up to his lips, he let out a grunt of satisfaction.

"Well, Solomon," he said. "It looks like sister here will be staying for a while."

Rebels and outcasts, they fled halfway across the earth to settle the harsh Australian wastelands. Decades later—ennobled by love and strengthened by tragedy—they had transformed a wilderness into fertile land. And themselves into

WILLIAM STUART LONG

THE EXILES, #1	12374-7-12	$3.95
THE SETTLERS, #2	17929-7-45	$3.95
THE TRAITORS, #3	18131-3-21	$3.95
THE EXPLORERS, #4	12391-7-11	$3.50
THE ADVENTURERS, #5	10330-4-40	$3.95
THE COLONISTS, #6	11342-3-21	$3.95

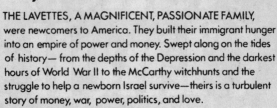